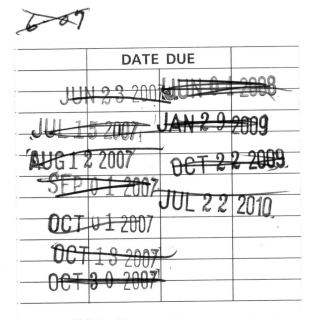

Also by Brendan Halpin

Long Way Back

Donorboy

Losing My Faculties

It Takes a Worried Man

DEAR CATASTROPHE WAITRESS

DEAR CATASTROPHE WAITRESS

a novel

Brendan Halpin

VILLARD/NEW YORK

Copyright © 2007 by Brendan Halpin

Published in the United States by Villard Books, an imprint of The Random House Publishing Group, a division of Random House, Inc., New York.

VILLARD and "V" CIRCLED Design are registered trademarks of Random House, Inc.

ISBN 978-0-8129-7702-8

Printed in the United States of America on acid-free paper

www.villard.com

2 4 6 8 9 7 5 3 1

First Edition

Book design by Susan Turner

For Suzanne Demarco

PHILIPPA
1983

She's wearing a white T-shirt with the artwork from the first Clash album on it. The sleeves are cut off. She drinks a St. Pauli Girl dark and sits on the hood of Brad Worthington's Camaro. She watches as a circle of stoners, fellow members of the Walnut Prep class of 1983, the last class to enter high school in the 1970s, pass a bong around, shed an occasional tear, and sing along with the words they can understand from Yes's "Starship Trooper," which is blaring from inside of Bobby Shiffer's house.

She hates Yes, but she finds that she has kind of warmed to her Yes-listening classmates in the last few months. There are, after all, only fifty of them here at Walnut Prep, and they've been together since the first grade, and the fact that they are not as cool as she is no longer seems like a reason to openly scorn them. In fact, Philippa finds as she looks down into the grass at her stoned classmates that she feels real tenderness for them simply because she remembers them all as little kids, and because she's never going to see them again after tonight and they are the only people who knew her before her parents split, before Mom started drinking, before she became the punk rock chick, back when she was just that little girl who really liked *H. R. Pufnstuf.*

She opens the graduation program again and runs down the list of the names of her classmates and where they are going for college. She doesn't know if Denison University is a stoner school already, but it certainly looks like it will be next year. She finds her own name: "Philippa Jane Strange: London Academy of Music." She smiles to herself, unable to believe she got away with this.

It's her little private joke to herself, because what she's going to do next year is what she's done every summer since the seventh grade: go live at her dad's flat in London and go to clubs and hear punk rock.

It's one in the afternoon. Philippa staggers down to the kitchen of her dad's flat, turns on the electric kettle, puts a PG Tips tea bag into a cup, and sits down at the table. She's only mildly hungover.

Dad, as he does whenever he spends the night here and not at Ella's, has left Philippa this morning's *Telegraph, Times,* and *Guardian* on the table. Once the kettle whistles, Philippa pours the hot water out and sits down to read the *Telegraph.* From there she'll move to *The Times,* and finish up with *The Guardian.* She and her dad have a joke about how she reads from right to left. Dad does the opposite, but with the same impulse: begin with the one you disagree with the most and work your way over to your side to see what the real story is.

Philippa's continued presence in her dad's flat is a rebuke to both of their political convictions. Philippa, like her friends, fumes with outrage over what the Thatcher government is doing to the welfare state. Unlike her friends, she lives for free in a very smart flat and has food and booze money supplied to her by Simon Strange, an investment banker who belongs to the class of people that benefit most from the economic policies of the Tory government.

Simon, like his friends and co-workers, yearns for the dismantling of the welfare state, for a more Americanized system where the government doesn't act as nanny and people are forced to show a little personal responsibility. Unlike his friends and co-workers, Simon runs a little mini welfare state of his own, with an endless reservoir of guilt over the divorce and his subsequent return to the UK fueling a micro-economy that would disgust him on a macro scale: Philippa pays no rent, is not expected to work, and drinks up her spending money.

Philippa is oblivious to any political irony in her situation, but Simon is not, principally because Ella points it out to him on a daily basis. Philippa's causing a terrible strain on Simon's relationship with Ella, but she's oblivious to this, too.

She does, however, notice that the date on all the papers is October 1. At this point, she realizes, all of her classmates from Walnut Prep, even the ones who went to school in California, are in their little college dorms, happily marching on the treadmill that will lead them back to their dads' companies, where they will be groomed to take over once they've gotten that BA under their belts. She feels superior to them, of course, but also, for the first time ever, a bit lost.

She's never been in London this late in the year. It's starting to get cool and rainy, and it's already getting dark much earlier, so that heady feeling of emerging from the pub two pints into a good booze-up at nine P.M. with the sun shining down is gone at least until next summer.

And she's starting to feel jaded about the music scene. The Clash are opening for the Who on a stadium tour of the US, for God's sake, and she remembers being thirteen and packing into a sweaty club to see them and hearing "White Riot" for the first time and having her life changed as a result, and nothing currently happening in the clubs can touch anything that happened then.

This is even true of Trevor's band, the NHS. (It stands for the

National Hate Service, and is supposed to serve as some kind of political commentary on the Tories' attack on the National Health Service, but Trevor reads three fewer newspapers every day than Philippa does and writes songs principally about booze and sex.) Philippa loves watching them perform, because Trevor is so very sexy when he sings, and she likes watching his hands on the guitar and remembering them on her the night before, imagining them on her after the show.

But she's been with Trevor for nearly three months now, and the fog of infatuation is lifting, and she is forced to admit that the NHS is not the Clash.

The phone rings twice in quick succession, and Philippa feels annoyed. Annoyed because she prefers the one long ring of US phones to the chirpy, insistent two-ring alert of British phones, annoyed because she's only halfway through *The Times,* and she really likes to read all three papers before speaking to anyone, and most of all annoyed because she thinks it's Trevor calling.

Trevor is terrible on the phone, inarticulate and clumsy, and his matter-of-fact proclamations of lust—"Thinkin' about your knickers today, Phil"—that actually seemed hot at first are now just kind of annoying. (She does enjoy the fact that the NHS's latest single is called "Thinkin' About Your Knickers," though.) Also, he's started stressing his poverty more and more recently ("I'm totally skint, Phil, buy us a pint"), and she's beginning to suspect that he likes Simon's money a lot more than her tits, which are another frequent topic of conversation.

So the phone trills—*Ringring! . . . Ringring!*—and it just won't stop, and she doesn't want to answer it, but she can't very well read *The Times* with that business going on, and she figures she'll have to talk to Trevor at some point today, so she may as well get it over with. She picks up the phone with her best punk rock attitude: "Yeah?"

"Uh, hello?" It's a woman. Not Trevor. Not Ella calling to tell her to get a fucking job, either. This is not a fear on Philippa's radar at the moment, though it's a conversation that Ella is currently planning. No, it's an American woman. But it's not Mom.

"Yeah?" Philippa says with more annoyance.

"Um, Philippa?"

"Speaking."

"It's your aunt Betsy, honey. There's . . . ," and Aunt Betsy starts to cry. Philippa knows that nobody cries on a transatlantic phone call if it's good news, and she knows Betsy wouldn't spend the money on the phone call just to talk to her, and she knows she should be alarmed, or worried, or something, but she searches herself and finds nothing. She does manage to de-snottify her voice, though.

"What is it, B? What's wrong?"

"It's your mom, sweetie, she's . . . there's been an accident."

Is she dead? Do you mean she's dead, Aunt B? Say what you mean, dammit! Philippa's relieved to find that she cares about the answer to this question.

"Is she okay?"

"She . . . her leg is badly fractured in three places, and the steering wheel knocked her two front teeth out, and she's bruised all over, but she . . ." More crying. "I'm sorry, sweetie. She's going to walk again, they say they can fix her face, and she's not in a coma or anything, but she's pretty loopy on the pain medication right now."

"Jesus." If she's not dead, I'm not flying to Cincinnati, Philippa thinks. She sends her aunt telepathic messages: Don't ask me to come back, because then I'll have to say no, and then I'll be a bad daughter, but I don't want to come to Cincinnati, so if you just don't ask, we'll be fine.

"She . . . she was drinking, honey." Well, duh, Philippa wants to say. I'm guessing it was a one-car accident, too. "She wrapped her car around a tree on Clough Pike." Silence. Philippa has nothing to say. The silence drags on for more microseconds, and Philippa knows this is where she's supposed to say she'll be on the next flight, that she's rushing to her mother's bedside.

Instead she says, "What hospital's she in?"

"Mercy." Of course it's the closest one to Clough Pike, but Philippa remembers her mom taking her out of Mercy when she'd broken her arm sledding, and they told her she'd have to wait until morning to get her arm set, and screaming at the emergency room staff, "You fucking quacks! You fucking incompetent quacks! I'm taking my daughter to a real fucking hospital!"

Philippa gets the address and the phone number and promises she'll call Aunt Betsy later. She hopes this will leave Aunt Betsy with the impression that she's going to call as soon as she knows her flight information. She hopes that Aunt Betsy won't call twice. She doesn't want Betsy to hate her.

What's strange, she thinks as she switches on the kettle for her second cup of tea, is that she cares if Betsy hates her, but she feels nothing at all about Mom. She tries to call up a picture of Mom with her front teeth knocked out, her face all black and blue, lying in a hospital bed. She does conjure up the image, but it does nothing to her. She slaps a tea bag into her cup, fills it with hot water, and sits back down to finish *The Times*.

Philippa slams down her pint glass on the table at the Junction Bar, a West End pub full of UCL students. She's just finished her third pint of Tetley's Bitter. She finished her second shot of The Famous Grouse ten minutes ago.

Three pints and two shots have not been enough to drown Aunt Betsy's voice from her brain, nor have they been enough to unlock anything she might be feeling about her mother's accident and hospitalization. She knows that many people drink to get numb, but tonight she's drinking in a fierce, doomed attempt to feel something.

She staggers toward the bar. On the way she stands behind Trevor, who's mesmerized by the fruit machine, feeding it her ten p coins, and grabs his butt. He grunts something then slaps a button, hoping to get the wheel to stop on a cherry. It doesn't.

Philippa puts a pound note on the bar, raises her finger, and gets her fourth pint. She weaves back to the table, not stopping by Trevor, who's suddenly pissing her off. She takes big gulps of the beer, thinking if she can only drink enough, she'll unlock some sadness about her mom, some concern, something that will make her want to go to her.

It doesn't happen, and Philippa's stomach begins to rebel instead. She feels it coming, and, since she's closer to the exit than the loo, she runs for the street and just makes it, hunching over the sidewalk, vomiting into the street. It's cold, and a light rain is falling. Philippa pukes again.

She hears the door open behind her, and she's glad that Trevor has noticed, that he's followed her, that he cares.

And then she hears Helen's voice. "You okay? Trev sent me to check on you."

What a prince that Trevor is. He sent Helen to check on her. "Yeah, everything's great. My mom's in the fucking hospital because she . . . ," and here she starts to cry, "she was in a car wreck, and she's lying in a hospital bed in the United States with her front teeth knocked out."

"Oh, hell, I'm so sorry. You must be so worried," Helen says.

"No . . . ," and more tears now, "see, that's the thing. That's the thing. I'm not worried. I don't care. I don't fucking care at all."

Helen is silent. "Oh. Well. Er, well, I'm sorry, then," she says, and returns to the pub. It's great to have friends.

Rain falls, and Philippa is cold. And she steps outside of herself for just a minute, and she's filled with hate for what she sees: a pathetic unemployed wretch puking in the street like a dog, with a so-called boyfriend who doesn't care, and a mother she doesn't care about, and no future except the road that leads to the hospital. Not to visit her mother, but to become her mother: some booze-soaked old bitch that nobody cares about, not even her own daughter, who'll die alone, probably with a bottle in her hand.

She wipes the puke from her face with one sleeve, wipes tears off her face with the other, and stands up. Unsteadily at first, she walks home.

MARK

Mark is thirteen. He's somewhere in Maine, on land owned by the Unitarian Universalist Association. He's at Camp Service, in cabin B-6, and he's lying on the third top bunk from the door with a painful erection. Below him, in a stage whisper, their CIT, Allen Spitz, is telling the story of how after campfire tonight Debra Fisher gave him a blow job. Mark knows enough to know that Allen is at least half full of shit, and he can't believe anyone as sexy as Debra Fisher would blow anyone who would say something like, "Shot my wad right between her pearly whites," which is what sixteen-year-old Allen is saying now.

And yet he does see the way girls look at Allen around the campfire. Their eyes glaze over, they cock their heads to one side, and they just gaze at him like he is the only guy in the world.

So even if Allen is three-quarters full of shit, and he is only getting one-quarter of the number of blow jobs he's described in detail here in the darkness of cabin B-6, he is still having a fantastic summer.

Mark thinks Allen is a stuck-up shit, and he obviously isn't very nice to girls, and he's not particularly good looking. But every night at campfire, he whips out his guitar, gives the ladies a little "Fire and Rain" or "Sweet Baby James," and pretty soon he's at least got his hand up their Camp Service T-shirts.

Mark knows Allen has reached the end of the story because all of his blow job stories end with the girl praising the taste of his ejaculate, which Mark very strongly suspects is something Allen saw in a porno movie rather than lived, and so when Allen says, "So damn sweet," Mark has two thoughts. The first is that he doesn't know what he's going to do about this erection because his bed squeaks. The other is that as soon as he gets home, he's getting a guitar.

1989

Mark is sixteen. He is sitting on a stool in front of a microphone stand on a makeshift platform stage at the south end of the mess hall at Camp Service. It's the last night of camp, and Mark is getting ready to perform his hit single, "Pukin' My Guts Out."

Mark never became the guitar-slingling stud of the campfire he envisioned that night on his bunk three summers ago. Too many of his fellow campers had had the same idea, and so there were so many would-be James Taylors crowding around the campfire that the girls decided they preferred the boys who were good at soccer. Mark bristled at the injustice of this. The soccer-playing jocks got all the best girls at Brookline High; did they have to take all the best girls here, too? This was a Unitarian Universalist summer camp for God's (or Great Spirit of Life's, or Goddess's, as you prefer) sake! If a sensitive guitar-playing guy couldn't get a blow job here, what hope was there anywhere on earth?

So by the time he was a CIT, he was playing guitar only for his own enjoyment. But then when he was assigned to the group of eight-year-olds that included his sister Janet, he brought it along, and when they were sitting around feeling cranky one sweltering Wednesday afternoon he brought it out, strummed a G–C–D progression, and freestyled a song he titled "My Baby Sister's Poop."

This was a riotous success with everyone but Janet, who scowled at him for two days until he promised to never, ever mention her in one of those dumb songs again or she would kill him while he slept. After this he treated the eight-year-olds to a daily diet of improvisational comedic folk songs dealing primarily with vomit, excrement, or bad camp food. He hit the trifecta with "Pukin' My Guts Out," and it wasn't long before the eight-year-olds—even Janet, who'd gone from humiliation to pride at her brother's status as a scatological celebrity—were singing it in the mess hall, which led to the nines and tens singing it, which led to the CITs singing it ironically at first, sincerely later.

And so Mark is about to experience the high point of his musical career. He strums the opening of "Pukin' My Guts Out," and before he can finish with his first couplet, "I don't think I can take much more of this / I got stuff leaking out of every orifice," all three hundred campers and CITs are singing along, singing so loudly, in fact, that they drown him out. When the song ends, there is lusty cheering, calls for an encore, calls for "Case of the Runs," calls for "Mystery Meat Mystery." Mark decides not to mess with success and plays "Pukin' My Guts Out" again, and the crowd stomps and claps, and Mark would probably play it again, but Tim, the camp director, steps to the mike and informs the campers that they must get to sleep so they can be bright-eyed and bushy-tailed for their parents' arrival tomorrow, that the last camp director who delivered three hundred hollow-eyed, sleep-deprived zombies to their parents disappeared in the vicinity of the lake and was never heard from again.

Mark feels higher and happier than he's ever felt, like he could fly home under his own power and save his parents a three-hour drive each way. He packs up his guitar, and Tim comes over and says, "Hey, Mark, that was really great."

"Thanks!" Mark says. Everybody says Tim is gay, and Mark

thinks it might be true, and that freaks out most of the male CITs, but Mark finds that he doesn't really care because Tim is really nice and funny and has never once made Mark feel uncomfortable. He sees no contradiction between his affection for Tim, whom he believes (correctly, as it happens) to be gay, and his habit of saying things like "Shut up, fag!" to his friends.

"So you wanna lock up the mess hall for me, just take a few minutes to soak it in, enjoy your success?"

"Yeah, that would be great," Mark says, thinking actually it would be great if he and Becky could make out in here tonight instead of in the storage shed.

"Okay then. I'm sure I can trust you," Tim says as he heads toward the doors, and Mark feels a twinge of guilt and wonders if he should really lock up the mess hall and meet Becky at the shed as usual. Tim smiles as he leaves, and Mark is sure that Tim is somehow reading his mind, and he turns purple with embarrassment.

Mark slowly packs up his guitar, and about two minutes after Tim leaves Becky sticks her head into the mess hall. Becky has bright red hair and the freckles that usually accompany it. She is a fantastic soccer player and is five inches taller than Mark, whose soccer feat of the summer was scoring an own goal and bloodying his nose on the same play.

"Hey," Becky says, and Mark's heart is pounding already.

"Hey, Beckster. I'm a big rock star, huh?"

"Yeah, I'm glad I got a backstage pass."

"Well, you know, only the prettiest girls in the audience get to come backstage," and Mark begins to laugh, both at the idea of his Raffi-like success singing songs about vomit being anything like rock stardom, and at the ridiculousness of a dork like him having this pretend grown-up banter with Becky Randall. Two weeks after their first kiss he still can't believe she likes him. She's tall and beautiful (though insecure about her height, her red hair, and her athletic build) and makes him laugh and, somewhat incredibly, wants to kiss a short, athletically challenged kid who sings songs about poop to eight-year-olds.

"So," Becky says.

"So," Mark says.

"Last night."

"Yeah."

"Are you gonna write to me?"

"Of course. I promise. And I'll call. It's gonna . . . it's gonna be weird not seeing you."

"Yeah."

"I'm gonna miss you."

"Me, too."

"I . . . ," and Mark is starting to get choked up here, and he can hardly get the words out, "I just like you so much, and I . . ." His voice is cracking, which he assumes is a terrible goof that will make Becky hate him for being a wuss, and he doesn't get that he is melting her heart.

"Shh . . . ," Becky says, and kisses him. And then they don't talk.

An hour later Mark is lying on a table in the darkened mess hall, feeling nothing but post-orgasmic contentment. He stands, and Becky leans down to give him a tender kiss.

He's only halfway back to his cabin when it all comes back: sadness about the end of summer, about missing Becky (for he knows in his heart that the letters and the phone calls won't last, that this will end, and, further, that Becky will end it), about what he believes is the end of a spectacular music career. He enters the cabin and, as he always does when he enters late at night, he hears Jamie Sibthorp's voice float down from the top bunk on the east wall.

"So did you get any? Did she give it up? Inquiring minds want to know!"

Mark smiles and thinks that he might actually miss this little ritual that he's found so annoying. He delivers his line for the final time this summer: "Shut up and go to sleep, Jamie."

1990

Mark turned eighteen three weeks ago. He's sitting in his room at Hill House at the University of Pennsylvania. He doesn't want to be here, but nor does he want to be home, where Mom and Dad are blaming each other and it's cold and dark even when it's sunny out.

So he sits in this tiny room that he shares, or rather shared, with Hyung Park. In his first weeks here he joked that the room was so small, he and Hyung could lie in their beds on either side of the room and hold hands if they were so inclined. It's an exaggeration, but if he and Hyung were much taller, it wouldn't be.

No one's seen Hyung in three weeks. Mark had seen lots of pamphlets about salvation by aliens on Hyung's side of the room (OUR LIGHTSPEED REDEEMERS and SALVATION HAS ENTERED OUR QUADRANT were Mark's favorites), and one day he simply vanished. Mark joked to everybody on the hall that Hyung had been beamed aboard the mother ship. And then Hyung's red-eyed crying mother had shown up looking for him, and Mark felt like a shit.

Now he's the one sitting in this room red-eyed. It's Sunday night, and tomorrow he'll have to go make the rounds to his professors, or, more accurately, grad student slaves of the professors, and give the dead-sister speech four times, explain his absence, ask about incompletes, ask about making up work that feels incredibly stupid and pointless.

The thought of doing that is like a rock in his stomach.

He opens the guitar case and brings his guitar out to try to calm himself down. He's randomly strumming chords, and he realizes he's playing "Pukin' My Guts Out." And suddenly he sees

Janet's face, smiling and happy and proud, listening to him play. And he remembers Janet's little hands on this guitar when he was teaching her the basic chords last year. He sees her smiling again, playing him her original composition, "I Get My Brother's Room," on the day he left, on the last day he saw her alive, and the memory is so strong that it knocks the guitar out of his hands and onto his ratty-mattressed bed.

He's crying now—sobbing really, so loud he's sure the whole hall can hear, and fuck them anyway, stupid hateful happy drunk motherfuckers, he hopes they do hear and that it stops their frantic booze-fueled humping for five seconds. He looks through blurry eyes at the guitar and realizes he hasn't changed the strings since the last time Janet played it, and it suddenly strikes him as bizarre and absurd that right here on the strings of this guitar there are traces of Janet, just the oils from her fingers probably, but more than is left of her anywhere else except in the urn at home.

He cries for thirty more minutes until his eyes are puffy and his throat hurts and he feels even more like he just got hit by a truck than he did before, and he realizes that he's going to need a new simile for this feeling, because he's probably going to feel it for a long time, and he doesn't want to think about people being hit by trucks anymore, ever.

He picks up the guitar and puts it back in its case. He will never take it out.

1991

Mark is nineteen. He's sitting in the lounge in the Public Service College House, a tiny dorm for people interested in public service. He sits on a maroon upholstered couch that was new five years ago and can no longer hide the stains very well, and he's slightly cold under the solarium glass. As usual, he has an exam on the last day of finals, so he is one of the very few students left here. Unlike most of the other people still here, he bears no resentment about this. He's not looking forward to another first—last year's misery fest was The First Christmas Since Janet Died, this one is The First Christmas Since The Divorce, and Mark doesn't even know where he's going to stay and whether he'll be the latest thing his folks decide to fight about.

And he doesn't even really have hanging out with his friends to look forward to, either. He was still embarrassed about what happened on the day after Thanksgiving, when a few beers and twenty minutes of sobbing about Janet had convinced him that Christine was not, in fact, just a good friend, but might actually want to drunkenly make out. Unfortunately, Christine had not been convinced that making out was a great idea and had told him she didn't want to ruin their friendship, which they'd had since preschool and which was incredibly important to her. But they'd had just a few awkward phone calls since then, so it looked like their friendship might be tanking anyway, so they might as well have made out. And Josh was off doing some kind of SuperJew thing—leading impressionable Reform Temple Youth Group kids on a ten-day kibbutz stay or something. And everybody else—it was nice to see them, but their conversations were getting limited to "Remember when Ms. Kean said this or that?" or "Remember that time Jeremy filled a beaker with puke in chemistry class?" This was fine as far as it went, but Mark often felt like he was watching these conversations from far away. Yeah, I remember stuff that happened when I was in high school and I lived in my real house and my parents weren't screaming at each other all the time and I had a little sister who was alive. So what?

So he is actually dreading the Christmas break and is happy to have an excuse to stay in Philadelphia for a while. Besides, there is always a strange but kind of exciting after-hours feeling all over campus when most of the students are gone. When Mark stayed here for spring break last year (no way he was going home right after Mom filed for divorce), he had this sense of possibility the whole time, like anything could happen, even though nothing did, beyond going to Chili's with one Mike and three Jennifers, and, after dinner, having Jennifer number two give him the "like you as a friend" speech he had heard so many times from so many girls that he could have said it himself and saved her the trouble.

So he's happy to sit here in the lounge and do pretty much nothing for as long as he can. Right now it's ten P.M. on December 19, and some chubby kid from the third floor has rented a bunch of Christmas movies and is showing them on the big-screen TV in the lounge. So Mark watches *Rudolph the Red-Nosed Reindeer* feeling blank and numb.

This feeling is abruptly replaced when Rudolph, sporting his fake nose, leaps into the air and yells, "I'b cuuuuute!" He had completely forgotten until just this minute how much he and Janet used to like that particular part, and as soon as Rudoph says it, he can hear Janet saying it like she's in the room, and it is physically painful.

And just like that, he's crying. At a cartoon. Or whatever one might call a filmed entertainment starring slightly disturbing puppets. He gets out of the chair he staked out at seven and staggers from the lounge into the hallway, where he sits on the floor, back against the cinder-block wall, and cries.

He's not sure how long he's there. But then he hears Raquel's voice. "Hey, Mark. You wanna watch *It's a Wonderful Life*?"

Mark looks up, embarrassed, and wipes his eyes. "Uh, nah, Rock, I don't think I can handle Zuzu tonight."

Raquel sits next to him. She's tall and thin with very short black hair. Everybody pretty much assumes she's a lesbian, but nobody's ever asked her, and there's been no evidence either way. This is at least in part because though she is in the lounge all the time, she is often silent and brooding, and while she's not big, she is tall and looks like she could probably take out pretty much any resident of the public service dorm, all of whom are just about as strong and athletic as you might expect people interested in devoting their lives to public service to be.

Mark likes to be around other people, too, so he usually sits in the lounge even when he feels like brooding, and so he's always felt like Raquel is some kind of kindred spirit. She's clearly pissed off about something.

But tonight, she's not pissed off, and their lounge rat comradeship seems to have been magnified by the fact that 60 percent of the residents of the dorm are home already.

"You wanna talk about it?"

Mark thinks for a minute. "I don't think so. Thanks, though. I don't even feel like thinking about it."

"I hear you. You wanna kiss me?"

This causes Mark to lift his head. He's never even considered this as a possibility, so he hasn't built up any excitement about the idea, but Raquel is sexy—long and lean and troubled and unpredictable. And kissing Raquel right now would feel good, and he certainly hasn't felt good in a long time.

"Yeah. Yes I do." And just like that, he does.

PHILIPPA

Philippa is in the dressing room at Harrods. It's been one week since Aunt Betsy called about Mom. Mom is out of the hospital, apparently fitted with something called a "flipper," which is a retainer with two false teeth attached, while she waits for the permanent false teeth to be done. When Philippa called her, Mom cried, insisting that this was a real wake-up call, that she was really going to stop drinking, no, this time she meant it, she was incredibly lucky not to be dead, and she had too much to live for to end it right now wrapped around a tree on Clough Pike, for Chrissakes.

Philippa had been at this long enough to know that while Mom believed what she was saying, addicts lied to themselves even more than they lied to everybody else, so she didn't have a lot of confidence in Mom's pledge to take the pledge.

Philippa's own pledge to stop drinking after she puked in the street lasted exactly two days, but the gnawing fear and discontent that surfaced on that day remain. So when Dad gave her a perfunctory invitation to the party he was hosting for his banking colleagues and assorted financial services people, she surprised him and herself by saying she'd love to. She wasn't sure she would actually love to, and going to a party wasn't much of a personal trans-formation, but it just felt like something she would never do, which is why she wanted to do it.

This is how she finds herself in a dressing room in Harrods trying on dresses with Ella on the other side of the door. Ella vol-unteered to help with this because she was not going to have Simon embarrassed by Philippa's inability or unwillingness to dress prop-erly, and also because she hoped that a day alone together would give her the opportunity to tell Philippa that she needed to stop being a sponge, that she was taking advantage of a wonderful man, or, anyway, a good man, that it was time to start acting like an adult instead of a spoiled child.

Philippa looks at herself in the mirror. She's not quite sure who this person in the dress is. If it weren't for the hair and makeup, she'd look pretty at home in this dress, and she has to admit it shows off Trevor's favorite features well—it's obviously ex-pensive, and her breasts look fantastic—but it still feels more than a little off.

She peels it off and puts her jeans and T-shirt back on. She throws the dress over her arm and exits the dressing room. Ella smiles and says, "Well?"

"I like it. If I can get my hair to calm down a little bit, I think it'll look great."

Ella smiles a genuine smile, surprised that Philippa is giving more than her usual series of grunts and hopeful that she'll man-age not to be an embarrassment at the party.

Philippa pays for the dress with Simon's money, and Ella sug-gests they have lunch. "Do you know any good places?" Ella asks. "I'm always on the lookout for something new."

Philippa wonders if Ella is fucking with her. Her experience with London cuisine is limited to what Trevor refers to as the three c's: chippie, curry, chinkie. "Uh, I really don't know anyplace good."

"Shall I pick a good spot then?" Ella says, and she hails a taxi, which she directs to a small restaurant where every item on the menu costs more than anything at Café Bombay, which is Phillppa's usual big splurge. On days when I get my allowance, she thinks.

They eat soup, and as the bowls are cleared away Ella makes her move: "So you've had a good summer, then?" She knows perfectly well that it's October 8, and that summer is long gone, and she hopes her question will be a subtle reminder that just as it's not really appropriate to be talking about summer in October, it's not appropriate for Philippa to continue living her carefree summer life this late in the year.

"I guess. No, the summer was great. The fall has been less great. And I don't know what the hell's going to happen in the winter."

"No plans, then?" Ella says. She believes she has just slid the knife between Philippa's ribs, and so she's completely unprepared for Philippa to respond sincerely.

"I don't know, I mean . . . look, I appreciate you being nice to me and taking me out and everything, especially because I'm usually such a bitch at home, which is usually just because I'm hungover."

"Well, you . . . your father thinks the world of you, and I think the world of him, so I feel like it's my—"

"Look, I know I'm a mess. You're nice to pretend I'm not a mess, but I know I'm a mess. It's . . . like I thought I was all superior to everybody at school who had the next ten years all planned out, but now I'm just . . . I'm not having fun. And I feel useless. I mean, I always figured Dad owed me for leaving me alone with Mom and Jack Daniel's all those years, but I'm getting . . . I drink too much, I'm not good at anything, and I don't really understand why I'm alive." Philippa pauses, not sure where all this came from or why she just unloaded it on Ella.

Ella is surprised to find herself feeling affection for this lost girl she wanted to berate. She is aware that Philippa may have pulled a stunning act of emotional jujitsu on her, shifting her weight and turning Ella's offense into a liability, but she just doesn't believe Philippa to be that guileful.

She's also aware of being terribly out of her depth. She's thirty-six, childless, and dating a man fifteen years her senior. She neither loves nor hates her job at the bank, and frankly doesn't know what she's good at or why she's alive, either. She sits silently for ten seconds, and Philippa rushes in to fill the silence.

"I'm sorry, Ella, I mean, I shouldn't drop all this on you, I mean, I guess it's kind of weird, we don't really know each other, but I never get to—"

"Hush. I was just—I mean, those are the questions, aren't they? What am I good at? Why am I alive? I'm sure many of your schoolmates are at university precisely so they don't have to think about those questions for a few more years. So maybe you're less of a mess than you think." Or perhaps I'm more of a mess than I think, she adds to herself.

"I wish I agreed with you."

"Well, let's get our hair done after lunch, and then at least you won't look a mess." Ella smiles as she says this last part.

Philippa squashes down her punk rock contempt for this whole scene—it's so shallow: Let's go shopping, and if we run up against any uncomfortable questions, we'll get our hair done. Still, she realizes, it's not like her normal life is very different—substitute booze and music for the shopping and beautifying, and vaguely Labour politics from people who don't vote for the Tory politics of people who do, and you've got much the same thing.

Well, her hair is a mess, and she'd like to look good for the party.

It's six thirty. Philippa, with her hair newly done by Ella's stylist in a style that is adventurous by banking standards and conservative by punk rock standards, walks into a Junction Bar nearly devoid of patrons, yet still reeking of smoke and stale beer. Trevor sits at a table sipping a pint she actually didn't buy for him. He looks up at her and spits a bit of beer back into his pint glass as he begins laughing hysterically.

"Bloody fucking hell! What the fuck's happened to your fucking hair, then? You look a complete fucking twit! Going to work at Daddy's bank, then?"

Philippa entertains an Indiana Jones fantasy in which she pulls out her revolver, shoots Trevor in the forehead, turns, and walks out. Fortunately for Trevor, guns are much harder to come by in the UK than in the US, and even if they were readily available, Philippa would not be carrying one in a holster on her hip.

She does the next best thing she can think to do with her sudden, volcanic anger—she walks over to the table, picks up the pint glass, and dumps the contents onto Trevor's crotch.

"Fuck! Bloody psychotic fucking cunt!" Trevor begins as he hops to his feet, and Philippa turns around and walks out.

Jeanie behind the bar calls out laughing, "Fucking brilliant! Your next pint's on me, Philippa!"

The offer of a free pint does very little to quell Philippa's anger, and her stomach feels tight and sour from being so angry. Of course, it really shouldn't surprise her that much that Trevor mocked her to her face. If it had been someone else who suddenly Torified her look, she probably would have joined Trevor in making fun. She decides to take an indirect, rambling way home in the hope of calming herself down.

She didn't really have time for a pint with Trevor anyway. In fact, she might not be finding much time for pints or anything else with Trevor in the future. She's tired of being the drunken loafer Trevor seems so fond of. But he is right to laugh at the idea of her working in a bank. And returning to Cincinnati doesn't feel like a very good option, either. Well, she'll worry about the rest of her life tomorrow. Tonight she has a party to attend.

She returns to Simon's flat as Ella says, "Philippa! Someone named Trevor rang twice!"

Philippa barely finishes saying, "Thanks, Ella," when the phone chirps again. She picks it up. "Strange residence, Philippa Jane Strange speaking," she says, knowing it'll be Trevor again.

"Fuck. I'm sorry. I'm such a stupid fucking cunt," Trevor says.

"If you're expecting me to argue with you, I'm not gonna do it."

"No, I just. Fuck. I'm a complete fucking shit and I'm sorry. The world's full of fucking prats who deserve to be shit on, but you aren't one of them, and I'm a fucking idiot, and I'm really fucking sorry. Let me buy you dinner."

Even including all the fucks, this is the nicest thing Trevor has ever said to her, and Philippa finds herself feeling all gooey inside, which is a rather strange thing to be feeling about Trevor so soon after wanting to shoot him in the head.

"I . . . I can't tonight. My dad's having a party, and I promised I would be here and not embarrass him with the way I look, and I feel like I owe it to him."

"Oh."

"But how about tomorrow?"

"All right then." He's sulking, and Philippa feels a strange urge to cheer him up.

"I'll bring my tits."

"Couldn't very well leave them at home, could you?" he asks, but she can hear the smile on his face.

"You don't know what I can do. I'll see you tomorrow."

"Right. Okay."

Philippa readies herself for the party, and when the guests start to arrive, they are greeted by the ever-dapper Simon Strange, looking especially sharp with his salt-and-pepper beard neatly trimmed and sporting new and expensive spectacles; Ella Roberts, slim, pretty, and sporting an appropriately conservative black dress; and Philippa, who is trying not to stumble in the one pair of heels she owns and who is wearing the expensive, breast-flattering dress she purchased this morning.

Philippa makes the rounds at the party and politely feigns interest in the many incredibly boring old people her father introduces her to. When they inevitably ask about her plans, she tells them that she is giving the UK an extended audition as she attempts to choose which of her home countries to live in. This usually gives the boring people an opening to either bash the United

States as a nation of boors or praise the United States as a bastion of free-market democracy where the poor can't leech off the hard work of others quite so readily as they do here.

Philippa has no interest in any of this and nods politely before excusing herself to get another glass of wine.

This happens at least five times, and Philippa is thinking that there is a damn good reason she never did stuff like this, which is that it's painful. These people are all exactly like the parents of her classmates from Walnut Prep—wealthy, self-satisfied, boring boring boring. Even the alcoholic parents who'd hosted keggers for high school students and creepily stalked around the parties with a Heineken in their hand observing the drunken sixteen-year-olds were boring, as Philippa had discovered one evening when she and Tracy had been stuck talking to Chad Morris's dad about the Bengals for half an hour. Philippa remembers that horrible feeling of being trapped, and it's coming back.

She pours herself another glass of wine. She doesn't know what number this one is, nor is she aware that continuing her alcohol consumption at this rate will cause her to embarrass her father with her behavior and potential vomiting rather than with her punk rock appearance.

She turns around, glass in hand, and finds herself face-to-face with a man in his mid-twenties who has the short, stocky body of a rugby player stuffed into expensive Italian clothes. He was in one of the circles Philippa fled from, and she hadn't looked at him twice.

But now he's in her face. "Have to flee from the boring old people, eh?" he asks.

Philippa is too drunk to lie. "Yeah, I just couldn't hear another word about Paul Volcker and US monetary policy."

"Can't blame you. Horribly tedious stuff. At least you don't have to be around it every day."

"Well, nobody makes you work there, do they?"

"No, quite right. Turns out, though, that I'm a bit of a materialistic shit with a talent for this kind of thing. So I do boring work so I can afford to live the way I want to live. At any rate, nobody's told you the main reason to live in the UK."

"Which is?"

"Fucking horrible beer in the States. I lived in New York for two years and barely survived on dusty bottles of Bass ale. Can't drink the stuff now—reminds me too much of those dark years in the land of Miller Lite. Tastes like piss! Less filling!"

Philippa smiles and introduces herself again to the guy she's been mentally calling Rugby Boy. Rugby Boy's name is Christian. He is flying to New York on business in a few weeks and plans to catch the Clash opening for the Who at Giants Stadium. He attended the same Clash show Philippa saw when he was nineteen. He perceives no contradiction between his love for the Clash and his employment as an investment banker. He appears to believe that calling himself a materialistic shit excuses him from actually being a materialistic shit, and Philippa finds that he seems to be at least partially correct about this.

The party drags on and on, but Philippa is enjoying talking to this guy, and she feels suddenly self-conscious. That is, she is suddenly, painfully aware of having a self. She feels as though she is outside herself, looking at this young woman being hit on by the young banker and wondering who the hell she is. She decides another drink would be a nice way to get this feeling to go away, but before she can pour it, Christian informs her that it's actually quite a pleasant night for October and would she fancy a walk?

Vaguely aware that this is a dumb idea, Philippa says that yes, she would fancy a walk.

Suddenly she's outside, and it's actually not that pleasant at all. It's cold, and it feels like it might rain, and Christian is saying something, and she is nodding but really just thinking about how having those beefy arms around her would be very different from Trevor's stick-thin limbs, and she's quite curious to make the comparison.

Walking down the block in the other direction, unseen by

Philippa and Christian, is Trevor. He's made a cringingly pathetic attempt to smarten up as much as he can, which means that his jeans are clean and do not have holes in them, his belt has no studs, his shoes do not have rubber soles, and his flatmate lent him an iron and showed him how to use it so that his button-down shirt would not be wrinkled. He spots Philippa and Christian, and sees Philippa lean her head on his shoulder. He follows them.

Philippa and Christian walk ten minutes, and Philippa says, "So, where are we going?"

"Well, my flat's just around the corner, if you'd like to go someplace quiet," Christian says, and Philippa thinks that this guy is completely full of shit with his pleasant night, just happen to know a quiet place with a bed and a dresser drawer full of condoms bit, and that agreeing to go to his flat and have sex with him is something one version of herself wouldn't do just to punish him for his cheesiness, but she's trying on a different version of herself, and the idea of cheating on Trevor, of being somebody else tonight, of having sex with someone she's just met, which she's never done before, is actually very exciting.

"Yeah, I'd like to go someplace quiet. And maybe make it not so quiet," she says, because as long as Christian is a cheeseball, she might as well be a cheeseball herself.

They round the corner, and it begins to rain. They laugh and run for the entryway of a building that turns out to contain Christian's flat. Before they can make it to the door, though, Philippa grabs Christian and kisses him, and the raindrops pelt them on their heads and her tongue explores his mouth, which tastes like scotch.

Half a block away Trevor ducks into a doorway, pulls out a Silk Cut, and lights it. He is crying, which he will never tell anyone. In his brain he runs down the street and throws a punch at the guy, but in real life he stays in the doorway, afraid of what a guy who obviously played rugby might do to him if he started throwing punches.

Trevor is not afflicted with the thoughtfulness and self-doubt that so often cause Philippa to have one more drink than she should; he does not ponder whether anything that he has done might have contributed to this moment. He merely stands there smoking and watching the rain run down Philippa's pretty lying face, and as she and Christian disappear into the building, Trevor stays in the doorway.

By the time he leaves, his anger and humiliation have given birth to the one great song he will ever write.

MARK
1992

It's May 7. Mark once again has a final on the final day of finals. He sits on his creaky dorm bed with a gigantic duffel bag half full of his clothes at his feet and boxes half full of his records and books all over the room. He is naked.

Raquel, in black cotton panties and a black cotton tank top, stands next to the bed. "Get dressed, stud boy. More packing to do."

"Ugh. Okay, okay. But if I start packing, that means I have to leave, which means I have to say good-bye, which means I don't see you for three months."

"We do have telephones in Nebraska. And the Pony Express brings us mail and notions from the Sears and Roebuck catalog once a fortnight!"

"Yeah, yeah. I'm gonna miss you."

"You're gonna miss having sex every day."

"That, too, but—"

"I know. You don't have to tell me. But you do have to pack."

"Okay." Mark rises, dons a pair of red boxer shorts with palm trees on them, and begins taking books off the shelf and putting them into a box. Raquel digs in the closet, bringing out a truly hideous shirt.

"Hey, this is sexy. How come you never wear this?"

"My grandma gave it to me, okay?"

"Sexy. Put it on!"

"Uh, how about no."

"Okay, into the duffel bag, then. Good thing you're gonna haul it on the train back to Boston and not wear it there, either."

"Yeah, yeah, yeah." Mark smiles. He does enjoy the sex, but he'll also miss this kind of conversation, this kind of easy companionship, which is really rare—it might almost be rebuilt with Christine after his attempted mauling last year, and certainly it was there with Josh, but neither Josh nor Mark would even be in Brookline for most of the summer anyway.

In any case, he's used to having this kind of companionship all the time, and he doesn't know how he's going to get through the summer without it. Mom is selling the house he grew up in, and Dad is already in his bachelor condo in some building full of ancient Russians in Coolidge Corner. He will head back to Camp Service and work as a counselor despite the fact, or possibly because of the fact, that it's going to remind him of Janet and rip his heart out every single day. There will be people he likes at camp, but they won't understand, and they'll probably be tiptoeing around him the whole time, afraid to say the wrong thing, and they won't understand. But Raquel . . . Raquel's mother killed herself two years ago, and there's something that happened in high school that she won't talk about, which kind of terrifies him, but the point is that he likes the understanding they have that life is dark and unpredictable and horrible, and that not knowing where you're going to score weed before the next Phish concert is not something that counts as an actual problem.

Mark gets up and begins throwing more clothes he never wears into his duffel bag, and he sees the guitar case in the back of the closet. He lugged it back to Brookline last year, and back again this year, and he still hasn't opened it since the first time he tried to play it after Janet's death. Suddenly it looks like it weighs about three hundred pounds, and the idea of squeezing onto the Amtrak holding this thing, this gigantic heavy reminder, this thing that might as well be a coffin to him, except that they burned up her coffin, is suddenly hateful.

"Hey, you want a guitar?"

Raquel stops. "Really?"

"I really can't stand to look at it anymore, and I don't want to carry it anymore. I used to . . . I wrote songs for Janet on it."

"And you want me to have it?"

"Yeah. Yes I do."

Raquel is silent for a moment. "Wow." She pauses again for ten full seconds. "Thank you." Another five seconds. "You know, I used to play in high school."

"Yeah, you told me."

"Here, I'll play you something," and she opens the case, and Mark has this sudden moment of fear, like he thinks Janet is going to pop out, which he knows to be crazy but thinks anyway. Janet does not appear, and Raquel begins something that she intends to be "Wild Thing" but is completely unrecognizable due to the fact that the guitar hasn't been played or tuned in a year and a half. She grimaces and smiles and begins to put the guitar back in the case, and Mark suddenly remembers about Janet's finger oils on the strings.

"Wait, wait!"

"Yeah?" She looks at him quizzically.

"Uh, this is gonna sound crazy, but I need the strings."

"You need the strings."

"Yeah. There's another pack in the case." Raquel looks at him like she wants to ask, but, sensing that she's stepped into one of Mark's dark places, she backs away as Mark always does when he steps into one of hers. Mark has seen enough movies to know that you are supposed to love someone for the things they say to you, but right now at this moment he loves Raquel for what she doesn't say. Without a word she digs the little lever out of the case, pops the pegs out, removes the strings, and hands them to Mark.

When he returns to Brookline, Mark will have his friend

Christine, whom he always teases about being artsy-fartsy, make him a bracelet from the E string. It will be ugly and uncomfortable, and he will wear it every day.

1993

It is a raw, rainy November morning, and Mark stands at a TWA gate in the Philadelphia airport. He's trying very hard not to cry. It's not working.

Raquel is rooting through her carry-on bag looking for lip balm. She finds a small yellow tin, opens it, and smears the balm on her lips.

"You know the air in there is so dry, it . . . Oh, geez, come here," she says. She stands and holds Mark, and he cries great gulping sobs.

"I'm just . . . I . . ." He's unable to speak. If he could speak, he would say something like I'm trying very hard to be excited for you, but I can't understand why you're leaving me, I can't understand why you won't wait, I can't understand why it's so goddamn urgent for you to go to LA now in November, instead of in the spring, and you're my best and, let's face it, only friend here, and what am I going to do without you, what am I going to do?

The agent announces that they will now be preboarding passengers traveling with small children or who need special assistance.

Though neither one of them is traveling with a small child and if anybody needs special assistance here, it's Mark, Raquel breaks off the hug, grabs her red-and-white ticket folder from her bag, reaches down, and picks up her hard plastic guitar case.

"I gotta go, sweetie," she says. "They're about to call my row."

"Okay."

"You have Amy's number, right?"

"Yeah."

"Okay, so call me. Everything will be okay, you know."

"If you say so."

She smiles. "I promise."

The agent announces that they will now be boarding their first-class passengers, and Raquel kisses him quickly and without tongue and heads for the gate. Mark stands at the gate watching the plane until the last passenger has been loaded on and the weird flat truck pushes it away from the gate.

He walks through the airport to the train that will take him back to campus. He tries not to cry, and he does a good job until the train comes. He sits on the vinyl seat and looks out the window at Philadelphia, which is certainly not looking its best this gray morning, and he feels bereft. What will he do? He's never been to Los Angeles, and he has no idea if he'd like to be there, and he doesn't know if being the rock star's boyfriend would be fun or just emasculating. Already he'd been getting jealous as she spent more time practicing, as she was surrounded by male and female fans after every gig, as she gained a career while he was floundering, not knowing what he was going to do after graduation, afraid because he didn't know and afraid because he didn't particularly care.

The train chugs absurdly slowly, and Mark wonders how SEPTA can unironically call this a high-speed airport train. Finally it pulls in to 30th Street Station, and Mark feels that he is, for the moment, all cried out.

He walks past the bronze statue of the angel lifting the fallen soldier to heaven and out the door to Market Street. He walks home to Public Service House and sits in his room. He pops Raquel's demo CD into his CD player and listens to her angry, percussive acoustic songs. He likes "Rotten to the Core" and her cover of Suicidal Tendencies' "Mommy" (which always struck Mark as an unlikely cover choice for someone whose Mommy actually is dead), but he wishes there were a tender love song in here.

Days pass in a fog, and Mark attends classes, does his required reading and writing, spends hours in the lounge talking to people he likes but has to admit are really just acquaintances, and feeling like a total idiot for not making any real friends besides Raquel.

He calls Amy's house and realizes for the first time that Raquel has a place to stay in LA because she actually made a friend last year. He calls at a variety of times for a week and somehow manages to miss Raquel each time. He's frustrated because he wants to leave a pathetic, lovelorn message, but Amy always answers the phone, and so he just makes his voice sound pathetic, which isn't much of an effort, and says, "Just tell her I called."

Frustrated with his inability to communicate, he stays up late one night writing a letter. He writes it by hand rather than typing it on his computer. He does this because it feels more immediate, more intimate somehow. He is unaware of this now, but an additional benefit to this mode of communication is that he will never have a copy of this pathetic, maudlin, clingy letter (or any of the seven that will follow) to read and feel embarrassed by. His exact phrasing will mercifully fade from his memory, which is a blessing, but he will remember telling her that she is everything to him, and he will remember telling her that he thinks it's fitting that she has this guitar with the strong connection to Janet, because she brought him so much happiness when he was wondering if he'd ever feel it again.

He gets two messages from Raquel, both of which arrive while he's in the dining hall. As a senior, he has snagged one of the coveted single rooms in Public Service House, which means his unheard-of-for-college privacy is going to waste with Raquel so far away, but his machine is his alone, so she has the opportunity to tell him very explicitly how much she loves and misses him, how much her body is aching for his touch.

Instead, she tells him this: "Hey, Mark, it's Rock. It's eighty degrees here! Talk to you soon!" and this: "Hey! I was swimming in the ocean today! The recording is going great! I met Clive Davis! He's so old! Bye!"

1994

It is March. It's a good day in Philadelphia: sixty degrees and sunny. It is that day when everyone simultaneously decides it's the first day of spring no matter what the calendar says. People are walking around campus in shorts, and all the green space along Locust Walk is crowded with people playing Frisbee or Hacky Sack or just sitting there, soaking up the nonwintry air.

Mark walks down Locust Walk and continues down Walnut Street toward Rittenhouse Square. On Rittenhouse Square there is a small variety store run by an ancient Greek man. Mark goes here to buy *Playboy* magazine. Of course they sell *Playboy* in the campus bookstore, but he's afraid of being spotted buying it there by that girl from his Islamic history class who is just painfully cute but whom he never talks to. He also has a fear—which he recognizes to be neurotic—that somehow he will be spotted buying porn and this will in some way jeopardize his graduate school plans to get an elementary education certificate back in Boston. As if somehow someone affiliated with the Massachusetts Department of Education might be in the Penn Bookstore, see him buying the "Girls of Wal-Mart" issue, and point a finger and denounce him as morally unfit to educate youth.

He ventured into one of the porno stores on Market Street a few months ago but hated all the pathetic men lurking down the aisles, and he just couldn't bring himself to be the kind of person who pays for a magazine called *Dripping Wet Teens, Cum Slurping Sluts,* or *Clean Shaven Squirters!* On his first visit to Rittenhouse Variety, he'd purchased a *Penthouse* magazine, remembering fondly the copies of this magazine that his childhood friend Spence Roberts had stolen from his dad and passed on to Mark when he was done with them. He was horrified to find that today's *Pent-*

house featured a number of urination shots, which was simply not a kink that appealed to him.

So he settled for *Playboy*, which was absurdly tame by *Cum Slurping Sluts* standards but still better as masturbation imagery than memories of sex with Raquel, which only made him sad at this point.

Mark spoke to Raquel for a total of ten minutes in her first month in LA. He got increasingly angry that his daily messages were so rarely returned, and always at times when he was in class or at meals, and that his twice-weekly letters were never answered in kind.

Finally his self-pity turned completely to anger, and he sent her this:

Dear Rock:

I don't know why you don't call me or write me back. I understand that you're busy, that you've got this exciting new career happening, and that you don't feel my absence as keenly as I feel yours because I was never there, and even now I still see you everywhere I go in Philadelphia.

Still, I guess I have to wonder what, if anything, the last two years meant to you if you can make such a clean break so quickly. I feel as stupid and pathetic as I probably look sending you all these puppy-dog letters and calling you all the time, so I'm going to stop now. I hope when the recording's done, you'll have more time and you will want to communicate with me again. I know I said this already, but I can't understand what sense you make of the last two years if you can just cut me off. I can't understand why you told me to write and call if what you really intended was to break up with me. I can't understand much, except that you don't want to talk to me right now. You know where to find me if you change your mind.

Sincerely,
Mark

He felt pretty good about putting "Sincerely" instead of "Love." That, he thought, would show her. He had no idea if it actually did, because she never wrote him back.

So three months later he grabs his copy of *Playboy* off the rack, puzzles briefly over whether the woman whose name and image are on the cover is an actual celebrity that he should have heard of, and glances briefly at the rest of the magazines looking for something else to cover up the *Playboy* purchase. He usually chooses *Rolling Stone* because it's printed in a larger format than *Playboy*, and he can slip the *Playboy* right into the center of the *Rolling Stone*, roll the *Rolling Stone* up, and hopefully get away with it as long as nobody looks too closely and notices that the *Rolling Stone* is much thicker than it should be. The top of the current issue of *Rolling Stone* is peeking out, and it says: THE NEXT ISSUE! WHO'S NEXT IN MUSIC, MOVIES, BOOKS, AND TV!

Mark walks home with the *Playboy* tucked into *Rolling Stone*, and he actually does pass that girl from class on Locust Walk emerging from the bookstore (!), so clearly all the soft-porn subterfuge was worth it. (Had Mark gone into the sex shop at 20th and Market an hour earlier, he would have spotted the same girl buying a ten-inch translucent pink dildo there, and they would have had at least one thing besides history class on which to hang a conversation, and both of their lives might have been different as a result. As it stands, Mark has his *Playboy* tucked into the "Next" issue of *Rolling Stone*, Katrina has her dildo nestled at the bottom of her bag, and they will never speak.)

When he returns to his room, Mark decides to delay his gratification by actually reading *Rolling Stone* before he even opens *Playboy*. He reads without much interest about which beautiful men and women will be the next big movie stars, which guy with close-shaven stubble is the next hot author, and the band of identically dressed Poles who are reinventing rock and roll.

Because Mark's every thought of Raquel involves her meeting with catastrophic career failure that brings her back to Philadelphia on her knees, he is shocked when he reaches the page with her picture on it. Something strange has been done to her hair, her face appears to be caked in makeup, and the words over her head say ROCK-L!

She is going by Rock-L, or possibly ROCK-L. Mark feels something he can't identify. He knows that the Raquel he knew would have laughed at the ridiculousness of this name. Who the hell is ROCK-L?

He wants to tear the magazine up, possibly spit on ROCK-L's face, but instead he finds himself continuing to read:

Singer-songwriter ROCK-L has been electrifying LA club audiences for months, and industry insiders are abuzz about this newcomer's stage presence and sure hand with an angry pop hook. Holed up for months in the home studio of her manager-producer, Aussie music legend Cal Tomkins (known for his work with Kylie Minogue, Whitesnake, and even Helen Reddy), ROCK-L is putting the finishing touches on an album that already has record execs in a bidding frenzy. "Cal brings a fine-tuned commercial sensibility to ROCK's angry pop, and the combination is dynamite," says Clive Davis, an admitted bidder for the album. "This is already the finest debut album I've heard since Bruce Springsteen's Greetings from Asbury Park.*"*

Of course, Springsteen never had this kind of sex appeal. ROCK-L is candid about her bisexuality, and tales of the parties at Tomkins's house in the Hollywood Hills have scandalized even jaded LA partygoers. ROCK-L draws throngs of male and female fans to every gig. While Tomkins tells us to expect a few songs "that should please the Howard Stern audience," he and everyone else agrees that her first single is the blistering rocker "Two Minute Man," a kiss-off to a boyfriend so sexually inept that he drove her into the arms of an unnamed older man who would seem to be Tomkins.

ROCK-L won't discuss the song's subject ("Everything I want to say about him is in the song," she says) or whether

Tomkins is the older man who compares so favorably with the titular sad sack. What's undeniable is that the song strikes a nerve with female listeners, and sounds like a huge hit.

Mark is overcome by a wave of feelings that he can't separate out. Anger, certainly. Humiliation, check. Shock. And, strangely, sexual excitement. He simply can't digest everything: She's bisexual? Is that just hype? Had she been cheating on him? With a woman? With Amy? Why hadn't he been allowed to watch? Two minutes? Behavior that scandalized jaded partygoers?

The person under all that makeup and under that ridiculous hairstyle is the actual human he knew as Raquel, the girl to whom he lost his virginity (for like the president of the United States, the Speaker of the House, and most American men, Mark didn't count receiving a blow job as actual sex), the girl he cried over for months, the girl to whom he gave the "Pukin' My Guts Out" guitar, the girl he'd told everything about Janet, the girl who, on the anniversary of her mother's death, had curled up in his arms, crying real tears all over him and saying, "I just want my mommy back." He knew Raquel. Who the hell is ROCK-L? And was she there all along, or did Sven Galli, or whatever the hell the ancient Australian pervert's name was, create her?

He masturbates quickly and angrily, remembering Raquel clutching his back, and the strangled cry she always gave at orgasm, and it's only after he's finished that he wonders if any of it was real.

PHILIPPA

Philippa does not sleep at Christian's flat.
The sex meets but does not exceed Trevor's standards, and is largely the headlong rush to (his) orgasm that she's come to expect. As Christian falls asleep, Philippa dons her party dress and sprints home in the rain.

When she gets home, the party is over, Simon and Ella are asleep in Simon's room (or so Philippa tells herself, simply because the idea of her father as a sexual being is not one she wishes to entertain), and Philippa heads to her own room. Surrounded there by her own clothes, her own stuff, she realizes that tonight's masquerade hasn't changed anything. She doesn't want to be the person who sleeps in this room, but she finds she doesn't care much for the girl who just came from Christian's flat, either. She feels stupid: she wanted to try to be somebody else, hoping it would change things, that she would somehow feel different, but the sad truth is, it's changed nothing.

Or so Philippa believes. In point of fact everything is about to change, but as Philippa stares at the ceiling with her buzz wearing off and the postdrunk self-loathing taking over, she doesn't know this.

Trevor, on the other hand, does. He calls the following day at eleven thirty, just as Philippa finishes *The Guardian*.

"So how was the party?" he asks.

"Oh, boring. Bunch of prats from Dad's bank. I was glad when it was over." Well, that much was true.

"Didn't meet anyone interesting, then?" There is no edge in Trevor's voice. He's not trying to get a confession or start a fight. He simply wants Philippa to lie so that his song will be completely accurate.

"Interesting? In a room full of bankers? Yeah, right." And Philippa does not feel that this is a lie, because now that she is back into her own skin, or anyway the one that she wears most often, she doesn't find Christian the least bit interesting, and she is comforted by the knowledge that he is a materialistic, self-absorbed shit (he doesn't cop to the self-absorbed part, but it's obvious) who won't call, and she can just pretend that last night never even happened. "So, Junction at seven?"

"Not tonight, I'm afraid. I've got a fucking brilliant song in my head, and I've gotta teach it to the band before the gig tomorrow."

"Do I get to hear it?"

"You'll hear it tomorrow, like everybody else."

"Is there anything I can do to persuade you to give me a private performance? Maybe I could give you a priva—"

"No, sorry, Phil, I mean, it's a tempting offer, but Evan thinks he can get us some cheap studio time after midnight, so we may go record some tracks after practice."

"Oh. Okay. Well, see you tomorrow, then."

"I'm counting on it," Trevor says, and he sounds for all the world like the dumb, lustful lunk that Philippa believes him to be. Later when she remembers this conversation, she will imagine him hanging up and laughing a maniacal mad-scientist laugh. In fact, he hangs up and whispers, "Fucking lying cunt."

Faced with two days without Trevor to distract her, Philippa decides to do some thinking. Or rather, she finds her mind wandering down uncomfortable paths and she doesn't particularly feel like drinking this early in the day by herself, so she decides to just let her mind have its way for a bit. She leaves the flat, intending at first to just walk to the corner shop for a tube of Smarties, but she ends up walking aimlessly, not paying much attention to the city around her and not getting chocolate.

She realizes she can't keep seeing Trevor. In fact, she needs to break up with him tomorrow night. She'll miss the sex, but one thing last night did show her is that she probably won't have much difficulty in that area. And she just hates hates hates Trevor's girl-friend, and she doesn't know how she can stop being that lazy alcoholic and still be Trevor's girlfriend.

She walks and walks. She stops at a chip shop and gets a gigan-tic bag of chips and a can of lemonade. She eats as she walks, and she keeps walking. She tries to conjure up some fantasies about the future, some idea of herself in one year, five years, ten years that will make her happy. Married? With kids? In school, out of school? She has no idea. She wonders what it's like to be able to picture a nice house in Indian Hill and a Beemer in the driveway and a hus-band who's vice president in charge of Bounty or Crest or Crisco or whatever at Procter & Gamble, which is undoubtedly where many of her classmates from Walnut Prep will end up. She tries to see herself there and can't, which is a relief in one way, but she also just wishes she could see herself somewhere, anywhere.

What about Trevor and her so-called friends here? Where do they see themselves in five years? Well, Trevor's pretty straight-forward about the British Rock Star Fantasy, which involves a big house that used to belong to Lord Somebodyorother, and how much he wants to have enough money to buy a house like that where all his mates could kip if they wanted and fuck the rich cunt who used to own it. (Philippa is aware that Trevor would then be the rich cunt who owned the big house, but Trevor seems unable to make the connection. But what about everybody else? On the dole and drunk as much as possible? Or do they just not think about it because they've got no future? Is that why the Sex Pistols were ac-tually popular here?)

Tired of walking, and tired of thinking, Philippa finds herself outside a cheesy tourist establishment on Oxford Street called EAT AT JOE'S AMERICAN BAR AND GRILL. On a whim she walks in. The place is done up like an American bar, with more baseball pennants, football helmets, and American flags than you'd ever see in a real American bar. There's even red-white-and-blue bunting hanging from the bar like it's the Fourth of July or something, though of course it's early October. She steps out of herself again, and watches as an attractive American girl with a haircut too radical for banking but too conservative to be a scary street punk walks up to the bar, asks for the manager, and asks if they need a real American for anything around here. Ten minutes later she's got a waitressing job, her first job ever. She'll start in two days.

When she gets home that night, Philippa's feet ache, but she feels strangely good. She eats dinner with Simon and Ella and relishes the surprise on both their faces when she reveals that she's gotten a job. She notices Dad looks like he just exhaled after holding his breath for a long, long time, and she has her first inkling that her freeloading may have been making him somewhat uncomfortable.

When Philippa arrives at the club the next evening, it looks for all the world like a typical NHS gig. There are the band's twenty loyal fans, of whom four are not former schoolmates or present girlfriends of the band, a handful of people who probably come out to this club every night, and another handful who are actually here for a band playing later in the night.

Philippa waves at Trevor as he takes the stage, and he nods in her direction. The NHS plays their typical set, but Trevor's performance is atypical. He's an emaciated spitting demon of rage, singing even the stupidest of his songs (and, Philippa reflects, the level of stupidity is so high throughout that she would have a hard time choosing which of the songs is the stupidest, though if forced she supposes she'd choose "Booze Up") with what appears to be real passion.

Trevor is really pouring his heart into this performance, and the NHS appears to be winning over the members of the crowd who came to see another band. The fans of Organ Doner Kebab are trickling in, and instead of huddling by the bar and looking scornful, they are pressing toward the stage. This is certainly the best show that Philippa's ever seen the NHS put on, and it makes her feel better about her plans to dump Trevor. He won't be completely lost without her.

The NHS winds up their typical set closer, "Servants' Entrance," an angry mix of class resentment and lust that Philippa believes to be Trevor's nastiest and best song. In fact, it is Trevor's nastiest and best song that Philippa knows of, which will prove an important distinction. The crowd roars its approval, and Philippa notices Dave, the bass player for the NHS, staring at her. She looks at him quizzically, and he jerks his head at the exit.

She looks at him more quizzically, and he mouths something that looks like *Go. Leave* while jerking his head at the door.

Philippa can't make any sense of that, and Trevor looks over at Dave, who stops trying to communicate silently from the stage. "Hang on," Trevor says, "we got one more. This one's for somebody special."

John, the drummer, bangs his sticks together, and the band rips into a chugging, propulsive song that Philippa doesn't recognize.

For many years Philippa will think about this moment and wish that she could somehow return to it and change things. Of course, the moment she left the party with Christian was the actual turning point, but this moment, when the first bars of "Philippa Cheats" begin, this is the moment she wants to recapture. She wants to go back, to understand Dave's warning, to run from the club straight to Heathrow, get on a plane, and go hide out in Cincinnati and go to secretarial school and listen to Jimmy Buffett and work downtown and never even know of the song's existence.

But of course, she doesn't understand Dave's warning, she doesn't leave the club, and she doesn't get it even when Trevor begins:

Saw you in the rain outside of his place
With the drops running down your pretty lying face
Saw you in the rain melt into his arms
Next time I see you gonna do you harm

The shame, the humiliation, the anger have not arrived yet. Philippa is feeling only two things. The first is that this song kicks ass, and is already the best thing Trevor's ever written. The second is a kind of confusion as her mind works prodigiously and successfully to avoid the obvious conclusion about what's happening here. Isn't it a strange coincidence, Philippa thinks, that the lyrics of Trevor's new song appear to correspond to something I did. I wonder how he ever thought of this.

Her stupidity clears up immediately when the chorus arrives:

Philippa cheats
Philippa lies
Philippa cheats
Philippa lies
Philippa cheats cheats cheats cheats cheats

Here, finally, are the shock, the anger, and the humiliation. She feels the eyes of the audience—the other nineteen NHS fans, anyway—turn to her. She looks at Trevor, and he catches her eye, winks, and sneers. She looks at Dave, and he sees her but then won't look at her as he adds a positively Beatlesque harmony to the chorus. She doesn't know what to do—cry? Rush the stage? Run from the club? There's simply no way to preserve her dignity in this situation. She can't stay here, but she'll be goddamned if she'll give Trevor the satisfaction of seeing her run out of the club.

The song continues, and Philippa's shock and humiliation turn to anger. Yeah, she might have cheated and lied, but she didn't humiliate Trevor in public, she didn't get up on the stage and yell about him while he was fucking standing there, she didn't do it because she's too . . . well, what? Kind? Probably not. She felt no guilt about her night with Christian, and she was preparing to dump

Trevor anyway, and let's not forget that she sponged off her dad and didn't care when her mom got in a near-fatal car wreck. No, kind simply isn't accurate.

Well, she thinks as they chant the final "cheats cheats cheats" for what seems like hours but is in fact only twenty-five seconds, maybe I am as bad a person as he says I am. Maybe I'm a lying, cheating bitch, and what would a lying cheating bitch like me do in a situation like this? She wouldn't take the high road. She'd . . . she'd . . .

Apparently she'd grab the nearly full can of McEwan's Lager from the hand of the spectator next to her and hurl it at Trevor while screaming in a voice that, she would later reflect, was her mother's, "You fucking asshole!"

Trevor's scrawny frame is a difficult target to hit, and Philippa's throw has velocity but not accuracy, and Trevor appears to have been expecting the lying, cheating bitch to throw something at him, because he dodges nimbly. The can bounces off the bottom of Dave's bass and hits the stage, and the lager dribbles out, and Philippa realizes too late that this gesture has only added to Trevor's victory, has made this piece-of-shit wannabe punk band that came six years too late look authentically punk rock.

"Thank you and good fucking night!" Trevor says in triumph as the crowd cheers. Philippa turns and walks from the club, making certain not to run until she is out the door.

Philippa immerses herself in work. Her feet hurt like hell at the end of every shift, which is something she strangely wasn't prepared for. It occurs to her that she may need more support than her Chuck Taylors are providing. The cooks speak in incomprehensible Cockney or West Indian accents and dialects, and *fuck* and *cunt* are the only words she's able to pick out reliably, but that actually covers a significant number of the server–cook interactions, and when Philippa offers to stick a burger and fries "in your mother's fucking cunt" when one snaggletoothed, acne-scarred cook is berating her with a string of rhyming words, she feels like one of the gang, though it must be said that the kitchen staff does not share this feeling. The customers, for the most part, are the kind of people that make Philippa embarrassed to be an American: loud, fat, clueless.

Of course Philippa spends all day playing up her American-ness in order to milk bigger tips out of the homesick American tourists, or occasional out-of-town British tourists who will never get any closer to America than this. Thus, she begins reading the *International Herald Tribune* so that she can follow sports scores, so that when, for example, a family from Houston waddles in, she can say, "Hey, your Oilers whipped my Bengals last week, huh?" and usually increase the size of her tip. She changes her name tag to read STACEY after one customer tells her she has a very English name, and she quickly finds that "Stacey" pulls in 25 percent more tips than Philippa did.

When shifts are over, all the pubs are already closed, and she's become too much of a beer snob to swallow the ice-cold Bud that EAT AT JOE'S AMERICAN BAR AND GRILL serves exclusively (to the delight of the tourists, who frequently exclaim, "Finally! A real beer!" when "Stacey" brings them a frosty mug of the stuff, and "Stacey" will frequently add, "Yeah, I can't drink that brown stuff," thereby assuring herself a bigger tip.). She can't very well end the night with no drink at all, though, so she usually ends up sitting at the bar with Kelly Sullivan from Peabody, Massachusetts, a fellow EAT AT JOE'S server who doesn't have to feign her all-American-ness, and drinking straight bourbon.

The work, the new schedule, and the new friend (Kelly's really not much of a friend yet, but she's funny and kind, putting her at least two notches above any of Philippa's punk rock "friends") help Philippa to forget the humiliation of being the subject of one of Trevor's songs that was not about her breasts or her panties. She's made a clean break from her punk rock self, and while she feels like she barely knows "Stacey," it turns out that she likes "Stacey," with her shallow knowledge of the sports that Philippa despises, with her clean-scrubbed, all-American disdain for fancy food and beer that's not yellow, a lot more than she liked the Philippa she was.

Then, on her night off, she puts Stacey away and turns on John Peel, and his soothing voice informs her that live on tonight's show will be the National Hate Service. She knows she should turn it off, but she doesn't, and so she hears "Servants' Entrance," "Booze Up," and, of course, "Philippa Cheats," all recorded live in the BBC studios. She's angry—she's left that whole thing behind, left Trevor behind, the whole scene, she just cut herself off, and that should be the end of it, but here they are on John Fucking Peel, and that means the NHS are about to enjoy their fifteen minutes of British Music Scene fame.

Sure enough, "Philippa Cheats" begins climbing the charts, the *NME* does a cover story with the title PUNK IS BACK!, and pretty soon it's damn near impossible for Philippa to walk down the street without hearing the song, seeing an NHS T-shirt, or seeing Trevor sneering from a magazine cover.

She enters Barclays to open her first bank account with her first check from EAT AT JOE'S, and the bank manager, a fatter, less successful version of Christian, on seeing her name says, "Oh, do you cheat, then? Heh, heh." She clenches her fists and says nothing.

She's grateful for Stacey, because seemingly overnight it gets to the point where every male in London under the age of twenty-five is either wearing an NHS shirt or singing the song under his breath, and Philippa is glad to escape into Stacey's skin for eight hours a day.

Kelly invites her to a party at her boyfriend's friend's flat, and no fewer than four people make a "Philippa Cheats" joke when she's introduced to them. The fourth one comes after her third beer, so rather than feigning a *heh heh*, she says, "Yes, okay! I cheat! And I lie! It's nice to meet you! You're a really handsome man with great teeth, and I'd love to sleep with you!"

She storms out of the room and out of the party altogether, and the guy runs after her. "I'm sorry!" he says.

"Yeah, thanks. Good night."

"Bet you're fucking sick of those jokes, aren't you?"

"You could say that, or you could just stop at sorry and let me go home."

"Must be a real pain to have idiots like me making these jokes, hanging someone else's bad behavior on you. I reckon you'd like to punch that Philippa if you ever—"

"Just stop, because you're fucking up your apology. It's me, okay. It's me."

"What do you—"

And three beers send this pouring out of Philippa's mouth before she even knows what's happening. "It's me, the fucking song is about me, okay, and the thing that pisses me off is that it's true. I mean, I was going to break up with him the next day, and I don't know what the hell he was doing following me anyway, that's kind of creepy when you think about it, he didn't write about that, how he was following me like a little fucking dog, and he's a scrawny idiot who only liked me because I bought him pints all the time, and I hate him, I mean really hate him, and he deserved it, such a fucking asshole."

The guy looks stunned. "Uh. Oh. I'm sorry."

"Yeah, well, thanks. I mean, lots of people do shit they're not proud of, you know, but I'm the only one that has complete strangers knowing about it and making jokes to my face about it because they assume it couldn't possibly be me, he just made that up, or he changed the name because it scans better than Clair, or something, but no, it's me, and everybody in this whole fucking country knows his side of the story. And now I have to go home and go to sleep. Like I said before, I'm a liar and it was really nice meeting you."

The guy looks stung. "Wait, wait. Look, my name is Andy. In college I had a girl at home and one in the dormitory, and neither of them knew about it until the home one decided to pop by for a surprise visit, and it would have been easy if they'd been angry, you know, thrown things at me and whatnot, but the girl from home—

her name was Anna—she just cried and cried, and I felt like a total wanker and I tried to apologize and sent flowers and the whole bit, but she's never spoken to me since and will probably never forgive me, and I'm fucking glad she never wrote a pop song about it."

Philippa stops. "Lucky you," she says, and sees the guy for the first time. He's in his early twenties, his dirty-blond hair is a little too long, his teeth are nearly presentable, he has gorgeous blue eyes, and his clothes are nice, particularly the shoes. He's just attempted to be kind to her, and while her tits may be a factor, his clothes suggest that her ability to buy pints is not a factor. So he's at least got that over Trevor. That, and he's never written a Top 10 hit about her.

"Yes," he continues, "well, listen, my name's Andy, like I said already, and I'd love to make it up to you by buying you dinner, and I promise I don't always say the first stupid thing that comes into my brain, I don't need you to buy me a pint, and I learned my lesson about two girls at once—er, you know, not exactly at once, I mean one behind the other's back, I mean . . . What do you say?"

"I say I would actually do it, but I have to work tomorrow dinnertime. I'm a waitress at EAT AT JOE'S AMERICAN BAR AND GRILL. I do hope you heard all the capitals there as I said it."

"Oh, absolutely," Andy says, smiling, and then, in a really bad attempt at an American accent in which he hits the r's way too hard and holds them just a little too long, he says, "Burrrrgerrr and frrries forrr the wife and kids."

"Pretty much. Though sometimes the kids have the grilled cheese."

"Fine. Lunch, then?"

"Okay. Where?"

"Giotto's. It's in Soho. They've got a brilliant pasta special at lunchtime, where—"

"I'm sold. I'll meet you there at noon."

"I can't wait."

• • •

Lunch is fantastic. For one thing, Andy is right about the pasta special—Philippa was unsure what a tarragon cream sauce would taste like, but it turns out that it tastes great. Andy's a writer, working on a novel and working "a dead boring job" at his dad's office to pay the bills. They bond about how living off one's father makes one feel somewhat less of a real adult. She tells funny stories about the tourists she meets, and Andy tells her about the novel he's working on—something involving football and a doomed love affair.

So it's a pleasant lunch, and Andy's cute and kind of fun, but what Philippa really likes about it is that this is the first time in a long time that she's felt comfortable in her skin. She isn't Philippa the drunken sponge dating an asshole, she isn't Stacey the Bengals fan, she's just some version of Philippa who's working and trying to become a grown-up and maybe figuring out how to live. It feels good.

When she gets to work and gets into her Stacey costume and character, Kelly says, "Hey, you look happy! What happened?"

"Nothing happened. What do you mean?"

"Glowing. Cut the bullshit. Did you get laid?"

"No, I just had lunch!"

"Lunch? What did you *eat*? Did you try the tube steak?"

"Jesus, Kelly, I had penne with cream sauce."

"Penne with cream sauce! That is so raunchy! I like it! Can I use it?"

"Kelly, I did not blow anybody! I ate pasta!"

"Okay, okay. Looks like you like the guy, though."

"Let's just say he's a big improvement over the last one."

"Good! You really do look happy."

"Hey—let me ask you a question about British guys. I mean normal ones, not like my piece-of-shit ex. Can I call him? Will I freak him out?"

"Well, he probably assumes that because you're American,

you're some kind of wacky take-charge woman, so you can use that to your advantage. It'll look like you're a sexed-up American taking charge instead of a pathetic clingy psycho."

Stacey's shift is uneventful, and she goes home and falls into bed. Simon, having slept at Ella's, is not home to fetch newspapers the next morning, so Philippa has to go out for her papers. She throws on some clothes and heads out to the newsagents.

She picks up the *Telegraph, The Times,* and *The Guardian,* and as she turns to pay, she sees the tabloid *Post* and *Mail* hanging up, with her picture on the cover, smiling and gesturing with a forkful of pasta. The headline reads PHILIPPA MYSTERY SOLVED! And below, in smaller print, TREV'S NO PRIZE, YANK REVEALS. The story, of course, is by Andy Townsend.

She does not buy a copy. The newsagent smiles at her, and she can just feel him thinking, So you're the bird in the song, as he takes her money. As she walks home, she feels the eyes of every other pedestrian on her. So that's Philippa! they think. Slut, they think. Poor thing, an old woman thinks. Wonder if she'd give me a go, a teenage boy inexplicably not in school thinks.

She reaches the flat and locks the door behind her. She goes to the phone, dials fourteen digits, and hears a groggy voice at the other end. "Hlo?" it slurs, and Philippa's first thought is that Mom is drunk already and it's only eleven in the morning, but then she realizes it's only six A.M. in Cincinnati, and she says, "Mom? I'm coming home."

MARK

      Mark graduates from college. Mom and Dad both come, and they all go out for Vietnamese food. Nobody talks much, and it's awkward and sad, because they can all see the empty space at the red Formica table where Janet is supposed to sit, three of them at a table for four, and Janet's absence occupying the fourth seat and the majority of their brains. It doesn't feel like a celebration. What's to celebrate? Janet's still dead, and all their lives are a mess.

      The summer passes uneventfully—Mark retreats to Maine, where he is now assistant director at Camp Service, which means he gets to deal with kids who get into trouble. They have two fights that summer, and Mark fervently wishes there were a little more guilt inherent in being a Unitarian Universalist, so he could berate the kids with *What kind of Unitarian are you? Didn't you learn anything in church school?* Of course, if their churches were like his, they learned a great deal about world religions and not so very much about ethical guidelines for their own lives. Which is evidenced by their punching each other in the nose.

      He also, in an irony that doesn't escape him, gets to bust the chops of counselors and CITs trying to act on their hormonal urges. "They can hump in the shed like bunnies for all I care," Tim tells him, "just make sure all the counselors know that the nurse's office stays unlocked and has a stash of condoms that are never inventoried, but try to act like you don't want them to know that. I am not sending any CITs home pregnant. Just make sure they keep it behind a closed door and away from the kids."

When Mark's parents wanted to give a plaque and a bench in Janet's honor, Tim placed it in a tranquil spot overlooking the lake that Janet used to love to go to during afternoon free time, apparently unaware that this was a favorite nocturnal outdoor make-out spot for the counselors during the week and a half when it was not too buggy to go outside after dark. Thus when Mark gives his opening speech to the counselors after Tim has left the room, he says, "At this camp there is a plaque and a bench dedicated to the memory of my late sister. I have been known to frequent that spot at all hours of the day and night, because I feel close to her there. [This is true.] If I ever have to interrupt anybody making out or worse up there [blushing from the fourteen-year-olds, wondering how on earth Mark read their minds], those individuals can count on an immediate phone call home accompanied by a graphic description of what you are or are not wearing at the time and where everyone's body parts are when they are discovered. I want you to take a moment and imagine your mother's reaction as I describe in graphic detail exactly what her little angel was doing on my sister's bench. Now, I do not particularly want to make that phone call, and you do not want me to make it, so stay the hell off the bench."

He never has to make the phone call, and, apart from the two fights, his disciplinary duties are pretty limited. On the last night of camp Tim announces that this is Mark's final summer at Camp Service, and a lot of kids cry, and the next day he is flooded with homemade cards from ten-year-olds that make him cry. When he returns to Brookline, he will place these cards in a box, and he will move the box everywhere he ever lives.

On his way back home, he is thinking primarily of how he's going to find an apartment this late in the summer, and what kind of roommate he's going to have to live with. The radio is on, but he's not paying any attention, until a familiar voice yells *Mark!* He knows instantly that it's Raquel, or possibly ROCK-L, and he turns his attention to the radio, where the song continues:

> *My words*
> *He's a two-minute man*

Raquel, Rock-L, whatever, is really snarling, yowling, and telling the world that he might be brokenhearted but he was done before she started. He pulls the car over to the breakdown lane on 95 South and listens and gets angrier and angrier. He'd known it was coming, but it's one thing to know somebody's written a song mocking your sexual prowess (and he was never going to scandalize any jaded LA partygoers with his sexual activities, but how, how can she do this when he can remember her curled up next to him, whispering "You make me feel so good"?), and it's another to hear it on a Sunday morning on pop radio, and then have the DJ come on in his cheesy broadcasting school baritone and say, "Boy, I'd hate to be that guy, huh? Have you seen the video? ROCK-L is *hot*. What kind of loser lets *that* get away?"

Well, Mark thinks, that would be me. The kind of loser who held her hand, the kind of loser who gave her the goddamn guitar that she used to humiliate me! *That* kind of loser!

He tries to take comfort in the fact that the song is the polar opposite of Raquel's punky acoustic numbers—it's got a distorted electric guitar, but it's just a little too slow and a little too slick to be credible to the fans who used to come to Raquel's shows on campus in their Sonic Youth shirts. He can just picture her in an LA studio surrounded by these fifty-year-old studio musicians with graying mullets, with Crocodile Dundee telling them to lay down some tasty licks like they did on the last Don Henley record. (Cal Tomkins did not actually use those words to the gray-mulleted musicians, but Mark's imagination of the recording is substantially accurate.)

The realization that Raquel has sold out provides cold comfort. She may not have any artisitic integrity, but it just means she can spread her premature ejaculation libel that much farther. With her original sound, she might have gotten some play on college radio; now he can only imagine what the limit is.

As it turns out, there is no limit. "Two Minute Man" becomes a cross-format radio hit, which means that it gets played on Top 40 stations, "Alternative" stations, and even "Adult Album Alternative" stations.

Fortunately MTV rarely shows videos anymore except at the times when other stations are showing infomercials for food preparation or exercise products or trade schools. Unfortunately, though, these are also times when young adults are awake and watching television, so Mark sees the "Two Minute Man" video several times, as, he is sure, does every other human his age in the United States. The video mostly features ROCK-L's face, though occasionally you get a glimpse of the video-friendly band they have assembled for her: the skinny, longhaired drummer, who Mark thinks may actually be the same skinny longhaired drummer from Hootie and the Blowfish; the young, good-looking-but-not-good-looking-enough-to-distract-from-the-star guitarist; and, of course, the black bass player with the long braids.

ROCK-L looks great, and she is just incredibly sexy. And she has stolen whatever macho thrill Mark might get out of knowing that lots of guys are going to want to nail her and he already nailed her, because of course the song is about how he was no good at nailing her, even though he certainly remembers it differently, but who's going to listen to that defense? *No, really, she came! And I mean, it's not like I was timing it, but I'd say the average time was closer to sixteen minutes . . .* There is no way he can rebut the song, even to himself. (Maybe she was faking? Maybe if I'd been a little better she wouldn't have left, none of this would have happened . . .)

And it simply will not go away. It stays on the radio, it's on in every store he goes into, and there are big articles in the Living section of the paper headlined WOMEN, GIRLS EMBRACE ROCK-L, and the album, *On the Rocks,* goes platinum and just keeps going. It will sell eight million copies in its first year of release.

Of course, except for the cheesy pause in the chorus between "Mark" and "my words," there's really nothing to indicate that the song is about him, and they knew each other in Philadelphia, so it's not like he's going to run into a ton of people up here who would be like, *Hey, I used to see you with ROCK-L! Are you the two-minute man?* Of course Christine knows, but she's backpacking through Asia with her boyfriend, and the odd postcards that arrive don't give any clue as to whether she's heard the song. (She has, beginning at the Shih Lin Night Market in Taipei and subsequently in pretty much every market in every country in Asia she visits. She figures, correctly, that Mark will not benefit from this information and leaves it out of her postcards.)

Josh also knows, and when he gets Sox tickets his dad isn't using, they sit in uncomfortable seats at Fenway Park watching the Sox lose to the Orioles and drinking overpriced, nearly tasteless beer while Josh provides an extended pep talk interspersed with color commentary on the game. It's the highlight of the summer. "Look," Josh says, "it's not like you're the only person to ever fall in love with a lunatic. Remember Amy Three?"

"I get confused, because there was some Amy overlap, if I remember correctly."

"Right. Amy Three came after that unfortunate business with the One and Two overlap. Don't you remember? I called you?"

Mark relished the memory—Josh, who always seemed on top of everything in life and who had always had girls falling at his unusually hairy feet, had called at a time when Mark was comfortably ensconced in his relationship with Raquel. He'd actually sounded rattled and was convinced that Amy Three was going to stalk him, and for the first and last time Mark had been the coolheaded one dispensing the love advice. Boy, were those days ever gone. "Stalker."

"Right! So I made a bad decision—balk! Jeez, did you see that? Obvious balk. Hump the ump! Anyway, so you happen to have been the lucky guy who hooked up with a crazy musician—"

"That's my fault! I made her a musician!"

"Oh yeah. Right. Okay. Well, you fucked up. Oh my God, that pitch was practically on the Mass Pike—what the hell kind of strike zone is that? Anyway, new city, new school, and I'm thinking that the ladies in ed school are totally going to fall for your sensitive-guy act."

"It's not an act," Mark says, smiling.

"Whatever!" Josh is wearing his shit-eating grin as he continues, "You happen to have picked a strategy for getting laid that was incredibly ill-advised in high school, but is probably going to pay huge dividends in grad school. These girls have learned their lesson dating all those assholes in high school and college, and they're moist and ready for some of your tiny, tiny lovin'. Elementary school teachers? They're gonna be eating out of your hands. You can feign sincerity with the best of them."

"Jesus, I only wish I could feign it."

"Oh, you just never even try. Jesus, is this inning ever going to end? What is it, like, eight to nothing?"

So when Mark starts education school, he feels like he's starting with a clean slate, and at first it goes well. At orientation they go around the room and introduce themselves and talk about why they want to be elementary school teachers. There are twenty-seven people in the room, and three of them are male. Mark judges (correctly) that he is the only straight man in this program. He is surrounded by attractive young women, he is a reasonably good-looking man, and he allows himself to hope that Josh is right, that everything that made him essentially undatable in high school will actually work in his favor here.

He seems to be on the right track, because when he introduces himself at orientation, he says, "My name is Mark Norris, and I'm originally from Brookline. I do not live with my dad a mere four trolley stops from here because I really wanted the experience of paying an enormous amount of money to share a disgusting apartment with many six-legged roommates and live over musicians who apparently never sleep." He checks the crowd. All are smiling, but some are smiling politely and nervously and have already written him off as too edgy. Three have actually laughed, and he immediately puts them atop his list of potentials. "I want to be an elementary school teacher because . . . well, for two reasons. One is that I've worked at Camp Service for the last five summers, and for reasons I don't understand, kids seem to really like me, and I always felt much happier and more alive when I was working with kids than when I was doing any other job. Also . . . well, my sister, Janet, died when she was ten years old, and it happens a lot when I'm talking to a kid that age that they will do something or say something that just reminds me of her so much. So I guess part of why I want to do this is that it keeps me connected to her." Now, Mark's mind is running on two tracks here. On the one hand, he is completely sincere. He's thought a lot about why he wants to be a teacher, and he really does believe it has a lot to do with Janet.

On the other hand, he is checking the crowd to see how this little speech is playing. And he finds that for the first time in his life, he is getting that Allen-Spitz-around-the-campfire look from every woman in the room (and, as it turns out, both men as well). A couple look like they are actually moist-eyed, and Mark believes that his list of potentials has just expanded beyond the three who laughed at his first joke.

So what if hateful, lying, cruel ROCK-L is emasculating him dozens of times daily over the airwaves? As far as the elementary education department goes, he is, for the moment at least, hot. Josh was right!

Mark's description of his apartment was, if anything, charitable, so he spends the bulk of his time on campus, hoping to run into classmates and make friends, though this process will be kind of painful to him. How does he start a conversation? "Hey, remember yesterday when we wrote stuff on big pieces of paper and hung them on the classroom wall and compared what we wrote with other groups?" It's been so long since he made friends that he kind of forgets how it's done. Christine is apparently settling in California, Josh has gone to Israel again, and he has a few acquaintances from college in Boston that he's seen for drinks, but Mark is lonely. It's a weird kind of loneliness, though—one that feels tinged with hope and possibility. He doesn't have anybody close by, but this means that in a weird way he's totally free—he has space in his life for something new and exciting and not at all like ROCK-L. He reads outdoors initially, but he finds that he is too distracted by the parade of undergraduate girls to concentrate on the barely comprehensible (and, ultimately, useless) education psychology texts, so he retreats to the library, where only the back of the carrel is competing with the ed psych reading. If there is any graffiti, it's a toss-up as to which gets more of his attention, but usually the text is slightly more interesting than a featureless slab of wood.

Ed psych meets at three o'clock and is only slightly more interesting than the textbooks, which means that Mark becomes very familiar with the top of his desk and is in a state of near unconsciousness by four, when class is over. He needs to head immediately to the student union for caffeine of some kind if he is going to be able to put in three or four more hours of work tonight. It seems that many of his classmates also need a caffeine jolt, and, though he should be confident after his get-to-know-you speech, he just doesn't know how to go up to their table and say "Can I join you?" even though, of course, that's exactly how to do it, and he rehearses it in his mind numerous times but does not sit with them until they see each other three times and they finally beckon him over.

A crew of six or eight of them are here three days a week after class, and Mark thinks that some of them might like him, but ROCK-L has dealt a pretty serious blow to his self-confidence and to his trust in his ability to understand what a woman is thinking. If, after all, a woman tells you that she loves you and that you make her feel so good and then she leaves you and humiliates you in front of millions of people, it becomes very difficult to believe that you can ever understand what any woman might be thinking or feeling.

He quickly and somewhat uncharacteristically divides the women in his program into two groups, which he dubs "the Mary Pats" and "the Potentials." There are actually two women in the program named Mary Pat, and both of them are Mary Pats, but the Mary Pats also include a number of young women with other names, such as a Molly, a Tricia, an Anne-Marie, and, strangely, a Shoshana. Most are Irish Catholic and hail from the Greater Boston area and are, Mark believes, the kind of girls who have a number of stuffed animals on their beds and posters on their walls with a cat hanging from a tree limb and the legend HANG IN THERE! FRIDAY'S COMING! Many of them wear the little pro-life roses that are an affront to Mark's Unitarianism. All of them appear to have relentlessly sunny personalities, and would, Mark believes, be put off by the hurt he's carrying around over Janet's death and ROCK-L's betrayal and, he further believes, don't possess the depth that an intimate knowledge of tragedy has given him. (In point of fact, one of the Mary Pats who is actually named Mary Pat suffered horrible physical abuse as a child, and behind her relentless sunniness is a stubborn refusal to allow these events to define her.)

The Potentials are a more diverse group—also primarily Irish Catholic (this is, after all, Boston College), but the majority of them do not attend mass (Mark knows from his childhood at First Church that lapsed Catholics count as honorary Unitarians, and that many of them will, in fact, become Unitarians). First on the list of Potentials is a short woman with brown hair and an amazing body whose name is Rebekah. Of course, Mark is immediately biased in favor of anyone named Rebekah because of his fond memories of Becky Randall. Rebekah defines herself as "culturally

Jewish," which, as near as Mark can understand, means she does not celebrate Christmas and reads *The New York Times* while eating bagels on Sunday.

Weeks pass, and Mark enjoys coffee with several Mary Pats and Potentials after ed psych. One Wednesday, Rebekah announces that she and her roommates are having a party on Saturday, and she hands out yellow postcards with a map to their apartment in Brighton, which turns out to be an easy ten-minute walk from Mark's own hovel. The invitation is printed in black ink, but on Mark's, Rebekah has written "Hope You Can Make It!" in blue Sharpie next to the map. Did she write this on everyone's, or was this a special message for him? Is there a double meaning to "make it," or has a year without sex scrambled his brain? Mark's eyes dart around the table, scanning for signs of blue Sharpie on the other invitations, but most are being tucked into bags, folders, or, in one case, a giant organizer-calendar.

The invitation says that the party begins at nine, and Mark debates whether to arrive on time, which would almost guarantee some time alone with Rebekah, or fashionably late, which would indicate a nonchalance and coolness he is not actually feeling.

Because he feels desperate, he chooses to arrive at a time that will not convey his desperation. This is a good choice, because ROCK-L's *On the Rocks* was one of Rebekah's get-ready-for-the-party CDs, and her roommate Katherine removes it from the changer just before Mark arrives. When he arrives, he is struck by the fact that while Rebekah's apartment is nearly identical to his own in terms of the layout and the shabby condition of the building, hers actually feels like a relatively nice place to be. She and her roommates have painted the walls a warm orangey yellow, and there are festive party lights in the shapes of butterflies, hot peppers, and dolphins hanging from the ceilings. Every room has at least one plant that is actually alive. Mark's apartment, by contrast, has an air of filth and decay that the rare guest actually finds palpable.

Mark stands in a corner feeling awkward, shy, ugly, and completely mingle-impaired. He's afraid to join any of the knots of conversation because the music is so loud that he would need to get right up in someone's face in order to have a conversation with them. After what feels like ninety minutes but is in fact only fifteen, Rebekah, on her way back to the kitchen for another one of those very strong drinks that Katherine keeps making in the blender (she's lost count, but it's ten fifteen and she's just finished number four since her party setup began at seven thirty), spots Mark and says, "Hey! I'm glad you could make it! Come to the kitchen and I'll get you a drink!"

He follows her to the kitchen, and Rebekah says, "She's calling these strawberry margaritas, but I don't think they taste like much besides tequila. Which is actually fine." She pours two vile, fruity drinks, and they spend fifteen minutes drinking them and dishing about which professors they hate. The tequila loosens Mark's tongue to the degree that he confesses his annoyance with one of the Mary Pats (her name is Margaret) who asks the most annoying questions in every class. Rebekah gleefully joins in and denounces "those creepy little pro-life roses those girls all wear. I think they might as well carry a sign that says, *I've never gotten laid.*"

Mark laughs despite the fact that there's an inner Unitarian minister yelling at him that he has to respect the religious and ethical convictions of all persons, even if, and perhaps especially if, he does not share those convictions. Fortunately, the sound of his inner Unitarian minister is drowned out by his inner pornography consumer (and how often these two have found themselves at odds, and how often has the minister found himself on the losing end of the conflict), who is fairly shouting that this woman just made a sex reference.

Mark finds himself unable to speak. Fortunately, Rebekah, now five very strong margaritas into the evening, bails him out, though the tequila has laid waste to her ability to be subtle. "So what about you, Mark? When's the last time you got laid?"

"Uh, I, uh, well, not lately, but, you know, yeah, though it ended badly. I mean, the relationship, not the . . ."

Rebekah gives him a smile. "Whew! I thought you were gonna tell me you were a two-minute man there for a minute."

Mark feels rage bubbling up inside him, that hateful ROCK-L's words should be coming out of Rebekah's mouth, and the inner horn-dog immediately makes some kind of joke about coming into Rebekah's mouth, and he is suddenly overwhelmed by a toxic combination of lust for Rebekah and rage at ROCK-L. Aware that rage is not the most attractive of his emotions, Mark excuses himself, runs to the bathroom, and splashes cold water on his face. There is a bottle of SERENE Aromatherapy Lotion on the sink, and Mark uncaps it and takes a deep sniff. He counts to ten. He counts to ten again. He sniffs the orangey aromatherapy lotion again.

He reflects that he didn't bring a condom to this party, that he in fact does not currently own any condoms, because, he tells himself, he's always been a relationship-sex kind of guy and not a party-sex kind of guy. (His brain uses those exact words, as though he has had enough party-sex opportunities to have been able to form a preference.) But that may be about to change.

Rebekah is planning to change that, and, though she has not normally been a party-sex kind of gal, it's been eight long months since she broke up with Jason, and she has a twelve-pack of condoms she bought three months ago and has yet to open sitting in her underwear drawer next to the vibrator she ordered from a catalog her friend Grace gave her.

Unfortunately for both Mark and Rebekah, at least in the context of this evening, Rebekah is not a habitual binge drinker. When Mark returns from the bathroom, Rebekah is still in the kitchen, but she has just polished off a tequila shot to calm her nerves, and she is beginning to stagger. "Uh . . . hey, Mark. Lemme show you my room," she says. "Smooth, huh?" And then she walks into the refrigerator.

Mark grabs her arm to steady her, and he walks her down the

hall to her room. She plants a very tequila-tasting kiss on him as soon as they enter her room, and she looks at him with heavy-lidded drunken lust.

Mark's penis is erect, but every part of his brain knows this is not going to happen. The Unitarian minister is clear on the ethical problems such an encounter would present, and the horn-dog prefers his women fully conscious, so he lays Rebekah down on her bed and kisses her on the lips without tongue and says, "I'd like to see this room again sometime."

"You will," she says, already half asleep. She fully believes this as she says it, but it's not true.

Mark goes to CVS on Sunday and buys condoms. This had become a routine purchase when he was with Raquel, but now he finds himself nervous and embarrassed as he hands the condoms and the breath mints over to the young man in the red vest. He is certain that the clerk is looking scornfully at his I-hope-I'm-gonna-get-laid care package, and/or wondering to himself why Mark is not buying the extra-large condoms that are clearly marked and easily available, and so Mark blushes, unable to look the clerk (who is actually thinking, Everybody in the world is getting laid except for me) in the eye.

He walks home holding the white plastic bag with a casualness so studied that he is convinced it gives away his nervousness to everyone on the street, though, it being Sunday morning in a student neighborhood, there is virtually no one on the street.

Once he returns home, he is unsure what to do. Should he call Rebekah? Or should he wait for her to call him? Perhaps she is so embarrassed by passing out that she won't call him. Or perhaps she doesn't even remember making a clumsy pass at him. He needs to find a way to communicate to her that he remembers, that he's still interested, that he doesn't think she's a disgusting drunk. But he can't call now. She may still be sleeping off her hangover or vomiting. (It's eleven A.M., and she's actually brushing her teeth after having finished vomiting, but Mark's instinct not to call is correct.)

So he sits and waits. At noon he goes to the bagel bakery he knows Rebekah frequents, and he gets a salt bagel with cream cheese and lurks in the doorway for half an hour, surreptitiously looking up and down the street, hoping he can feign casualness if he does see her. He doesn't.

He walks home and spends the rest of the afternoon wondering whether to call her, then searching for the yellow invitation with her number on it, which seems to have vaporized (it's actually serving as a coaster for a half-consumed strawberry margarita back at Rebekah's house). He looks her up on the online student directory, only to find that she's opted out of being listed.

He thinks about walking over to her house, possibly with some flowers, but decides that might be over the top, might, again, communicate the exact level of his desperation rather than communicating the cool indifference he thinks he's supposed to communicate.

He makes a desultory attempt at reading from the course packet, which appears to have been photocopied from books too stultifying to stay in print even for education school, which is saying something. He remembers that Rebekah once said something about liking Vietnamese food, and he recently read in a free paper that pho was good hangover food, so he takes himself out for dinner, once again hoping to spot her and not getting his wish.

He watches *The Simpsons* and goes to bed early, but he finds that he can't really sleep. Tomorrow he will certainly see Rebekah in class. What will he say to her? What are the perfect words to say? *Should you still be interested in intercourse with me, I am amenable to that, but should you not be interested, it is as nothing to me, for I can have my pick of the ladies.* Mark comes up with no answer to this question, and eventually he falls asleep and dreams that ROCK-L is on a bus to Cuba with him and David Hasselhoff.

Mark arrives early to class the next morning. He wants to have some time to exchange a few words with Rebekah if that's possible, but, more important, he wants to be seated when she arrives so that he will not be faced with the decision of whether to sit next to her and be paralyzed by the implications of sitting with her and the implications of not sitting with her. He reads his *Boston Globe* and feigns nonchalance.

Rebekah chooses the opposite tack and arrives five minutes late to class, thus forcing herself to take whatever seat is available, which happens not to be next to Mark. All through class Mark's heart pounds, and he wonders what, if anything, to say to her when class ends. She is seated in the front row, so he stares at her throughout class. She does not look in his direction once. Does this indicate that she is not thinking about him, or does it indicate that she is thinking so much about him that she doesn't dare appear to be thinking of him?

Finally, class ends, and Mark stands slowly, fumbles with his notebook, folds his newspaper neatly, and waits for the rest of the students to clear out. Rebekah is also packing up slowly, and now she has looked in his direction. Is she blushing, or is she flushed because of the poor ventilation in here? She seems poised to turn and speak to him when Mary Pat who is actually named Mary Pat bounds into the room and says, "Rebekah! Let's get some lunch! Come on!"

"Uh—" She casts a glance in Mark's direction. "—sure." She pauses for what seems like five minutes but is in fact only seven seconds, and then she says, "Hey, chivalry boy! You wanna have lunch?"

"Uh, yeah, sure!" Mark says, and then realizes he's beaming, because the fact that she called him *chivalry boy* indicates (a) affection and (b) that she remembers the events of Saturday night more or less clearly. He tries not to beam and walks over to the student center with Rebekah, Mary Pat, and three other women.

They sit at a round table and eat, and Mark is conscious of his eating and conscious of the fact that this time, Rebekah has carefully maneuvered herself next to him, and she keeps giving him this smile that he interprets to be the we've-got-a-secret smile.

And then he hears a familiar voice call his name. And he realizes that ROCK-L is playing on the sound system here in the student center, and he tries to pretend he's not hearing it, and he wonders if it's obvious that he's gritting his teeth, he wonders if it might be possible for him to grit his teeth in a not entirely literal way, and he experiments, trying to envision his teeth clenched while holding his mouth slightly open, but this experiment is derailed by Anne, a Former Potential (for, with one Potential about to become an Actual, Mark has begun considering the others Former Potentials): "I know it's overplayed, but I really love this song!"

Nods of agreement from all the women around the table, even the Mary Pats, which surprises Mark because he assumes they'd be offended by the sexual nature of the song, that Rebekah's read on the pro-life rose was correct, but here they are all nodding about how much they like a song about premature ejaculation. Well, Mark thinks, perhaps they've gotten laid but just never enjoyed it. He makes a mental note to tell this to Rebekah later, but he's interrupted by her saying, "I just admire her so much. This song is so empowering."

And Mark suddenly has an important choice to make, but he responds so quickly that it doesn't even feel like a choice, and it will only be later, as he sits alone in his apartment kicking himself, that he will realize he actually had a choice here.

"You know," he says, and his voice is shaking with anger all of a sudden, "that is just such bullshit. That's the thing that just drives me nuts. That is a really nasty song. Why is it empowering? If it was produced by the great oppressed half of the human race, it couldn't just be nasty, could it? No, women can't ever be mean, or unfair or wrong, can they? No, women's anger is always righteous anger. So nobody can admit that it's cruel, that it's nasty, because then what does that make you if you like it? So you have to say it's 'empowering,' so that you can believe that feeding your spite is somehow making the world a better place. This idea that women are morally superior just means you can shit all over everything and call it fertilizer. It's just the basest kind of hypocrisy, and it makes me sick."

And with that, he gets up from the table, his hands still shaking. He is confident that he has demolished the "empowering" argument about "Two Minute Man," and it is only after he cools down that he will realize he has also demolished his chances of ever getting laid by pretty much anyone in this program. There is, suddenly, no more Actual, and there are almost certainly no more Potentials.

PHILIPPA

Philippa's appearance on the cover of one of Britain's leading tabloids causes Simon Strange a great deal of personal and professional embarrassment, and so he is only too happy to put Philippa on the next available flight, which ends up being a British Airways flight to Philadelphia followed by a connecting USAir flight to Cincinnati.

Simon, busy at work and fearing that he'll be photographed in the company of his daughter, sends her to the airport with Ella and a check for five hundred pounds. Philippa wants very badly to refuse the check, to show Simon that, despite the evidence of the last four months, she doesn't need his money, she needs a father to care about her, she needs somebody she can depend on when Mom is being flaky. But she knows that Mom is nowhere near as generous or wealthy as Dad, and that approximately $750 will go a long way in Cincinnati, so she swallows her bile and her sarcasm and places the check inside her American passport. (Simon actually had not been intending to give Philippa a check at all, as his anger over her tabloid celebrity had temporarily eclipsed his guilt over abandoning her, but Ella, uncharacteristically, had insisted.)

Ella drops Philippa at Heathrow, hands her a business card with her home address written on the back, and says, "Do let me know if you find out what you're good at and why you're here. I'll do the same. It seems you've set me thinking."

"Thanks, Ella," Philippa says. "I'm sorry I was such a bitch all summer."

Ella waves her hands. "Please. You should have seen me at your age. We would have got on quite well, actually," and Philippa doesn't know if she means *if you had stayed,* or *if we had been eighteen at the same time,* and she feels the tiniest twinge of sadness that Ella is disappearing from her life.

Ella drives home from Heathrow and realizes that she wants a child of her own. Philippa boards her plane and never sees or hears from her again.

When she arrives at the Greater Cincinnati and Northern Kentucky Airport nine hours later, Mom is waiting there, looking better than she has in years. She enfolds Philippa in a hug that lasts far longer than Philippa expects, then pulls away, tears in her eyes, and says, "I'm just so happy we get a second chance, sweetie. I've been going to meetings, I haven't had a drink since the accident, and I really think I'm going to make some positive changes in my life."

"Well, that's great," Philippa says, and she smiles.

She spends the next few days waiting uneasily for the other shoe to drop. When Mom's at work, she searches the two-story wood-frame house in Hyde Park for hidden bottles and finds nothing. She gives her mother a big hug every time she comes home from work. Candace Strange believes that Philippa's sojourn in London, coupled with her own sobriety, is responsible for her sullen daughter becoming suddenly affectionate, and she never suspects that Philippa is smelling her breath for evidence. Philippa, for her part, is unaware that she is running the same scam that countless parents run on their teens every time they come home, because on those occasions when Candace had actually been home when Philippa got home, she had never been sober enough to check anyone else's sobriety.

Candace does not drink, and so Philippa gradually turns her attention to herself. While she's happy to be back in a city where most people will not even hear of punk until 1991, where she would have to position the radio in her room in exactly the right place on the second-highest shelf of her bookcase in order to even pick up Handsome Clem and the Hockey Punk spinning punk records on WAIF, a place where she is not defined by that fucker Trevor, a place where she doesn't have to live up to being a cheater and a liar, she doesn't know who she is or what she's doing.

She doesn't know why she fell for Trevor in the first place, she doesn't know why she didn't see through Andy's deception, she wonders what's wrong with her. She sits around the house all day, and she finds she can't even listen to the music she loves because every single record she owns leads her mind back to Trevor and the NHS. Trevor's taken her music and her father's country away from her, which seems like a pretty harsh punishment for cheating on somebody she'd only been with for three and a half months, and who, she reminds herself, was an idiot and a moocher. How many stupid guys were there in London who might have been attracted by big tits and an endless supply of beer money? And she had to pick the only one out of that rather large pool of men who would have the ability to humiliate her in front of fifty million people when she got tired of him.

While Candace's sobriety brings a refreshing break from the torrent of verbal abuse that Candace spent the last five years dishing out, it also makes it harder for Philippa to adjust to being back in Cincinnati. If Candace were drinking, Philippa could at least distract herself with her favorite game from high school, which was drinking up her mother's secret stash of booze and then seeing whether it was more important to Mom to maintain the façade that she wasn't drinking or to yell at Philippa for her illicit boozing.

Usually the façade won, but now it isn't a façade. And Philippa has many hours a day in which to think, and she doesn't like any-

thing that she's thinking. She calls up Danni, who was a sophomore at Walnut Prep when Philippa was a senior, and who kind of
idolized her for her firsthand punk rock experience, and Danni invites her to a party.

Philippa picks Danni up at her gigantic house in Indian Hill,
and they drive half an hour to another gigantic house. They walk
into the party and Philippa immediately wonders what the hell she
was thinking. She hated these parties even when she still went to
Walnut Prep. As she walks through the room greeting her acquaintances, she can feel them scorning her for the pathetic loser she is.
Why the hell is she here? she can feel them thinking. Doesn't she
have any college parties to go to? (While she reads the thoughts of
the girls fairly accurately, missing only the envy of her breasts and
the fear that she'll steal a boyfriend, the thoughts of most of the
boys she greets are considerably less scornful than she believes and
far more pornographic than she imagines.) In just a month she's
gone from hanging out in real clubs in London with real adults, or
anyway legal adults, to walking around some kid's basement in Anderson Township with fourteen-year-old girls drinking wine cool-
ers with a straw.

Two more days pass, and Philippa decides she should probably
get a job, simply because she doesn't know what else to do. She
spends two nights going out to various restaurants and bars in
Cincinnati and quickly decides to apply in Mount Adams, where
the young professionals go, and avoid Clifton, where the University
of Cincinnati is, and where she'd undoubtedly spend every shift
being pawed by drunken frat boys.

On Saturday afternoon she decides to make the rounds in
Mount Adams. She's decided to tell all the managers that she
worked at EAT AT JOE'S for her entire four months in London,
figuring that there are few bar managers in Cincinnati willing to
make a transatlantic phone call to check on her work experience.
Just in case, though, she dons a T-shirt far too small for her, figuring (correctly) that her breasts are actually a far more important

qualification than her waitressing experience, and that she would stand a good chance of getting hired in this outfit even if she had no experience at all.

She goes to her first choice, the Mellow Melon, a small place wedged into a rehabbed town house with a patio in what was once the backyard. The Mellow Melon has live jazz on the weekends, and while she doesn't like jazz, or know anyone who likes jazz except for Simon Strange, he is always an extravagant tipper, so the Mellow Melon seems like a good choice.

She speaks briefly to the manager, who hires her on the spot. (He is impressed by Philippa's formidable breasts, but also believes that her having lived in London will help him to create a sophisticated, classy atmosphere. He actually does call EAT AT JOE'S, where he speaks to the manager Philippa listed on her application. Kelly Sullivan happily states that she is the manager, that Philippa was a model employee for four months, and that she was sad to see her go. The last part is true. She also tells the manager to have Philippa call her, but he forgets to deliver the message.)

When she returns home, Mom greets her at the door. "How do I look?" she asks. She's wearing a black dress, heels, and more makeup than usual, and Philippa is happy to be able to tell her truthfully that she looks fantastic.

"I've got—I mean, I met this guy at a conference, and he works across town, and we . . . well, I guess I have a date," Mom says.

"That's great, Mom!" Philippa says. After a few very bad relationships following the divorce, Mom had dated Jack Daniel's almost exclusively for the last few years. "I got a job!"

"Oh, honey, that's great!" Mom says, and gives her a hug. Philippa checks, and her mother's breath smells only of Crest.

The guy, Adam, comes over to pick Candace up at seven thirty, and, though her urge is to flee, Philippa stays downstairs to greet her mom's date cordially, figuring that if Mom is starting over and remaking her life, she can do the same thing. Adam says it's nice to meet her, Philippa says it's nice to meet him and thinks that he looks a lot like Dad, only with more of a gut. Candace and Adam leave, and Philippa microwaves a Lean Cuisine and eats it in front of the TV while watching a bad slasher movie on cable.

Philippa is asleep in front of the television when Candace returns. "Get your ass down here!" she yells, and Philippa's stomach drops as she springs awake. Mom's drunk.

"Mom, I'm not talking to you when you're drunk," she calls out, and this brings Candace running into the TV room.

"You goddamn well will talk to me!" she yells, and she's between Philippa and the door, so it looks like this will actually be the case.

"Mom, please, save it for the morning, okay?"

"No I will not save it for the morning, because you're not going to be here in the morning!"

"What the hell are you talking about?"

"I'm talking about you, you and your slutty little outfit, trying to steal Adam away from me, and you think I didn't notice the way you looked at him? And he couldn't keep his eyes off your tits, not that you were trying to hide them, dressed like a whore—"

"Jesus, Mom, are we back on 'whore'? I thought we moved to 'ungrateful little bitch' when I was seventeen. I'm pretty sure 'whore' was 1981's drunken insult."

"How dare you call me a drunk, you little whore!"

"Mom, you are a total cunt when you're drunk. Why don't you go for a drive on Clough Pike and calm down?"

"How dare you! I could have died!"

"Yeah, well, I wish you had." Philippa pushes by her mother, who attempts to slap her face but hits the door frame instead.

Candace collapses in a heap crying, holding her hand, and Philippa can hear her crying, "I'm sorry, baby," before she's even reached her room.

She throws her stuff back into the suitcase she only recently brought back from London. She looks at her clock and sees that it's eight more hours until the Fifth Third bank opens. She hopes

Simon's check has cleared, because she's obviously going to need that money to get an apartment.

Candace is sleeping off what promises to be a killer hangover, and she has left a note on the table that says, "I'm sorry. Please don't go." Philippa writes "Fuck you" at the bottom of the page, considers ripping it up, picks it up off the table with the intention of ripping it up, stops, considers writing something about how betrayed she feels, not by the verbal abuse, which she's sadly used to, but by Candace's suckering her into hoping she had a mother again. She decides to go with her original, concise seven-letter message and places the note back on the table.

Philippa leaves in her car—it's actually a '78 Audi that Simon left behind when he left and that Philippa drove while her mom went through a succession of I'm-a-single-hottie cars, the latest of which, a new Honda Prelude that replaced the Honda Prelude Candace destroyed on Clough Pike, is parked in the driveway.

She quickly procures an apartment—a cheap one-bedroom in a brick building on Madison Road between Hyde Park and Oakley. It's not that close to work, and it's not a cool neighborhood, but it's cheap and clean, and best of all it's hers. She figures it will be a decent starter apartment.

Work at the Mellow Melon turns out to be far better than she could have hoped. She quickly makes a friend in Martha, the black-haired thirty-two-year-old bartender who is an artist on the side. The Mellow Melon's clientele turns out to be an interesting mix of artists and young professionals aspiring to sophistication. There are always men with money there, and this has one very important implication for Philippa: this being the mid-1980s, they are able to offer her cocaine pretty much whenever she wants it. Martha's third job is coke dealer, and she gives Philippa her first taste on her third night on the job, and she likes it so much she wonders why she ever bothered with booze.

So life is mostly good. She parties relentlessly. Being young, female, and attractive, she could have sex whenever she wanted it, but she'd always rather have coke than sex, and she's always able to get the coke without the sex. Given her experience with Trevor, Christian, and Andy, she has no desire to get involved with any-body right now, and she doesn't feel like there's anything missing in her life.

Except in the morning. She wakes up in the late morning, fixes herself a cup of Twinings English Breakfast, reads *The Cincinnati Enquirer,* and tries desperately not to think. She's having fun, but after a while this nagging sensation that there might be something else she should be doing besides waiting tables and partying creeps in. This is intensified a year and a half into her tenure at the Mel-low Melon when her English teacher from senior year, Mrs. Mertz, comes in with her husband to hear some quartet from New York that apparently has a big following. Philippa can't really tell any of the bands that play here apart. Jazz is just background music to her.

She tells Mrs. Mertz no, she's not in school, she's just taking a few years off to think things over and figure things out. But she's not thinking anything over—she's doing her best not to think, and she sure as hell hasn't figured anything out. Mrs. Mertz tells her she hopes that she does get it all figured out, because she has a great mind and a strong spirit, and Philippa wonders if that's true and if Mrs. Mertz really means it or if she says that to every former stu-dent she runs into.

She comes straight home from work for three nights following this encounter. She does no cocaine. By day four she's impatient with the fact that she hasn't figured anything out yet, and she spends the following night after work doing cocaine with Martha and a jazz- and coke-loving middle manager from Cincinnati Mi-lacron who's old enough to be her father and "accidentally" touches her left breast three times.

More time passes. Philippa eventually thinks she might have less time to think about how lost she feels if she were with some-body, so when a handsome, jazz-loving relief pitcher for the

Cincinnati Reds asks her out, she says yes. They date for six months, and it's fun—there are nice dinners out, flights to New York when the Reds play the Mets, a really nice week off from work at spring training in Florida (during which a drunken backup outfielder staggers up to Philippa and says, "You must really be something special—Teddy gave up road pussy for you"), and, of course, a great deal of cocaine. Best of all, she's able to wake up in the morning and have sex instead of thinking about where her life is going, about why she's taking up space on the planet.

Finally Teddy takes her to the Maisonette, the most expensive restaurant in Cincinnati, when they both have a night off. The lights are dim, the sauces are rich, and a small army of apparently psychic servers anticipate and fulfill their every need. After dinner, Teddy hands her a box with a gigantic diamond ring inside. She tells him she'll think about it, and she does—the proposal sparks two more coke-free days of introspection. She likes Teddy, maybe she even loves him—she doesn't really know whether what she feels is love or not. Should she know before she gets married? She's not 100 percent happy with her life right now (indeed, the percentage of unhappiness is growing daily), but she has met various Reds wives, and she's not ready for that life—nice clothes, nice house, sure, but lots of time getting beautiful every day and popping out a kid or two and raising it by yourself while your husband is on the road and may or may not still be chasing road pussy, though of course they all tell their wives it's the other guys who do that. And then there are the trades, the demotions, where you leave behind whatever friends you might have made and uproot your kids—it seems like you have to love either your husband or baseball or money a whole lot to be a baseball wife, and while Philippa likes money as much as the next person, she's indifferent to baseball and can't say for certain that she loves Teddy. She doesn't like where her life is going right now, but she doesn't want it to go in that direction. She goes to Teddy's apartment downtown with the river view and stares out the window at a barge with blinking lights chugging slowly under the suspension bridge as she tells him she cares for him but she's not ready to get married; he calls her a heartless bitch, shatters a wineglass on the floor, tells her to get the fuck out, and never speaks to her again. He is traded to the Padres two months later. He spends the remainder of the season in San Diego, is traded to the Cubs, marries during his two seasons there, tweaks a hamstring, messes up his mechanics, and retires at age thirty.

Three months after that she meets a nice guy at a party at Martha's. He's a twenty-six-year-old painter named Sam, and, un-like most of the other painters she's met at Martha's, he does not immediately ask her to model. He's tall and thin with black hair and blue eyes. He's wearing a Clash T-shirt, and when their hands collide reaching for the cheese knife at the same time, Sam says, "Oh, I'm sorry," and Philippa says, "Nice shirt. I saw the Clash in London when I was thirteen." She immediately kicks herself for adding the *in London* part, because it makes her sound like she's posing, trying too hard to come off as sophisticated. But the dam-age is done.

"No kidding? How was it?" He appears to be unfazed by her error. Martha invited him to this party with "I know a great girl you have to meet," and he has been trying to work up the courage to talk to her all night, and now he's so delighted that she's actually talking to him that he doesn't even notice she sounded pretentious.

"It knocked me out. It changed my life."

"So are you still into punk? Have you heard this new Hüsker Dü album?"

"No. I, uh, I kind of had to give it up." Sam looks at her quizzi-cally, and Philippa finds herself suddenly standing next to herself watching this hot cokehead waitress tell the story of how a hot boozy teen had a Top 10 song written about her. She has never told anyone in the United States, even Martha, this story, and yet it sud-denly seems silly, like something that happened to somebody else, which maybe it did. She's too far into the story to back out when she realizes that her having cheated on Trevor might be a red flag for Sam, but it's too late to back out now, and she just hopes that it will make her seem sexy and alluring.

Even though she feels a million miles away from the person that song is about, she's not sure why Sam is the person she chose to share this with. He looks kind, and he's very cute, and he's unlike most of the guys who come into the Mellow Melon in that he is close to her age and doesn't have any money. Maybe that's why. Maybe she'll figure it out later. (She will, but it will be much later, when she is a different person from the one who is at this party tonight.) She ends the story with Andy's article and her departure from Britain and says, "The worst part is that I know it's a good song. Like, I know why it was popular. I just wish it wasn't about me."

"Wow. I'm sorry. But at least you can take comfort in the fact that the album sucked."

"Did it? I never heard it."

"It's just horrible. They broke up almost immediately. I actually saw that guy at Bogart's a few months ago. He was doing this solo acoustic thing opening for the Alarm. He was fat, he sucked, and some guy next to me pegged him with a plastic cup full of Hudepohl."

"Whoa." So Trevor'd gone from the top of the pops to having beer thrown at him in some club in Cincinnati. Good. She suddenly feels a whole lot better about her own life. She may not know what she's doing with herself, but at least she's not getting beer thrown at her opening for the Alarm. (She's getting beer spilled on her while middle-aged men try to peek down her shirt.) Nor is she fat, due to the fact that coke has replaced booze as her drug of choice. She can only imagine how much Trevor started drinking once he got enough money to buy his own pints. Enough to make him fat, apparently.

After the party Sam begins showing up at the Mellow Melon. Philippa doesn't believe for a second that he's interested in jazz, particularly since he sits there sketching while the music plays. He nurses one beer over the course of the night, tips extravagantly, and always gives Philippa little sketches of the other customers at closing time. Philippa finds herself doing less coke than usual, because doing coke almost always means disappearing for a few minutes with some guy in a suit, and she doesn't want to give Sam the wrong signals.

Except she keeps trying to give him the right signals, and all she has to show for her efforts is a pile of little sketches. Why doesn't he ask her out? Doesn't he get that she's available? (He does, but spends what little money he has on drinks at the Mellow Melon, and he's not going to ask her out for a quarter pounder or something, and he believes her too sophisticated to be impressed by *Let's take a walk through Eden Park.*)

After three weeks, just as Philippa is beginning to lose patience, he calls her over to his table. "Uh, hey, I, um, are you off tomorrow?"

"Yes," Philippa replies. Finally!

"Well, there's this kind of benefit thing down at CAGE, and I know you gave up punk rock, but some local groups will be playing, and there'll be art and stuff, and I've got a new piece I'd like you to see."

"That sounds fun!" She takes the red postcard he's offering, wondering what exactly the hell "cage" is, and sees it's a nonprofit gallery down by the warehouses on the west side of downtown.

"Great. Well, I'll see you there, then," he says, and practically runs out.

He'll see me there? Philippa wonders. The shy thing was cute, but this may be getting a little extreme.

She shows up the following night at a small brick building nestled among big brick buildings just a few blocks from where Al Schottlekotte does the news at eleven. She finds the gallery, or artist-run collective, or whatever it is, small, dingy, and packed with people. The bands are playing in the basement, but you can hear the music down the street, and when she walks into the gallery she can feel the bass and drums vibrating through her feet.

The singer is screaming something about leather dresses, and Philippa thinks this sounds a little more metal than punk, but she hasn't paid any attention to what's happening in music for years (Martha is deeply into the Stones, so Philippa has listened mostly to *Exile on Main Street* and *Sticky Fingers*). She scans the tightly packed crowd for Sam, and, not finding him, she begins squishing her way through the hot, sweaty mass, looking at the art on the walls and trying to guess which is Sam's new piece.

She finally pushes through a group of teens she assumes are here for one of the bands and sees both Sam and his new piece immediately.

"Hey!" Sam calls out. "I'm so glad you could make it! What do you think?"

Philippa is speechless, and she initially has no idea what she thinks. Hanging from the brick wall on a wire attached to a masonry screw is a painting of her. In the painting she is wearing a white veil and holding a bouquet of flowers in front of her stomach. She is otherwise naked.

She suddenly feels the eyes of all the teenagers upon her, feels the eyes of everyone in this shitty little gallery on her, is convinced that the musicians and their fans can see her from the basement, and she suddenly doesn't feel that different from the girl who had "Philippa Cheats" written about her, because she's once again in a crowded room being defined by some asshole.

She's angry at Sam's presumption, and more than a little creeped out at the way he's portrayed her. They've talked for a total of less than an hour in the last three weeks, and he's already envisioning her as his naked bride? What the hell is it with her? Why does she end up being taken in by these guys?

"Uh, do you like it?" Sam asks, and Philippa considers a variety of responses before simply spitting in Sam's face. He looks stricken, and as she walks out of the gallery, Philippa thinks that spitting in his face was a much better response than the sucker punch in the gut she had also spent a split second considering.

She drives home in a rage, wanting to kill Sam, wanting to kill Martha for inviting Sam to her party, wanting to kill pretty much anybody who pisses her off.

When she gets home, though, her rage suddenly switches off, and an almost unbearable sorrow takes over. She finds herself on her kitchen floor in front of the fridge, sobbing uncontrollably. She hates herself, she hates her life, she just wants to be happy, she just wants everything not to suck for once. After twenty minutes of crying she's able to crawl into bed, where she falls instantly asleep.

In the morning her determination to make changes in her life has faded almost completely away, and she thinks that she is going to party especially ruthlessly tonight. She calls Martha to see if there's anything happening after work, if there's anything they can do, if there's any yuppie's house they can go to and do lines, if there's anything that can help her forget herself, get her out of the skin of this disgusting girl she's starting to really hate.

Martha doesn't answer, and Philippa decides to take herself out for breakfast, though it's much closer to lunchtime now. She walks down to the foyer of her building and sees a large cardboard box that says PHILIPPA STRANGE on it sitting just inside the glass door to the street. Her first thought is that creepy Sam is actually inside the box, that he's staked out her apartment and has disguised himself as a package in order to get in the building and make her his naked bride. She sticks out a foot and shoves the box with it. It rocks easily, so it's too light to contain Sam. She has a moment when she fervently hopes that the box contains what remains of the painting after Sam has chivalrously cut it into pieces.

Philippa peels the tape back and opens the box. On top is a piece of yellow legal paper that says this:

Hey Philippa,

I've gotta go, and I've gotta travel light. I can't tell you where I'm going because I dont want the Hilbilly Mafia to find me and believe me I woudnt blame you at all for telling them if you knew. Heres some stuff I cant really take, I hope you get some use out of it. Im sorry but Ill probly never see you again. You are a good kid and I'm glad you were my friend.

—Martha

Philippa stands there staring at the paper for a minute. This must be a gag, she thinks. Right? Martha had always joked that she got her coke supply from the Hillbilly Mafia, and Philippa had never asked, because she didn't want to know, but now Martha's leaving her a note and a box of—art supplies and Stones records, it turns out—and saying she has to leave town because she's pissed off the Hillbilly Mafia?

Philippa is still not convinced it's real that night when Jeff, the Mellow Melon's owner, is behind the bar and visibly pissed off because he has no bartender and no coke. She knows Martha must have gotten the coke somewhere, but she never really believed in the Hillbilly Mafia, and she doesn't believe any of this is for real until a week later, when a guy who looks like a member of Lynyrd Skynyrd afflicted with gigantism comes into the Mellow Melon and asks for Martha. He disappears into the back with Jeff, and Jeff emerges alone fifteen minutes later visibly shaken.

So just like that, Philippa's only friend is gone. She considers briefly the fact that she could have lost her only friend and been in a nice baseball wife's house in San Diego right now, but she pushes the thought out of her mind, putting it next to her fears that Martha will be killed, and her sadness at Martha's departure.

Martha lived two blocks from the Melon, and when the first of the month rolls around, her landlord puts all her stuff in the street. Philippa walks by and sees the small painting of the fountain from Fountain Square that Martha had done in garish Day-Glo colors and hung over her toilet. She grabs it, and the blank canvas behind it.

That night after work she hangs the painting over her own toilet. She likes having it there, but it feels like an inadequate tribute to Martha. Philippa stares at the blank canvas for an hour, then roots through the cardboard box of Martha's stuff, finds some supplies, and begins to paint.

MARK

Word of Mark's outburst spreads through his program, and he becomes radioactive almost immediately. Rebekah, who was genuinely charmed by Mark's sensitivity and chivalry, was especially stung by Mark's cruelty to her over a stupid pop song, for God's sake, and feels that she's dodged a bullet by not getting involved with him. She speculates aloud that Mark is probably a premature ejaculator himself, and wonders if maybe he didn't start with her on Saturday night because he was already finished. She also says, "I just said I liked the song, and he totally abused me."

She is partially overheard by two other women, and it's not long before this rumor spins out of control, and a group of concerned young women approach the dean of the graduate school and ask why Boston College chose to admit a man with "a known history of abuse."

Rumors swirl for weeks, until finally, when it's time for student teaching to start, Mark, like everyone else in the program, submits to a criminal record check. He makes twenty photocopies of his completely blemish-free record and posts them all over the education school. He considers adding an empty threat at the bottom about pursuing legal action for slander against anyone who continues to spread lies about him, but he stops himself, realizing that though he is innocent, that sounds kind of psycho, and he will be needing recommendations from the professors here, and he doesn't want the phrase *easily unhinged* to appear in any of them.

At home in front of the television, he wonders often if he's doing the right thing. Every morning he has to psych himself up to go sit in classes with everyone looking at him, hating him, thinking he's something he's not. He is astounded by the stupidity of anybody who'd think he was some kind of wife beater because he overreacted to their moronic adulation of the song, and he thinks that he could probably get out of the social hole he's put himself in if he could just tell them that the song was about him, that's why he went nuts, wouldn't you, he's not crazy, he's just very hurt. But that would mean admitting the song was about him, and though he's not at all pleased with this, Mark finds that he prefers to have all these women think he's a nutcase to having them know (or at least believe they know, because *the song's about me but it's a lie* would never fly) that he's no good in bed.

He feels completely alone. He's in sporadic touch with his friends from high school, and he's beginning to feel like he leans on them too hard, like he's no fun to talk to and they'll probably stop returning his calls; he doesn't speak to his only friend from college because she's touring behind a record about how he comes too fast, and he's obliterated any chance at making friends in grad school.

Fortunately student teaching begins, and he gets another chance at a fresh start. He tells himself that he absolutely won't fuck this up, that if every woman at this school sings "Two Minute Man" nonstop, he will suck it back and not say a word, because, after all, if you think about it, that song is really about Raquel's own sickness—what it purports to reveal is his sexual incompetence, but what it actually reveals is her cruelty, her willingness to sell out something that was (probably, he hopes) important to her just to get fabulously wealthy.

This rationalization doesn't really take, but it does help him stay determined not to say anything. Fortunately, when he arrives at the John Fitzgerald Elementary School in Brighton, which he delights in calling "the Honey Fitz" as the entire staff does, he finds that while he is still the only straight man, he is also the youngest adult in the building by nearly twenty years. There is one fourth-grade teacher who is forty, and everyone else in the building is at least fifty. This is not ROCK-L's fan base.

Mark is assigned to a third-grade class currently taught by Kathy O'Brien. Kathy O'Brien is fifty years old, dyes her hair red, and sneaks behind the building to smoke with a couple of the other teachers after school. She is kind to Mark, telling him when he screws up, which is frequently, but never making him feel stupid or incompetent. She acts and feels maternal toward Mark, and thinks that if only her daughter Elizabeth hadn't married that idiot last summer, she could have fixed him up. She considers briefly setting him up with her niece Jennifer, but rejects the idea when she realizes that her sister Meg would have one more reason to feel superior to her if she had such a nice son-in-law.

Mark is initially concerned that the mothering he gets from Kathy O'Brien, and from many of her colleagues, will mean that he won't be taken seriously as a teacher, that they won't really respect him, but as he goes to his weekly seminar class and listens to a few of his classmates talk about how their mentor teachers are nasty, sharp-tongued bitches who undercut them at every opportunity, he thinks that being the cute, somewhat incompetent son is way better than being seen as the competition. He also makes a superhuman effort not to point out how the evil mentors are kind of undercutting the benevolent-nurturing-sisterhood-of-women mythology.

So life is improving because he gets to spend his days surrounded by women who think he's wonderful, even if there isn't a single Potential in the group, and because he gets to feel smug in class whenever the complaints start, which is not the same as having a friend to joke with and have coffee after class, but is at least something. Principally, though, his life is improving because he gets to spend his days with twenty-one nine-year-olds. There are certainly times when he wants to tear his hair out, times when he despairs of ever being good at this job, and times when he has to take a deep breath and step back to stop himself from getting into an argument with a nine-year-old. But overall he is happier and more content when he's with his class than he is at any other time. Working with them just makes him feel alive in a way that he hasn't felt since ROCK-L left. He feels completely certain that he's doing the right thing, and feels lucky to have that certainty.

It is bittersweet, though. He really hadn't been lying in his introductory speech back in September: he just feels Janet everywhere when he's teaching. Not in any literal sense—he certainly doesn't believe that her benevolent little spirit is watching over him or anything like that; but he feels closer to her here than anywhere else. She'll be ten forever, and as long as he works with kids, he'll be close to her in a way he couldn't be otherwise. When Julia complains about her big brother Julio, or when Katya offers that she wants to "dance on Ben's grave," or when Khadija laughs, Mark is immediately put into the same space with Janet, and he likes it there very much, even though he knows that most of these kids will grow up, and Janet never did. He also knows that while very few students at this school will die as young children, not all will live to be adults—it's just a statistical certainty in a school with 350 students—and this makes his work feel that much more critical. For some of these kids a year spent with him will be a blip, one year out of seventy or eighty they will live. For others the time they spend with Mark will be 5, 8, 10 percent of the time they spend on earth. Since he doesn't know which ones these will be, he really feels that he needs to act like this year is that important to all of them.

And when he is invited to go out for beers on Friday afternoons with Kathy O'Brien and five of her co-workers, he reflects that there does actually seem to be a benevolent sisterhood of women in this building. He finds out that four of the five have worked together in this building for twenty-five years; that Kathy and Eileen, a first-grade teacher, roomed together for five years; and that they have seen each other through children, divorces, and two cases of cancer. They also swear like truck drivers when they aren't teaching, and after a few beers Mark finds himself privy to details about the sex lives of fifty-year-old women that he suspects few men ever get to hear. After hearing a rather detailed account of Eileen's husband's shortcomings in the sack, Mark suddenly feels that having a song that calls him a premature ejaculator but doesn't name him might be preferable to having five women whom you see at barbecues several times a year cackling over your impotence quite loudly in the middle of The Cliffs of Moher Irish Pub and Grill. It's just light-years from the prim, prissy atmosphere he'd been expecting. They appear to be from a different planet than all the Mary Pats who are in his classes. He wonders if any of these women were Mary Pats when they were in college and if it's just living for fifty years that gave these women their sharp edges.

One Friday night, after several beers and many plates of fried appetizers, Mark goes to the bathroom and returns to find that he is alone at the table with some empty plates, a three-quarters-empty pitcher, a stack of cash atop the check, and Maureen, the forty-year-old fourth-grade teacher.

"Hey, where'd everybody go?" he asks.

"Home. Husbands, kids, that kind of thing."

"Okay, then. I guess I'll be staggering back to my hovel then."

"Hang on," Maureen says, and puts a well-manicured hand sporting a wedding ring and an engagement ring with a gigantic diamond on his arm. "I, uh, it's a long drive to West Roxbury from here, and I need to just sober myself up a little bit."

"Oh, okay, sure. I mean, it's not like I have a husband to get back to, ha ha."

"Well, neither do I, tonight. Lewis is out of town, and the twins have some kind of team-building sleepover thing or something."

She looks at him, and Mark suddenly has the erection-causing, stomach-chilling realization that she may be hitting on him.

No. It couldn't be that, could it? He looks at Maureen. She wears too much makeup, and has the lines on her face that reveal that she's sixteen years older than him, but her body is in fantastic shape for a forty-year-old, which Mark has noticed before, since she's ten years younger than any of her colleagues and therefore the hottest woman in the building.

"Can we go get coffee or something?" she says, and Mark barely hears her and wonders if his erection will be visible when he stands up. "I think maybe walking around and just getting out of this bar will help me sober up."

"Uh, um, sure, yeah, okay," Mark says, and they leave the bar to head for the coffee shop two blocks away. By the time they have reached the door of the bar, Mark has pretty well convinced himself that Maureen is not hitting on him, that a year and a half without sex has addled his brain, and that she really just needs to sober up.

On the walk to the coffee shop, though, Maureen is walking just a little too close to him to be just companionable, and she somehow steers the conversation so as to get Mark to reveal that he lives a mere five-minute walk from here, and that he lives in a studio apartment without any roommates. His erection comes back and rages the whole time he and Maureen are drinking coffee.

There is some kind of flirtatious conversation going on, but it's like Mark is watching someone else having the conversation while the horn-dog and the minister in his brain stage a boisterous debate.

"She's totally hitting on me!"

"She is not. She's forty years old, she's married with two kids, don't make an ass of yourself assuming that she's hitting on you."

"But let's assume she is hitting on me. Should I?"

"Should you sleep with a married woman sixteen years older than you? I think the answer to that question is self-evident."

"You're right. I totally should. It's been so long, though, I really hope I've got more than two minutes in me."

"You totally should not. It's not the right thing to do."

"Hey, if she's breaking vows, that's not my business! I never made any promises! Besides, it's ideal! No commitment, no messy relationship—just get this two-minute monkey off my back!"

"Are you sure there'd be no mess? What if you fall in love with her? That would be messy. What if she falls in love with you? That would be even messier! What happens when she tells you she wants to leave her husband and kids and be with you?"

"She doesn't want to marry me, for God's sake! She just wants to get some while her husband's out of town!"

"This is the wrong thing to do. You know that. Act accordingly."

The minister gets the last word and prevails. When the coffee cups are empty, Maureen says, "So, would you like me to walk you home?"

And Mark desperately wants to say, *Yes, I do want you to walk me home, thank you for wanting me, thank you for this excitement, walk me home and I'll make you come so hard your hair will curl.* But what he actually says is, "Uh, Maureen, I think maybe that's not a great idea," and then, because he doesn't want to humiliate her, he says, "I mean, I would really love the company, but, you know, uh, this neighborhood really changes block by block, and, uh, you might regret it."

"I don't think I would," Maureen says.

Mark wants to give in, but instead, he finds himself saying, "It's actually kind of dangerous. I think I'd worry too much."

Maureen stares at him hard for what feels like a full minute but is actually only five seconds. "Are you sure?" she asks.

"Yeah, I think I am," Mark says.

"Okay then. Well, thanks for the coffee," she says, and walks out.

Mark kicks himself the whole way home, cursing himself for a coward and an idiot, and imagining how Josh is going to yell at him that this was exactly the kind of thing he should have done, that he'll only regret the things he doesn't do. He masturbates as soon as he gets home, thinking about Maureen's hand with its red nails and big diamond ring.

On Monday he hopes for a note thanking him for being a gentleman, telling him how great he is, how he'll make someone very happy someday, something that will make him feel like less of an idiot for turning down what undoubtedly would have been hot, no-strings sex. His mailbox is empty, though, and Maureen, though she does feel that Mark is wonderful and that she is glad he said no because sleeping with him seemed like a profoundly stupid idea by Saturday morning, is so full of embarrassment and regret that she wants only to pretend that nothing ever happened. So she does.

PHILIPPA

Over the course of the next few weeks, Philippa uses Martha's paints to make a self-portrait. She does this mostly so that the only image of her on canvas won't be Sam's creepy naked bride painting, but she finds that the process of creating the painting has another interesting benefit: while she's sketching out the image on the canvas, and while she's using Martha's paints to bring it to life, she is able to get outside herself. She spends hours at it, and while she would never say it's as immediately fun as cocaine, it is like a drug in that it allows her to just forget herself, to not just be her boring self thinking her boring thoughts and living her boring life but just be elsewhere. She copies Martha's painting of the Tyler Davidson Fountain in downtown Cincinnati, but she puts herself at the top, where, on the real fountain, the longhaired, androgynous figure stands with arms outstretched, water pouring from his or her palms onto the rest of the fountain.

Philippa has no art training beyond art classes she took at Walnut Prep, so she doesn't even attempt a face but just paints the fountain from the distance, with the *Genius of the Waters,* as the figure on top is called, suddenly having her hair, her breasts, and her favorite outfit. The water that pours from her hands is electric blue, and Philippa likes the image, but she doesn't really know what it means except that, for the first time, she's the one who's created an image of herself, instead of having herself interpreted by some asshole musician, lying reporter, or scary pathetic painter.

If she's done a good job creating herself on canvas, she is, she believes, doing a horrible job of creating a self she can stand in real life. Work at the Mellow Melon is much less fun since Martha left. For one thing, there's no more cocaine, which makes everybody on the staff edgy and irritable, and, on a related note, fewer customers are coming in now that there's no reliable source of blow behind the bar. Jeff was informed rather forcefully by the Hillbilly Mafia that they believed he and Martha might have been working together to cheat them, but that they would refrain from killing him if he would pay them the money Martha owed them, and that both he and his establishment are now off-limits to all of their distributors, which, in fact, is every distributor in the Greater Cincinnati area.

So business is down, and due to the rather rigorous payment schedule the Hillbilly Mafia has set up, the Mellow Melon is hemorrhaging money and will close in six months, though Jeff, having finally paid off Martha's debt, will consider himself lucky that his body is not in the same ruined state as his business.

The staff starts jumping ship immediately after Martha disappears. One of the last to go is Patrick, the chef, who calls Philippa and tells her he's gotten a sous-chef job at this little upscale bistro that some guy from J's seafood restaurant is starting in Hyde Park, and they need servers. Philippa goes over on her night off and meets Charlie, the owner, and begins working at Jekyll Drive Bistro a week later. As she walks out of the Mellow Melon for the last time, she feels a twinge of sadness. This, after all, is the place where she effectively became an adult, and if she is not exactly happy with where her life is right now, she has many, many memories of good times she had here, or with Martha, or even with Teddy. Partying is getting kind of old, but it certainly wasn't when she got here.

While she will always consider people older than thirty who identify strongly with their college through window sticker, sweatshirt, and alumni gatherings to be vaguely pathetic, Philippa will always feel a similar nostalgic pull for this institution where she went from teen to adult, and she will never throw out her Mellow Melon T-shirts, even when she won't feel safe wearing them.

Work at the Jekyll Drive Bistro is quite similar to work at the Mellow Melon with a few important exceptions: the clientele consists mostly of couples having romantic dinners, so Philippa gets hit on with much less frequency than she did at the Mellow Melon; the kitchen staff's criminal records are mostly for nonviolent offenses; and there's nobody dealing coke here. Though she initially craves coke terribly, Philippa is now back on booze, having convinced herself that if she actively sought cocaine, this would indicate that she had a problem, so she will do it if it is offered to her, but she won't go looking for it. Though Philippa isn't aware of this, she saves both her septum and 80 percent of her sense of taste with this decision.

In any case, partying is less fun than it used to be. While she will still have a drink after work now and again, she doesn't find any of the rest of the staff here very interesting—she feels kind of lost, and so she doesn't enjoy hanging out with Kathy, who's also lost; Alex talks only about his drug use and sexual escapades, which does allow Philippa to find out which local celebrities are gay but is otherwise pretty boring; and Pam is so dull that Philippa begins to yawn reflexively in her presence.

So on her off nights, Philippa paints. She's started buying supplies at the art store over on Calhoun Street, and she has fun experimenting with different types of paint. Her technique is still pretty limited, but she does have a gifted eye for color, and she's pleased with what she creates, though, apart from the fact that she's able to lose herself while she does it, she's not completely sure why she's painting. But then, she's not sure why she's doing anything. Years have passed since she told Ella that she didn't know what she was good at or why she was taking up space on the earth, and she's no closer to any kind of answer. She's a good waitress, she can hold her liquor, and she makes paintings that she likes. That's it.

She considers applying to art school, the first time that any kind of higher education has seemed even remotely appealing to her, and she even gets the applications, but she immediately comes up with reasons not to submit them: the creation of a portfolio is too much work, too much of a hassle, and then there's the financial aid form, and she doesn't like to take on any debt, and, anyway, she can enjoy her art without any formal training. The last is the only reason with any validity; the rest are simply cover for the fact that Philippa suspects that she's not a very good artist, and to be officially rejected would only confirm that suspicion, and then she'd lose what is currently the best thing in her life.

So she continues to wait tables, but life begins to seem somewhat brighter than it did there at the end of the Mellow Melon experience. Still, it takes her nearly a year to work up the courage to approach Charlie with one of her paintings—it's an eight-inch square of canvas with a long view of four backlit figures on a small stage surrounded in golden light inspired by her first Clash show, and she calls it *Strange Epiphany*—and Charlie informs her she can hang it over the worst table in the place, the two-top right by the kitchen door, and if anybody says anything bad it's coming down. Nobody says anything bad—in fact, nobody appears to really notice it at all, except for her co-worker Alex, who tells her she has "a real gift"—but it makes her smile every time she goes to work to see her work hanging on the wall with paintings by real artists that Charlie actually paid for. (Or so she believes—they are all actually by servers and cooks at Charlie's various restaurants, only one of whom has ever sold enough work to meet Philippa's definition of a "real artist.")

One night a young couple is seated under *Strange Epiphany*, and it's not until she brings their dessert—a fantastic, enormous concoction for two that the Parliament-Funkadelic-loving pastry chef calls "The Chocolate City Mothership Connection," though nobody ever orders it under that name, preferring instead "that chocolate thing"—that the woman says, "I'm sorry, but did you go to Walnut Prep?"

"Uh, yeah," Philippa says, searching the woman's face for any trace of familiarity and not finding it.

"I'm Kim. Kim Simons? I was class of '84. We were in gym together. You were my fencing partner. Remember?"

Philippa does not remember, but she decides to fake it. "Uh, yeah, of course, Kim! Right! So what are you up to?"

"Well, I'm in med school—oh, I'm sorry, this is my fiancé, Eric—"

"Nice to meet you," Philippa says, extending her hand, and Eric says it's nice to meet her as he attempts to look down her shirt while she's leaning over to shake his hand while pretending he's not trying to look down her shirt. He fools Kim, but not Philippa.

"Anyway, I'm in med school, planning a wedding, even though it's a year away and my groom lives five hours away"—Eric grins sheepishly—"all that stuff. What are you doing? Are you in school?"

And Philippa doesn't think that Kim, whoever the hell she is, is trying to be mean—it's just a natural assumption for anyone who went to Walnut Prep that a fellow alumna who's waiting tables is actually pursuing something interesting.

"Uh, no, actually. I took some time off."

"Well, I think that's great," Kim says without missing a beat, which is a far cry from the awkward pause Philippa had been expecting. "I mean, you always did do your own thing. I really admired you in high school, you know."

"Good God, why? I was a mess."

"Well, you were just never afraid to be yourself, and I spent a lot of my energy trying to be like everybody else, and I always kind of wished I could just care a little bit less about what everybody thought of me. I mean, I don't mean—I mean, you know, in a good way."

"Well, thanks," and Philippa now wants out of this conversation, wants out really badly, but it's a slow night and no other tables are demanding her attention, so all she can say is, "So what kind of doctor are you going to be?"

"Oh, I think I'm going to be a pediatrician. At least that's what I think now, but I won't get seriously into the rotations for another year or so, so maybe something else will appeal."

Philippa has nothing to say to this and feels awful. "Well, uh, good luck. It's great to see you again. I need to just go check on something in the kitchen, but it's really nice to see you."

"You, too. Good luck."

"Thanks," and Philippa nearly runs through the kitchen and into the filthy employee bathroom, where she begins to cry. Kim was certainly one of those kids that Philippa had had contempt for—this is evidenced by the fact that she has no memory of fencing with her in gym class—one of those girls she felt superior to, who went to all the right parties and dressed the right way and would have an empty life raising some P&G executive's kids. Except she doesn't have an empty life—she knows what she's doing, she knows what she's good at and why she's on the planet.

Whose life is empty now? And stupid Kim didn't even have the decency to be a shallow catty bitch so Philippa could hate her. She was just kind and smart and was probably going to be nice to sick little kids, and Philippa is nothing but a drunken waitress who does bad paintings.

A few splashes of water from the sink and Philippa is able to put a lid on her pesky emotions for a few minutes. When she returns to Kim and Eric's table, she finds a tip that is on the generous side, especially given what one can usually expect from a couple in their early twenties, but not so large as to scream, *I feel really sorry for you,* which Philippa appreciates. Kim had inwardly debated the size of the tip for about a minute and a half, taking back a few dollars when she feared she had strayed into pity-tip territory.

On the back of the check is Kim's phone number and a note: "My mom is driving me insane and maybe if you're not too busy you could help me do some girly wedding stuff sometime. Call me if you're interested; I'll tell you which of our teachers I slept with in the eleventh grade."

Philippa smiles: it was a ballsy move for Kim to leave that note, since she imagines Eric doesn't know about Kim's eleventh-grade adventure (correct—the note was left under the ancient I-think-I-left-something-back-on-the-table ploy). She's not that intrigued by the gossip part—she's fairly certain that it's Mr. Fellowson, because the rumor mill always insisted he slept with students— but the idea of doing some girly wedding stuff, or even suffering through girly wedding stuff just to have some company, is actually kind of appealing.

So she does call Kim, and they go together to a dress fitting and then have lunch with too much wine and laugh about the insane women in the shop, and Kim reveals that of course it wasn't Fellowson, he was gross and pervy, it was some guy who'd worked as a math teacher for one year who was fresh out of college that Philippa didn't even remember working at Walnut Prep at all.

Kim is incredibly busy, but she is always up late at night, so she and Philippa talk on the phone regularly. Kim is actually really smart and funny, and Philippa wonders briefly how many interesting people she missed out on knowing because she was so busy feeling superior to them in high school.

Philippa's hobby expands: she goes to yard sales and buys crappy old furniture and paints it, and soon her entire apartment is furnished with pieces she has decorated in bright colors and crazy patterns. It makes her happy to come home and find herself surrounded by things that she has created, or at least beautified. At least this one element of her life is both beautiful and under her total control, and when Kim comes over, she gushes her appreciation and admiration for Philippa's art, which also makes her feel good.

It's nice to have a friend, but Kim is free pretty rarely, and, anyway, it's been a long time since Philippa had sex, and she finds herself missing it very badly, to the extent that even her abstract paintings start looking sexual to her.

Though she's not being hit on every night at Jekyll Drive Bistro, it does happen, and so she is able to secure a few dates this way. She dates a guy who works at the Contemporary Art Center for a few months, until he mysteriously stops calling. She has a brief, passionate fling with a divorced professor at UC's College Conservatory of Music, which ends when she finds out he is not, in fact, divorced, or even separated, and she puts her foot through a twelve-hundred-dollar Martin guitar in his office. A month later his wife finds some evidence and calls Philippa, berating her for being a "little fucking whore" (which has the effect of making Philippa wonder how her mom is doing these days), and insisting "you will never ever in your worthless life have what I have," to which Philippa replies, "If you mean a husband who cheats on me, I hope you're right," and hangs up.

Kim, upon hearing the story, insists on buying Philippa a bottle of very nice wine, which they share, laughing.

When she goes to buy the new Rolling Stones record at the record store (a terrible mistake from a musical perspective), she pays by credit card, and the guy behind the counter says the only time he's heard that name before was in that old punk song, and Philippa clams up, and he says, "I bet you hate that, huh? Remember that song 'Keith's on Drugs'? I don't know why you'd write something like that anyway, I mean it's like pretty obvious, but anyway, what, uh, what I'm getting at eventually is that my name is Keith, and so morons are always singing that to me, and I hate it."

Keith therefore recovers from a beginning that appeared disastrous. Though Philippa feels (correctly) that she is much smarter than Keith, and though Kim, when she meets him, has a very difficult time hiding her contempt for him ("Is he high or just really dumb?" she asks Philippa, who, sadly, knows it's the latter), she does enjoy his company, and she figures that, at age nineteen, he's unlikely to be secretly married. They are together for six months until he unexpectedly tells her he has to go back to Chicago for "family stuff," which is mostly true—his family in Winnetka has been calling to remind him that he really needs to take advantage of that deferred acceptance to the University of Illinois, that he can't work in a record store for the rest of his life, and that he's not with that Faith girl he followed to Cincinnati anyway.

Keith leaves Philippa his phone number in Chicago. When she calls it, a nice woman thanks her for calling Comiskey Park and asks her if she'd like to buy White Sox tickets.

Kim's wedding is in three weeks, and Philippa doesn't have a date. Kim has offered some guy she knows from med school with the tepid recommendation, "If you can get past his breath, he's really kind of okay."

Philippa hopes to do better, especially because Kim's wedding is kind of stressing her out. This is not because she's given so much assistance in choosing colors, thus sparing all seven bridesmaids the horrible teal prom dresses with the pouffy sleeves that Kim's mom was eyeing: Philippa is uncharacteristically confident that she's made good choices in this area. Rather, it just reminds her that, even though Kim spends an undue amount of time agonizing about whether she's cut out to be a doctor, whether Eric is really the right one—I mean when you think about it they're still really young and he's been in Pittsburgh for the last two years, so they've never even lived together—she has skills, she has a plan, she has a fiancé. Kim may or may not be steering in the right direction, Philippa thinks, but at least she is driving. Philippa feels that she's not even spinning her wheels—she's never even made it out of park.

Two weeks before the wedding, the Jekyll Drive Bistro is closing up, and Ken, a wine salesman who supplies the bulk of the Bistro's wine list, is pulling corks with Charlie and the staff.

"Now, while it is certainly true that my company currently has a surplus of this particular cab, I think you'll find that I'm not trying to unload caseloads of junk. Now, Charlie, I think—I had that Rosemary Chicken tonight, which was delicious, by the way, and I think this cab would really be perfect with that. You'll sell a ton, and we're both winners."

Charlie sips the cab skeptically. Philippa sips some and agrees that it would be fantastic with the Rosemary Chicken, though of course she doesn't say this aloud.

"Now, we're not dumping all the extra in the stores, so your customers are not going to go down to the pony keg and see it for four bucks a bottle. I think it wouldn't be unreasonable to price it around twenty."

Charlie sips, considers, and orders four cases. Everybody relaxes once the business negotiations are over, and Ken pulls a really nice port from his sample bag, and everybody has some.

As Ken talks, Philippa wonders if he'd be good wedding-date material. He probably would be—he's good at socializing, he's tall and blond and good looking, and while he's flirted with Philippa and every other woman in the place, he's never actually asked her out, and doesn't come across as some sleazebag on the make.

She's never asked anyone out before—she's never had to—but maybe she should. Then again, here is a guy who's obviously successful, you can tell by the clothes he wears and the car he drives, and probably the reason he's never asked her or any of the other women here out is that he prefers a more professional type.

She downs a second glass of port, and Charlie is back in the office doing something, and Alex gets up to go to the bathroom, and she's alone with Ken.

"So," he says.

"Yes?"

"Why haven't I ever asked you out?"

"I was just wondering the same thing."

"Okay. I have to drive to Indianapolis tomorrow, but I'll be back in two days, and I think we should have dinner on Monday."

"Okay, but I have conditions."

Ken smiles. "Fantastic. Negotiations. I have to warn you, I kind of do this for a living."

"And I charm big tips out of people for a living."

"Duly noted." He's smiling. "Proceed with your conditions,

and let's see if we can come to an agreement that will be mutually beneficial."

"My friend is getting married in two weeks . . ."

"And you want me to be your date."

"Well, yeah."

"So in exchange for a dinner alone, I have to get dressed up, go out, and eat rubbery chicken and drink bad champagne—"

"I don't think it'll be bad champagne. Kim's parents are loaded."

"Okay. Decent champagne. In that case, it's a deal. However."

"Yeah?"

"I really have to draw the line at the Electric Slide. I really won't be able to participate in that activity."

"Thank God. I'm hoping to just be lurking by the edge of the dance floor making fun of everybody when the Electric Slide starts."

"Fantastic. When's the date," and Ken whips out his Franklin Quest planner and writes the date of Kim's wedding in pen.

The date goes very well. Philippa never goes out to restaurants, and Ken gets good tables and service pretty much anywhere in town, so they go to a very nice Italian place with a lot of empty tables where the owners stare resentfully at the packed LaRosa's pizzeria across the street. "That's what people want. That sweet sauce—tastes like pancake syrup!" one of the owners laments to Ken.

"Yeah. People in this town are fuckin' idiots—no offense, Philippa, I obviously don't include you in that—you should really try your luck in Chicago," and he goes on for a minute before the owner goes off to attend to something, and Philippa marvels at Ken's charm. It's not that she really disagrees with his assessment of Cincinnatians—indeed, having lived in one of the five great cities of the world and having been surrounded by fuckin' idiots there as well, she believes that most people in most places are fuckin' idiots—it's just that he's said this thing that was potentially offensive, and Philippa's only response is to be thrilled that he excluded her. He's just completely, completely sure of himself.

He proves a good wedding date—he makes great conversation with their table-mates, and Philippa is enormously grateful. They are seated primarily with Philippa's fellow Walnut Prep alumni, law school, business school, med school, starting their own businesses, and Philippa, who had nothing to say to these people when she saw them every day, has even less to say now that she is completely adrift, never went to college. She looks great, but she feels stupid and useless compared with these people. So she's grateful when Ken answers the "how did you guys meet" question with "Our companies do some business with each other," which is the absolute best face he could put on the truth.

Ken is also very knowledgeable in an area where most people, even those as accomplished as the other people at this table, feel terribly inadequate, and he holds forth on wine for quite some time, criticizing the champagne harshly—"This stuff is actually crap, but people buy it because it's forty bucks a bottle. You can spend half as much and get a much better wine, but I guess at an event like this you have to impress Aunt Doris with the label."

She's thrilled to be in the company of somebody with insider information, and it must be said that the rest of the table feels the same way, and no fewer than three of them will serve the sparkling wine Ken recommends (and, not coincidentally, sells) at their next celebration, and will tell their guests variations on "This is really a better wine than ones you pay twice as much for."

Ken is out of town a great deal, but he calls Philippa every night. He does most of the talking, and he spends a great deal of time lamenting the stupidity of everyone he meets, which again has the effect of making Philippa feel something she's never really felt in a good way—special. Ken has a lot of contempt for most of the world, but she's on the inside with him looking out at all the idiots and assholes, and so she must be special.

And she is.

MARK

Though he never expected this, Mark finds himself a very desirable commodity, at least on the job market. There simply aren't that many men who want to be elementary school teachers, and he has his pick of job offers. He settles on a job at the Emily Greene Balch Elementary School in Boston. He chooses Boston because the pay and benefits are better than most of the other systems, but also because he feels like the need for his services is greater in Boston than, for example, in Newton or Wellesley, two systems he rejects. (Need for his services is, of course, subjective and not measurable, but during the following school year, a little girl in the school in Wellesley is killed in an accident similar enough to Janet's to endanger Mark's mental health were he in the building.) He chooses the Balch, as it's known, because he likes the principal, and there aren't any openings at the Honey Fitz. He also chooses it because it's in Jamaica Plain, at the corner of Centre and Sedgwick streets, adjacent to an old municipal building, and he gathers from reading *The Boston Globe* and the *Boston Phoenix* that Jamaica Plain is a funky, up-and-coming neighborhood with a lot of new restaurants, and he figures this might be a good place to both live and work from a romantic and sexual perspective, so he procures an apartment—a two-bedroom that is actually way too big for him on the second floor of a three-family house—on a quiet side street ten minutes away from the Balch on foot.

Mark has unfortunately missed any of the articles that might have given him a clue to the fact that a very large percentage of the young single women in Jamaica Plain are lesbians. Thus, he is a bit surprised when the young woman he admires from afar while he's in the coffee shop marking papers every afternoon greets a female friend with a kiss a little too enthusiastic to be just friendly. He chalks it up to bad luck when he spots the rainbow patches on the bag belonging to his second coffee shop crush, but when it happens for the fourth time Mark realizes he may have made a tragic miscalculation, neighborhood-wise.

Fortunately, he appears to have made a good career choice. His students like and respect him, parents consider themselves lucky that their children are in his class, and on his annual evaluation, his principal writes that he is "a born teacher." He certainly doesn't always feel like a born teacher, though. He kicks himself mercilessly for every mistake, and every day he has something to kick himself for. He also feels the traumas of his students very keenly, and he wonders if he feels them too keenly to make working in this job a viable long-term plan. He finds himself in his house sobbing in front of the television the day he collects a reading journal in which a third-grade boy writes, "At nite my mom beets the crap out of me." He files a 51-A report of abuse and neglect, and the phone call from the Department of Social Services causes Derrick to get the crap beaten out of him again, but he ends up moving to his aunt's house in Brockton and escaping any further beatings.

Despite all this, Mark never doubts that he's in the right place. His work feels important, he loves his students, and at the end of every day, if he is not completely satisfied with his own job performance, he's satisfied that he's doing his little part to serve the world and the community. He finishes his first year of teaching feeling exhausted but very good.

But not quite good enough to make up for the fact that he is lonely and desperately horny. Both Christine and Josh blow into town occasionally, and this always leads to big get-togethers with other members of the old gang whom Mark likes but somehow never finds time to call. These are always bright weekends, but too many weekends remind him of weekends in the seventh grade, when Mr. Rourke's hot blond assistant, who looked so fetching in her white suit, was the highlight of Saturday night. Work does help somewhat with the loneliness—though the staff at the Balch are not as cohesive as those at the Honey Fitz, there are regular beers-after-work kind of get-togethers, and he often has lunch with Cassie, a twenty-six-year-old second-grade teacher who is funny, nice, married, and unattractive. Two of his older co-workers set him up with young friends (he ducks all attempted setups with blood relatives of his co-workers, figuring it might be difficult to work in an environment where one is known as "the asshole who broke my daughter's heart"), he goes on dates, they are painfully awkward, and there are no second dates.

He watches MTV at night and marvels at the fact that if one is a well-muscled simpleton, it appears to be relatively easy to get laid whenever one wants by a variety of breast-flashing drunken hotties, whereas a thoughtful, sensitive guy—an elementary school teacher, for God's sake—sits here alone with pay-per-view porn. MTV, in the rare moments when it is covering something musical in nature, also informs him that ROCK-L's "eagerly awaited" second album, whose full title is *Occasionally Malicious Meanderings Through the Haunted Forest of My Memory and Imagination,* is about to be released, that it was not produced by Cal Tomkins, and that, furthermore, the first single is an incendiary three-minute rocker called "Ausshole." (The album, perhaps weighed down by its title, sinks like a stone.)

So things appear to be both personally and professionally

bleak for ROCK-L, who is now inexplicably going by rock_l, which does provide Mark with some cold comfort in his own personal bleakness. As his second year of teaching begins to wind down, hope may be on the horizon. Camp Service is facing a rather large budgetary shortfall, and Mark has been getting mailings advertising a big alumni reunion gala sleepover on Memorial Day weekend. The director hopes that the proceeds from the weekend will get them through the summer and, further, that bringing the alumni on site will help remind them of their formative sexual experiences on that site, and that this will lead to an increase in donations that will secure the camp's financial future.

Of course, Mark hopes he'll see Becky Randall, that she will still be attracted to him, that she will not be married or engaged, and that she'll be willing to engage in at least one weekend of fervent sexual activity if not begin a relationship. And if not Becky, there will certainly be other women there who remember him as the "Pukin' My Guts Out" guy, who might be impressed with his career choice, or, failing all that, who will be drunk and willing to give it up on short notice.

One day at lunch in early May, Cassie says, "So Jim and I are having this big barbecue over Memorial Day weekend. You wanna come?"

"I'd love to, but I am . . . well, I'm going to a summer camp reunion. In Maine."

"That's cute! Are you going to like raid the girls' cabins or something? I mean, what exactly does one do at a summer camp reunion?"

"I don't really know. This is the first one they've ever had. I guess if you're me, you nurture pathetic hope that you'll be able to reconnect with your summer camp girlfriend."

"Aw, Jesus, Mark, that is a bad strategy."

"Yeah, well, what exactly are my options? More dates with Andrea's daughter's psychotic co-worker? Pining after hot lesbians in the coffee shop?"

"Listen, my friend Elaine just broke up with her boyfriend,

she's perfect for you, and she's coming to the barbecue, so bag the camp reunion and come to my barbecue! Do you know if this girl's even going to be there?"

"Uh, well, not exactly, no."

"So what if she's not there, and you dragged your ass to Maine for nothing? Or what if she is there and married? Or fat?"

"Well, she was very athletic, I don't think—"

"You think she looks exactly like she did when she was seventeen? Sure, why not, everybody else does! Well, actually, you probably do, but most of us have changed."

"I know this is pathetic, I know it's lame, and I know I'm setting myself up for a huge disappointment here, but I have to do it anyway. You think Elaine is going to evaporate after this weekend?"

"No, she'll probably still be in solid form, but I gotta tell you, she's really hot and Jim has been talking her up all over his office, so she may be off the market by Tuesday."

"What, she's going to fly to Vegas and marry one of Jim's buddies immediately following the barbecue?"

Cassie laughs. "She well might. And then you'll be sorry you missed my barbecue, you asshole!"

Mark laughs, finds he prefers *asshole* to *pathetic deluded loser*.

When he arrives at Camp Service at six thirty on Friday night before Memorial Day, Mark's heart sinks. The camp looks shabby. He parks his car and walks up to the dining hall, which does not appear to have been painted since his tenure here as assistant director. Whoever is running the camp now has clearly focused resources on maintaining the screens. Granted, given the blackfly and mosquito population up here, this seems to Mark to have been a wise decision.

He walks into the dining hall and has a brief flashback to what, sadly, still stands as the great triumph of his young life: bringing the house down with "Pukin' My Guts Out," and getting blown by Becky. That, of course, was while Janet was alive, and while he came back here after Janet's death and therefore has memories of this place from the post-Janet part of his life, he still feels like she haunts him here. Not that he has any real sense of her presence; it's just that every spot has a Janet memory attached to it, and even the chill in the air in the late-May evening feels a lot like the chill in the air in a mid-August evening, and it seems to unlock feelings in Mark that he can usually keep a lid on.

He finds a seat at one of the long metal tables with Formica tops with the benches attached that have been unfolded especially for this occasion by Kathy, the director who took over for Terry, who took over for Tim.

Mark looks at the crowd: there are very few people here, and none of them is Becky. He recognizes some faces and even manages to pull out a few names, but, again, none of them is Becky. None is even Liza, whom Mark had always had nice conversations with and considered his emergency backup girlfriend if things went sour with Becky, though she never gave him any indication that she was available for that role.

He doesn't see Andy, Ted, John, any of the kids he used to get in trouble with; more important, he doesn't see Becky. Well, she might not even be here, she might not even live in New England anymore, she might not be a Unitarian anymore, she might have moved to Brazil, changed her name, and begun a career as a cabaret singer for all he knows. Or perhaps she plays in the WNBA—has their season started yet? She certainly had what the commentators would call a dominant low post presence when she was seventeen.

As he thinks this, it occurs to Mark that *dominant low post presence* sounds kind of dirty. And he'd always thought *dribble penetration* was the dirtiest basketball phrase.

Mark entertains himself with word games, makes small talk with some of his fellow former campers, who persist in not being Becky despite Mark's best efforts to magically transform them into Becky with the power of his mind.

Kathy gets up and makes a speech about how the camp has

meant so much to generations of kids, how the service ethic must
have taken because their questionnaires reveal that they have in
their midst people studying to be doctors, people who are doctors,
people who are social workers, teachers, public defenders, founders
of nonprofits, employees of nonprofits, that if they want to live in
a world where places like this can still inspire people to lives of service, they'd damn well better pony up to keep the roofs from leaking. (These are not her exact words, but the message is clear, and
Mark brought his checkbook expecting to be hit up, and seeing the
condition of some of the buildings, he's now planning to write a
much bigger check than he intended, especially since now, with
Becky not here, he's not going to need any extra money for calling
her in Burlington or wherever the hell she lives. Rio?)

After the depressing fund-raising, Kathy wheels in a keg on a
dolly, somebody else pushes PLAY on some kind of early-1990s mix
on the CD player, and it feels almost like a party, except for the fact
that Mark feels like exactly as much of a chump as he expected to.
More people trickle in, most lamenting the horrible traffic on 95,
but none of them is Becky. He wonders how big a check he's going
to have to write to get out of here in time to get to Cassie's barbecue tomorrow night and line up with all of Jim's co-workers to
meet The Fabulous Single Babe Who'd Be Perfect For Him.

This strikes him as a pretty depressing scenario, but so does
staying here all weekend feeling like an idiot. After about an hour
of pleasant, dull conversation with his fellow campers, Mark's
about to head to his bunk in cabin B-6 (and his imagination has
cooked up a pretty horrifying scenario for what the mattresses are
like given the state of everything else here) (and his horror-movie
scenario is only slightly worse than the actual condition of the
mattresses) when Kathy rolls out a big TV on the kind of wheeled
metal cart that Mark recognizes very well from his work in elementary schools, and she says, "Hey—if I can have everybody's attention for a minute. I have here a piece of history that I'd like to share
with you. It's a song that many of you undoubtedly remember, that
campers here still sing with stomach-churning regularity, and

here, captured on videotape, is an early performance by the young man who started it all. So without further ado, ladies and gentlemen, I give you 'Pukin' My Guts Out.' "

She pushes PLAY, and there is Mark, sixteen years old, with his guitar (his guitar he gave to Raquel, ROCK-L, rock_l . . .), singing his greatest hit.

Memory turns out to be much kinder than videotape, and Mark can't believe that this awkward, zit-covered dork on the TV screen is actually him—he was sure he'd looked a lot more like Kurt Cobain and a lot less like Screech from *Saved by the Bell*.

But the tape's cruelty doesn't end there. Because, as the song is ending, the face of a girl with shoulder-length auburn hair appears in the frame, smiling right at the camera, smiling right at Mark from beyond the grave. "That's my big brother!" she says, smiling and jerking a thumb toward the stage behind her shoulder, and Mark feels his entire body become hollow. He's suddenly an empty shell, unable to think, unable to speak, not really aware that he's smiling and waving politely as his fellow campers applaud the end of the tape, not aware of anything until he stumbles out of the dining hall and runs to his car to collect his sleeping bag. He opens the door, slides into the driver's seat, and begins to cry. How could that happen? How could she be there, eight years old, mouthing "That's my big brother" at the camera, alive and not dead, how can that possibly be? And how can it possibly be that he's still here and she's gone, poor little Janet . . .

After fifteen minutes Mark collects first himself and then his sleeping bag and heads off to cabin B-6. He half expects to hear Jamie Sibthorp's voice asking him if he got any, but if Mark's math is correct, Jamie is currently in college, probably, in yet another cruel twist of fate for the evening, getting some even now while Mark pines after someone he hasn't seen in nearly eight years.

Mark breakfasts at a long table, eating buckwheat pancakes that are surprisingly tasty. He talks to someone named Melissa, who was a CIT here when Mark was thirteen. He remembers her (as everyone in his cabin would remember every female CIT), and he listens politely as she talks about her job teaching English to refugees and wonders if he can work up enough of an attraction to her to make this weekend interesting.

It's not that she's unattractive—if he saw her on the street, he'd probably describe her as cute, and they are both teachers, and she lives in Boston, and he should probably ask her out just so that he can have a date with someone not related to any of his fellow teachers.

There is a postbreakfast tour of the camp, and Kathy skillfully points out every single thing that needs repair or updating, which is pretty much every single thing at the camp, so the tour takes nearly an hour.

At the end of the tour, they are heading back to cabins to change for canoeing (and a few masochists insist they are going to try to swim in the lake, a bone-chilling proposition in May in Maine) and a car pulls into the lot. It's a black Lexus, and Mark can practically see the cartoon dollar signs bugging out of Kathy's eyes as she spots the Japanese luxury sedan.

The door opens, and a tall woman with red hair emerges. It's Becky! It's Becky! Mark orders his legs not to go running down the hill, orders his arms not to wrap themselves around her, orders his mouth not to yell, *Becky, please save me, I'm so lonely!*

All of his orders are carried out successfully, and Becky comes up and introduces herself to Kathy—"Rebecca Randall," she says, and then offers to the group, "I got caught up in something at work. Did I miss anything entertaining?"

"We watched the 'Pukin' My Guts Out' tape," somebody says, and Becky catches Mark's eyes and says, "I'm sorry I missed it!"

"Well," says Kathy, who is still bedazzled by the Lexus sitting in the lot next to all the Honda Civics and Toyota Tercels, "I'm sure I can arrange to show it to you. And here, you've just missed the tour, but I can give you the quick version," and she leads Becky away to show her the ravages of time on the camp and hopefully get her Lexus-driving self to underwrite some repairs.

Becky looks over her shoulder as she goes. Was that a look for me? Mark wonders. He straps on a life jacket, swipes most of the cobwebs from a battered metal canoe, and takes a little spin around the lake. It's quiet and beautiful, but Mark stubbornly resists serenity. Does she have a boyfriend? Why does she drive a Lexus? Is she some kind of money-grubbing investment banker or something? Who has she become? Will he even like her? And, whether he does or not, will he be able to sleep with her?

And what about him? Will she like him? Who has he become? He knows that Janet's death took forever the sunny outlook he had when Becky knew him, and if it had been in any danger of reemerging, rock_l's betrayal kicked it down for good. But overall, he feels distressingly like the kid he saw in the video last night— occasionally sure of himself, but mostly just uncomfortable in his own skin, needy and lonely. He paddles around some more and finally comes back to the dock in a terrible funk, convinced that nobody, much less Becky, will ever be interested in him.

He wanders around the camp looking for Becky and doesn't find her. He walks up the bench dedicated in Janet's honor and sees that it is missing a slat and is in terrible need of painting. He wonders why Mom and Dad didn't follow up on this. Well, Dad obviously has his trophy wife and her kids to obsess about, and in a way Mark doesn't blame him—he's got two little kids who are both alive, so why dwell on the fact that he once had one who isn't. But Mom has no such excuse.

He sits on the bench and keeps sitting even after Kathy signals lunch by ringing what everyone has always called "the Bataan Bell" because apparently some Unitarian GI had come across it on Bataan and brought it home, though Mark never understood how a soldier in the South Pacific who wasn't Douglas MacArthur managed to get a hundred-pound bell back to the Middle Of Nowhere, Maine, in 1945. A Unitarian miracle, he supposes.

He thinks he should go down to lunch, because Becky is there, but he's wrapped up too tight in his doubt and insecurity to move. Because the minute he goes down there and finds that Becky is dating some manager at Fidelity, or the governor of New Hampshire, or something, then he'll know for sure, and the Getting Becky Back fantasy will be over forever. The fantasy will end one way or the other when he walks down the hill, and it's kept him company through many a long night since rock_l rocked the pop charts, and he finds that he can't stand the idea of saying good-bye to it.

He should just walk down there and ask her. And then, if she's got a boyfriend, he'll write Kathy a check and still be back in Boston in time for the barbecue and the rest of his life, which will be fine, goddammit, which will involve someone beautiful and wonderful and not crazy who might not be Becky but who is probably looking for him right now in Boston while he's chasing his adolescence in Maine.

Maybe he'll just skip seeing Becky altogether. It's just not healthy. Even if she has a boyfriend, he can't guarantee he won't make a pathetic play to win her away from him. No, that's ridiculous. He's going to go down there and just find out.

He stands up from the bench, turns toward the dining hall, and sees Rebecca Randall, Esq., walking toward him up the hill.

"Hey there," she says.

"Hey," Mark believes he says, though he can't really hear his words over the pounding of his heart, which he is sure must be audible for a ten-mile radius.

"So were you gonna duck me all weekend, or what?"

"Uh, no, I wasn't ducking you, I was just . . ." And Mark watches in awe and horror as Mr. Ballsout takes over his mouth and says, "Well, what the hell. I came up here just to see you, and I did actually look for you earlier, but then I was afraid that I'd find you, and you wouldn't like me, or you'd be married, or something, and I had this wonderful idea about reconnecting with you that was probably stupid, but I got kind of attached to it, and I would have hated for it to end when you told me about your wonderful boyfriend."

"Or when you found out I was fat, right? I mean, come on, you were worried I was going to be fat, right? Because I was worried about you being fat."

"Well, okay, but I could see that as soon as you got out of the car. Nice car, by the way."

"Yeah, it's my little nod to conspicuous consumption. I've found that people just don't take you very seriously as a lawyer when you show up in a Honda Civic."

"So you're a lawyer?" Mark says, and hopes that he's kept the disappointment out of his voice, because of course if she's a lawyer, she's not saving the world, and this could be a deal breaker, because the kind of people he'd known in college who became lawyers were one of the classes of people that Mark despised and felt vaguely superior to. He understood why people would go chasing money, he certainly would have liked to have nicer stuff, but how could you possibly spend your life in pursuit of something so hollow when there was so much important work to do?

"Yeah, I work at one of these white-shoe firms in Boston, even though the closest thing I have on my personal shoe tree is a pair of conservative cream-colored pumps, ha-ha. But anyway, they have a division that does mostly civil rights work, though I have worked on some asylum cases, too. I'm actually incredibly lucky, because I get to get paid like a real lawyer without feeling like I've sold out. And I'll need real legal experience if I want to run Amnesty or Human Rights Watch or the UUSC or something someday. Everybody who runs these big NGOs is a lawyer."

And suddenly Mark finds himself looking up at Rebecca from what he was convinced was his high horse. "Uh, I teach elementary school in Boston."

"That was actually going to be my guess. Either that or like pediatrician or something. You were so great with the kids here."

Well, Mark thinks, this is going badly, but not in the way he might have predicted. He had always been comfortable with her being a better athlete than him (indeed, he'd found this strangely arousing, particularly when she was dripping sweat after a soccer game), but now she's a better world saver than him, too. She's high-powered! She's ambitious! So, okay, the Lexus doesn't mean she wants a guy with an MBA making mid-six figures, but she very well might want the junior senator from wherever, or like some globe-trotting war correspondent, or something. But then why did she come up here and seek him out?

There is an awkward pause. Mark steps in with "So the camp looks shitty, huh?"

"Yeah."

"I was actually going to bag this whole thing if you didn't show up."

"You're really sweet. Let's bag it now."

"What do you mean?"

"I mean it's three in the afternoon, and we're an hour from Portland, and we are grown-ups and don't have to eat shitty camp food and sleep on those mattresses anymore. I came here to see if you were here and single. Check on both. I am also here and single. So let's go have a nice dinner!"

They fling checks at Kathy, and though Mark doesn't see Rebecca writing hers, he knows it dwarfs his own, because when Kathy takes his, she says, "Thank you very much. I'm sorry you can't stay," whereas when Rebecca gives Kathy hers, Kathy says, "Oh. *Oh!* Thank you so much, this is very generous. Listen, we can certainly arrange some kind of naming—"

"No, that really won't be necessary," Rebecca says, then looks at Mark. "Well, you know what—name something else after Janet Norris."

Mark follows Rebecca's Lexus to Portland with at least half an erection the whole time. Because if they have dinner in Portland, that puts them two and a half hours from Boston after dinner, which is a drive they could certainly do, provided they don't have too much wine with dinner, they'd easily be home by midnight, but who wants to drive so far when there are so many hotels in Portland?

They eat lobster and kill a bottle of pinot grigio, and talk and laugh, and if he needed any more encouragement after the *name something after Janet* comment, Mark certainly has it after two hours of easy conversation. It's not just like it used to be—it's far better. Mark talks passionately about his work, Becky does the same, they argue about movies, they agree about politics, and, as awkward as Mark and Rebecca feel on the inside (Mark feels dwarfish, ugly, and poor, not good enough for her, not good enough, he keeps hearing inside his head) (Rebecca feels just as awkward, feeling every inch of her six feet, thinking herself a freakish giantess, hoping he won't see how much she actually likes driving the Lexus), on the outside they are not teenagers but real adults who can actually make conversation and who turn out to enjoy each other's company.

Rebecca allows him to pay his half of the check (Don't emasculate him! she'd screamed at herself when she reflexively reached for the Amex card), and they walk along the cobblestone streets of Portland's Old Port area, looking at the touristy shops without really seeing anything. They find themselves holding hands, though neither one remembers initiating it. It's electric, Mark thinks, and can't keep his brain from following up with *boogie oogie oogie.* He laughs.

"What?"

"Well, this is dumb, but I was just . . . I've just been thinking so long about touching you, and then here we are holding hands, and it's electric, I mean I actually feel like there's a current from you running through my whole body, but when I thought, It's electric, my brain just had to start singing that Electric Slide song."

"Careful there, killer. They play that song at weddings," Rebecca says aloud, and then says to herself, Shut up! You haven't succeeded in scaring him away with your freakish height, so now you want to talk about weddings? You idiot! and, simultaneously, He's really good marriage material. He'd anchor you in what's important.

Mark, for his part, smiles, and figures this is as good a time as any to broach the subject of exactly where the two of them will be sleeping tonight. "So, uh, there's no way I'm driving to Boston tonight."

"Goddamn right. Not when I booked us a nice hotel room on the drive down here."

Mark takes a moment to digest this. "Uh, okay. Great!" It's very hard to stroll nonchalantly when your penis suddenly feels like it's covered in steel and filled with molten lead. It's also very hard to speak coherently when so much blood is suddenly redirected. "Uh, I don't . . . I mean, I didn't exactly prepare for . . ."

"Well, it's your lucky night. There's a CVS right there."

Becky waits outside while Mark goes inside and buys condoms. The clerk appears uninterested, but Mark wants to hug him and scream, *I'm gonna get some! Thank you, shopkeep, for making this moment possible!*

He emerges from the CVS with a big smile on his face.

"You know," Rebecca says to him, "I was just thinking."

"Yeah?"

"Well, you were my first blow job."

"Uh, yeah, and you were mine." And how many have there been since me? Mark suddenly thinks.

"Well, I was only seventeen."

"Yeah, so was I. It's not like I took advantage of you or something."

"That's not what I mean. What I mean is that I'm sure my technique was kind of lacking."

"I couldn't really complain."

"Of course you weren't going to complain! You were seventeen! Now, I don't know how much experience you have in this area, but I think you'll agree that my technique wasn't what it could have been."

Mark takes a moment to ponder this. The blow job was a rare part of Raquel's sexual repertoire, so his experience is not as broad as he wishes. And it's difficult after idealizing Becky for so long to admit that anything could have been less than perfect with her. But the truth is there.

"Well . . . ," he begins. "Nah. Nothing."

"What?" She digs a finger into his rib cage. "Tell. I have two siblings. I do know how to tickle you to death."

"Okay, okay. There was . . . I mean, it's not that I wasn't grateful, it's not that I didn't enjoy it . . ."

"Yeah, yeah. Get to the point."

"There was a little bit of a teeth issue."

"A teeth issue."

"A little bit—you know. There was the occasional tooth scrape."

Becky smiles. "Well, I think I can guarantee that's not going to be a problem tonight."

Becky is as good as her word. On Monday, Mark's students will wonder why he seems so patient, so happy, so glad to be alive. His colleagues will have no such confusion. When he floats into the teachers' lounge for lunch, Cassie shouts, "Oh my God, look at Mark! He got laid!"

Mark smiles, tries to protest, and can only smile as he takes a big bow to acknowledge the sudden outbreak of applause and cheers.

PHILIPPA

Philippa walks into the Camp Washington Savings and Loan and finalizes her plans to kill herself. This seems like a funny place to plot her destruction, Philippa thinks, but then, she'd known it was going to end here for at least eighteen months.

This is the Bank That Time Forgot, one of the few little banks that hasn't been swallowed by a bigger bank, and certainly one of the few banks of any size that does not appear to have renovated its interior since the 1950s. Philippa walks up to the teller's window, which is an actual window in a wall of glass atop a gigantic slab of oak that runs the length of the bank. Every time she comes in here, which has been every week for the last eighteen months, she half expects George Bailey to come out from behind the counter and beg her not to withdraw her money.

Today, though, even George Bailey couldn't stop her from withdrawing her money. She passes the passbook—dirty from living beneath the floor mat on the driver's side of her car—across to Marie, the white-haired teller who is another fixture that's been here since the 1950s, and says, "Hey Marie. I guess I need to close out my account."

"Oh," Marie says, "I'm so sorry. I thought you were so smart to start a college fund before you were even married, and now here you have to clean it out. Well, when my Fritz was out of work, we had to dip into Jacqueline's college fund, and it broke my heart, it really did, but little by little we paid her back with interest. I'm sorry, dear. Brighter times are ahead."

Philippa waits for Marie to go get Ellery, the manager, and she feels bad. She feels bad that she's not the person this kind old woman thinks she is, that the truth is just so much more pathetic than even the pathetic story Marie believes.

And she thinks about how she got to this point, on the verge of destroying Philippa Jane Strange. She has time while Ellery completes the paperwork and counts out the money, so, though it fills her with self-loathing, she engages in that process she's come to think of as "picking the scab" and runs over Ken's Greatest Hits in her brain.

Certainly there were warning signs she can't believe she ignored: Ken's temper and foul mouth in traffic, the way he twice hopped out of his car to try to fight another motorist. The number of times he'd driven home completely shitfaced. It wasn't that bad, she told herself. He was drunk on really nice wine, and somehow that was a lot better than downing a case of Milwaukee's Best in front of the Bengals game or something. Wasn't it?

And then there was The Baseball Incident. She'd awoken late one Sunday morning to find Ken already awake and rooting through boxes in her closet.

"Umm . . . wha . . . what are you doing?"

"What the fuck is this?" Ken turned around, his fair-complexioned face bright red, holding a baseball in his hand.

"Uh, looks like a baseball to me," she said, tentatively, and feeling suddenly afraid. She recognized this as his road rage face, but they weren't on the road, and he wasn't mad at somebody else, and he was between her and the door.

"Why is it signed? Why do you have a baseball signed by some piece-of-shit relief pitcher for the Reds? You don't even like base-ball!"

It suddenly seemed like there was no right answer to Ken's question, and while Philippa sat there contemplating how quickly she might get her window open and what she could possibly say to Ken to calm him down, he said, "Did you fuck him? Huh? Did you fuck this guy, you fucking slut?"

Well, of course she'd fucked him, but this didn't seem like the time to get into that, so she came back with "Jesus Christ, Ken, I knew that guy years ago!"

"I didn't ask that! I asked you a simple question! Did. You. Fuck. Him? Are you so fucking stupid that you don't understand what I'm asking you?"

And she started crying, and she said, "Ken, I went out with him for six months five years ago. Why are you doing this?"

"So why do you still have the goddamn baseball? Huh? If you're with me right now, why do you have fucking Teddy's fucking baseball in your fucking closet?"

"I don't know, Ken. I don't care about him. I haven't spoken to him for four and a half years."

"I thought it was five years! You fucking lying slut!" And Ken grabbed the baseball, and Philippa saw clearly in her mind's eye Ken giving her the high heat, the old brushback pitch, a little chin music, a ninety-five-mile-an-hour fastball straight to the cranium. Instead he ran from her bedroom into the living room and fired the high heat straight at the plate glass window that overlooked scenic Madison Road, and the baseball shattered it spectacularly and bounced into the road, where it deflected off the tire of a passing Honda Accord and came to rest in the gutter, where later that day a twelve-year-old Reds fan named Norman found it and took it home and placed it next to his Tom Hume and Ron Oester signed balls.

Ken ran out of the building, screaming "You fucking whore!" at the top of his lungs, got into his car, and drove away.

The problem with having a violent altercation early on Sunday morning in an eight-unit apartment building is that everybody else is home to witness it. An emergency board-up company came and bolted a piece of plywood over the plate glass window, and Philippa's eviction notice arrived twenty-four hours later.

Ken arrived shortly after the eviction notice bearing Belgian chocolates, roses, and a bottle of high-end champagne, and Philippa, cringing, remembers how she did what she thinks "any sensible young woman would do," and moved in with him. She told Kim she was moving in with Ken, but didn't tell her about The Baseball Incident. When she tells the story in the future (and she will tell it only once), she will be at a loss to explain this decision. Even now, with nearly two years to think it over, she can't really make sense of it. Ken at least had apologized, which is something Philippa's mother had never done. (If you can count, "I'm sorry I did that, but you should really know better than to keep shit like that. Guys get jealous!" as an apology, which, sadly, Philippa does.)

Ken lived in a very nice three-story town house in Mount Adams with a breathtaking view of the Cincinnati skyline. Ken was very helpful and kind as they made trip after trip from Oakley to Mount Adams, and the move was feeling like a good decision. When she brought in a pair of stools that she had painted lime green with little red squiggles, Ken had looked at them and said, "Oh, you're going to have to put that hideous shit in the basement. I sometimes have clients over here."

"Jesus, Ken, I made these!"

Ken smiled. "You do woodworking now?"

"No, you know what I mean. These are my work!"

"Well, first of all, your work is waiting tables, and you're damn good at it, and second of all, I'm sorry, but they're hideous! Put them in the basement!"

"You're an asshole, Ken."

"Yes, I pretty much am," he said, and that was the last word about that.

. . .

It wasn't all horrible, she would try to explain one day. There was still Good Ken, who was attentive, bought her nice things, and was genuinely fun to be around. He knew people at every restaurant in town, he had a large number of friends and acquaintances, and was a great party host and guest, never losing the power to mesmerize and delight people, to make them think that his attention and approval were precious commodities that they were lucky to have. That Philippa was lucky to have.

But Bad Ken came out at unpredictable times, and the longer they lived together, the more often Bad Ken came out.

There was the parking thing. Parking was tight in Mount Adams, and Ken liked to be able to park his car right in front of the house so that he could load his samples into the car without having to lug them down the block. One week a Toyota Camry had appeared in Ken's spot and stayed there for three days.

Ken's first salvo was a letter he put under the windshield. "Cincinnati law REQUIRES you to move your car every TWENTY-FOUR HOURS. This car has been parked in this spot for THREE DAYS. Please comply with the law by this afternoon or STEPS WILL BE TAKEN."

The car was moved, and two days later, while Ken was out, it reappeared. It had this note in the driver's-side window: "No notes please. I am a Mount Adams resident parked legally in a public spot."

Ken responded with this: "Nobody gives a FUCK where you live. This is about THE LAW."

The Toyota Camry remained in the spot for two days, in violation of Cincinnati's rarely enforced parking ordinance, and Ken called "a buddy over at the police" (actually a police dispatcher he had been sleeping with irregularly since his brief stint as a Cincinnati police officer eight years earlier). He found that the Camry's owner had one conviction—a public lewdness conviction he'd gotten for administering a blow job to a forty-year-old closeted married man in Eden Park. One night Ken had gone outside with red spray paint and written FAGGOT on the back window and CALL ME I SUCK DICK along with the owner's phone number on the passenger side.

The Camry thereafter disappeared entirely, and Ken parked his Pontiac in the spot in front of the house for four days without moving it. Though this incident was not directed at Philippa, Ken's power to reach out and hurt almost anyone in a horrible way was a key factor in her decision to erase herself from the earth. It was not long after this that she started her escape fund at Camp Washington Savings and Loan, figuring, correctly, that because Ken made so much money, her own was insignificant to him, and he wouldn't even notice as she socked away an ever-larger percentage of her tips in this little one-branch bank in a low-rent part of Cincinnati where nobody who didn't live there ever went unless they were going to Camp Washington Chili, which in any event was four blocks away from Camp Washington Savings and Loan.

Bad Ken had come out more and more regularly at home: Once, on their anniversary, Philippa had cooked the Rosemary Chicken from Jekyll Drive Bistro. Ken came home late, took one look at the chicken on his plate, and tossed chicken and plate in Philippa's direction. The plate shattered against a cabinet next to her and Ken had called her a fucking whore and demanded to know if she was fucking the chef at the Jekyll Drive Bistro.

"Jesus Christ, Ken, that's crazy! I made this for our anniversary! You had it the night you first asked me out!"

"Don't you fucking lie to me!" Glassware was flying everywhere, and Philippa was glad she wasn't wearing open-toed shoes. "You fucking slut! Fucking the goddamn kitchen help and too fucking stupid to cover it up!"

Somehow, and she really wished it wasn't so, this struck Philippa as very funny. This was because she had a Julia Child cookbook on the shelf, and she wondered if she ever cooked anything from it would Ken accuse her of being a fucking dyke, fucking Julia Goddamn Child, and despite the fact that she was surrounded by broken glass at the time, or possibly because she was surrounded by broken glass at the time, she couldn't get the idea of going down on Julia Child out of her mind, and this struck her as absurdly funny, and she began to laugh and laugh and laugh, and would have continued to laugh if Ken hadn't doubled her over with a single wind-knocking punch in the stomach, the only time he actually struck her.

"Next time you laugh at me it's your fucking face," he said and stalked out.

It wasn't long after this that Philippa stole a knife from the kitchen at the Jekyll Drive Bistro and hid it under the mattress. Every night as she went to sleep, she would reach between the mattress and box spring and pull out the eight-inch chef's knife and place it under her pillow as insurance in case Bad Ken emerged at three A.M. with murder on his mind.

Thus every night Philippa went to sleep with visions of burying a knife in Ken's neck multiple times.

One night Philippa was tired and not feeling incredibly sexy, but had consented because it was easier to consent than to have an argument. Her attraction to Ken was inversely proportional to her fear of him, so it is fair to say that during this particular session, she was not as enthusiastic as one who felt active passion might have been. Ten minutes after sex Philippa was lying on the bed, not really thinking anything, and Ken had been up brushing his teeth and putting pajamas on. He got back into bed, grabbed Philippa's left arm, and twisted it behind her back. Her immediate fear was that he had found the knife and was getting ready to use it on her.

Instead he just pulled her arm farther up her back until she'd cried out, "*Ow!* Jesus, Ken that really hurts! *Ow!* What are you doing?"

He released her arm, said, "Yeah, you can be loud when you want to," lay down, and turned out the light. Philippa grabbed the knife and spent the night not sleeping, but analyzing the pros and cons of killing Ken with the knife while he slept.

One afternoon, randomly: "I know you're thinking about leaving me."

"What are you talking about?"

"I'm talking about how you think about leaving me. I know I'm an asshole, and I know you think about leaving. You'd be pretty fucking stupid not to."

"Ken, I don't know why you're bring—"

"I just want you to know that I would find you. You know I have buddies in the police, buddies at the DMV. I will find you if you ever leave me. I will find you."

This was, in some ways, the most unnerving of all the incidents, because Ken was so far from enraged when he said it. She'd gotten pretty good at seeing Bad Ken lurking behind Ken's eyes, and had gotten fairly skilled at dealing with Ken's anger, but now he was threatening her and he wasn't even angry. And yet she didn't leave. Kim had been telling her for months (sixteen, actually) that she had to leave Ken, that she wasn't safe, and yet Philippa did not leave. In some senses it was just a failure of imagination—she couldn't picture a future where she was free of Ken, where she had another job, where she lived somewhere else. It's also the terrible success of the human ability to adapt to a bad situation. In the future she will be talking about commuting with someone with a two-hour commute who will say, "It's amazing what you can get used to," and she will think that sums up her life with Ken as well as anything. Eventually she just kind of disconnected from it. When Bad Ken came out, she saw it happening, but in an important way she didn't feel it happening. She continued to make her weekly deposits at Camp Washington Savings and Loan, but the idea of flight that once seemed so urgent began to seem less and less likely, and eventually the deposits became just a habit, and the lie that this is Unborn Junior's college fund begins to seem increasingly plausible.

• • •

Then, a month after Ken's cold threat, Philippa peed on a piece of plastic she'd bought with cash at a Walgreens in Western Hills (Cincinnati's east–west divide had served her clandestine purposes very, very well: she could do whatever she needed to do on the west side, fully confident that neither Ken nor any of his friends would ever see her) and found that she was pregnant.

She cried all afternoon. She briefly considered getting an abortion. It would be easy, and she could probably do it without Ken noticing (for she knew for certain that he would not believe that they'd been the victim of an unlikely birth control failure, and would not believe the baby was his, but that, paradoxically, he would never agree to an abortion), but she found that she didn't want to terminate this pregnancy. Faced with the prospect of bringing one person into the world who would love her above all others, she found that she couldn't bear the idea of not doing it.

She thought, though, of bringing this child up in a house with Ken, and, even, with Philippa: Would he (for she knew as soon as the stick she peed on turned blue that she was carrying a boy) (or thought she knew, anyway) grow up to think that women were weak, like Philippa, that to love a woman was to verbally abuse her and break things? Would he hate Ken for what he did to Philippa, or would he hate Philippa for allowing it? And what would happen the first time the baby ripped something important, or erased Ken's Illinois spreadsheet when he was trying to play Minesweeper, or caused some kind of unintentional destruction, as children do? Would the child even survive making his father angry?

Or would she? Kim told her in no uncertain terms that domestic abuse is the number one cause of death among pregnant women. "Number One, Philippa. Your doc will screen you for all kinds of stuff that is twenty times less likely to kill you than an abusive partner. You have to get out of that house now."

Philippa appreciated Kim's concern, but she had already made her decision.

Once this decision was made, the rest became surprisingly easy. She spent two days planning, and, peeking into Ken's organizer, saw that he was leaving Cincinnati for a five-day, four-state swing through his Midwest territory. She decided to leave a day after Ken did in order to get herself a head start. She knew he would call from the road (what she didn't know was that it was almost always after he'd had sex with another woman, though this wouldn't have surprised her), and that he would leave increasingly abusive messages on the machine, and that he would come home full of rage and ready to beat her, and that he would probably destroy something expensive when he didn't find her.

She wrote four letters. As she leaves the bank, life savings in hand, she slips them into a mailbox. This is the second-to-last act she will perform before killing Philippa Jane Strange. The first letter is to Simon Strange. Though she knows her tabloid celebrity has probably been forgotten by every resident of the UK, the idea of going back to London doesn't feel possible—Simon resumed his benign neglect almost as soon as she returned to the US, and though there was no big falling-out, they haven't spoken since he called on her birthday last year, or maybe the year before, and she doesn't feel she can either show up on his doorstep or blow a huge percentage of her escape money on a plane ticket. And even in London she'd still be Philippa, and this idea is intolerable, so she says good-bye:

Dear Dad,

Haven't heard from you in a while. Fair enough. It's not like I've been in close contact with you, either. I don't have a lot to say except thanks for your hospitality. I know you love me even now, and I don't blame you for leaving Mom. I left her years ago, too. Anyway, it's been a year and a half since we spoke. Not much has changed, but I am going to be very hard to reach for . . . well, forever. So I guess this is good-bye. I want to end on a good note, so here it is: I really appreciated the way you accepted me unquestioningly when I was a pain-in-the-ass, fucked-up teenager. I love you, and I always will.

Love, Philippa

The second is to Kim:

Kimmy-baby:

You are my best friend, and I am sorry I didn't take your advice a lot sooner. Anyway, I need to disappear, for obvious reasons. This is hard for me to write, so I'm not going to go over everything you've meant to me, but you are a real friend, and I hope maybe someday I will be able to talk to you again. But right now I have to disappear. I have it all planned, and I think I'm going to do a good job of it. But just in case, please destroy this. Also, Ken will be back on Friday and will probably show up at your house pissed off and looking for me. So, I don't know how you feel about this ethically, but just for your safety, you might want to tell the police that you haven't seen or talked to me in three days on Thursday and give them the other letter in this envelope.

Thanks, and I love you.

Philippa

The third, mailed in the same envelope, reads as follows:

Dear Kim,

Ken has gotten worse. I really think he is going to kill me. I am really scared, but maybe it will turn out to be nothing. So call me when you get this, and if you don't get ahold of me, please please call the police and tell them that Ken killed me. Don't let him get away with it.

Love,
Philippa

After writing this letter, Philippa had taken the eight-inch chef's knife and made a substantial cut in her thumb. She had then walked around the house, leaving drops of blood in nearly every room.

The final letter was to her mother:

Dear Mom,

It's been years and my number has been listed so I guess you haven't been interested in contacting me, and I obviously haven't been interested in contacting you. For our purposes, I will be dead soon, so I wanted to tell you a couple of things. One is that I'm sorry I said I wished you had died on Clough Pike, because I really don't. The other one is that I really don't blame you anymore. I have gotten some insight into how people get themselves into situations they wouldn't even dream of getting into just because of bad choices or whatever. Basically I have fucked up so much and so consistently, and now so seriously, that I really can't blame you for fucking up anymore. I guess it runs in the family, and I'm sorry we won't get a chance to sit around and laugh about it all someday. But know this: I am happy that you are still alive, I hope things get better for both of us, and I love you.

Philippa

Philippa mails the letters. Simon will cry upon receiving his. Kim, too, will cry, but, in an act of deviousness she wouldn't have believed herself capable of, she will destroy Philippa's real letter and take the fake one to the Cincinnati police. Though she has never been an actor, she will call up all of the worry she has felt about Philippa for the last two years and give a heartrending performance convincing the detectives that she believes her friend might be dead. (As, indeed, she soon will be.) The attentions they lavish on Ken will be enough to distract him from threatening Kim and will significantly delay his efforts to find Philippa.

Candace Strange will later regard the letter as her personal "bottom," and will tell meeting after meeting about how she lost her daughter forever, and how that broke her heart in two and also saved her life.

Philippa sells the Audi for far less than its value at a small used-car lot in Western Hills, then takes a Cincinnati Metro bus downtown and walks up to the Greyhound station.

She buys a ticket for Atlanta with cash, and thus begins her multistep plan to kill Philippa Jane Strange. Philippa Jane Strange may have conceived this child in Cincinnati, but Stacey Kimberly Phillips is going to bear it in Boston.

MARK

It is late June, and Mark stands in the door of the luxury apartment overlooking the Boston Common that he and Becky have shared for the last three and a half years. He is holding a FedEx envelope, which he's just picked up from José downstairs.

It's from Becky. He can't imagine what it's going to be, especially since it's strangely lumpy. Something she forgot in her rush to get to the airport, something in Boston he has to take care of for her, but what could he possibly take care of that her assistant couldn't take care of?

He turns it upside down, zips it open, and Becky's engagement ring—an exquisite antique work of gold and platinum that Mark took a long time finding, a thing of beauty he was especially proud of because it did not contain a diamond, a diamond that might be financing a bloody civil war in Sierra Leone, a diamond that might have come from a mine in Africa using slave labor, a diamond that would have appeared clear but that Mark would have known was stained with blood. It was a ring that perfectly symbolized everything he and Becky had together—they didn't need a big diamond engagement ring, even though every other woman in Becky's office had one; this ring showed that they were different, that their love was special, that their love was unique.

And here it is in Mark's hand and not on Becky's. Faced with a cataclysmic change in his life, Mark is temporarily afflicted by incredible stupidity that doesn't allow him to even guess at the reason Becky's engagement ring is sitting in his palm. Maybe it set off a metal detector at the airport? Maybe she was going rock climbing and didn't feel safe leaving it in the hotel. Maybe her ring finger had unexpectedly swollen up, and she needed him to resize the ring immediately so that she could put it on as soon as she got off the plane.

Well, surely the note would explain. And it does. Mark reads it three times, because the first time he is sure he must have been struck by some kind of learning disability that prevents him from making the proper sense of the printed word, and the second time it really sinks in, and the third time, he's just picking it over and over because it hurts, but he can't stop.

"Dear Mark," it reads,

I am sorry I am such a chickenshit, that I'm doing this like this. You deserve better, but apparently I'm not the person to give it to you.

Three years ago, you went to Maine looking for Becky. I did the same thing. I am not a good person, but I am a damn good lawyer. Every company I ever litigated against offered me a job after the trial. Every one. It was getting harder and harder to turn down the big money, to do what I knew was right. I thought if I found that sweet, sensitive guy who cared about justice, the one who had been in love with Becky, that that would help me keep Becky alive, because Rebecca was getting very, very tempted.

It worked for a while, but I keep getting better at my job (I know that sounds arrogant, but measure it against the fact that my heart and soul seem to be hopelessly stunted) and the offers kept getting better. It turns out I want to be rich and successful more than I want to save the world. I found myself feeling embarrassed about showing up with someone so much shorter than me, someone who doesn't have a high-powered job. I know these are petty, stupid things to feel, that in terms of what's good about you, you tower over most people on earth. And yet I felt them anyway. I tried to explain the diamond-free engagement ring at work, to tell everybody how sweet it was that you cared about African slaves so much, but I found that I just couldn't muster the enthusiasm I wanted. I'm not telling you this to embarrass you or humiliate you—I'm trying to illustrate the fact that I am not the person you think I am, that I'm not as good a person as you are, and that eventually you would have found that out and been miserable with me. As it stands, we are both still young, and you have plenty of time to find someone who deserves you more than I do.

So, as you've probably guessed, I'm not coming back from California. I've taken a job in the legal department at Markbreit, which probably shows you more powerfully than anything else I can say that I am simply not right for you. (My starting salary at Markbreit is twice that of the executive director of Amnesty. I looked it up.) I know, though, that you are fiercely loyal, which is one of many qualities I admire in you, and I know that you would be on a plane out here later today if I didn't tell you this, which is the only reason I am telling you this. I would spare you this if I thought I could, but I couldn't stand you coming out here and finding out. So, yes, there is someone else. It's James, who you may remember meeting at office gatherings. He's just made partner, and he's taking over the firm's San Francisco office, and I think we're probably going to get married. I'm sorry—one more piece of evidence that I am pretty much a piece of shit compared with you. Well, I'm good at making persuasive cases. I will say, if it makes a dif-

ference, that I never slept with him while I was engaged to you.
I felt I owed you that much.

   I actually owe you so much more. I owe you the life you
wanted with Becky. But Becky, it turns out, is dead, and I'm
just,

Rebecca

PS—I gave Denise a key. She's going to come with some people and pack up my stuff at the end of the week.

PPS—Rent is paid through the end of the summer.

PPPS—The Lexus is still in the parking garage. I've signed the
title over to you.

Mark stands there, reads the note, and just says, "Fuck me. Not
again. Not *fucking again*!" He starts crying, and his tears turn to
great, gulping sobs, as Becky surely knew they would, that fucking
chickenshit bitch, and this is exactly why she sent a note instead of
telling him in person, so she wouldn't have to see what she'd done
to him. Fuck.

   She even gave him the Lexus, so he can't even take his anger
out on her car, because it's his fucking car now, not like he ever
wants to drive it, to have people see him on the street, here comes
Mark in the Cuckoldmobile! Becky probably actually believes that
giving him the car is a nice thing to do, that he will appreciate it,
that he won't understand that the new corporate counsel at Markbreit can't show up for work in a five-year-old Lexus, that he will
actually think she's done something for him.

   Markbreit! She really couldn't have sold out any more if she
had tried. Markbreit busted unions in its retail stores in the US, ran
child-labor sweatshops in Vietnam, and, according to Human
Rights Watch, had fully participated in partnership with the In-
donesian government in what amounted to enslaving several hundred East Timorese to work in its plant there. The Unitarian
Universalist Association had passed resolutions calling for Unitar-

ians "and all people of conscience" to boycott Markbreit at the last five General Assemblies. And his Becky was going to work for them. Except she wasn't his, and she wasn't Becky.

She was, apparently, Rebecca, and she was James's. James Neighbors, for God's sake. The guy has the same name as Gomer Pyle. This, however, is the only thing that would allow just about anyone to feel superior to him. James is handsome, six foot five, and has a really fantastic smile. He played basketball at Stanford and then went straight into Stanford Law. And he apparently just made partner at thirty.

But she's not coming back. And James will certainly buy her the big diamond she wants so badly. And sometime close to her fortieth birthday, Becky will start pumping out superbabies, tall, brilliant, beautiful, and charismatic, every one of them, and maybe one day one of them, maybe James Junior, will ask his Guatemalan nanny, his Filipina nanny, or his Haitian nanny, "Rosita, do you have any children of your own?" "Paring, do you have any children of your own?" "Dieudonné, do you have any children of your own?" and the nanny's eyes will fill up with tears as she tells James Junior of how she had to leave her children behind in order to come and care for him, and this will spark in little Jimmy an understanding of his complicity in oppression and a desire to make the world a better place, and after his long career with the Lakers, he will go to Stanford Law just like his dad, and then he'll run for governor of California and win handily, and eventually be a president who inspires the best in America, who tells America that morality doesn't stop in the bedroom, that we have to start behaving in a way that's less selfish and more sane, and so Becky's leaving will turn out to be a blessing for the whole world.

Well, it may be. Or it may be that James will reevaluate his priorities after an early heart attack. Or perhaps Becky will snap one day, will realize that her life is empty and leap from the Golden Gate Bridge. Or, most likely of all, it may be that Becky and James will raise children as shallow as themselves, will grow old together and die happy amid the luxury they've bought at the expense of poor children in other countries.

It's only the beginning of the summer, and Mark has all summer to contemplate everything that's gone wrong with his life, to try to figure out how the hell he did it again, how he is ever going to put his life together again, and, apparently, to mourn Janet's death some more. Because he hasn't read Rebecca's letter more than twenty-five times when he starts feeling that familiar stabbing in his gut that signals Janet's absence. How he wishes she'd lived, she'd grown up, that he could call her up at college, and she'd say forget that bitch, she doesn't know a good thing when she sees it, you're better off, and someday she'll come crawling back to you, but you'll be too busy eating your way through a supermodel sandwich to bother with her. (For dream Janet, the one who lived, Earth-2 Janet, as his comic-book-informed imagination always thinks of her, has a very raunchy sense of humor.)

But of course Janet's dead, her body burned to ashes, and Mark's done it again, thrown himself completely into a life with the wrong woman. He gave his entire self to Becky—he just gave her everything, even parts of himself that a normal, sane person would probably save for friends. When was the last time he'd called Josh? How long had Christine's last letter been sitting there unanswered? When was the last time they'd had Cassie and Jim over for dinner instead of one of Becky's friends? And the whole time she was holding back ever bigger parts of herself and preparing to shit all over everything he'd given her, except for the ring, which apparently wasn't even worth shitting on, so she just gave it back.

And now he has to live in a city where every location is tainted by memories of Becky, where all his happy memories have lost their warm amber glow and been tinted in sickly shades of yellow and green. Here's where I started living a lie. Here's where we went to dinner the last time we had sex that was anything but routine, and yeah, I just thought that was the normal dimming of passion that comes with a long-term relationship, and no, I didn't make anything of the fact that she didn't want to kiss me in bed anymore, it never struck me as funny that she hadn't initiated sex for a year and a half, because we still did it weekly, or biweekly anyway, well, a little more often than monthly, and no, I never suspected anything when she suddenly needed to work late so often. Here's where she told me she loved me when she was probably already blowing her co-worker. For while Mark feels that he doesn't know Becky at all, that he never really knew her, he actually wishes he knew her even less, because he reads her declaration that she never slept with James while engaged to him to mean (a) "James is going to slip it into me as soon as I slip the envelope with the ring in it into the FedEx box," and (b) "I've blown him a lot, because obviously you don't move across the country and talk about marrying somebody whom you've had no sexual contact with, and blowing someone is not sleeping with them."

What is it with him? What has he possibly done to deserve this same goddamn thing happening to him twice? And how can he keep living in a world where being kind only gets you shit on, where little kids die, good kids, nice, kind, goodhearted kids die and these stupid hateful selfish bitches live and thrive and spread their misery, their soul sickness through the world?

He drops the envelope. He'll be fucked if he's going to keep living here, caged in the house that traitorous lying bitch paid for. No.

And he'll also be fucked if he's going to be the kind, understanding, goodhearted person Becky—sorry, Rebecca, because of course "Becky" is dead—no she isn't, you stupid, selfish cunt, Janet is dead, that's what being fucking dead is, Becky isn't dead, Becky's just a fucking asshole, and how dare she compare herself to Janet in any way at all. He'd like to kill her.

But he won't. But neither will he be kind and understanding and open the apartment for Denise and the movers to take Becky's stuff. No, Becky's stuff is going to be long gone by the end of the week.

He immediately grabs garbage bags and empties Becky's

dresser and closet. Loaded down like some deranged Santa, he walks four blocks to the homeless shelter in the Combat Zone and donates them. The people who receive the donation are effusive, thank you so much, we're always so desperate for interview clothes, you have no idea what an obstacle it is for people trying to get back on their feet that they simply have nothing to wear to an interview, he's done a great service, and does he mind if they ask how it is that he has tens of thousands of dollars of women's clothing to donate?

"My . . . my wife," Mark says, choking up—yeah, he's lying to people who work at a homeless shelter, so much for Saint Mark, he'll be asshole enough to get a good woman soon enough at this rate—"She was an attorney. She . . . she died of breast cancer," he says, and his tears are real though his story is not. Would he like a letter, something to indicate that he's done this in her honor? No, she believed that charity should be anonymous, but thanks all the same. It's what she would have wanted. (Ha! What she'd have wanted was that fucking navy suit back, but tough shit.)

Mark returns home, picks up the keys, and drives the Cuckold-mobile to Beacon Hill Toyota/Lexus, and finds that a five-year-old Lexus, immaculately kept, with only thirty thousand miles on it, brings a shocking amount of money, especially considering that the sleazeball he sells it to is probably screwing him as severely as legally possible. He considers donating the money, spending some small amount to help Becky's other victims, the ones whose blood will be flowing into her bank account, but that's something a nice guy would do, somebody who cared about the world.

He goes to the bank, deposits the check, and withdraws one hundred dollars. He goes to the hardware store and spends twenty-eight on a sledgehammer. He returns home and smashes Becky's dresser, computer, bed frame, stereo, and anything else he can find that belongs to her that is of any value, that anyone might possibly want. He puts a few holes in the walls to ensure that she will not get her security deposit back, either.

"Yep," he says, swinging the hammer, "I'm not on the lease!"

He grabs a garbage bag and throws away all of her cosmetics. He realizes he should probably take the tampons over to the shelter, but he's going to feel like an idiot walking in there with two boxes of tampons, so he empties them out into the garbage bag and finds that one large box of Tampax Super Absorbency is actually full of notes from James. He reads one, two, and then ten, and finds himself strangely disappointed. They are just completely banal and boring and never mention him at all, not a single "I admire the fact that you're taking your time letting that wonderful man down" or "I can only hope to someday match the sexual prowess of that pint-sized stud you're currently living with."

He knows Becky will want this bland evidence of her bland, poetry-free love with James, and so he considers burning them, but in the end he just sticks them in the recycling with the newspapers, and hopes that someday those fibers find themselves part of a roll of toilet paper.

PHILIPPA/STACEY

In Atlanta, Philippa buys a ticket for Nashville, and, once in Nashville, it takes her only one day to secure an apartment. She chose Nashville because she knew no one there, and there were enough students and musicians that people were used to strangers blowing in from out of town and then just as suddenly disappearing. She supposed there were any number of large cities like this, but Ken knew she had dated a kid from Chicago, and he'd never even think to look in Nashville.

On her second day in Nashville, Philippa secures employment in a bar that hosts bands she supposes to be the country equivalents of the National Hate Service: guys with maybe one good song in them, but not enough talent to make a career of it. She gives her name as Kay Lastima, a sad little joke left over from her high school Spanish class: What a Shame. It's Philippa's last moment of self-pity before she disappears. She will never be able to cash her paychecks, but the tips will be cash, and the work involves an easy component and a difficult component. The waitressing itself is the easy part—the bulk of Philippa's job consists of loading up trays

with Bud longnecks and carting them to a table and giving the customers the cleavage reveal she's perfected in her food service career
and securing a nice tip as a reward.

The difficult part involves fending off the advances of the customers, bartenders, and, especially, musicians. After only a few
days she concocts a story about a boyfriend in prison—"But he
didn't do it, they just thought he was the one who struck the fatal
blow because he's so big"—and how he's up for parole in just a few
short weeks. She considers the story ridiculous, but she delivers it
with such conviction that she finds herself on the ineligible list for
everyone who hears the story.

For one month, as required by law, she runs a classified ad in
a newspaper—in this case, a free paper called *Nashville Nights*
that Philippa imagines is immune from LexisNexis searches, and
that no library in Cincinnati will carry or archive—stating that Philippa Jane Strange intends to change her name to Stacey Kimberly
Phillips, and all creditors should consider themselves sufficiently
informed.

At the end of her mandatory month, she goes to the court-
house, appears before a judge, swears again that she is not running
away from any debts (they don't ask her about a potentially homi-
cidal ex, so she is not forced to lie under oath, though of course she
would), and, just like that, Philippa Jane Strange is no more, and
Stacey Kimberly Phillips is born.

Though Stacey is technically born in Nashville, she will always
tell people she was an army brat, a little time here, a little time
there, basically rootless, and tragically lost her mother to cancer as
a child, then tragically lost her father in a training accident involving a helicopter as a young adult, then, in the final blow, lost her fiancé, the father of her child, to a traffic accident.

Stacey is most nervous that Philippa's ex will track her at this
point—when she is creating a paper trail, a record of her existence
that somebody with contacts in law enforcement might eventually
track down. But she comforts herself with the knowledge that if

Ken comes looking for Stacey Phillips in Nashville, he will be a thousand miles away from where she lives.

Ken will never get this close to her. He will, with the help of pictures and a sad story about his mentally ill sister, find that she had been in the Greyhound station, and that "she bought a ticket to, I don't know, Chicago, or Atlanta, or Philly—all those buses leave at the same time." This will not help Ken to find her, but, once the police interview the Greyhound clerk, it will be enough to close the investigation into Philippa's murder. Ken will never receive an apology from the detectives for his five-hour interrogation, during which he had ground his teeth so hard he actually lost a filling while the detectives asked him if he liked hurting women, if that made him feel like a big man, did he get off on seeing women cry, did he kill her because maybe she'd laughed when he couldn't get it up, was that it, a little bit ashamed that he couldn't be a man when it counted?

Given three cities to search, Ken will not even try, will tell himself that he's better off without that crazy bitch anyway, that there is probably somebody else out there with tits like that who won't enrage him, that if he can only find a better woman, he'll be a better man.

Stacey suffers through a really long bus ride to Boston, and, as she disembarks at South Station, she vows to herself that she will never take a bus again. She's chosen Boston only because Philippa's old pal Kelly Sullivan came from the Boston area and seemed to have an affection for it that Philippa (The Late Philippa, Stacey thinks) never felt about anywhere but London until London betrayed her.

Stacey spends what remains of her escape fund paying for her first month as the roommate of two grad students and sets about immediately to secure a Social Security card and then to find a job. When The Late Philippa worked at the Jekyll Drive Bistro, Alex had eventually left to work at the restaurant in the new boutique hotel on Fountain Square, and he had come back once raving about the

salary and benefits—"actual honest-to-God health insurance!"—
that the unionized hotel provided.

Philippa had never really needed health insurance, but Stacey
knows she will need it if she's not going to deliver her baby in the
apartment, which is spotless but lacks certain critical medical
amenities, so she spends a week walking from hotel to hotel applying for any job they happen to have. At three months pregnant she
is still not showing, though she does find that she is constantly
hungry.

A week goes by, her Social Security card arrives, and she gets a
call from the Harborside Hotel, a four-star hotel with stunning
water views nestled in the heart of Boston's Financial District, as
the brochure would have it. Yes, she is willing to work weekends.
Yes, she understands that housekeeping is hard physical work and
that physical fitness is a Bona Fide Occupational Qualification, and
yes, she can lift forty pounds. (She's not sure if she's going to be
able to heft forty pounds over and over for an eight-hour shift
when she's eight months pregnant, but she'll worry about that
when the time comes.) Yes, she can start tomorrow.

Her benefits won't kick in for three months, which will certainly put a damper on her prenatal care, but Stacey Phillips is
happy: she has a real job, she has a future growing inside her, and
she is finally, decisively free of Philippa and all her stupid fuckups,
her terrible decisions, her drug use, her alcohol use (for Stacey has
never done drugs, has never so much as taken a drink of alcohol,
and she never will), her entire stupid, hateful, fucked-up past that
weighed her down like an anchor.

If Philippa had a grave, Stacey would be dancing on it.

MARK

Mark got the FedEx on Monday. Denise is coming to pick up Becky's stuff on Friday. It's now Wednesday, and after two nights of sleeping on the mattress he and Becky shared, Mark is ready to get out, to take the Cuckoldmobile money and just go somewhere, just take off, even if it's just to the Copley Plaza to stay with the rich people for a few nights.

Secure in the knowledge that he will never have to pay the long-distance bills, he tracks Josh down at his flat in Edinburgh, where he's doing some kind of incomprehensible research project on the Scottish Parliament for his incomprehensible graduate program in international policy, or some such thing—Mark has been guilty of tuning out whenever Josh tries to explain it to him.

After telling Josh the whole story, including the part about wrecking the apartment, which he's already getting embarrassed about but which Josh heartily applauds, Mark says, "I just don't know what to do. I mean, I should probably go get an apartment or something, but I just . . . there's nothing I feel like doing."

"So why don't you come over here and hang out? I've got this apartment through the end of the month. Spend some of your

Lexus money on a plane ticket and just come here! It's beautiful, and the beer is great, and it might stop you from moping your summer away."

Mark is stunned into silence and prepares himself to come up with a list of reasons why it would simply be impossible for him to just pick up and go to Edinburgh. He searches his mind and finds nothing—he can't find a single reason not to do it.

He hangs up the phone and books himself a flight out of New York, so in five days he'll be on his way to a month in Scotland. He's never had any burning desire to go to Scotland, but he has a burning desire to get as far from Boston as he can for a while, and even given the fact that Josh will be working and probably spending an hour on the phone with Elizabeth every night, it'll still be more consistent quality time with him than he's had since high school.

Friday morning he'll take the train to New York, stay in a hotel for a couple of days, and then fly away. That leaves today for packing up his stuff to take to the U-Store warehouse in the South End—shouldn't take more than a couple of hours, there's not that much stuff that's really his, that's untainted by Becky, that he wants to keep. Some books, his work clothes, photos, though with no photos of rock_l or Becky, one album seems to do it. Two trips in a cab to U-Store should just about cover it.

As he contemplates the wreckage of his almost-former apartment, Mark feels a weird mixture of emotions. He's both embarrassed and happy about the damage he's caused. He hates Becky, hates her like death for stealing three years of his life, but he also misses her, or anyway he misses the idea of her that he thought was real that turned out to be such a sick, awful lie.

Later that night Mark sits in an apartment empty but for the wreckage of the furniture and a notebook he found where he used to keep a little scorecard. He was so proud of Becky—whenever she won or settled a case, he would write down the offending corporation and keep a tally of how much she'd gotten out of them. There was Markbreit, with two million dollars next to it. He'd considered that a great victory against those horrible union-busting slave masters, but now it looked like an okay deal for them. They gave up some of their tainted money and got her tainted soul.

The phone rings, and, though he hates this, he finds his heart beating faster, hoping it's Becky calling from California to say, *I've made a terrible mistake, please, Mark, please take me back, I don't know what I was thinking.* He wonders through three rings whether he will take her back or tell her to fuck off.

"Hello," he says.

"Uh, Mark?" It's not Becky. It's an unfamiliar female voice. Not Denise, either. One of Becky's co-workers who knows of his humiliation and wants a date?

"Yes?"

"Uh, hi. It's Raquel."

"Oh, you have got to be fucking kidding me. Why on earth would you be calling me?"

"Well, I'm in Boston on tour—" Had he been following music news at all, Mark would have known that rock_l is now a DIY icon who owns her own record label and who makes a good living playing sold-out theater shows with no radio airplay. "—and I'm doing some personal work, and I got your number from the alumni office—" Ah, the alumni office. It's bad enough they have to hit him up for money all the time, and that he's too polite to say you fuckers should give some money to the school where I teach, but now they have to give his number to rock_l. "—and I just needed to contact you and make amends for what I did, for the song, for how totally I betrayed you."

"Well, you know, I am really interested in your personal growth, but I actually just got left by somebody else, I mean I am literally sitting in the empty apartment we used to share as we speak, and this is actually kind of a bad time for me to accept your apology, so why don't you stick your apology somewhere small and tight, like your heart."

"Oh, Jesus, Mark, I'm so sorry. Jesus, that's awful. I'm so sorry.

I just, if you'll just let me explain, I just, I thought I was, I thought I needed to do something to really show that I belonged out there, that I was on board with the whole drug-addiction and Svengali thing that was being peddled, no, I'm sorry, it's not—it wasn't Cal's fault, it wasn't anybody's fault but mine. I made a series of terrible choices, and I'm sorry that what I did hurt you."

"You know what, it really did, but that just feels like a million years ago. What kills me, what really kills me, is that in grad school, when that fucking thing was on the radio eight hundred times a day, I was too pissed off to go out with any of the hot, available women I saw every day. Which led me into another fucking train wreck of a relationship. And you can't possibly do anything to give me those opportunities back, so I'm sorry, but your apology doesn't mean shit to me. Because if you really care, if you are really ashamed of that song, why don't you donate all the money it made you to charity? Huh? I can recommend several."

"Well, I mean, I don't have that kind of money anymore. A lot of it went up my nose, and the house is really the only thing—"

"So sell the fucking house! You built your career on being nasty to me, and now you want to just say you're sorry but keep everything that song got you. So how sorry could you possibly be? You're a fraud and a liar, and you always always were. I hate that I wasted five seconds thinking about you, sleeping with you, telling you I loved you, when there were so many women who deserved it," and he's crying now, "when there were good people out there, wonderful women who were everything you're not. I hate that. But that's *my* bad decision that I have to live with forever."

"Okay," rock_l says, "I can tell you're not in a space right now where you are ready to accept my amends—"

"You are not making amends! Give the money away! That's making amends! You're not doing anything but trying to involve me in your fucked-up life *again* when I have my own problems to deal with! I hate you!"

Raquel hangs in there, he has to give her credit for that. "Well,

Mark, I am sorry you feel that way, but I really can't blame you. I'm sure I'd hate me, too, if I were you. But I do want you to know that I spent a lot of time kicking myself for pissing on you when you were never anything but kind and understanding to me while I tied myself into knots trying to please people who didn't really care about me. Our time together did mean something to me, and I really hate that neither one of us can look back on it with any kind of affection now. I look at that time and think about what I threw away, and you probably wonder why you wasted your time on such a nasty bitch. Oh, I guess you actually said that, didn't you?"

Mark can't help smiling, and this annoys him because he wants to stay pissed off. "Well, words to that effect, yeah."

"Yeah. Well, listen, I am sorry, for whatever it's worth. I guess it's probably nothing to you. Oh, yeah, you said that, too. I'm sorry you're suffering, and I'm sorry that I added anything to that suffering. You really don't deserve this shit. You're a good man."

The angry guy, whom Mark thinks of as Sledge Hammer, recedes, and Mark finds himself powerless against Raquel's sincerity. "Uh, yeah, well, thanks. I feel meaner than you can imagine right now, but thank you. Listen. I know it's bad to put conditions on forgiveness, but it's the best I can do for you right now. So I have two."

"Okay. What are they?"

"One. I want a guitar. And I don't want the one I gave you, because that's kind of tainted. But you got into this whole thing because of the guitar I gave you. So I feel like a guitar is the least you could do."

"Okay." (She is glad he didn't ask for the actual guitar he had given her, because she broke that one years ago in a drunken rage while using it as a club to destroy the display case in which Cal Tomkins stored his Grammys.)

"And a nice one, too. Nicer than the one I gave you. With a hard case."

"Done. What else?"

"I want a song. I mean, I want an apology, a mea culpa on the CD, so it's not just for me, but for the same public who bought the first one."

"Aw, geez, Mark, there's been one on each of the last three CDs."

"Really?"

"Yeah."

"Well, you know, I haven't really been following your career that closely. Okay. Send 'em to me, then."

"I will."

"I'm going to be at the Berwick Tower hotel on Thirty-eighth Street in New York as of tomorrow night, so I guess you can send stuff there. I'm leaving the country for a month in five days."

"Okay. Everything will be there by Saturday."

"Okay then."

"Really okay, okay?"

"I mean, okay, I'm still angry, but apparently I'm a nice guy, too nice for most women apparently, but I guess that means I will have to forgive you. I think maybe it'll be a relief to stop hating you."

"Yeah. I'd like to stop hating me, too."

"Well, good luck with that."

"Thanks."

"All right. Bye."

"Good-bye, and thank you."

It actually felt better to forgive her than it did to tee off on her. Mark basks in the warm glow of forgiveness for a few minutes and wonders if he might somehow get to sleep with Raquel again. But reconnecting with somebody from the past hadn't exactly worked out last time, so maybe it's not such a great idea.

STACEY

Stacey finds that the HR people didn't lie, that hotel housekeeping is hard physical work, and she finishes each shift completely exhausted, with aching limbs. After two weeks she is pleased to notice some muscle tone emerging on her arms. She figures she'll need that for holding her son.

Stacey finds housekeeping strangely contemplative. She has sixteen rooms to clean in an eight-hour shift, and, after the first few days, the bed making, vacuuming, and toilet cleaning are completely automatic, and her mind is free. She thinks about Philippa's life, and about how she will not repeat Philippa's stupid mistakes; she fantasizes about the life her son will have, how he will grow up strong and smart and happy, how he won't do the stupid shit she's done, how he will be a nice person who won't mistreat the women in his life, how he won't be a doormat who goes looking for people to be mean to him, how Stacey will do a much better job of raising him than Philippa ever could have.

She also spends hours inventing Stacey's life, creating "My Bobby" and imagining their courtship and actually moving herself to tears as she imagines his tragic death.

After three months her benefits kick in. She feels a thrill as she presses hard—she's making three copies—on the enrollment form for her health insurance, and as she chooses a doctor. She feels like a real person, a real person with a real job and a real doctor and a real life.

She gets a prescription for some horse-pill folate supplements as well as an ultrasound, which reveals that her son is actually female. It takes her a day or so to adjust to this news, and she actually finds herself worrying that she may have done irreparable harm to her daughter by imagining her as male for all this time.

She figures that she should inform her roommates of what's happening. Her name's not on the lease, so they can pretty much give her the boot anytime, and she'd prefer it to be sooner rather than later, so that she won't be apartment hunting with an infant in her arms.

Tiffany Park and Phoebe Varoudakis are never home, and certainly not at the same time, so Stacey posts a copy of her ultrasound on the fridge with the following note:

Dear Tiffany and Phoebe,

Below please find an image of my daughter, in utero. She should be ex utero in three months. I would certainly like to stay here until the term of your lease expires in eight months, but I recognize that you never agreed to room with an infant, so I will certainly understand if you don't want us to stay. I'd appreciate it if you'd let me know sometime soon. Thanks,

Stacey

Several days later she returns from work, pizza box in hand, to find Tiffany and Phoebe together on the couch, waiting for her.

"So," Tiffany says.

"So," Stacey says, thinking, Shit, I am bone tired and all I want to do is eat an entire pizza and a pint of ice cream and go to sleep, but now I guess I have to have the goddamn roommate conversation.

"We've been talking," Tiffany says.

"Oh, just look in your room!" Phoebe says.

Stacey walks gingerly over to her room, expecting to find a suitcase full of her stuff or her bedding slashed or something. Instead she opens her door and sees a new bassinet next to her bed.

Overcome, Stacey begins to cry. It's not little trickles of tears, either—it's real crying. Even though she is Stacey, Stacey who likes herself, Stacey who doesn't have a history of fuckups, Stacey whose poor dead mom never called her a cocksucking whore, even though Stacey has cleaned many many toilets while trying to convince herself of all this, she still can't believe that she deserves to have anyone be this kind to her.

"I ... I ... ," she says. "I can't believe ... I'm so lucky, you guys are the nicest people on earth, I'll bet there aren't twelve people in Boston who'd let me stay." This, as much as anything, convinces Stacey that she exists, that Philippa really is dead, because nothing like this would ever have happened to Philippa.

After four months on the job, Stacey hears of a minibar opening. Minibar is vacation compared with housekeeping: nothing heavier than an eight-dollar bottle of Miller Lite to lift, and no complaints from the guests if there's a single pubic hair in the shower drain. Stacey, for whom cleaning has become a kind of spiritual discipline, as though every pubic hair removed from the shower is another stain on her soul erased, has impressed her supervisors with her thoroughness, her punctuality, and her attitude. (Though her co-workers figure nobody knows when they are watching soap operas in an empty room, it's quite noticeable that their carts sit in the corridor immobile for an hour and the television just happens to be blaring from behind a closed door.)

Stacey is promoted to minibar, so she is now doing easier work for more money. Restocking minibars is such a quick task that it does not offer the opportunites for contemplation that cleaning did, but neither does it demand things that Stacey's aching back and swollen ankles would have complained of.

Stacey has grown much closer to Tiffany and Phoebe since throwing herself on their mercy, especially after Tiffany accepted that she was not necessarily going to be able to bring the wayward Stacey to Jesus. Both women take a keen interest in Stacey's pregnancy—and are very good about fetching stuff when Stacey is on the couch and that jar of kimchi in the fridge seems a mile away. Still, neither one is home very often, and there are limits to what kind of friendship one can build in fewer than three hours a week, and so when Stacey goes into labor, she calls herself a cab to the hospital, where, alone but for the nurse and doctor, she delivers a healthy baby girl eighteen hours later.

There are any number of remarkable things about becoming a mother, but, for Stacey, the most remarkable is simply how she instantly, the moment Kelly Phillips emerges, is handed to her, and pees all over her chest, becomes the second-most important person in her own life. Even when she was practicing her meditation by cleansing, Stacey had focused on herself—what her future was going to be like, how she was going to change her life, never make the same mistakes Philippa made—and now, suddenly, Stacey is a distant second in Stacey's thoughts. Everything she thought was important is suddenly upended.

Not only that, but she feels like her heart and soul have just expanded; Stacey simply would not have believed she had the capacity to love this completely, this fiercely, this much. She knows what it must be like to be a mother bear—she knows in her heart that she would not hesitate for a moment to kill anyone who harmed her child. She's glad this child doesn't belong to Philippa, because, as strange and powerful as this protective urge is, she thinks Philippa might well have had it scared out of her, might never have known this precious feeling of imagining herself killing to protect her child.

Fortunately, Stacey will never be called upon to kill for Kelly, but she will bring her fierce love to bear on giving Kelly a life she can be proud of, a mother she can be proud of, a chance for happiness that poor dead Philippa never had.

• • •

Through the union, she finds a family day care that caters to hotel workers and is therefore open on the weekend, and though it tears her heart out to have to drop her baby daughter into the hands of a stranger, Stacey does it so that she can continue to put a roof over Kelly's head.

(Since the day care caters to hotel workers, Kelly is the only white child there, and, as she begins to speak, she will come home with some Spanish words that Stacey recognizes and some Haitian words that she doesn't. Stacey thinks briefly that Ken would burst several blood vessels at the thought of his child spending all day in the company of Haitian children—and under the care of a Dominican day care provider—but then she reminds herself that Her Bobby's freshman roommate and best friend in college had been named Dashawn Jackson, and that he was a kind, openhearted man, that Stacey, at least, had made a good choice about the father of her child.)

(Of course Stacey knows who Kelly's father is really, and she knows that Her Bobby never existed outside her imagination—and would that the same could be said of Ken!—and she knows that she was born Philippa Jane Strange at University Hospital in Cincinnati, and yet she feels that it's critically important to stay in character, not only for her, but for Kelly.)

Tiffany and Phoebe are very good about not complaining (though both have very uncharitable thoughts and tell themselves that they would have kicked Stacey out in a heartbeat if they had only known about the incessant crying, but it's too late now, they can't go back on their word), but Stacey feels guilty nevertheless.

Thus it's a relief when Phoebe announces that she and her fiancé, a loan officer at BayBank, are buying a gigantic Victorian home in Jamaica Plain, an up-and-coming-but-still-slightly-dicey-could-go-either-way neighborhood. The house, she says, has this strange little in-law unit in the basement, and it's very small and probably not up to code, but would Stacey and Kelly like to move in?

Stacey says yes she would, and she thanks Phoebe profusely. (And well she should, for Phoebe's insistence on offering the apartment to Stacey when her fiancé, Steve, had his heart set on bilking some student out of an unreasonable amount of money had led to a massive argument—did she know that people with infants can legally compel you to put them up in hotels if the apartment isn't deleaded?—and Phoebe had expended a great deal of Marital Argument Capital on Stacey's behalf, which would lead her to driving cars she hated for the next ten years.)

Stacey continues to work hard and get regular promotions and raises, but she begins to feel an itch to get a more family-friendly occupation, one that doesn't require her to work on the weekends. The weekend work isn't really a problem now, but what about when Kelly starts school? But where else can she get these kinds of benefits and this kind of money? Though hotel work was a good choice, she feels like she's boxed herself in—she's got all this experience in the hospitality industry and sees no way to make the jump. Inspiration strikes when she and Kelly attend two third-birthday parties for kids in the neighborhood, which has continued to steadily gentrify to the point that Stacey is beginning to feel slightly out of place. Both take place in winter. The first is at King of Plaster, where the kids get to pick out a hideous plaster objet d'crap and paint it, and the second is at Captain Craft, where the kids get to stick little (and very chokable, Stacey notes, thinking this activity is really inappropriate for three-year-olds) pieces of foam onto picture frames.

Stacey has been painting furniture for Kelly and improvising craft projects for the last two years (it's a hobby she got into with the help of her late friend Philippa), and it strikes her that this kind of thing would be really easy to replicate. She gets literature from both businesses pretending that she is interested in throwing Kelly's next birthday there. Knowing how much the supplies cost and how much parents pay to be able to make a mess somewhere other than home, she quickly figures that with a wealthy enough customer base, she could actually make a comfortable living doing this. Health insurance would be exorbitant, but she could probably clear just a little less than what she currently makes at the hotel and have more time to be a mom as well.

She spends the evenings after Kelly goes to sleep reading *Business Plans for Morons!* and then, she hopes, writing a nonmoronic business plan for a modest small business called Kids' Creation Station. Phoebe practically begs to be allowed to put her Sloan MBA to work by giving Stacey some free consulting services on her business plan, and though it rubs her the wrong way to take anybody's help, Stacey finally consents and gets a few helpful suggestions.

Having already accepted help from Phoebe, Stacey's determined not to use Steve's influence at whatever the hell they're calling BayBank these days unless she has to, so she takes her business plan to another bank and secures a loan. She finds empty retail space in Chestnut Hill, an area fifteen minutes and several tax brackets from where she lives. The space is relatively cheap, and the clientele won't mind paying Stacey's exorbitant prices for the privilege of having their kids paint something or put beads on something away from home. And Stacey will get to play all day, and will get to use two of her best skills—making beautiful things and playing with kids—to make a living.

Everything is going wonderfully. Stacey's plan has worked flawlessly.

Except that it's proving somewhat harder to be the self-denying saint, She Who Serves Her Child, than Stacey had at first imagined. It had actually been relatively easy when Kelly was an infant and a toddler—she demanded so much time and so much attention that Stacey was exhausted by nine every night and was perfectly happy to fall asleep with Kelly curled up next to her.

But Kelly's on the verge of starting kindergarten, and she's still sleeping in Stacey's bed, and sometimes Stacey just needs some space, just needs a few inches on either side of her to keep her from going crazy, and she finds herself losing patience with Kelly because she doesn't feel like she has a single moment in the day to be a grown-up. Or maybe she's losing patience with Kelly because Kelly is so demanding, and those toddler tantrums still haven't gone away, and what the hell is she so angry about? She and Phoebe often have drinks—wine for Phoebe, herbal tea for Stacey—after Kelly's safely asleep, and while she does value this time (especially because hearing about Phoebe and Steve's marital problems makes Stacey feel much less like she's missing out on anything), it's simply not enough, and their adult conversations are often interrupted by Kelly calling "Mom? Mom!" from her bedroom, and needing another ten minutes of Stacey at nine thirty, at ten fifteen, at times when any normal kid should be sleeping like a log, goddammit. And so she yells at Kelly, and then she cries and cries, because isn't that just what Ken did? Find somebody smaller and weaker and yell at them when they didn't do exactly what he wanted? And Kelly pats her on the shoulder and says, "It's okay, Mommy. I'm sorry I was bad," and this, of course, only makes Stacey feel worse.

So she is very guarded. There was an opportunity, back when she still worked at the hotel—another minibar attendant, a fifty-five-year-old guy whose wife had early-onset Alzheimer's, and they used to talk on breaks, and, though Alan was old enough to be her father, they found their conversations turning flirtatious. Neither one of them had been getting any for quite some time, and they did work in a hotel, where, if you were more careful than the soap-opera-watching housekeepers, it would certainly be possible to have a break-time tryst.

She thought about it seriously for several days. It would certainly be different from anything Philippa had ever gotten involved in—she felt real tenderness for Alan, and his main attraction was that he was kind, not that he was incredibly hot or had easy access to drugs or could make her feel like she was better than anybody else. Finally, though, she decided against it. Alan's wife was slipping away, but she was still alive, and she was his true love, and Stacey didn't want to be the piece of ass on the side. That was far too Philippa.

And strangely, Stacey felt sentimental about her virginity. (For, despite the compelling evidence of Kelly's existence, Stacey considered herself a virgin, as, technically speaking, the legal entity that was Stacey Phillips had never had sex.) Philippa had never had any such sentimentality—she'd believed that the whole mythology of having the first time take place on some canopied bed with Prince Charming dismounting his white steed and mounting his princess was just a myth meant to keep girls from having sex. She much preferred the model offered to boys—get it over with as soon as possible—and so she had, at age fifteen, in a squalid squat in London with a boy who was very sweet, very eager, and very unskilled.

But that was Philippa, and look where it had gotten her. Stacey was not going to sleep with anybody until such time as she felt like she really loved him. Since this had never happened to Philippa, Stacey wasn't sure it would ever happen to her. When, after deciding against sleeping with Alan (not that he'd asked, and, had Stacey proposed it, he would have said no, believing he would be unable to face the shell of a human that once was his own true love if he'd broken his vows, even under such extreme circumstances), Stacey decided she needed a little more excitement than her hands in the bath could provide, she'd gone to a "woman-centered erotica boutique" called D'Isle D'eaux and purchased a few mechanical aids that had proven very successful in keeping that part of her body and mind occupied.

MARK

Two days after he speaks to Raquel (for, though she still records under rock_l, she is once again Raquel in Mark's mind) Mark gets a phone call from the front desk at the Berwick Tower on 38th Street, where he has been lost in a fog of scotch and exorbitant pay-per-view porn, telling him that there's a delivery for him, and would he please come down and sign for it? It's his care package from rock_l. It is a black acoustic guitar in a hard case, suitable for checking on an airplane, he notes approvingly. Three CDs are tucked into the case: *Omnivore, That Stupid Girl,* and *My Left One.* Each of the CD cases has been marked with a highlighter, and Mark cues up the relevant tracks in chronological order. "My Left One" actually makes Mark cry, not simply for the verse about him, in which rock_l sings, "I'd give my left one not to do what I did," but also for the verse in which she reveals something she'd never told Mark: that she was the one who found her mother after her suicide, with her left eye shot out: "The note said, 'I'd give my left one to get out of this place' / so she shot her left one right out of her face.' "

"That Stupid Girl" details how "That stupid girl threw you away / I know she hates what she did today," and the apology song from *Omnivore*, titled simply "I Fucked Up," reveals how "I stare at my ceiling at three A.M. / thinking about how I fucked up / I see a guy that looks like him / and think about how I fucked up."

It is actually a pretty impressive display of contrition, and Mark can't help thinking that there could be a chance to reconcile. What the hell, he got back one girl from his past (and yes, that had been a disaster, but this time he'd be going into it with his eyes open), and wouldn't it be weirdly symmetrical to get the other one back?

But as he listens to the rest of rock_l's confessional oeuvre, Mark is reminded that, as screwed up as he is, rock_l, whose songs reveal political certainty, deep self-loathing, an apparently insatiable sexual appetite for both genders (the title track of *Omnivore* is quite clear on the fact that she won't be limited in what she eats), and, most tellingly, a narcissistic urge to reveal everything to everyone all the time, is probably even more screwed up, and is probably not the person he'd like in his life while he's trying to get mentally healthy, or at least when he's trying to stop being attracted to the wrong women.

Not that she'd offered. (Nor would she, for, to tell the truth, it never even occurs to her—she's very well occupied both sexually and romantically by a total of three people, though never by all three at exactly the same time—and while she could stand to apologize to Mark, it would simply be too painful for her to have any kind of regular contact with him, because he's a living reminder of the beginning of a string of horrible hateful choices that That Stupid Girl made all those years ago.)

Mark is once again titillated by the notion of being involved with someone with Sapphic leanings, and, fortunately, pay-per-view porn provides several variations on this scenario, and he's paid for the all-day, all-channel porno package. But it's not long before the porn just becomes depressing because it reminds him of how much he misses real sex. There are still all kinds of memories of Rebecca stored in Mark's brain, but masturbating to these images would just be depressing—so depressing, in fact, that his body won't cooperate when he tries. So, in a move Sigmund Freud would be proud of, Mark takes his hands off his genitals and puts them on the guitar.

He's in free fall now, but in eight weeks he'll be back in school. He wonders if he could find an excuse to play "Pukin' My Guts Out" to his class. He wonders if he could play it all the way through without being overcome by grief. He wonders if he has any more inspired scatology to share with the world.

He uses the tuner rock_l has helpfully included to tune the guitar and then, tentatively, his fingers form the G chord, and he begins to play.

Mark spends four weeks in Edinburgh. It goes quickly. During the day he plays guitar, drinks tea, does the crossword in the *International Herald Tribune* (having tried and failed miserably to do the incomprehensible cryptic crosswords that the British newspapers run), and walks around the city. He knew nothing about it before getting here (to the extent that he was confused when his cab from the airport took him to "South Clerk Street" when he'd clearly asked for "South Clark Street"), but he feels like he was fortunate to get here. He finds that being surrounded by beauty every day—the hulking rock of Arthur's Seat, which he can see from his kitchen, the castle that he walks to nearly every day, and pretty much all the buildings in the Old Town—helps him to feel some hope for the future, helps him to feel like he's not necessarily mired in misery, that maybe there's still a way he could have the life he wants.

He goes to used-record stores. In one he hears a fantastic old punk song called "Philippa Cheats" that just about perfectly captures the way he feels, and he buys a vinyl copy of the National Hate Service album, long out of print, for twenty pounds, though he has no record player here. But surely he'll be able to pick one up at home when he's furnishing his apartment in Jamaica Plain.

At night when Josh is done with whatever the hell he studies at the Scottish Parliament all day, they go to pubs and, though Mark quickly finds himself downing more beer than he ever has in his life, it's an otherwise completely rejuvenating experience. They don't talk about how Mark fucked up his life, they don't talk about how Josh is on the fast track to being president of something (The World is Josh's stated ambition, but Mark thinks he'd settle for a small country), and, thankfully, they don't discuss the Scottish Parliament and the devolution of centralized power in the context of an increasingly muscular European Union more than once. Mostly they just drink, look at girls, and laugh in a way that Mark just never laughs with anyone else.

They see a lot of women, many of whom are too young for him, many of whom are American tourists, German tourists, and Australian tourists. They have a game of guessing the nationality as soon as the backpack-laden girls enter the pub, and Mark is proud when he can tell the Germans from the Swedes, but Josh can accurately tell a German from an Austrian or a Swiss at twenty feet. Josh is being characteristically faithful to Elizabeth (except for the unfortunate Amy overlap several years ago, he's always been faithful to his girlfriends, despite going through a rather staggering number), and Mark is feeling far too timid to even speak to any of the women they see, despite the fact that Josh is always encouraging him to. "You just need to get your pipes cleaned," Josh says, which leads them to use "plumber" as secret code for any eligible backpack-toting tourist babes. They never get tired of this and laugh hysterically over it on a nightly basis—"Plumber!" Josh will call out when a longhaired Australian enters the pub, and Mark will insist that he's had it with tall plumbers, or that he doesn't think that particular plumber works on his kind of plumbing. It's fantastic to be sophomoric without actually being a sophomore who has to go to Algebra 2 in the morning.

Mark has decided it'll be a long time before he's ready to date again, but maybe he can contract with a succession of hot young plumbers. He's not going to lie to anybody, he's not going to break anybody's heart—he'll just get laid a lot, just have a parade of young women through his apartment, and that won't be the future he wanted, the family he wanted to build with Becky, but the hell with that. Chasing that fantasy just broke his heart. Who knows— maybe if he pursues this program of casual sex, he will actually learn how to treat women as badly as they seem to want, learn to stop being so nice that they just want to shit on him or, worse yet, be his friend.

Being with Josh, a personal and professional go-getter, makes Mark realize he's had a problem with passivity. Raquel came to him. He went to Maine in search of Becky, but she's the one who came walking up the hill, the one who said, *Let's go to Portland and I'll blow you like you've never been blown before* (and which business trip was it when she made James the same offer? Was it before or after she'd agreed to be Mark's wife?). Maybe there is such a thing as a woman who's not completely insane, a woman who knows what her name is for God's sake, and maybe she's waiting for him to ask.

So it's his last night in Edinburgh, his stuff is all packed up, he's written a song he thinks has real potential called "Vomit and Snot," which was inspired by the tremendous quantities of both he saw one night when five bouncers at Preservation Hall were beating a belligerent drunk senseless. (There was a lot of blood, too, but this was, after all, a song for kids, not some Tom Waits number about the seamy underside of barfly life.) Elizabeth has come to visit, which means Mark is on his own while Josh and Elizabeth work on the plumbing.

He's decided he's going to try to talk to an actual live woman tonight. He's got nothing to lose except the ten pounds Josh bet him that he'd be too chickenshit. He scans *The List* to find out where there's live music tonight and settles on a singer-songwriter named Maebh McConnell, figuring that the women will be better looking at this gig than they would be at Vatican Shotgun Scare, or at least that singer-songwriter fans will be more likely prospects for a short smart guy trying not to be so goddamn nice than the metal fans he'd be likely to find at the other gig.

He arrives at the pub early, before the music starts. There is a pale young woman with dark hair and green eyes sitting at the end of the bar wearing a Ramones T-shirt. She looks about twenty. Couldn't even drink legally in the US, Mark thinks, and she was in eighth grade when he graduated from college. He suspects that hitting on her might be ethically dicey, but he doesn't care.

He really has no idea how one approaches a girl in a bar—it's just not the kind of thing he's ever had to do before, and he's terribly shy and bad at small talk. Give him an opening to talk about early childhood education, or grief, or corporate malfeasance, and he's fine, but this hateful *hi how are you what's the perfect thing I need to say to get you into bed* routine is completely foreign territory.

Well, guys in movies are always buying drinks for girls in bars, so maybe he'll go with that. He sits for ten minutes and watches as the girl sips at her pint, and when it looks low enough that it might conceivably be replaced, he signals to the bartender and says, "Pint of heavy for me and another of whatever the lady's having."

"Whatever the lady's having." How fucking cheesy is that? So cheesy that she'll probably either throw the drink at him or else blow him in the men's room. The bartender delivers the pint to the girl, who raises it in his direction, says, "Cheers," and takes a sip.

Okay. What now? He thinks this is the part where he moves down the bar and asks if he can join her, but even with nothing to lose, with a virtual guarantee that he'll never see this girl again, he can't bring himself to do it. At least not without a few more sips of beer. He takes three great gulps, picks up his glass, and walks to the end of the bar, making his legs move though he is paralyzed with fear.

(What are you afraid of? he asks himself. That she'll tell you to fuck off? How could that possibly be worse than what you've already been through? You've been rejected epically twice—this girl

simply doesn't have time to humiliate you as thoroughly and completely as Raquel and Becky, or should I say rock_l and Rebecca,
did. If she agrees to talk to you, you'll fly home a loser tomorrow,
and if she tells you to fuck off, you'll fly home a loser tomorrow, so
the stakes are really impossibly low here, so get your heart to stop
hammering and just talk.)

Nervous, Mark babbles. "Hi, my name's Mark, and as you can
probably tell, I'm American, and I'm flying home tomorrow and
I'm just wondering if I could sit with you for a while, just to talk,
you know, not, I mean, well, I don't want to say I'm not hitting on
you because I guess that's what I'm doing, but what I mean is that
I would be content to just sit and talk for a while if that were all you
were interested in, because I've been here for four weeks and I
haven't really met anyone Scottish or anything, which is pretty
lame, but as you can probably tell by my babbling, I'm actually
quite shy." This wasn't the smooth invitation to clean the pipes he
was hoping for.

The girl smiles. She actually smiles! "Have a seat, Mark. I'm Jo."

"Okay. Hey, Jo, just so we're clear, I'm guessing that even
though you're here by yourself, you probably have boyfriend. Is
that correct?"

"Yes, it is."

"And I'm guessing he's like a big, good-looking guy. Am I
right?"

"He's a great hulking prat, actually."

"So, uh, Jo, are you in the mood to cheat on the big hulking
prat, or are you thinking more along the lines of go out and have
some fun, maybe be seen flirting with somebody so that somebody
can run back and tell him and make him jealous enough that he'll
be sorry for whatever it is he did?"

"I suppose I'd have to go with the latter."

"Great. Well, now that that's clear . . ." I have nothing to say to
you, you beautiful child, but I'll keep trying. "Uh, is this Maebh
McConnell any good?"

"She's crap."

He's dying! This sucks! He tries again. "So, uh, are you a student?"

"That's right."

"What are you studying?"

"I'm studying to be a teacher, actually."

Score! God, that sick bastard who killed his sister, who sent not one but two crazy women pretending to be something they weren't into his path, has finally smiled on him. Or did he make his own luck? In any case, he has something to talk to Jo about, and when Maebh McConnell turns out to be just as crap as Jo promised, they go to another pub, and then another, and Mark's lost track of how many pints he's had, and they get kicked out of the last pub at closing time trying to teach each other to imitate each other's accents.

They are standing in the street, and the evening is over, and Mark decides he still has nothing to lose, so he says, "So, Jo, I want to respect your desire not to cheat on Fergus, though he does sound like a total asshole who doesn't deserve you, and he has a funny name besides, but so I was wondering if a good night kiss falls under your definition of cheating."

"It does, but I'd like to do it anyway," Jo says, and kisses him sloppily, and says, "Good-bye, Mark. I hope you find somebody who deserves you."

"Me, too. Thanks." She turns and walks away, and Mark looks after her, and after about twenty feet, she turns around and says, "If you were staying . . . ," smiles, and runs off down the street.

Mark staggers home, collapses on his bed, and the following day he collects ten pounds from an incredulous Josh and flies from Edinburgh to New York with a brutal hangover.

Back in Boston, Mark finds that the carefree drunk who hit on college students (college students!) (well, just one college student, but still) is gone. He's not going to be able to sell a Lexus every summer, so this is his real life, here. Here in a nice but rather sparsely furnished apartment in JP that is no bigger than the first apartment he rented here six years ago but costs him five hundred more per month. Here planning his lessons for the coming school year. Here in the city that is horribly tainted by memories of Becky, except for those parts tainted in a different way by memories of Janet.

And who was he kidding with that parade-of-babes fantasy? For one thing, he simply doesn't believe he's the type of guy some hot twenty-year-old jumps into bed with on a whim. He's just not what that kind of woman is looking for. And, anyway, while he would certainly like to have sex, he doesn't want to waste his time hanging around with stupid young women. (Though Jo wasn't stupid. Beautiful, inaccessible Jo.) That isn't where his life is going— he wants to get married, he wants to be a dad. That was the life he thought he had coming, and now he has to start fresh. He's almost thirty, and he had hoped to be married with a kid by thirty, but that plan is probably out by now. So what's he going to do? Waste a year, two years, three years chasing hot girls and then try to start finding somebody he can settle down with, be happy with for the rest of his life? And make that decision in haste and regret it later? Settle down, or just settle?

He's tired of thinking about it, tired of giving his life over to women who mistreat him, tired of obsessing about women, of not having any friends who live in the same state. And, anyway, he's damaged goods. So for now he's just going to go to work every day, come home, shut down, and do it again the next day.

The day after Labor Day is a "professional day," which means they will listen to a boring taped message from the superintendent and a boring live message from Principal Inez Jackson, and then they will be turned loose to set up their rooms. Mark seriously considers calling in sick, but then when would he get his room set up?

He does not sleep the night before, and in the morning he gets up, sets up the ironing board in front of the TV, and irons his Mr. Norris clothes. He remembers how Becky had insisted on sending his shirts out, he remembers how they were actually supposed to be married by now, and he cries, with his tears splatting on his shirt and turning to steam when the iron hits them.

Walking his special back way to the Balch, he realizes that people are going to be coming up to him all day and rubbing his nose in it. He told Cassie to tell everybody, so that nobody says, *Gee, Mark, I never got my wedding invitation. Are you still getting married?* or maybe, *Where's your ring?* or, worst of all, *How's married life treatin' you?*

So he'll have to endure everybody's pity today—you poor sap, left at the altar, do you want to meet my sister-in-law? Ugh. When Cassie sees him, in front of the table of gigantic, ice-cold, flavorless muffins in shrink-wrapped trays from Costco, she just approaches him, squeezes his upper arm, and says, "Welcome back." Following this, his day is far less painful than he'd feared. The messages from the superintendent and principal are, of course, stultifying, and his initial encounter with every member of the staff except Cassie is horribly awkward, but it is wonderful to finally have something to do, to finally be able to feel like he has a purpose in life besides being sad, masturbating, and playing guitar. And, he realizes at the end of the day as he's finishing stapling a chart to his bulletin board, this is a place where he never saw Becky, where it's not at all bizarre or surreal not to be seeing her, where she never belonged. This was his place alone, and goddammit, it's still his.

The following day Mark feels a jolt of joy as the kids walk into the building. He may be the walking dead, but these kids are alive here today, and Mark feels wonderfully parasitic—like he's just drinking up all the excess life energy they're exuding all the time and slowly, slowly, bringing himself back to life.

Several members of the class he taught last year scream "Mr. Norris!" when they see him, and they run up and hug him. One, Emilia, says, "Mister! Did you get married?"

"Uh, no, Emilia, I didn't. Looks like I'm not going to."

Emilia looks genuinely sad. "Oh, I'm sorry, mister."

"Okay, thanks, Emilia. Who's your teacher this year?"

"Miss Huffman."

"Okay, then, you be good for Miss Huffman, okay?"

"Okay!" And off she goes.

Once inside his own class, Mark introduces himself to his students. During his short introduction, one kid raises her hand and says, "Do you have any brothers or sisters?"

Mark thinks about invoking the only-child lie, just to make it easier, but he can't betray Janet that way, can't pretend she never existed.

"I have a sister, but she died ten years ago." There is a moment of silence, and three or four kids look like they're planning follow-up questions, but, thankfully, they don't ask them. He then tells them to write a brief introduction to themselves for him. This works as a good diagnostic for where their reading and writing are as well as serving the purpose of getting to know them a little bit. He helps Karina and Max, who start misbehaving as soon as he asks them to write their name on the index card, and thus, he figures, probably can't write a sentence.

The day goes by in a blur, and, that night, Mark works on a new composition he titles "Sticky Booger Blues," inspired by some rather messy trouble that Diego had that afternoon. Once he believes he's explored the subject of mucus enough, he gets out his bag and sits (working! Not contemplating his loserdom, not kicking himself, but actually doing something worth being alive for!) matching the cards with the photos.

As usual, there is a wide range of abilities in his class. He'll do the official testing in a few weeks, but he can already guess the entire range: coming in below kindergarten level is Max, who, with Mark's extensive help, came up with "my nam Max." And, up at the high end, this one:

"Mr. Norris. I am sorry about your sister. My dad died too. I know it's very sad. Sincerly, Kelly Phillips."

STACEY

Years pass in a blur of art projects and movies. Kids' Creation Station is doing very well—well enough that Stacey was able to pay off her loan early and is amassing some savings for a down payment for a house of their own. There is certainly a great deal she likes about living in the apartment in Phoebe and Steve's house, but she feels like it's time for S & K Phillips, LLC, to find a new headquarters.

Steve and Phoebe finally get married, and Phoebe, usually the calm professional, goes completely to pieces during the planning process. Stacey helps extensively with color selection, dress selection, invitation selection, and general hand-holding. She works very hard at not remembering Philippa doing the same thing for Kim and focuses instead on how much she enjoys not being the one who's a mess, how much fun it is to be calm and competent and helpful.

Stacey attends a number of insufferable meetings with a bunch of worrywarts trying to decide which Boston Public Elementary School to choose for their precious little angels and eventually decides to send Kelly to the Emily Greene Balch Elementary School, primarily because it's an easy walk from their house, and secondarily because a bunch of the worrywarts will be sending their kids there, and she figures they'll be up the principal's ass making sure everything is perfect so she won't have to be.

Kelly is occupied at school for six hours a day, and Stacey finds that the extra time is a tremendous boon to her mental health, and the closeness they have after school and on the weekends starts feeling cozy again rather than just suffocating.

Phoebe is always trying to set her up with some hot young professional she meets on a consulting job, and even swears she will babysit whenever Stacey wants to go out with any of these eager men she has lining up. "I know how much you loved Bobby," Phoebe says, and Stacey feels a little knife of guilt slide between her ribs over the lie she continues to tell her best friend, "but life does go on. Anybody would say that you've honored his memory, and you are doing a fantastic job of raising his daughter, and you don't need to be alone forever. You deserve to be happy."

Stacey's not so sure she agrees. What she deserves, and what she has, is cleanup duty for the mess Philippa made of her life. She is happy—proud of her business, proud of her savings account filling up with down-payment money, money she earned herself, all on her own, not because her dad was rich, not because of the school she went to, not because of anything but her brain and her hard work. That makes her happy. And Kelly makes her happy. Sure, raising her is hard work, but she is a funny, smart, creative, and sensitive kid. And yes, her flashes of irrational anger are worrisome—are they just childhood tantrums, or are they Ken's DNA asserting itself?—but Stacey is proud when she thinks of what she's saved Kelly from. Kelly will grow up thinking that being a woman means being strong, being in charge of your life, not living in fear and being called a dumb cunt all the time.

She nearly convinces herself that she is completely happy, that she doesn't need anybody.

But it's not just Phoebe pushing the whole dating thing. During Kelly's first-grade year Camille, a fortyish woman with two preschool-aged children, starts coming in to the Kids' Creation Station at least three times a week. After two weeks, Stacey ventures this after a conversation about Glitter Glaze: "So, uh, I take it you don't work outside the home?"

"Honey, I don't even work inside the home. I play with my kids all day and hire people to do everything else."

"Wow, that must be nice."

"Well, I earned it. Have you heard of the Caswell Company?"

"Uh, no."

"Well, they own gated town-house communities all over the South Shore. I was married to Warren W. Caswell the Third."

"Yeah?"

"Well, to make a long story short, Warren was fond of getting drunk and violent and calling me any number of horrible things, and thanks to a fantastic attorney, he's now paying me to stay home and sleep with my personal trainer!"

"Good for you!" Stacey says, and wants desperately to say, *me, too, I left an abusive man, too, I know what it's like, you are my sister,* but of course none of that is true of Stacey.

Weeks later Camille, after describing in vivid detail her latest personal training session, says, "So what about you? Anybody interesting on the horizon?"

"Well, it's hard with Kelly and everything, and I honestly don't even know where I would meet anybody."

"You're kidding, right?"

"What do you mean?"

"Honey, you don't go into your competitors' places of business very often, do you?"

"No, I mean, I'm pretty much here or at home with Kelly, and whenever there's some new product people want, they usually come in and ask for it."

"Do you want to guess how many dads I've ever seen at a birthday party or even on a random weekday afternoon at Captain Craft?"

"Uh, I don't know."

"Zero. Zero, Stacey. Fathers do not come to these goddamn girly things and watch their little angels stick beads on stuff. Except here. You ought to issue them a drool cup when they walk in. Don't you honestly even notice that you're being ogled all the time?"

"No, but thanks very much for pointing it out, it'll make work so much more comfortable for me from here on out." Camille is of course exaggerating—she's actually seen five fathers in eleven visits to Captain Craft—but her point is valid: Kids' Creation Station is a big hit with divorced dads, widowed dads, and even married dads, and, as Camille points out, it is not the visual appeal of the art supplies that draws them in. And Stacey is being completely truthful. It's never even occurred to her, which suddenly strikes her as bizarre. Is she so far gone? She spent years manipulating her attractiveness to her advantage at work, and now she's apparently doing it unconsciously. It's somewhat dispiriting—she wants customers because she's created a superior business, not because of her fantastic rack.

"All I'm saying is that this place is full of potential dates every Saturday. Check the left hand, dearie."

"Ugh, I don't know."

"Sweetie, if I had tits like yours, I wouldn't settle for just one personal trainer."

"Uh, I'll keep that in mind." And she does, filing it away in the back of her mind. Maybe if some dad comes in here someday, one who isn't too creepy, too pathetic, too fat and bald, too old, too inept at parenting, then maybe, just maybe she would consider it. But months go by, and no one matching that description comes in.

After Kelly's first day of second grade, Stacey peppers her with questions she knows are annoying, but she can't quite make herself stop. Is she happy to be back in school? ("Sort of.") Is she glad Grace is in her class again? ("Duh!") What's her new teacher like? "Well," she says, "well, he said that he had a sister who died, and I kind of thought he would be a really sad guy, but he doesn't seem like a sad guy. He's pretty nice, I guess. But he did have to yell at Kevin and then turn out the lights. I don't like it when the teachers do that. I told him my dad died, too."

Stacey says nothing to this. "So, did this guy give you homework or what?"

"Yes! Can you believe that? Homework on the first day? What's with this guy?"

Stacey smiles and looks at Kelly in the rearview mirror. "Don't look at me like I'm cute!" Kelly says. They arrive at Kids' Creation Station and Kelly sits right down in the office and does her homework without any complaining or fighting, which is a relief, because she's been really into the mural she's doing, and Stacey was afraid they might have a Homework Battle.

It being the first day of school, Kids' Creation Station gets an unusually large after-school rush, as the wealthy parents try to console their kids about the end of summer. Stacey runs around for two solid hours, during which time Kelly sits quietly and works on her painting of the two of them in a rain forest surrounded by red-eyed tree frogs.

They head home and Stacey heats up leftover lentil stew. "This sucks!" Kelly says. "I want grilled cheese."

"You can't have grilled cheese every day of your life, sweetie, and please don't say 'sucks,' " Stacey says.

So far it's been a great day despite the stress of the new school year beginning. And then it's time for Kelly's bath, and Stacey realizes that with all the hurry of getting out the door this morning, she never put detergent in or started that load of laundry she'd put in the washer at 6:30 A.M., so Kelly has no pajamas. Kelly stands there, naked and dripping wet, and screams, "You are so stupid! Why can't you ever remember to do the laundry? That's fine, I'll just wear rags like an *orphan*! You're an *idiot*! You *suck*! You're the worst mother in the whole stupid *world*!" and slams her door.

Stacey yells, "Well, I hope you didn't want to watch *Fairly Odd-*

Parents in the morning, Miss, because you just lost TV for the whole week! You do not speak to me that way!" But she does speak to her that way. And Stacey keeps upping the punishment for name-calling, and it keeps not helping. And did she really just say "Miss"? "I hope you don't want to watch *Fairly OddParents, Miss*"? How the hell did Candace Strange, lost for all these years, suddenly find her way into Stacey's mouth?

She gives Kelly a few minutes to stomp around her room while she cleans up the dinner dishes. When Stacey's sure that she's calm enough to face Kelly, she grabs *Harry Potter and the Prisoner of Azkaban* from the shelf, knocks gently on Kelly's door, and asks if she's ready to read. Kelly gives a quiet "Yeah," and they spend the next half hour at Hogwarts. When they reach the end of the chapter, Kelly, perhaps chastened by Harry's desperation to hear his dead mother's voice, says she's sorry she was mean, she doesn't think she's stupid, she knows she works really hard, she's sorry, she's so sorry, she has the best mom in the whole universe.

Stacey smiles and kisses her good night, and when she's sure that Kelly's asleep, Stacey thinks about calling Phoebe, who's consulting in Chicago, but instead she just sits on the couch in the dark and cries. Stacey wonders what she can do. Medication? Therapy? What the hell is Kelly so angry about?

Or maybe she's the one who needs therapy and medication, Stacey thinks. Are Kelly's tantrums actually getting objectively worse, or is she just less able to handle them? Why does she find herself crying so much at night? Why is she so impatient with Kelly? Maybe Kelly's getting worse because Stacey's getting worse. A bad parent raises a bad kid. Fantastic. During the day it feels fine, it feels like she's got it all under control, like she's built a nice life for S&K Phillips, but at night she just feels like her whole life is balanced on a knife edge, and she doesn't know how to keep it from tipping over.

When she's all cried out, she climbs into bed, exhausted. In the middle of the night, Kelly appears by her bedside, crying, she's scared of the dementors, can she please sleep here? Kelly climbs into bed and she's warm and soft and sweet, and they both sleep until morning.

During the next few weeks, the roller-coaster ride continues. Perhaps emboldened by what she hears on the playground, Kelly tries "Fuck you" out on Stacey when she's mad. The demon she becomes when she's angry just seems completely at odds with the sweet, thoughtful kid she usually is, and Stacey keeps thinking she'll grow out of it, or she'll get better when she's not stressed by what's currently stressing her. And sometimes the beast has gone away for weeks at a time, and Stacey believes that they're finally out of the woods, it was just a phase after all, and now things are going to get better. But she's reaching the conclusion that things aren't getting better.

Phoebe encourages her to check in at school, and Stacey reluctantly agrees. Three weeks into the school year she calls and leaves a message for Mr. Norris. He calls her at Kids' Creation Station at four o'clock that day.

"Hello, Kids' Creation Station!"

"Uh, hello. I'm trying to reach Stacey Phillips?"

"Yeah, this is Stacey."

"Hi, this is Mark Norris, Kelly's teacher? I got a message that you called?"

"Yeah, I did. Hang on, let me just go into the back—Aileen, I'm going to the office, you're in charge . . . Okay. Yes, I just wanted to . . . I'm not sure exactly how to say this . . ."

"It's okay. A lot of people have questions about the new math curriculum. They really are learning the basic skills, it's just that we try to put them in context so they're not just—"

"No, no, it's not about the math curriculum." Shit! Calling Kelly's teacher seemed like such a great idea before, but now how does she say I'm a shitty parent, and is my little angel being as demonic at school as she is at home? Or is she even being that bad at home? Please, Mr. Expert who sounds like he's about twelve, re-assure me! "It's just that, well, Kelly's been acting out a lot at home, and I just wanted to check and see if that . . . what you've seen from her at school."

"What I've seen? I mean, I've seen only good things. She's reading well above grade level, she does her work, she listens, she works well in groups, she's very patient with the other kids—depending on the task, I try to group them by ability, or else put a mix of levels in one group, and whenever she's in one of these mixed groups, she's just incredibly patient with the kids who are not getting it as quickly as she is. I mean, I don't say this to every-body, but she's just a remarkable kid."

"Well, thanks. I like to think so."

"It's just true. She did mention . . . well, she mentioned her fa-ther's death once, but it's never come up again. I'm sorry, by the way. I don't know if that was recent . . ."

"No, it was before she was born."

"I'm sorry. I . . . I lost my sister when I was nineteen."

"Oh. I'm sorry about that. Life is so hard sometimes."

"Yeah," Mr. Norris says, "it sure is."

MARK

When he sees the note in his box, Mark winces, and as he opens it he braces himself for what he is sure is going to be a very annoying conversation. In his few years of experience here at the Balch, when the parents of the smart white kids call, it always leads to a really annoying conversation along the lines of "Why is my Madison only reading one year above grade level?" or "What are you doing to prepare Aidan for the Boston Latin test in the sixth grade?"

So Mark gets out his Kelly Phillips folder, notes with relief that she's reading two years above grade level, and prepares his standard response about the Latin test. He's shocked, then, when Stacey Phillips asks if Kelly has been misbehaving in school. Kelly? He tries to keep the shock out of his voice. Kelly is one of those if-only-I-had-a-class-full-of-Kellys kind of kids. The closest she's come to acting out is getting a little bit frustrated when she runs out of room on a page to write one of her stories.

He feels bad that he can't help Mrs., or possibly Ms. (he's been yelled at for using each honorific, so now he just always goes with full names) Phillips sitting there at the Kids' Creation Station, whatever that is, worrying. He can almost see her in his mind—probably worrying the strap of her Birkenstock, or tugging absent-mindedly on the hair on her plump calf as she talks to him, wanting him to say, *Yes, Kelly's a pain in the ass here, too, it's not just you.* But he can't tell her that. He wonders what Kelly did—maybe she announced a desire to one day wear makeup or high heels, he thinks, and then feels bad as he remembers Kelly's grief and how much harder it must be for Ms. Phillips to grieve while trying to be strong for a kid.

He tiptoes over to the subject of her husband's death (or, anyway, the death of Kelly's father, he reminds himself, you can never take anything for granted in Boston), and as soon as she tells him life is so hard, it's all he can do not to pour his heart out to this woman. Which would be a horrible mistake, he thinks, terribly unprofessional, not to mention that she might think he liked her, and all he needed was some middle-aged earth mother stalking him.

And yet he just wants so badly to say something. But all he can say is "Yes. It sure is."

There is a pause, and then Kelly's mom says, wearily, "Well, thank you." And the conversation is over, she doesn't say, *What happened to you that makes you say life is hard?* and what she's obviously thinking is, Stop right there because I've got my own problems, buddy, don't even think you can weigh me down with your shit, I've got myself and Kelly and that's all I can handle right now.

"Yeah. Well, I will certainly keep you posted if I notice any change in her behavior. So far, though, she's really a model student."

"Well," Ms. Phillips says, "that's certainly a relief," and he can hear her thinking, Goddammit why does she give me all the shit, I devoted my life to her!

"Feel free to call any time you have questions or concerns," Mark says.

"Okay, thanks," Ms. Phillips says, and Mark can hear her thinking, Thanks for nothing.

He hangs up, but the call stays with him. He will keep an eye on Kelly, see if he notices her face darkening at any unusual times, see if he can detect anything that might be helpful.

And, furthermore, he will figure out how to live.

If Stacey Phillips can raise a wonderful kid, or one who is wonderful in public, anyway, with the shadow of an actual death hanging over her, then he should be able to construct a life in the shadow of betrayal.

He mentions this to Cassie at lunch one day. "I just feel like I want to start fresh, but I don't have any ideas of what to do."

"Well," Cassie tells him, "when we bought that treadmill, even though it obviously hasn't done anything for the size of my butt, it really helped my head a lot. Maybe you should try getting some exercise. I mean, other than walking to work."

Well, he thinks, what the hell—being in better shape might actually help him get laid, or attract a potential life partner, or whatever the hell it is that he wants. He joins the Jamaica Plain branch of the Y, and, since he's awake at five every morning anyway, obsessing over every bad choice he's made, he goes to the Y to exercise. He feels awkward and embarrassed and out of shape, and he is extraordinarily disappointed that the spandex-clad hotties he expected to find on every machine are simply not here, and he's the only person under retirement age in the place.

One bitterly cold Tuesday morning, Mark has the beginning of a cold, so with some trepidation he enters the steam room. The whole cult of geriatric nudity there makes him terribly uncomfortable, as does the weird geriatric machismo. Clearly it's not the place where a guy like him can feel comfortable.

And yet, what exactly is a guy like him, anyway? Becky's fiancé would never have taken a steam with the old guys at the Y, but Becky's fiancé doesn't exist anymore, and neither does Becky, if she ever did. So what the hell.

Inside the steam room there's a lot of sweating and not too much talking, and after a few weeks he gets companionable grins and waves from the old guys, and he can feel himself getting stronger.

Three student teachers start at the Balch. Cassie has one—a twenty-four-year-old named Mary with blond hair and a scorching hot body—and Annie Rooney, a stern first-grade teacher, has Karyn, a twenty-seven-year-old with a body somewhat less scorching hot than Mary's, but whom Mark vaguely remembers being in a Spanish class with in high school. The third is Althea, a tall, pear-shaped, unattractive twenty-five-year-old. All three seem perilously close to Mary Pat territory—perky and with no hint of an edge. Still, the new Mark, the one who works out, the one who is done giving his entire heart to unsuitable women, finds that there's another part of him he'd quite like to give to either Mary or Karyn, which he is just sure means that Althea will be the one to develop a crush on him.

One Friday after school the three student teachers are congregating in the hall, and Mark is walking to the office in the probably vain hope that the copier will cooperate enough to let him make twenty-three copies of a handout he needs for Monday morning. "Hey, Mark," Karyn calls out. "We're all going out to Bumpers for drinks later. You wanna join us?"

"Uh," and again, his initial impulse is to say no, thanks, I can't go out drinking with young hot student teachers, I've got to get home to my fiancée and snuggle on the couch because *Law and Order: SVU* is on tonight, but that's Becky's fiancé talking, and he is not Becky's fiancé, he is Mark Norris, Single Swingin' Stud, and are not hot student teachers the very kind of women he has the best chance of scoring with?

"Yeah, okay. Where is it?"

Karyn looks at him like he's from space. "You don't know where Bumpers is?"

Mark wants to say no, I spent the last three years living in a delusion of pre-marital bliss with a woman I wrongly believed was wonderful, not looking for some bimbo in some crappy bar, but of course he doesn't, he just says, "Yeah, well, I'm really not any cooler now than I was in high school."

Karyn laughs. "It's at Faneuil Hall. Meet us outside at five thirty. There'll be a bunch of people from our program there."

"Uh, okay," Mark says. He leaves work and goes directly to the mall, figuring that his Mr. Norris clothes are not cool enough for some downtown after-work meat market. He has casual clothes, a couple of suits, and a bunch of oxfords and ties to wear to work, but nothing that might be considered meat-market casual.

He stalks fretfully through Banana Republic, finally shelling out a shocking sum for a sweater and some pants he hopes are fashionable. He doesn't buy mints or condoms—he doesn't believe he's going to get laid tonight, though he entertains fantasies of Mary or Karyn (or Mary *and* Karyn) making a drunken pass at him. So why is he even going? Just because it seems like it might be better than sitting home and playing songs about vomit and snot on the guitar, because it might make him feel alive, and because he is, after all, a Swingin' Single Stud. And maybe, with enough drinks in him, he can actually approach somebody like he did in Edinburgh, and maybe she'll be as sweet as Jo, and he's been thinking about Jo way too much, pining again for some ideal in his brain that might or might not match the reality, though experience suggests it wouldn't.

He stands outside the bar for five minutes feeling like a complete dork, and finally he sees Karyn walk up, and they are quickly joined by Mary, Althea, and six other people, including two attractive women, two unattractive women, and two men whom Mark supposes are neither hot nor repulsive.

After ten minutes in the bar Mark knows he has made a terrible mistake. The girls are all drinking drinks with funny names and interesting colors, many of them are smoking, which Mark finds an indicator that they are either weak-minded sheep or self-destructive idiots. The music is so loud that it's difficult to converse unless you're willing to get right up in somebody's face and yell, which he isn't, and there is constant motion of young, attractive people bouncing back and forth, hitting on people and getting hit on, and Mark sits at the table feeling about a hundred and fifty years old, and wondering if it was really just a couple of months ago that he actually hit on somebody in a bar.

He is only slightly older than most of the people here, and there are a good number who are his age or even a little older, but they just seem to live on a different planet from him. A planet where you try to meet people without actually being able to talk to them. A planet where you drink too much, dance to bad music, and have no idea that life can be unbelievably, unbearably sad and unfair, and that Death is standing outside, scythe in hand, waiting for the people you love, waiting for you, and maybe tonight is your night. None of these people appear to have any idea of the horror that life offers. If they did, why would they spend any of their precious time on this earth doing this?

Mark finishes his beer and skulks out the front door, convinced that no one will even notice he's gone. He goes home, takes out his guitar and runs through his entire scatological repertoire, and despairs of ever meeting anyone, of ever having sex again. He's far more comfortable hanging out with naked old men than with provocatively dressed young women. This couldn't possibly bode well.

Parent conferences are approaching, and Mark, for the first time in a while, is actually nervous. He's been making an effort to observe Kelly, to see if there's anything he can tell her mom, but there's just nothing. He feels that if there's just one bone he can throw, the conference will be over quickly and painlessly, and if not, he'll have to sit there with her mom while they hash out "what could be wrong with my baby," which he's certainly done before, but he just doesn't want to do it again.

But he just has nothing. Kelly devours *Freckle Juice* in about a day, and she keeps him on his toes finding extra books to give her in addition to her reading-group books. She's clearly as interested in the adults in the building as she is in the kids—she sits by the doors and eavesdrops on everything that happens.

Mark finds this out when he stops by her table to see how the penguin project is going and she asks him what a restraint is. He explains that sometimes when a kid isn't being safe, a grown-up needs to hold them in a special way to stop them from hurting anybody. It seems like a completely random question, and it's not until the end of the day that he realizes she overheard the conversation he'd had in the hall the previous afternoon when he was sure they were all working on their math problems. Lynn, a special ed teacher, had begged him to go to restraint training, saying, "I'm the only trained person in the building right now, and I had to do two goddamn restraints yesterday while I was supposed to be teaching. I can't keep being the only one—it's ridiculous in a school with three hundred kids."

Kelly was obviously listening to every word, and Mark just hopes she didn't also hear the conversation later that same day when he told Cassie how he was doing fine, really, he didn't need to be set up, but he'd love to come over for dinner, no, really, he was still reeling from being jilted. He wonders what he'll do if Kelly asks him what *jilted* means.

So Kelly is comfortable with and interested in adults, which Mark supposes is what you'd expect from an only child. She laughs at all his jokes, she's a good ally, and, unlike most of the really smart kids, she doesn't seem to have been so convinced of her own preciousness by her doting parents that she can't get along with other kids. He looks for her famous temper, for any sign that she's keeping something volatile under control, but he just doesn't see it. He wonders if he and Stacey Phillips could possibly be talking about the same kid.

STACEY

Kelly's tantrums come and go, and Stacey is still resisting getting Kelly any professional help. She's terrified that the therapist will see right through her, will tell her that she has to work on her own issues, that the sins of the mother are affecting the daughter, and then she'll have to dig up Philippa, and the whole beautiful house of cards that is her life will come tumbling down. No thanks.

She wonders if the problem is just too much togetherness, so she arranges for Kelly to go to Grace's house to play every Wednesday. "I think it'll be fun, honey," she tells Kelly, "and it'll be good for you to hang out with somebody besides me all the time."

Kelly suddenly erupts. Tears are falling and she throws the mug she spent two days painting to the floor, where it shatters, sending slivers all over. "No! I do not want to go to Grace's stupid house! I want to stay with you! You don't want me! You hate me! Shit! Shit you!"

Kelly's inability to curse properly almost makes Stacey laugh and defuses the "Goddammit, you can't just break stuff, what the hell is the matter with you?" that was on the tip of her tongue. She takes a moment to stifle the hysterical laugh that wants very badly to come out and is finally able to say, in a calm, quiet voice, "Now, honey, you don't really think that, do you? I mean, you really don't believe that for a second, do you?"

"Yes," Kelly says, but she says it quietly and without conviction. Stacey is instantly proud of herself for defusing the situation, and this turns quickly to self-loathing: if she could always just respond correctly, maybe this wouldn't be a problem. Kelly apologizes and tells her that she just likes having playdates at "our place"—Kids' Creation Station—because other moms just aren't as fun as she is. They quietly pick up the pieces of the mug together, and after this Kelly seems only happy and excited to go to Grace's house.

But she still doesn't sleep through the night, and when Stacey wakes up the next morning, Kelly is asleep next to her.

On Wednesday, when she gets to Grace's place to pick up Kelly, Kelly is so involved in the game she and Grace are playing that she barely acknowledges Stacey's arrival.

Opal, Grace's mom, invites them to stay for dinner, and Stacey, relieved that she won't have to figure out what to throw together out of the meager contents of her fridge, happily accepts.

Opal pours herself a glass of wine and, in deference to Stacey's tragic history ("I had some trouble with alcohol after Bobby died," she told Opal two years ago, when Grace and Kelly had first become friends, "so I just like to leave it alone now"), a big tumbler of seltzer for Stacey.

They talk about business, and about the kids (though Stacey doesn't get into Kelly's anger problem, because she knows deep down that it's her fault, and she's sure Opal will, too), and it's refreshing to just hang out with a grown-up. She really likes Opal—why haven't they done this more often?

Then the doorbell rings.

"Oh," Opal says, trying and failing miserably to feign nonchalance, "I guess that would be Glenn from Shawn's office. He must be here to pick up those Celtics tickets!"

"Oh, hell no," Stacey says. "Please, Opal, please tell me you didn't do what I think you did."

"Oh, just relax," Grace's mom says. "He's just picking up Celtics tickets. I mean, I don't know if he actually has anyone to go to the game with . . ."

"Evil bitch!" Stacey says through clenched teeth she's trying to force into a believable facsimile of a smile.

"You'll thank me," Opal calls back musically as she opens the door.

Glenn from Shawn's office is good-looking and tall and wears a very nice suit. He also happens to have nobody to take to the Celtics game on Thursday. Stacey smiles and pleads parent conferences that night, sorry, and there's no way for her to avoid giving Glenn her number.

Maybe she's numb from so many years alone—she knows she should want to go out with a good-looking, not obviously horrible guy, but she just doesn't feel anything about him. This never would have stopped Philippa—she would have gone out with the guy on the grounds that it might be fun and you never knew if an attraction might develop. And Stacey knows she should—this is the way to find a normal life, go out, have some fun, get some distance from Kelly—but she can't do it, she just can't.

Kelly sulks on the way home and Stacey asks if she had a bad time.

"No! I had a good time with Grace! But you're going to marry that stupid guy and forget about me!"

"What? Marry what guy?"

"Glenn from Shawn's office," Kelly says in her snottiest voice.

Stacey just looks at her. "I thought you were playing in the basement."

"Well, I wasn't! And I saw you smiling and laughing, and you're going to marry him and then you won't love me anymore! I hate him! I hate stupid Glenn from Shawn's office! You won't pay any attention to me anymore!"

"Sweetie, I wouldn't even go to a basketball game with Glenn from Shawn's office. I am not going to marry Glenn from Shawn's office. He wasn't my type."

"But you might get married someday. I don't want you to. It has to be just you and me forever. That's what you said."

"Well, I don't know. Let's worry about that when it happens, okay, kiddo? There's nobody I want to marry right now, or even go to a basketball game with."

"You can't get married. Ever. You're not allowed."

"Like I said, sweetie, this is not something we really need to be worrying about right now."

"Okay." Kelly sounds like she's been convinced. A minute passes and then she comes with "Mom?"

"Yes, sweetie," Stacey says, unable to keep "I'm just so tired" out of her voice.

"You were using bad language."

"I . . . oh. Yeah."

"You said Grace's mom was the b-word. How come you're allowed to use bad language and I get punished if I use bad language? You said that name-calling is disrespectful and dehumanizing, and that's why I can't watch TV when I do it, so I can learn a lesson. So how come *you* get to do it?"

"Uh . . . I don't know, sweetie. Sometimes when you're a grown-up—I mean, if you heard me, you could tell I wasn't really serious, right? That I wasn't, like, yelling that at her?"

"So it's okay to call somebody the b-word if you say it right?"

"Ugh. No. I tell you what—no TV for me tonight, okay?"

"Okay."

STACEY

        It's parent conference night. Phoebe has Kelly, and Stacey's appointment is for seven o'clock, the last appointment of the conference period. She has always chosen the last appointment of the night ever since Kelly was in kindergarten, when she'd made the mistake of making an early appointment and had run into and joined a knot of parents talking in the hall. She'd had to make up all kinds of elaborate lies in order to avoid being pressed into service on the Parent Council or the School-Based Site Management Council, or the Council of Trent, or the Second Vatican Council, or any of the other five hundred committees and activities that the activist parents were always doing.

    So now she stands at the corner of Centre and Sedgwick streets, watching as three or four of the most involved parents stand guard at the door, waiting to pounce on unwary potential volunteers. It's not that she's repeating Philippa's mistake of dismissing people out of hand—surely Philippa would never have been friends with Phoebe or Opal, though she probably would've liked Camille—it's just that work takes so much energy, and whatever's left goes to Kelly. Tonight, for example, she is debating firing the latest BU student she had hired to supervise young artists. Aileen has been late three times, and two bottles of Shimmer Glaze #3 have gone missing. (Camille has been urging her to fire the kid because "I guess BU stands for Butt Ugly—you better fire that kid before you drive your entire customer base away! Aren't there any hot art students out there?" Stacey believes that Aileen's tardiness and probable theft are more serious issues, but she and Camille have agreed to disagree on this point.)

Stacey waits until her watch says 7:01, takes a deep breath, and walks briskly to the door of the school.

"Stacey!" Frederick, chair of the Parent Council calls out. "Got a minute?"

"Ooh, I'm sorry, I'm already late for my conference. Catch me on the way out!" If you can, she adds to herself, hoping the principal doesn't alarm the back door before conference time ends.

She walks down the hallway, eyes the bulletin boards, and notes to herself that she could certainly make more eye-catching bulletin board displays for parents' night. She takes the piece of paper out of her purse and sees that Kelly's classroom is 112. The even numbers appear to be on the left, but then she walks directly from 110 to 115. And, of course, the odd-numbered side jumps from 109 to 116.

Finally she backtracks to an unmarked fire door, pulls it open, and finds the four missing classrooms on a little spur of hallway.

When she enters room 112, she sees Mr. Norris, or, anyway, a male figure she assumes to be Mr. Norris, sitting at his desk with his head in his hands.

"Uh . . . hello?" she says, and Mr. Norris's head pops up. He's really young looking—she figures he's maybe twenty-four.

"I . . . uh, I'm sorry," he says, and for just a microsecond she sees what she believes to be almost unbearable pain and weariness drain from his face as the professional, sociable, Mr. Norris face appears. "I've been here for eleven hours. It's a very long day, and my last two appointments didn't show . . . well, anyway, I'm sorry, hang on a second and let me get Kelly's folder out." Even professional, he's flustered. It makes him kind of cute, she thinks. No wonder Kelly likes him so much.

"It's okay, take your time, I need to duck the Parent Council people outside before they make me chair of something."

"Yeah," Mr. Norris says, "now that I'm not engaged anymore, I'm running out of excuses to duck them." He pauses. "Uh, I'm sorry. Long day. Oversharing."

"It's okay." There is an awkward pause, and Stacey kind of wants to fill it by dishing about the other parents. This is something she never really gets to do: Phoebe's daughter isn't school age yet, and anyway there is no way Steve would stand for her going to Boston Public Schools, and Opal is friends with Frederick and Tina and Caroline, and so she's never quite sure exactly where the line is in terms of what she can say about them without creating an awkward moment. Of course, Opal had no compunctions about creating an awkward moment with Glenn From Shawn's Office, she could tell already that sitting through a Celtics game with him would have been mind-bendingly dull, and anyway, he was good-looking and had money and Philippa would've gone out with him in a second, which was reason enough to reject him.

Finally Mr. Norris says, "Okay, well, here's Kelly's folder. I mean, what can I tell you—she's reading above grade level, she's doing math above grade level, she's a gem socially, and I really enjoy her sense of humor and the fact that she's always spying on what goes on in the hall."

"Well, I'm glad that's not just at home," Stacey says, smiling, but thinking, Then why is she only a monster at home? What am I doing wrong?

"I've been looking for anything that might give you more information in terms of the behavior stuff. I mean, there's the competitiveness with Grace and Keianna, but that's just girl stuff, I see that every year." It's not exactly what Stacey wants to hear, she wants him to say, *I've got it all figured out, you're not a terrible mom,* but still, there's something about him that's reassuring. He has a kind of calming presence.

"Yeah, I used to . . . ," Stacey finds herself saying, remembering how Philippa, in her plaid skirt in fourth grade at Walnut Prep, was always competing with Patricia Onwall, who was probably mayor of Cincinnati by now or something, but that's Philippa's life, not Stacey's, and she never fully fleshed out a childhood for Stacey, and how could it possibly be that her guard came down so far that Philippa almost came out? ". . . well, I used to be the same way."

"Yeah. I mean, boys compete, too, but it's usually about kickball or something. And those of us who suck at kickball become teachers, where we have to watch kickball games daily . . . Oh, jeez, I'm terribly sorry. My professionalism is in tatters here. I'm sorry about the language."

"The language?"

"Well, maybe it just got past you. We are pretty sensitive to language issues around here."

"I know—it was all I could do not to laugh in kindergarten when Kelly came home talking about 'the s-word,' and I found out she meant *stupid*."

"Yeah. That's a big one around here. Anyway, here is the only thing, and I have no idea if it means anything, but we were doing this thing with fingers and toes for the tens unit, and they had to figure out how many fingers and how many toes in their family, and Kelly looked really distressed, and after a couple of minutes she came up to me, obviously kind of upset, and asked if there was any way she could please, please count Aunt Phoebe and her family because they live upstairs. She said she thought the math would be too easy with just the two of you, and maybe that's all it was, but I don't think that was all it was."

"Yeah, she's embarrassed about the size of our family. I get a lot of Why can't we be a normal family like everybody else?"

Mr. Norris's face darkens, and Stacey's afraid she's just stepped in something here. Parent gossip says he got jilted at the altar, so maybe the subject of families is a little sensitive.

"That must be so hard," he says. "I mean, you can't explain some things. I don't know what I'd do if I had to try to explain what happened in my family—I mean, my sister's death."

"Yeah. It is hard. Most things are hard." There's a pause.

"Yeah. I know," he says, and there's a pause again, but it's not an awkward pause. It's . . . it's . . . companionable. He doesn't have to say anything else, because he does know. He doesn't know what it's like to fuck up so badly you have to destroy your identity, but if he really did get left at the altar, he's probably familiar with feeling like you've fucked up. And he seems to know that life is hard in a way that most people, certainly most people his age (how old is he really? If she were waiting tables, she'd card him . . .), don't.

Mr. Norris looks like he's about to say something else, but all he says is, "Well, listen. I don't have any children [does he wince when he says this? Does he regret it?], but I've been at this long enough . . . well, I mean, this is my seventh year [so what does that make him? Twenty-eight? And why is she thinking about it? Why could it possibly matter?], so I've taught a little over a hundred kids, and a lot of them come from single-parent families, and Kelly is really a fantastic, fantastic kid. As hard as she might be at home, you're doing a fantastic job."

And this, finally, is reassuring. Because he's an expert, right? Baby face and all, he sees a lot of parents and a lot of kids, so he must know. "Well, thank you. It's just that she—she gets so mean at home, it's like she has so much . . . it's like *anger* doesn't even begin to cover it, it's just rage, and it's always directed at me, and it's exhausting." Whoa! Now who's oversharing? It's just that there's something about this guy—twice now she's found herself watching in amazement as things tumble out of her mouth that she thought she could keep to herself.

"I'm sorry," he says. "I mean, I think it's only natural, in a way, when you're angry about something, you just . . . my folks split up after my sister died, and they had some vicious fights. I think they were both so angry, and they took it out on the closest person they could find."

"Jesus, I'm sorry."

"Oh—yeah, I think I must've been really bad in a past life. But I was . . . all I was trying to say was that everybody tends to take their anger out on the people closest to them."

"Hmm. Well, if you're angry, you don't seem to take it out on the kids. Kelly adores you."

"No, they're what gets me out of bed in the morning."

"Yeah. Me, too."

"Hey . . . " he says, and then stops.

"Yes?"

"Uh, uh . . . well, nothing, I guess. I just hope you know this isn't a typical parent conference for me. I mean, I have this . . . I have this Mr. Norris persona that I seem to have misplaced, and you're just getting Mark, and I'm sorry."

"You know what, Mark? Don't worry about it. I'm not a typical parent."

"Yeah, you haven't asked me how I can ensure your kid will get into Boston Latin in four years."

Stacey laughs and sits for a minute. There's really nothing else to say, there's really no reason to continue this conference, there wasn't really any reason for it to go this long in the first place, but she doesn't want to get up. She gets up slowly, and Mr. Norris . . . or, apparently, Mark . . . gets up, says thanks, and then she is walking out the door, and she forgets to sneak out the back, and goddamn if Frederick isn't there asking her if she would like to work eighty or ninety hours on the silent auction they have coming up, and she's donating a birthday party for fifteen at Kids' Creation Station, which is going to cost her a bundle but will be worth it if it will get her off the hook for volunteering for a while.

She walks home feeling calm and contented for the first time in a long time. It's too bad, she thinks, that she won't get that many opportunities to talk to Mr. Norris.

MARK

Mark wakes up grumpy. It's parents' day, but that shouldn't be bothering him. His first one had terrified him, but it was actually pretty reassuring to have all these parents trooping in and looking at him like they thought he knew what he was doing just because he was the teacher. It actually helped him a great deal to start feeling like a real teacher and less like an impostor.

And sure, some parents will be annoying, and, for the most part, the parents of the kids who are doing great will show up, and the parents of the kids who cause problems or are having problems will stay home, but overall it should be a good day.

So why does he feel so poisonous today? He exercises vigorously but still feels mean and cranky afterward.

Work is bad—the kids don't seem to be understanding anything he says, and he gets impatient and frustrated and ends up yelling at Kadeem, and that kid gets yelled at enough to judge by the way his grandmom acts when she's in here. He shoots his eyes over to Kelly Phillips, his little barometer, just after he yells, and she's shaking her head.

He hates the fact that he's silently checking in with a seven-year-old on his teaching, and he hates even more that she's right. When the kids go off to specials, he hears Keianna, one of his four horsemen—Kelly, Grace, and Diego are the others—who are the allies he depends on to bring everybody else along, say, "Mr. Norris is mad cranky today."

Kelly, ever loyal, says, "Maybe he's having a terrible, horrible, no good very bad day. Maybe he needs to go to Australia."

He sits at his desk not planning or correcting during his precious hour of planning time. He just straightens things up, makes sure the room looks presentable for the parents tonight, though he still has an hour and a half with his class after specials, so he'll have to do all of this again after school, but it's all he can do right now.

The end of the day is uneventful. The class is worn out from gym, and he and the kids come to the tacit agreement that they're just going to phone it in until two thirty.

School ends and he straightens up again and checks his schedule. Great. Of course somebody's signed up for the very last time slot of the night, there's no way they could come in at five thirty or five forty when he has openings, no, they have to come at seven, and look at that, it's Kelly's mom. This could break either way. Either it'll be a quick, painless conference in which he says, yes, your little angel is doing great, or else it'll be a long and painful one in which she seeks more reassurance that the fact that Kelly's a monster at home doesn't mean she's a terrible mom.

He sits at his desk and puts on his Mr. Norris face, and he has nice conversations with Keianna's dad, Grace's mom, Diego's mom *and* dad, and the parents of four other kids who are not the superstars that his four horsemen are but are generally well behaved and learning on schedule. As predicted, the five he needs to see most are not here. Kadeem's grandmom is actually scheduled, but Mark doesn't believe for a minute that she's going to show up, and, sure enough, she doesn't. So he's sitting alone at his desk, and he realizes he's really hungry.

And now, finally, he realizes why he's been in such a shitty mood all day, and he marvels that he could have possibly been so stupid as to not know it. Because every parents' night since they'd been together, Becky had come to pick him up at school, and they'd gone out for a really nice dinner, and it was always great after working a twelve-hour day to be able to look forward to something besides collapsing on the couch.

He closes his eyes, and he's back, a year ago—could it really have only been a year ago? Is that possible? Is it possible that everything could go so sour in such a short time? He walked out of school after parent conferences, and Becky was there with the Lexus, which was not yet the Cuckoldmobile (or was it?), and Keyon, a fourth grader he'd had two years earlier, had been standing there with his mom and said, "Oh, snap! Mr. Norris rollin' in a Lex! Okay then!"

Mark smiled and got into the car and beautiful Becky was there, her seat pushed back, her legs impossibly long, a little black band at the top of her stocking just showing. He was starving, and they went and ate really spicy food and drank too much wine, and they'd gone back to the apartment, and she'd left her stockings on, and the anesthetic effects of the alcohol had given him superhuman endurance, and they'd both woken up with rug burns, and if he closed his eyes, he could still see her above him . . .

At some point the motion-detector switch turned the lights out on him, sitting at his desk motionless. So he's sitting here in the dark, aching for Becky's touch, aching to hear her voice, her laugh, the story she told at dinner that night, and wishing that any of it, any of it at all, had been real, that there really was a person on earth who was as wonderful as he had stupidly believed Becky to be.

Suddenly Becky's absence and the lie of her whole existence is a hole in his midsection, one that's being gnawed ever bigger by rats that will surely consume him entirely.

He sits with his head in his hands, not crying, just despairing.

And suddenly the lights flicker on. Somebody's moving in here. Probably just Bill the custodian here to empty the trash or something. He doesn't even raise his head from his hands.

"Uh, hello?" a female voice says. Shit. It's Kelly's mom. Mark looks up, says, "Uh, I'm sorry," and struggles to put his teacher face on. It's a struggle made all the more difficult by the fact that Stacey Phillips is not exactly the earth mother he'd been expecting.

She's stunning. Certainly her face is beautiful, and certainly her body is amazing (can those possibly be real? Could he possibly bury his face in them right now?), but more than that, she's . . . she's sparkling. Widowed single mom and all, she is definitely, vibrantly alive. The air is crackling around her.

Instantly Mark has a flash of clearing off his desk and just fucking Stacey Phillips senseless right here on the desktop, of drinking in all the life from the place where life begins . . . he forces the image from his mind so that he can have an actual conversation and not just sit here drooling.

He says something stupid about what a long day it's been and fumbles around for Kelly's folder. She smiles this wonderful, kind smile and tells him not to worry, she needs to hang out here to duck the activist parents.

"Yeah," he says, "now that I'm not engaged anymore, I'm running out of excuses to duck them." Whoa. That's too much, that's not professional, and though they have already consummated their relationship in his mind, this woman isn't even his friend, much less anything else, and she certainly never will be. He remembers girls like this from high school, from college—they always had guys coming to them, and yeah, sometimes Mark was one of them, and, given their pick of the guys, they always preferred large, dumb, and mean to small, thoughtful, and kind, at least in Mark's experience, and he is certain that this woman turns down more dates in a month than Mark's had in his whole life. So yeah, she might be widowed, and yeah, she has a kind smile and sparkling eyes, but get ahold of yourself, he tells himself, and then gets sidetracked thinking that he will definitely need to get ahold of himself later if he's ever going to be able to think of anything but Stacey sprawled across his desk, fingers tugging at his hair, breath coming quickly and heavily . . .

He's embarrassed. "I'm sorry. Long day. Oversharing."

She says it's okay, and Mark is convinced she can read his mind. Surely women as sexy as this have some kind of built-in radar about stuff like this.

He puts that horrible pervert away for a minute, opens Kelly's folder, and tells Stacey that Kelly is doing great, that he really enjoys her sense of humor and the fact that she's always spying on the adults. He is always paranoid, as a male teacher, of being misinterpreted. When he was student teaching, his supervisor took him aside for a little talk, told him that he had the potential to be a lightning rod, be very careful, and it's not fair, but his female classmates were going to get to hug their students, and he was just going to have to forgo that if he wanted to remain a teacher, he couldn't do anything that would even give anyone an opening to think the wrong thing, because people were automatically suspicious of a man who wanted to work with children, and it wasn't fair, and it wasn't right, but that was the way it was, and so he'd damn well better always be aware of it.

So he's careful. He wants to go even further over the top, to tell Stacey that Kelly is his number one ally in class, the chief of the four horsemen. He wants to tell her that Kelly is, thus far, his favorite of all the students he's taught in the last six years. But he also wants to remain employed, so he just leaves it at that.

"Well, I'm glad that's not just at home," Stacey says, and Mark sees a flash of something incredibly familiar in her eyes. Behind the sparkle, behind the flash, there's a profound sadness and what looks like fatigue. Mark knows this look all too well from seeing it in the mirror, and suddenly Stacey is not just an object of his lust (though, of course, she is still that), she's also a fellow sufferer, probably one of the few people he's seen tonight, one of the few anywhere close to his age (she is close, right? Most of the parents of the white kids are at least forty, but Stacey Phillips looks much younger. Could she be as young as thirty?) who has any idea of the incredible shitstorm that life can be.

He wants to help her, to comfort her, so he blathers about how Kelly competes with Grace and Keianna, then says something stupid about how girls are like that or something that's probably offensive.

But there's a pause, and Stacey says, "Yeah, I used to . . . ," and then trails off and comes back a second later with ". . . well, I used to be the same way." She gets this look like she's said too much, which Mark thinks is weird because she's actually said nothing at all.

But she let him get away with his stupid generalization, which he appreciates, and he still hasn't done anything to comfort her, to reassure her, but now he needs to make sure she knows he's not some kind of misogynist, so he says something ridiculous about how he sucked at kickball. And he actually said *sucked*! At a parent conference! He doesn't think Kelly's mom will complain, but he is embarrassed anyway. Somehow his guard came way, way down. Is it the fact that he's finally in the presence of someone who understands? She must have been even younger than me when Kelly's dad died, Mark thinks. We've both seen the futures we thought we had evaporate—she looked death right in the eye, and here she is looking a little scared, a little sad maybe, but not defined by it, not living under a cloud. Of course, he's just told her he was a loser in elementary school, which feels even worse than the professional lapse. He babbles while he's trying to regain his brain.

"Oh, jeez, I'm terribly sorry. My professionalism is in tatters here. I'm sorry about the language." Stacey looks confused. She didn't even notice! Beautiful. Mark feels temporarily back on top of his game, and he remembers that weird thing with Kelly and the math problem, probably the only time he's seen her upset like that, so he tells Stacey. It's probably nothing, but he feels like he really wants to tell her what she wants to hear, like he has to give her something. (Oh, I'd like to give her something all right, Mark thinks, then feels ashamed, and comes to as Stacey is saying "I get a lot of Why can't we be a normal family like everybody else?")

And Mark suddenly thinks, But you are a family, which is something that seems hopelessly out of reach to me now, and you're normal, you've obviously achieved some kind of normalcy, the kind of normalcy I can only dream of. How did you do it? You've been through much worse than me, how did you get so normal, and will it ever happen to me? And how did you do it with a kid looking at you, making you explain what the world's really like: "I'm sorry sweetie, there's no Santa, good people suffer, bad people usually thrive, and sometimes people die young, and it damn sure could happen to you or me, I can't even throw you that bone"? How do you comfort a kid when there's no comfort to be had?

"That must be so hard. I mean, you can't explain some things. I don't know what I'd do if I had to try to explain what happened in my family—I mean, my sister's death." The one that destroyed the only family I ever knew, the only one it looks like I'm ever going to have.

"Yeah. It is hard. Most things are hard," Stacey says.

"Yeah. I know," Mark says, and for a moment he doesn't think anything except this. It's so nice to sit with somebody who knows, not somebody he has to put on a brave front for, somebody who understands, and he almost tells her this, that it's just an incredible relief to sit across the desk from somebody who understands, that, with the exception of one drunken evening, he's spent the last six months (Jesus, has it been half a year already? Has he already been without her for one-sixth of the time he was with her? How can that be?) feeling like the only person with a dark cloud floating over his head in a sea of shiny happy people who have no idea about what life really is. Yes, it's hard. Fuckin'-A-right it's hard. *I can think of something that's getting hard just looking at you,* his filthy, perverted mind offers. Why can't he shut that guy up?

He can't bring himself to tell Stacey how much he is treasuring the seconds he spends with her, so instead he tells her that she must be doing a fantastic job, because Kelly is so great in school. He believes this—it is obvious to anybody here who spends five minutes with Kelly that she's loved and supported at home—but he mostly just wants to give Stacey something nice, something to take the cloud away from her beautiful face.

And it seems to work. He can see her relaxing, and she says that Kelly just has all this anger, and before he knows what's happening, he's telling Stacey about how his parents split after Janet died. Mom told him he'd missed the worst of the fights while he was at college, so apparently there were even worse ones than the barn burners he'd witnessed at Thanksgiving and Christmas. "... everybody tends to take their anger out on the people closest to them," he says, and he's thinking mostly of Mom and Dad.

"Hmm. Well, if you're angry, you don't seem to take it out on the kids. Kelly adores you," Stacey says, and Mark is taken aback to realize that she thought he was talking about himself, too. And maybe he was. *I've got anger like you wouldn't believe, lady*, he wants to say, *but I can't take it out on anyone close to me because I don't have anyone close to me*, but instead he says, "No, they're what gets me out of bed in the morning." Perfect. Way to reward the nicest moment in months. With some pabulum cliché that sounds like he read it in *Chicken Poop for the Teacher's Soul* or something.

"Yeah. Me, too." Stacey says, and the conversation is obviously winding down, and he just never wants it to end, and he's on the point of asking her, *Hey, if you don't have to get right home, maybe we could grab something to eat, I'm starving*, or, *God, it's such a relief to talk to somebody who understands the dark side, please please please meet me for coffee, I'm drowning here.*

He gets as far as, "Hey," which is going to be *Hey, I know this is unprofessional, which seems to be the theme for the night, but would you like to meet for coffee sometime? I just so rarely get to talk to anybody who has the vaguest idea of how tough life can be ...*

But his internal censor stops him. What if she took it the wrong way and complained to Ms. Jackson, *can't a woman come in here and have a parent conference without some perv hitting on her, this is totally inappropriate?* Worse yet, what if she said yes, let's meet for coffee, and then they met for coffee, and then they came to the point that every girl in high school pre-Becky had, that every girl in college pre-Raquel had, that point where they say, *I really like you, you're a really nice guy and I really like talking to you, but I just like you as a friend, because why would I want to date somebody kind and intelligent when there's a tall, athletic idiot down the hall whose idea of conversation is tallying up his drinks from last night who's just dying to mistreat me?* Or worse yet, what if they hit it off, and he fell in love with her, then she said, *Oh, I have to leave town and start a new career with a new name, and by the way I'm fucking the Boston Celtics, the BU women's rugby team, and the cast of* Blue Man Group?

So the internal censor steps in, midsentence, and says, Wrong move, wrong time. He feels as guilty as if he had actually asked her out, and he blathers something about how this isn't a typical parent conference for him, that he's usually more professional, et cetera.

Stacey tells him not to worry, that she's not a typical parent. You sure as hell aren't, Mark thinks, but what he says is, "Yeah, you haven't asked me how I can ensure your kid will get into Boston Latin in four years." They sit for a moment, and then Stacey gets up slowly, and Mark wants to beg her to stay, but of course he doesn't, and she smiles and leaves. Mark steals a look at her ass as she walks down the hall, then returns to his empty room.

The Lexus still exists, somewhere, but Becky is long long gone, and she's not picking him up, not tonight, not ever.

But tonight, for the first time since Jo, he's had a human connection with someone, with a woman, and neither of them was drunk. And there are any number of reasons why he won't see this woman any more than three times a year, not the least of which is that she's ridiculously hot and he wouldn't stand a chance, but maybe it's an encouraging sign for the future. Maybe he won't be alone forever, maybe he won't be miserable forever, maybe there is some hope after all.

STACEY

Stacey realizes early that it was folly to think that donating a birthday party worth many hundreds of dollars would get the other parents off her back about volunteering for the silent auction. Eventually she gives in and agrees to chaperone kids' entertainment from six thirty to seven so that she doesn't have to spend hours setting up or cleaning up, and so she doesn't have to stand there at the end and try to collect checks from the highest bidders.

This at least gives her an excuse to blow off all her friends trying to set her up. Opal seems to have written her off as hopeless after she blew off Glenn From Shawn's Office ("He's a really nice guy! And he makes shitloads of money!"), but Phoebe may be gearing up for another round, and Camille has already told her that she has several young fitness professionals in mind for her should she ever desire some personal training of her own. This actually has some appeal, because it wouldn't involve vetting anybody for a potential relationship, worrying about how he got along with Kelly, stuff like that. But she's not just horny—she's lonely, and if she can't talk to somebody about work, about what's going on with Kelly, about life, she really doesn't think she wants to sleep with him.

So she tells everybody she's really busy, she's just had to fire an assistant (caught her stuffing a box of brushes into her bag!), she has to interview for a new one, and she just got roped into volunteering for this event at Kelly's school, there's no way she can even think about going out with anybody at least until the silent auction is over.

So that's covered, and she actually manages to find another BU student who is honest, talented, and very hot to be the new assistant. Life at home continues—Kelly is either her best friend and her number one fan, or her most dedicated enemy. Mr. Norris was very kind to try to pass this off as just her anger over her situation, but Stacey knows, she just knows, that this is Ken's DNA, that the sick bastard followed her into her new life, he'll never ever let her alone, and she might build the best life in the world, but he'll always be there behind her daughter's eyes, ready to call her an idiot and a bitch now, and a stupid whore as soon as Kelly learns that word.

And yet, for all this, Kelly is really fun, and really smart and actually quite compassionate about everyone but her mom, and even usually to her mom, and it's not like every moment is hell, and it's not like there's even an outburst every day, it's just so very tiring when it happens, because it just drags Philippa out of her grave again, it drags Ken back into her life, and she hates it.

One day she goes to pick up Kelly and stands there with the other parents waiting for the walkers to come out as she does every day. She's wearing her rock_l shirt that she bought online, the one that says ROCK_L in tiny letters up by the collar and MY LEFT ONE across her left one. She kind of hopes she scandalizes the other parents with stuff like this, and she's glad that Kelly is still too young to be completely humiliated by her mom showing up at school with a shirt like that on.

It's probably cold enough for her to wear her hooded sweatshirt that she also bought online, the one that says ART SAVED MY LIFE (not 100 percent true, as a talent for deception and hotel housekeeping also played a big part, but she likes the sweatshirt anyway), zipped up, but if she zips up the sweatshirt, then nobody will see the T-shirt that says MY LEFT ONE on her left one.

The walkers come out two minutes late, and, after the kindergartners come out with Ms. Jimenez, there's a new face leading the first and second graders out. It's Mr. Norris, and he's holding Kelly's hand. Due to some nonsense with the buses, the walkers have to come out the side door on Sedgwick Street and then walk outside the entire length of the school up to Centre Street, so Stacey gets a few minutes to observe Mr. Norris and Kelly. He leans down to listen to something she says and comes up laughing. Then he leans down and says something to her, and she bursts out laughing. She looks completely joyful, and Stacey always feels all gooey inside when Kelly's like this.

Finally they reach the fence, and Stacey, without thinking, says to Mr. Norris, "New duty, huh?"

"Yeah," he says as Kelly releases his hand and runs over, crushing Stacey's ovaries with a bear hug around her midsection. "Yeah, but it's okay. I like this duty, because I see the kids at the time of day when they're happiest." He seems to actually mean this. He's so cute! "—Keianna, your dad's over there—Grace, is that your new babysitter? Okay, see you tomorrow."

Stacey looks down at Kelly. "Are you happy, sweetie?"

Kelly nods, obviously too freaked out that her mom and her teacher are speaking to be able to say a word.

"Even though your mean teacher gave you so much homework?" Mr. Norris asks Kelly.

"You were only mean that one day," Kelly answers, and then she runs behind Stacey and hides.

Mr. Norris smiles, and then his eyes flit down to her tits, as all men's eyes eventually do. He smiles and says, "Nice shirt."

"Oh." Oh shit! She's wearing the My Left One shirt! Shit! She never would have worn it if she'd known she was going to see Kelly's teacher! "Oh, yeah, I, uh . . ."

"Uh," Mr. Norris begins, and now he's blushing, because he's basically announced that he was looking at her tits, "I mean that's her best song."

"You like rock_l? I didn't think men were allowed to like rock_l."

"There's a story. I'll tell you sometime," he says, and then he disappears into the swirling mass of kids and parents as he leads the kids who haven't been picked up yet back into school.

"Finally!" Kelly says, and Stacey realizes that Kelly's been tugging on the back of her sweatshirt ever since she ran behind her to hide. "Can we go? I want to try the new gem finder!"

Kelly's referring to a new apparatus at the Kids' Creation Station that allows kids to sift through a big pile of sandy dirt in order to find cheap pieces of quartz they can stick on something or else make a necklace out of. Stacey thought it was a complete piece-of-crap waste of time when she saw it in the catalog, but she'd bought it on the strength of Kelly's enthusiasm for the idea, and it was now the biggest hit at Kids' Creation Station and generated a pretty ridiculous amount of revenue considering it was basically just a pile of dirt with a couple of rocks in it.

"Yeah, let's go," Stacey says, and Kelly is great, fantastic, a perfect angel for the rest of the night.

And the next night, she's telling Stacey that she hates her, she's the worst mother on the face of the earth, she wishes her dad was alive and her mom was dead, and Stacey can't help thinking that Kelly doesn't know it, will never know it, but her wish has already come true.

Without even realizing it, Stacey begins paying attention to her appearance when she goes to the Balch to pick up Kelly. It's not that this is completely new—as Camille and legions of divorced (and married) dads who are loyal customers at Kids' Creation Station know, Stacey always looks good—in fact, she can't help it. But she just starts thinking about what kind of image she's projecting at school, and aims for hot and funky but not slutty or freakish. If anyone asked her about this, and no one does, because it's not a big enough change to be remarkable to anyone, Stacey would simply say that she doesn't want to embarrass Kelly, that Kelly's getting older, and also that as she gets involved in this silent auction business, she finds that she actually likes several of the parents she had previously dismissed, and she no longer feels the urge to scandalize as strongly as she once did.

Every day she sees Mark come out with the first and second graders, always with a different kid by his side. Sometimes he is holding their hands, sometimes he's just walking, but he's always engaged in conversation with them, talking and laughing, or stopping the line in order to talk to the kid who just stole somebody else's hat. This is in marked contrast with Ms. Jimenez, who always looks bored and/or annoyed as she brings out the kindergartners.

It's a chaotic mess when the kids come out, so they don't always get a chance to talk, and when they do it's usually something along the lines of "Freezing today, huh?" or something like that, though sometimes it's "Kelly wrote a fantastic story today. I told her she had to show it to you, but I wanted to tell you just in case she forgot." Of course, any communication always leads to Kelly expressing her disapproval. Sometimes it's just a scowl, but sometimes it's tears when they get in the car: "Why do you always have to talk to him? It's *so embarrassing!*" Stacey always tells Kelly that it's a good thing for parents and teachers to communicate, that's why they send those fliers home with the teacher's e-mail address, and didn't she notice that Mr. Norris always says hello to Diego's dad, too?

Kelly doesn't exactly buy this, but it's not like Stacey can (or would) start ducking Mr. Norris at pickup time just because it makes Kelly uncomfortable. They don't always speak, but even when they don't, she always catches his eye and smiles. He's a good egg, she thinks, and she's happy he's Kelly's teacher. She's really curious about what his rock_l story is, but this is obviously not the time or place to hear a story at all, since it's a struggle to even exchange three sentences.

Well, she thinks, maybe at the next parent conference. And maybe then Kelly's anger will have subsided, her tantrums will have gotten better, and she'll be able to tell Mr. Norris that she was all worried about nothing last time, ha-ha, isn't it funny how parents get so neurotic about these little phases?

Except it's not really a phase. And it's not really getting better. One night after the playdate at Grace's house, Kelly has a fit about dinner, about how she wants goddamn chicken nuggets, and so she goes to her room without eating and eventually comes and eats her cold grilled cheese before bed.

Phoebe is out of town, so Stacey calls her on her cell phone. She listens to Phoebe vent her worries for ten minutes, and provides her customary reassurance—no, you're not a terrible mom because you're out of town, no, Steve's not fucking the nanny, no, really, Steve's not fucking the nanny, no, you're not a terrible mom, yes, I'm really really sure Steve's not fucking the nanny. Wait, what's that squeaking sound from upstairs?

After she assures Phoebe that she honestly was just joking, she can't hear anything from upstairs, she says that she's really worried about Kelly, that the time at Grace's hasn't helped at all, she totally lost it tonight.

Then she hears an angry whisper over her shoulder. "Who are you talking to? Why are you talking about me?"

Suddenly furious that she can't even have ten goddamn minutes to have an adult conversation, Stacey whips her head around and barks, "Get back in bed *NOW*!"

She listens as Kelly retreats to her room and then as stuffed animals and books go flying into the hallway. "I'm sorry, I'm gonna have to call you back," she tells Phoebe, and she's grateful that she hung up the phone in time so that Phoebe didn't overhear Kelly yelling, "Fine! I'm getting back in my bed, you fucking idiot!"

Stacey charges for the bedroom door, and just as she begins to yell "Never *ever* speak to me—" Kelly chucks the framed picture of the two of them smiling next to the pond at Larz Anderson Park at the door frame. The glass shatters and a shard flies into Stacey's leg, which begins to bleed.

"Ow, Kelly, Jesus Christ! Goddamn it!" she yells, and then she collapses next to the door and begins to cry. She's a failure, she's the worst mother in the world, and now she'll have a little scar on her calf to prove it to the world. She fucked up, she fucked up so completely, and no matter how far she runs, no matter how much she pretends to be somebody else, she is cursed for life.

Despairing, she cries and cries and cries and cries. And she hears somebody else crying. It's Kelly, and she's saying, "I'm sorry, Mommy, I'm so sorry, Mommy, please don't die, please, Mommy, don't die, please . . ."

Stacey lifts her head. "I'm not gonna die, sweetie." She walks over to Kelly's bed and hugs her. Kelly clings to her and it feels nice. And suddenly there's a break in her clouds of despair, and she says, "Kel-Bel, we've gotta go talk to somebody about this."

"That sounds really suckish, mom," Kelly whispers. "It doesn't sound like any fun."

"Well, Kel-Bel, how fun was this?"

"Not very much."

"I'd say it was pretty suckish."

"It was, Mommy," Kelly says. They lie down together in Kelly's bed, and Kelly is asleep in five minutes. Stacey cleans up the glass and then tosses and turns all night.

The next day she calls Kelly's pediatrician, and the receptionist, after silently judging her the worst mother on the face of the earth, transfers her to Behavioral Health, where the receptionist, after silently joining in the other receptionist's judgment, grants her an appointment with Dr. Karen Haver, who will give her professional opinion that Stacey is the worst mother on earth two weeks from today.

MARK

At the beginning of the second trimester, the principal, Ms. Jackson, whose first name is Inez but who insists that everybody call her Ms. Jackson (Ms. Jackson if you're nasty, Mark can't help thinking whenever the issue comes up), comes to his room and tells him that, as he is aware, the contract allows her to assign duties and to change them at the trimester, and she knows that he had an inside duty for the first trimester but now she needs him to take over taking the first- and second-grade walkers out in the afternoon, and she's sorry but her decision is final.

Mark is happy to do this—he actually likes this duty, but he can't help but get mad at the way Ms. Jackson acts like Mark is some kind of slacker, or some kind of malcontent who's going to file a grievance when he didn't say a word and actually preferred outside duties.

So on the first day, he takes the walkers out, and Kelly, his second in command, walks by his side. She reaches her hand up, and though he knows he needs to be careful and avoid any physical contact, he's not going to refuse to hold the hand of this sweet kid with the dead dad, so he just hopes her incredibly hot mom will be cool about it. He suspects she will be.

When he hands Kelly off to her, Stacey is smiling, and Mark wonders if she understands how electric her smile is, if she knows that she's lighting up the sidewalk here. Probably not. He also sees that she's wearing a rock_l shirt with MY LEFT ONE written on the left side of her formidable rack.

"Nice shirt," he says, and then blushes, because how can you admit to noticing a shirt like that without admitting that you're noticing the fantastic breasts beneath it? You can't, so he keeps talking: "Uh, I mean that's her best song."

"You like rock_l?" Stacey asks. "I didn't think men were allowed to like rock_l."

"There's a story," Mark says. Is there ever. "I'll tell you sometime." And then he is drawn away from Stacey and her incandescent smile, and later on he reflects that he managed to say something that actually sounded sort of cool even though he felt like he'd felt when he was a ninth grader in the presence of Lauren McCormick, Senior Girl.

After this, he has an extra reason to look forward to his afternoon duty. He finds himself feeling really disappointed whenever Kelly's going to Grace's house after school, because that means he won't get to see Stacey that day. It's not that the chaotic pickup time is very conducive to conversation; it's mostly just little bits of conversation—Wow, it's cold today, Kelly really liked that book you gave her, this kind of stuff. But it feels nicer than the interactions he has with the other parents. Is this just because he's far more attracted to Stacey Phillips than he is to any of the other parents?

She always looks fantastic, and Mark begins to feel self-conscious about the fact that Stacey Phillips is so funky and stylish, and he looks like a dorky elementary school teacher. So he begins adding to his wardrobe, one piece at a time—a blazer here, a nicer shirt there, some uncomfortable shoes there. He wonders if she notices. Even if she doesn't, it couldn't hurt his chances with her or with anybody else. He doesn't feel quite himself in nice clothes, but he finds that this is a sensation he enjoys.

In the meantime, there are parents in and around school all the time doing silent auction stuff. Grace's mom comes to address a faculty meeting and says, "Of course this is being done by the parents for the benefit of the school, so we are not asking you to help out or supervise or anything, but we would really love to have you all there just to enjoy it as a community event. We're going to be having entertainment for grown-ups outside, and entertainment for the kids on the inside, so those of you with children [Not me, Mark thinks, I got jilted!] can bring your kids and drop them off, we're going to have a magic show and some other things we haven't booked yet . . . ," and she drones on and on about all the wonderful things that the parents are going to do with all this money. After the meeting, Mark approaches her.

"Uh, hi, Opal."

"Mark! What's up?"

"Well, I, uh, I play guitar, and I used to do a bunch of kids' entertaining, and I'd really like to do a few songs, if that's okay."

"Oh my gosh, that would be great! Are you sure you really want to do that? I mean, you spend all day with our kids every day, and I can certainly understand if you want a break."

"No, I think it would be fun for me. I haven't done it in a long time."

"Well, okay, then, great!"

So Mark is committed to rockin' out on his rock_l guitar with some songs about poop. He's immediately nervous. Will it make him too sad? He doesn't think so. Even though it reminds him of Janet (and of Becky blowing him back when she had never blown anyone else and certainly wasn't lying to him about blowing anybody else at the same time), it's also something he did before everything in his life started to suck, and it was something he might have picked up again a lot sooner if he hadn't given the guitar to rock_l. Then she would have just cheated on him without writing the song, and then he never would have yelled at Rebekah, and maybe they'd be married by now, raising little culturally Jewish Unitarians and arguing about what holiday to celebrate in December.

Maybe there's some way that making kids laugh about bodily functions will help him to recapture that time in his life when he didn't know so much, when he didn't know that God is a thug who kills children, that people—well, okay, women—have a seemingly unlimited capacity for deceit and betrayal, when he didn't understand so completely that there is no earthly or celestial reward for being kind, it's just something that suckers do because they are too weak to be cruel.

He begins devoting all his after-school time to rehearsal and planning for his appearance. He scours the used-record stores looking for cool stickers to put on his guitar. He rejects any number of band stickers and finally settles on a red sticker with black letters that reads: WARNING: MAY CAUSE IRRITATION. He slaps it on the guitar and feels cooler than he has in his entire life. He heads to the used-clothing stores, braving the musty smell of the merchandise and the patchouli reek of the twenty-year-old customer base in the hope of finding a cool rock-and-roll outfit. Or at least a cool Raffi-with-an-excretory-fixation outfit.

Finally, at four o'clock one Saturday, he spots a shiny purple suit on sale for only forty-five dollars. He buys it up, gets the sleeves and pant legs shortened, and is ready to go.

The silent auction is on Friday, and it's now Thursday. The Balch is a hive of activity with busy-bee parents doing their dances all over the place. Mark wonders grumpily why the lovely Stacey Phillips is not among them. When he walks the kids out, she is there waiting for Kelly, and she waves twice, first at Kelly and then at him. (Ah, Lovely Stacey, he thinks. Do you have any idea what that wave does to me? And why must you be so far out of my reach?)

"So," Mark says, "are you coming to the silent auction, or did you manage to duck the organizers?" He figures this is safe, because it's a big school event, it won't look like he's asking *Are you going to the school dance?*, it'll just look like he's interested in this big thing that's happening at school, and he's trying to bond about the way the parents try to rope you into stuff.

"Oh, yeah, I got roped into supervising the kids' entertainment. So it looks like I get to see a magic show," she says, rolling her eyes.

Yes! She's supervising kids' entertainment! Thank you, God, and I'm sorry I called you a murderous thug! "Well, make sure to stick around after the magic show—there should be some good music."

She looks at him quizzically, and then he is swept away by the tide of kids.

He can't fall asleep on Thursday night. He is nervous about his performance, of course, but he's even more nervous about the fact that Stacey Phillips is going to be there. He keeps trying to think about something else, but he keeps seeing her every time he closes his eyes. At one o'clock he gets up, turns on Conan O'Brien, and tries to clear his head. You don't even really know this woman, he tells himself. You're doing it again, you're getting obsessed with an idea of somebody without knowing a thing about her, it's just like Becky, you wanted her to still be Becky, but she was really Rebecca.

And, anyway, you can't date the parents of your students. And, anyway, she's older—you don't know how much, but she probably is in the market for somebody—somebody as good looking as she is, somebody different from you. After all, every other woman you've ever gotten involved with was actually in the market for somebody quite different from you.

Stacey is kind, and she has a wonderful kid, and she is so sexy it makes him sweat just to look at her, but she's no more than an American version of Jo—a fantasy he can escape to so he can forget the reality of Becky, of Raquel, of the fact that he's doomed to be lonely until he settles for some kind of socially awkward, unattractive girl who writes Buffy fan fiction in her spare time or something.

Having decided that Stacey is just a fantasy, Mark gives in to a rather elaborate fantasy in which she is the star, and soon after he's finished, he's able to catch three hours of sleep before waking up at five, terrified.

After school Mark hangs around, his stomach too sour to eat, his brain too muddled to do any work. He settles for running through his set list again, quietly singing his scatological hits while he strums his guitar quietly with his thumb.

Finally, after what feels like days, he walks around outside and sees what items are up for bid. He listens to the band of parents calling themselves Nina and the Blackwoods doing painfully sincere covers of 1980s songs. When "Nina"—actually Jennifer Martin, parent of a kindergartner—makes a little gun with her hand and "shoots" the audience for the "bang bang" part of Scandal's "The Warrior," Mark decides that even the worst magic show would be preferable to this. Besides, Stacey is in there.

He walks in and finds Stacey at the back of the room while The Amazing Zev is making foam balls disappear from one hand and appear in the closed hand of Patrice, a third grader.

"I don't know if it's appropriate for that guy to be playing with his balls like that in front of the kids," he ventures. This is a calculated risk—he doesn't think anybody who wears a My Left One shirt is going to be offended by a seventh-grade testicle joke, but if she is, better to just end his hopes now before he starts singing his poop songs.

Stacey doesn't miss a beat. "Yeah, he really shouldn't play with them so much—they're all red." Mark laughs, and Stacey continues. "So I hope your act will be a little more appropriate."

"Oh, it's actually going to be terribly inappropriate, and I can probably tell you right now which three parents are going to complain about it."

Stacey gives him a puzzled look. "Should I remove my daughter?"

"I don't know. What are your feelings on scatology?"

"I feel like I don't know what that word means."

"It's, uh, I suppose it's the study of excretory functions."

"You're doing a poop act?"

"Well, I mean, it's not exactly a poop act, I don't think anybody's going to poop, although if you look over there, Jasmine's little sister kind of looks like she may have left a present in her diaper. But, no, I mean, for some of the songs, the subject matter is fecal matter."

"Well, how much am I going to want to kill you when Kelly starts singing this stuff?"

"Less than I'm going to want to kill myself when my whole class starts singing when I'm trying to do math with them."

"Okay then," and she smiles. He feels like this is going really well, except that he's now feeling incredibly stupid for having volunteered to do this in the first place, because he knows he's going to catch a bunch of shit for it, no pun intended, ha-ha, but more than that, he doesn't seem to need it. It looks like he can actually hold a real conversation with Stacey without being the bard of the bathroom, and suddenly this feels like a terrible miscalculation, one more time when he's going to look back and say, Jesus, why the hell did I do that anyway?

"So can I ask what your rock_l story is?"

"Oh! Yeah. I'd love—" *I'd love to tell you the whole thing over a cup of coffee, baby,* he wants to say, but actually says, "—to, but I am actually kind of nervous, and I need to go put my rock-and-roll clothes on. But how about after my, uh, performance?"

"Great!" Stacey says. "Break a leg!"

"Ugh, I kinda wish I could. This seems less and less like a good idea."

She smiles again and says, "I'm sure it'll be great," and Mark thinks, If I can get another one of those smiles at the end of this, then it was definitely a good idea.

He returns to his classroom, dons the purple suit, grabs his guitar, and returns to the cafeteria. He's feeling very close to panic. Certainly some of this is stage fright, but it's also just the fact that the last time he sang for a group of kids, one of them was Janet. Well, there's really no point in thinking like that, so he stops thinking altogether.

He sings, and plays, and the kids go crazy. He can't bear to look at Stacey while he sings these songs, he can't even check her reaction out of the corner of his eye, so he looks directly at the kids. Certainly Kelly and Grace are enjoying the show—they are laughing really hard, and they both have this amazed look on their faces, this I-can't-believe-my-teacher-just-sang-about-the-sticky-booger-blues! look.

Mark's five songs are over in what feels like two minutes, and he takes a bow and exits to the raucous cheers of the kids. He goes to the back of the room for a drink of water, and as he's emerging, he sees Stacey. She's smiling, which is probably a good sign.

"That was great. Kelly was howling."

"Yeah, it was fun."

"So do you teach second grade because it allows you to stay close to your subject matter?"

"Well, I suppose that's as good an explanation as any," he says, though of course the dead sister explanation killed in grad school, and it might be worth pulling it out to see if Stacey would get those googly eyes, but that explanation is a bummer, and he's feeling really good.

"So anyway," he says, "rock_l. Our story begins many years ago, within the hallowed cinder-block walls of the University of Pennsylvania . . ." This is as far as he gets before Frederick's wife, Marisa, approaches, looking red in the face.

"Mr. Norris," she huffs. "I just want you to know that I was really offended by your performance, and you can be sure I will be talking to Ms. Jackson [If you're nasty, Mark thinks] first thing on Monday morning. Your conduct is totally inappropriate for a teacher."

"Uh," Mark says—he was expecting some grumbling, but not right in his face—"I'm sorry you didn't like it."

"Jeez, Marisa, lighten up," Stacey says. "The kids loved it."

Marisa looks shocked and angry and like she is just about to uncork some rather serious words about how Stacey lives, and dresses, but she just walks off instead.

"Well, that was pleasant," Mark says.

"Yeah, she needs a sense of humor implant. I'm surprised she didn't ask for it when she got the tit lift."

"When she got the what?"

"Oh, it's obvious—she's forty-eight years old. Nobody's tits point to the ceiling at forty-eight without some kind of assistance."

"Uh, okay. I see." Tit lift. Who knew? Mark is wondering whether he could somehow keep the topic of breasts on the table here for a while, and then wonders whether that's a good idea, and then he looks to the door and sees Frederick approaching, which couldn't be good news. "Oh, hey, here comes another enraged parent. You know, I think maybe I'd better do a little 'Elvis has left the building' routine here."

"Okay," Stacey says. Is she disappointed? She sounds kind of disappointed. He thinks maybe she's disappointed.

"Talk to you later," Mark says, and scoots out the back.

He all but runs home, still wearing his purple suit. When he gets home, he's really wound up—too hyper to read, too hyper to concentrate on television. So he just thinks about Stacey and fantasizes about asking her out until sleep finally comes.

STACEY

Stacey spends her last forty minutes at the silent auction defending Mark to the four parents who are outraged by his performance. She makes a note to herself to ask him which three he had picked out beforehand as the ones who would be offended and to tell him that he missed one. She hopes he doesn't get in too much trouble. She really enjoyed talking to him, and he was so cute during his show—the songs were gross but actually kind of clever for all that, and very catchy—Stacey found herself humming "Vomit and Snot" all weekend, and Kelly was running around the house yelling about the sticky booger blues, too.

Stacey is having the annual Kids' Creation Station sleepover next month. It's a nightmare of an event, but a terrific revenue generator, and Kelly always enjoys it. Stacey usually likes to provide some kind of entertainment in addition to the art activities, just to give her time to get stuff cleaned up and get ready to unroll the sleeping bags. She wonders if she could hire Mark to play a few numbers. It seems like a good idea. Maybe she'll call him.

She finds herself thinking about him until late that night. The parent grapevine has informed her that he was engaged and his fiancée left him—ran off with either a member of the California legislature or a player for the Golden State Warriors—the grapevine is unclear on this point, and partisans of each story are unwavering in their belief. It's a shame, she thinks. He's such a nice guy, and really great with kids, and smart and kind and so cute. And he's got a great sense of humor—kind of edgy and irreverent—maybe that's what happens when you're pissed off about being pissed on. And, she thinks, as bizarre as this seems, he was actually sexy when he was singing about snot.

She's thinking about him through Saturday, and so, during a slow patch at Kids' Creation Station, she calls Phoebe. She tells her at length about the silent auction, about Mr. Norris and how great his performance was, about the bite-in-the-ass parents who got all prissy about their children hearing the word *booger*, about how funny Mr. Norris was, and how he mysteriously liked rock_l, and should she ask him to perform at the sleepover?

"Sounds like a good idea to me. He is a teacher—I'm sure he could use the money."

"Yeah. Okay. There's something else, too."

"Yeah?"

"Well, I'm just wondering if you know any like really cute young female consultants or dot-com millionaires or something we could fix this guy up with. He's just such a sweet guy, and really cute, and the parent gossip network says he got jilted at the altar or something, and I was just thinking it would be really great if we could find him a nice woman."

"You want me to find him a date."

"Yeah! I just think it would be great for him—I hate the idea of a guy this sweet not having anybody."

"So you want to know if I know anybody who's single and hot who might like to date an elementary school teacher."

"Yeah!"

"Yeah, I'm pretty sure I can think of one."

"Great! Who is it?"

"Stacey, please tell me you're messing with me."

"What do you mean? He's a nice guy!"

"Yeah, and I happen to know somebody who is beautiful and single and has a killer body who happens to live downstairs from me who obviously wants to date an elementary school teacher."

"Me? What are you talking about? Me?" Her? She doesn't want to date him! Does she?

"Jesus, Stace, I love you but you are being so thick I can't believe it. Have you been inhaling paint fumes or something? You spent ten minutes telling me how wonderful this guy is, how great and how cute and how funny he is, and you want me to find a date for him while your lonely horny ass sits home alone with the vibrator?"

"I . . . I . . . I don't know, I'm not ready, I . . ."

"Don't be chickenshit. You obviously like this guy."

"No, I was just . . . uh . . . Jesus. Maybe I do like this guy." Well that's weird. Could that be true? It's just a bizarre feeling. Stacey has just been shut off for so long that she didn't even allow it as a possibility that she might be interested in a guy. And Philippa always had guys coming to her, never really knew what it was like to have a crush on somebody, because it was always just about choosing the best one—okay, actually, it seemed like it was actually about choosing the absolute worst one—from the pack of men chasing her. She never really had time to develop a crush on somebody, because they were always there asking her out. Was this what it felt like to be a guy? And could she possibly ask him out? Philippa had never done that, which is probably a good reason why Stacey should, but she didn't know how. And anyway, what twenty-nine-year-old wants an old bag like her, an old bag with baggage, when there are probably all these women his age and younger, childless and with bodies as tight as Philippa's used to be, who are just begging to be knocked up with that kind, intelligent DNA?

And what kind of Ivy League graduate wants to date somebody who never went to college, who doesn't know what *scatological* means? No, she couldn't possibly ask him out, because she couldn't face the inevitable rejection when he told her that there was a twenty-five-year-old brainiac astrophysicist Playmate of the Year probably blowing him under his desk even now.

But, she supposes, she could get him to come to the sleepover, because she does have a vacant half hour on the schedule, and then she could maybe get some information about the Neurosurgeon/ Supermodel he was inevitably dating, and then it would all be professional, above board, and not humiliating.

She prints up an extra flyer for the Kids' Creation Station sleepover, circles the store's number with a Sharpie, and then writes: "Four parents were actually outraged. Can you name them?—SP"

On Monday she arrives early for pickup and stands nervously at the fence, shifting from foot to foot, reminding herself that she is not asking the guy out, she is simply offering him a professional opportunity. There is no reason to be so nervous.

Still, she finds herself getting that too-much-caffeine adrenaline buzz when Mark—Mr. Norris, she reminds herself—emerges from school at the head of a line of children who follow him, smiling and laughing. He reminds her of the Pied Piper, and while that's not an image she ever would have believed was appealing at all, it somehow makes Mark—Mr. Norris—even more adorable.

When he reaches the fence, she shoves a flyer at him, says, "I have a slot I'd like you to fill, from seven thirty to eight, if you'd like to come and sing some booger songs. I can pay you!"

He does not tear up the flyer and throw it in her face. He does not laugh at her. He smiles, takes the flyer, and says, "That sounds like fun. You have to promise you won't put a letter of reprimand in my personnel file, though."

"Is that what happened?"

"Well, I'm gonna grieve it and it will be removed. It's a gigantic pain in the butt, but apparently they needed to pacify the antibooger brigade."

"I'm sorry."

"Eh, it's okay. Thanks for the job offer! Gotta go," and he's off in the tide of kids and parents.

Stacey leans down and asks Kelly how her day was. "It was fine," Kelly replies, "but you really talk to Mr. Norris too much. You know it embarrasses me."

"I'm sorry, sweetie. But don't you think it would be fun to have him sing at the sleepover?"

"Yeah! But you can't talk to him."

"So he's supposed to come in to my place of business and perform, and I'm not supposed to speak to him."

"Yeah. I'll take care of saying hi and thanks for coming and that stuff."

"Well, we'll see, Kel," Stacey says, and revisits the conversation. Was he really excited about the sleepover? What would she do if he agreed to do it? What would she do if he didn't? And oh my God, did she really tell him she has a slot she wants him to fill?

MARK

Mark sits in his apartment eating a burrito from Purple Cactus and staring at the crumpled yellow piece of paper on his table. Of course he's going to play the sleepover, but that means he's going to have to call her.

What should he make of the Sharpie-scrawled message on the flyer? When Rebekah had used a Sharpie to write him a special message on a party invitation back in another lifetime, it had actually meant something. Is there some code that everybody but him knows about the use of the Sharpie? Stacey runs an art store, so she must have access to all kinds of fancy pens and markers. Why did she choose a stinky permanent one?

Mark finishes his burrito, flips through channels for a few minutes without really seeing what's on. He realizes he has to ask her out. Because what if he goes and she's all friendly like she is after school and then she tells him how she likes him as a friend, she couldn't possibly date Kelly's teacher, she couldn't possibly date somebody who had never been good at sports, she couldn't date such a hideous gnome, but she'd love to be friends and feel powerful by keeping herself close but forever out of reach.

Well, he supposes, it's best to get it over with. He picks up the phone three times, and on the third try, he actually dials the number on the flyer.

"Hello, Kids' Creation Station!" a female voice answers. Is it Stacey? Does she have employees? She must. He can't just act all chummy with somebody who isn't Stacey, because then that person will go running back to her to tell her what a freak he is. What should he say? He decides to go professional.

"Uh, hello, this is Mark Norris calling, is Stacey Phillips available?"

"Yes, Mark Norris, this is Stacey Phillips speaking." Shit. Now he looks like a freak anyway. He decides to keep the exaggerated formality thing going, so it will look like he meant to do this all along.

"Wonderful. Stacey Phillips, I'm calling about your employment offer with regard to the event you are hosting at your place of business next week?" Actually, I'm calling about that slot you want me to fill, he thinks.

"Yes, Mr. Norris. Have you reached a decision?"

"Uh," he didn't rehearse this in some formal way, so he begins to babble. "Yes. Well, this is probably inappropriate for at least three reasons, and of course I am confident in my ability to maintain a solid professional relationship with all members of your family whatever your answer would be, but I find myself in a position— that is to say, I do believe I can do the sleepover, but, uh, well, okay, I just want to . . . uh, would you like to have dinner with me? I mean, just to be clear here, I'm talking about a date, and like I said, I understand why that's inappropriate, but I just think you're delightful and I would really like to go out with you."

Silence. How long till he fills it with something stupid? He holds his breath and counts, one one thousand, two one thousand, three one thousand, four one thousand, five one thousand, and he tells himself that on seven he will apologize profusely, get off the phone, and dig a hole through his kitchen floor into which he can crawl and die.

"Uh, would I like to have dinner with you? Like a date date?"

"Well, that was what I had in mind, but if you're not comfortable . . . ," or if you'd never dream of such a thing, or if you are even now pointing at the phone and making the finger-down-the-throat sign to your smirking co-workers . . .

"No, I'm comfortable. I'd like that. I'd like it a lot."

Whoa. Success, it turns out, is actually just as terrifying as failure. "Hey, that's fantastic! Well, I don't know what your schedule looks like, I mean it's obviously more complicated than mine, which mostly revolves around television, but how's Friday?"

"Well, I've already agreed to watch Phoebe's kid on Friday, and anyway that's movie night with Kelly, which I would be killed in my sleep if I missed. Uh, I, uh, Mark, I really want to do this, but the rest of the week is crazy with getting stuff ready for the sleepover and stuff. I am not trying to blow you off, in case you're wondering. I'm also not regretting saying yes and trying to make it difficult."

"Oh, no, I didn't think that." Yes I did, and thank you for reassuring me, you beautiful goddess of love. "Well, how about, like we could just go ice skating on Sunday afternoon or something." And where are we going to go, Mark wonders. To the Frog Pond on the Boston Common, with its poisonous memories of skating with Rebecca The Corporate Whore, believing she was Becky The Crusading Lawyer?

"I'd like that. That sounds fun. I have a stack of babysitting chits as tall as this house that I can call in. Tell me where and when when you come to the sleepover."

"Okay. Sounds great!" He doesn't want to end the conversation, but he finds he has nothing else to say. "Uh, how many kids are you expecting?"

"Oh, I'm not expecting right now, I've been alone for seven years!"

"No, uh, I, uh . . ."

"I'm joking, I'm joking. I mean, no, I'm really not expecting, but I did know what you meant. Right now it looks like fifteen."

"Okay. I'll plan accordingly." Of course, the size of the audience has nothing to do with Mark's performance, but he hopes it's credible as filler until he thinks of something else to say. He really wishes he'd been a little smoother with that pregnancy joke. And what does *alone* mean? Was she actually telling him that she hadn't gotten laid in seven years? She must have broken one hell of a mirror to have luck like that. But why would she tell him that?

"Great. I'm really looking forward to it."

"Me, too!"

"I mean, Sunday, too. Not just Saturday."

"Yeah. Me, too."

"Okay. Well, I have a four-year-old here who is about to do something really unfortunate with glue, so I gotta run. Okay, sweetie, no, put that down—that's okay, we can clean it up, don't cry—okay, I gotta go."

"Okay. Bye!"

"Bye!" And she's gone. Except that she isn't gone. She won't go away at all. Not when Mark is trying to sleep, trying to watch television, trying to do anything. He feels manic, frantic, like he needs to be doing five things at once, or possibly ten, as long as none of them involves sleeping, because that seems impossible. He reads three pages of a book, watches eight minutes of television on twelve different channels, he plays fragments of nine songs on the guitar. Finally, at two A.M., he goes to bed and sleeps until five.

He needs an extra cup and a half of coffee to feel human the following morning, but the students demand so much of his attention that he is actually able to focus on his work, mostly. He does get distracted from time to time wondering if Kelly knows anything. When his class goes to specials, Mark sits at his desk and begins stuffing the word study homework into every student's homework folder, and he thinks of Stacey.

He briefly considers slipping a note for Stacey into Kelly's homework folder, but he can easily see how she might get freaked out and/or resentful about his using Kelly like that, and it wouldn't be fair to Kelly, and there are twenty reasons not to do it.

So he won't slip it into Kelly's folder. But he will write it. He pulls out a piece of paper and writes:

Stacey,

I've been thinking for a long time that, given the scarcity of mirrors there at the Bars of the Cage (secrets of the Balch faculty: that's what we call that fence that separates parents from teachers on the Centre Street sidewalk! You can decide for yourself which group is the zoo patrons. But I digress), you probably don't have any idea that your smile lights up the entire sidewalk. It's practically twilight by 3:30, and of course it's freezing cold, but it always feels bright and warm out there when I see you.

Mark

He reads it seventeen times until his class returns from specials, at which point he puts it in a Boston Public Schools envelope, writes "Stacey Phillips" on the front, and sticks it in his pocket. He will just carry it out there, of course. He won't actually give it to her. It's far too corny, it's tipping his hand, it's creepy, and, worst of all, it reveals him to be a nice guy, the kind that finishes last, the kind with an unused engagement ring quietly mocking him from the top of his dresser every morning.

As he walks the kids out, Grace says something to him, and he barely hears. Stacey is at the fence, illuminating the sidewalk as always, and Mark catches her eye. He can't wave without dropping Grace's hand and Keianna's hand, so he gives this nod that he is sure looks incredibly dorky.

For some reason it takes an hour and a half to walk to the Bars of the Cage, and when he finally arrives his hand whips back to his butt pocket, pulls out the Boston Public Schools envelope, and hands it to Stacey. "Important communication from your child's teacher," he says, and smiles, and flees down the sidewalk with his charges.

He looks back over the sea of small people and sees Stacey still standing there, reading.

STACEY

Stacey is so wired after Mark calls and asks her out that she has a hard time concentrating on or remembering anything at all, including the appointment with Karen Haver to get her official stamp of approval as the worst mother ever. She finds a little slip of paper with the appointment scrawled on it under the passenger seat of her car while she's looking for some gum that she could swear she bought at 7-Eleven today, though maybe that was yesterday, or last week.

She curses herself for an idiot, calls Kids' Creation Station, and begs her new assistant, Katerina (the hot one, the one who will surely steal Mark away the second he walks in the door), to stay for an extra couple of hours, and then steels herself for the tantrum from Kelly when school gets out.

She smiles at Mark as he emerges with the walkers, and he smiles and waves, and her heart is pounding and her brain is wiped clean until she gets back into the car with Kelly.

"So, Kel-Bel, guess what we get to do today?"

"Something crappy. I can just tell by the way you're talking."

"We get to go see Karen Haver and talk about how we can be

better with each other!" Stacey holds her breath and waits for the explosion that doesn't come.

"Great. She's just gonna say I'm a bad kid."

"You don't know that. She might say I'm a bad mom."

"You're not a bad mom. You're the best mom."

"Thank you, sweetie. You know, I was thinking it would be funny if Karen Haver's middle initial was B, and then she would be Karen B. Haver. Like Karen Behavior? Caring Behavior?" A glance in the rearview mirror shows Kelly suppressing a smile and trying to stay annoyed.

"You're corny."

Karen Behavior does not pronounce Stacey the worst mom in the world. She listens carefully to both of them as they talk about what happens at home, which they substantially agree on—sometimes Kelly just gets so mad and she doesn't know why. Stacey cries, and Kelly cries, and Karen Behavior is kind and calm through the whole thing, and she does not reproach Stacey for her awful parenting that caused all this, though Stacey is sure she must be thinking this.

When it's almost time to stop, Karen Behavior asks them both if they ever have any apart time at home.

"When she's in trouble," Stacey says.

"Well," Karen Behavior says, "I can see that you two are very, very close. And sometimes it's good to be close, like it's very cozy, right?" She looks at Kelly and Kelly doesn't nod. "But sometimes when you are really close, like if somebody comes and gives you a hug that's really, really tight—"

"Like Diego does in the morning sometimes, right, Kel?" Stacey offers. Kelly glares.

"It can kind of hurt, right?" Karen Behavior continues. "It's too close?"

"Yeah," Stacey says and looks at Kelly. Kelly doesn't say anything.

"So it might be helpful for both of you to have a space where you can go if it starts to feel like a hug that's too tight. Not when anybody's been bad, but just when you think you might get too mad. It doesn't have to be a punishment to be by yourself."

"What do you think, Kelster?" Stacey says.

"I think it would be a lot easier to have a place to go to be alone if we had a real house to live in instead of living in Aunt Phoebe's basement."

Stacey gets angry, feels the everything-I-do-for-you speech welling up inside her, and with difficulty she forces it down and says, "Yeah. It would. Soon, sweetie. I promise."

Karen Behavior says thank you and come back next month, and while she didn't say Stacey was a bad parent, neither did she offer any magical solution. Still, for the first time she can remember, Stacey feels slightly hopeful about Kelly's tantrums—just the fact that Karen Behavior didn't gasp with horror and suggest that one or both of them needed to be hospitalized makes her feel like maybe there's some hope.

Sleepover night finally arrives. Every other sleepover night, Stacey has been nervous and cranky, worried that something horrible would happen, unhappy about the prospect of not getting very much sleep, concerned about getting all the logistics right. Today she is completely confident in her logistical ability and unconcerned about not sleeping, since she's been too excited since Mark asked her out to sleep much anyway.

But she is horrified about her body, her store, and herself. Once Kelly is off to school, Stacey comes home to shower and get ready and worry. She always opens Kids' Creation Station late on sleepover days, since she's going to be putting in a full night of work, so she has all day to get ready.

After the shower, she takes a long look at herself in the mirror. Her hair is good—short and stylish—but she wonders if it's time to lose the platinum-blond dye job and go for pink or magenta or something. Maybe magenta. Pink is too young. Her breasts remain fantastic, though now that she looks at them carefully, they do appear to have begun their inevitable, unstoppable march to her waist. She quickly puts on a bra and puts them in their place. Her stomach is not as flat as it once was, but still a damn sight flatter than the stomachs of all the Newton and Brookline moms who come in with their six-year-olds. But those moms are forty-seven, and anyway, those aren't her competition. How does she compare to the twenty-eight-year-olds? And will Mark even look at her with hot Katerina, who is from BU but certainly not Butt Ugly, right there? And speaking of butts . . . no, she can't even look. She puts clothes on and begins applying her makeup. Jesus Christ, she has wrinkles by her eyes, small now, but they'll be the Grand Canyon in just a couple of years.

She's a mess, and for the first time in years she wishes that just a little bit of Philippa's confidence was left. Philippa never would have doubted herself or her attractiveness like this. But then again, for Philippa, the stakes were always incredibly low. She had never really aspired to be friends with a guy before, she'd never wanted so much from a guy in her short, pathetic life. She never expected a guy to understand her, she never expected any kind of meaningful companionship from a guy, she never wanted a father for her child.

Jesus, she chides herself, you will terrify this man, you will send him screaming for the exits if you reveal just how much you need, how much you want. She hates it.

She feels her insecurity rising up again, so she goes over to her bedside table, opens the drawer, and pulls out the Boston Public Schools envelope with her name on the front. She reads the note again and smiles. She doesn't have to be twenty-five, she doesn't have to be Philippa, because Stacey's smile lights up the sidewalk. So there.

Eventually she picks Kelly up from school, with her heart in her throat. She'd given Mark a little Thank You card that said, "Thank you for your note. That was the sweetest, kindest thing anyone has ever said to me. Or written to me. You know what I mean."

Will he have another note for her? He walks out at the head of the kids, and she sees him scanning the fence, looking for her. She wants to jump up and wave, but she keeps her cool and just gives him a smile. He approaches the fence, smiles, and hands her an envelope.

"What is that, Mom?" Kelly asks. "Why are you always passing notes?"

"It's, uh, it's Parent Council stuff, Kel," Stacey says, hoping Kelly will buy it, that she won't say, *You are a fraud, Mother. You've never been to a Parent Council meeting in your life.* She doesn't say it, whatever she might be thinking.

Stacey suddenly feels dread. This is crazy—she can't date Kelly's teacher. What is Kelly going to say? Will she make it impossible? Or, worse yet, will she get too attached too quickly, believe she's found a dad at last only to have her heart broken when Mark tires of Stacey and finds somebody his own age? What was he thinking asking her out? Doesn't he know how dangerous it is?

She opens the note as she and Kelly walk to the car. It contains a flyer printed on red paper. "Mark Norris," it says in big, balloony letters. Below, in smaller type, it says, "Disgusting songs for children," and below that, his phone number and e-mail address. He's written in Sharpie on the flyer, "Performing tonight at Kids' Creation Station! I'm very nervous because I have a big crush on the owner.—MN."

Kelly talks about her day in the backseat while Stacey daydreams all the way over to Kids' Creation Station. Stacey tries to imagine what Mark might think as he drives up. Nondescript glass-and-cinder-block box, typical strip-mall architecture. Plaster corner confronts her as soon as she walks in, and she's suddenly aware of how tacky everything there is—the unicorns, the big-eyed puppies, the World Wrestling Entertainment logo. She wants to put up a sign: *I know how tacky this stuff is, but it puts a roof over my head and Kelly's head, and anytime kids are being creative, it's a good thing, even if they are putting sparkly orange paint on the wrestling logo.*

She hates the hideous squares of blue industrial carpet that cover the floor. They are anything but funky, but you can spill anything on them, and they will take the abuse that dozens of little kids tramping around every day dish out. Maybe he won't notice the horrible carpet. The ceramics corner is pretty inoffensive— mugs and bowls, mostly, and stuff done by kids drying on the shelf, which looks good . . . the beading table is fine, if covered in glue . . . it's really just the plaster that's tacky. Well, that and the carpet, but that's really more utilitarian than tacky. She has to remember to say something about the plaster.

The time drags by, and Stacey tidies up, checks the computer for the guest list, checks the permission slip file, calls the caterer, and, with Kelly's help, hangs the decorations. She tries not to think about the fact that Mark is going to be here, tries desperately to focus on the fact that she is a responsible businesswoman with a very important event to manage tonight. "Professional, professional," she says to herself, and tries to push from her mind the thoughts of taking Mark into her office and making out while the kids fend for themselves making beaded necklaces and key chains. Just one kiss, she thinks, I'll know after one kiss, I won't need to stick my tongue down his throat, though I want to, I just want one kiss to know if it's right, I swear to God I'll know after one kiss.

Jesus, who is this woman with the Sleeping Beauty fantasy, and what happened to the comfortable, if somewhat tight, shell she used to have?

The sleepover participants begin to trickle in, and Kelly acts as the mistress of ceremonies for the kids: "Okay, now you can put your sleeping bag over here. We'll be having snack in just a bit. What's your favorite activity here?" and Stacey has one of those so-proud-of-my-kid-I-think-I-might-explode moments.

She doesn't explode, which is good, because she needs to greet, joke with, and reassure the parents. Most of the kids here tonight are regulars, and Stacey knows their parents by their first names, but there are two newcomers—an Asian girl with two white moms and a tiny, black-haired white boy. The girl attaches herself to Kelly and appears completely content, barely noticing when her moms come to say good-bye after ten minutes of trying to burden Stacey with their irrational worries and giving her both cell phone numbers *again*. The little boy's mom is dressed in heels and expensive jeans, with just a tad too much jewelry and way too much makeup—she reminds Stacey of the baseball wives Philippa saw when she was dating Teddy, and Stacey wonders briefly if she's looking at some alternate-world version of herself if she'd married Teddy. Baseball Wife flees, giving her son a quick peck on the top of his head, and the kid starts to cry almost as soon as his mother leaves. Stacey leans down to give him a hug, and he buries his face in her breasts and cries. Suddenly Stacey hears Camille's voice whispering in her ear: "Another future tit man. Just remember, he's going to be asking Kelly out in six years."

Stacey looks up at Camille, smiles, and says, "Don't you have some personal training to do?" Camille smiles, waves, kisses her kids good-bye, and departs. "Kelly!" Stacey calls out.

Kelly runs over with Stephanie still attached to her.

"Yeah?"

"I think James here is feeling a little homesick. Do you want to show him the SpongeBob stuff? D'you like SpongeBob, James?" James looks up and nods, and Kelly reaches out and takes his hand and leads him over to the wall of plaster crap, where he stares, wide-eyed, as Kelly describes how he can paint his own Sponge-Bob, or, if he'd prefer, Patrick or Sandy.

"I like Sandy!" Stephanie calls out, while James whispers that he likes Patrick.

Stacey reflects that she should really pay Kelly something for this, since she's far more help than Katerina, who's not even here yet.

Five minutes later Katerina arrives, and Stacey wishes she'd stayed home. She's wearing her BU sweatshirt, and sweatpants, so far so good, but her hair is really long and naturally blond, and it's pouring out like honey from the back of a baseball cap that says JUICY on the front. She's got the waistband of her sweatpants rolled down, which is a fashion Stacey can't understand, except that it seems to say *I'm half undressed already and simply waiting for you to finish the job,* and a hot pink thong sticking up at the back, which really makes no sense for a kids' party unless she's trying to, for example, steal Stacey's date.

Still, given how Stacey dresses in here, it's not like she can tell the kid to go home and change, and with fifteen kids here, she's definitely going to need Katerina's help, but God—does she have to be so hot? This is undoubtedly her frumpy casual wear, and yet she's just oozing sex, like she couldn't bother to put any real clothes on because some dorm stud spent all day wearing her out.

Well, there are kids to entertain, and after huddling with Katerina and reminding herself that the kid is actually very sweet and the best assistant she's ever had, and she'd be useless with her eyes clawed out, Stacey gets down to the business of beading, painting, and snacking, and before she knows it, it's seven fifteen, and where the hell is Mark?

He arrives at seven twenty, dressed in his purple suit and carrying a guitar case. He opens the door, scans the room, and lights up when he catches Stacey's eye. She smiles right back, and asks herself if he could have possibly noticed Katerina, who is crouching down next to Camille's son over at the beading table. Probably not. Stacey begins to walk toward him, but Kelly shoots her a dirty look and waves her off, mouthing *No,* and walks up to Mark.

"Hello, Mr. Norris," Kelly says.

"Hi, Kelly. You know, since we're out of school, and I am at least a temporary employee of S&K Phillips, LLC, and since you are K Phillips, you can call me Mark."

Kelly looks kind of stunned at this. It's a jolt to her worldview.

Get ready, kid, Stacey thinks. If things go well, more jolts are on the way. But, being the hostess with the mostest, Kelly quickly recovers and says, "Okay, Mr. uh Mark. Would you like to see where you'll be performing?"

"That sounds wonderful."

"Great. Follow me!" and she leads him over to the little riser that the kiln sits on. NEVER ON DURING BUSINESS HOURS, the sticker that Stacey made screams from the side of the kiln.

"Cool sticker. I might need one of those for my guitar," Mark says, and smiles over at Stacey, and she hopes the look he gives her actually means, *Your kid is a complete delight, and I am happy to see you, and who is the hag-like twenty-year-old over there?* because that is what Stacey wants it to mean.

Stacey and Katerina corral the kids, and they all sit on little mats on the floor and Mark begins to play. Once again Stacey is baffled by the fact that a guy in a purple suit singing about mucus can seem at all sexy, but he has the kids eating out of his hands, and he even leads them in a lusty sing-along version of "Vomit and Snot." His time is up at eight. He looks at Stacey and says, "I can stop or keep going," and Stacey checks her clipboard. She has to get at least one more project done tonight, because the parents are expecting four projects to come home, but she was going to try to keep them up till nine thirty anyway just to make sure they were all good and tired and wouldn't wake up wanting their mommies at two thirty in the morning, so she calls out, "Fifteen minutes," and Mark gives them fifteen more minutes, though he appears to be out of vomit songs, so he does Beatles covers, which Stacey thinks is a good choice, because he's leaving the kids' brains stuffed with catchy songs that probably won't enrage their parents, and he's also calming them down from all the scatology, which is a word Stacey has been looking for an excuse to use.

Finally he finishes, and Stacey and Katerina get the kids started on project number four, making sure that one through three are all in the boxes labeled with the kids' names, and Mark talks to Kelly and some other kids. By the time the kids are all set up, Mark has five kids completely enthralled as he pretends to pick out a piece of plaster. "So this is Sandy?" he asks James as he picks up a plaster Patrick, and James and three other kids shout "No!"

"Sandy Squirrel!" James says, laughing. "Get it? Sssssssandy is a Sssssquirrel."

"I see," Mark replies. "So Pppppppatrick is a . . . pppppp-poooooop?" James laughs so hard he has tears coming out of his eyes. Stacey can't believe this is the same wimpy little kid who buried his face in her chest just a couple of hours ago.

Mark looks over at Stacey and says to the kids, "Well, I think maybe I'll stick with SpongeBob. You guys get started, and I'll be back in a second," and he starts walking over to her.

She walks toward him, only to find Kelly in her path. "Mom!" Kelly stage-whispers. "No! You said I could do all the talking with Mark!"

Stacey leans down and says, "No, Kel, you said that. And only S Phillips can sign the checks for S&K Phillips, LLC, so if I'm going to pay our entertainer for tonight, I need to take him to the office [and maybe, she thinks, he could take me in the office] and write him a check."

Kelly's eyes are suddenly little smoldering coals of rage. "You could mail him a check," she spits out.

"Yeah, but I don't want to. Now you need to let me get by."

"Fine!" Kelly whispers, and stomps away to one of the painting easels. Now if you are able to contain yourself here, Stacey thinks, if you can be mad at me here without calling me names and break-ing stuff, why the hell can't you do that at home? Why won't you do it at home?

She goes up to Mark and says, "Hey, that was great."

"Thanks," he says, and smiles. He's blushing. How cute is that?

"So if you want to follow me back to the office, I can cut you a check."

"Uh, well, I'm not in any hurry to get pa . . . oh. Yeah, why don't you cut me a check."

"Great. Let me just tell Katerina that she's in charge for a few minutes." She scans his face, looking for Katerina lust there. She doesn't see any. He doesn't even take the opening she's provided by speaking her name to look over at her. He's just looking at Stacey, or else at his shoes.

"Kat, I'm just going back to the office for a minute," Stacey says.

Katerina barely looks up from the gem finding she is assisting with and says, "Okay."

She trudges through the two feet of molasses that suddenly cover the floor, opens the door that suddenly weighs three hundred pounds, and finds herself in her tiny office. She looks at it with what she believes are Mark's eyes: desk a complete mess, papers everywhere, out-of-date computer, stupid screensaver that Kelly picked. She turns around to apologize for the condition of the office and suddenly finds Mark kissing her.

And, just as suddenly, she finds herself kissing back. He's kissing her slowly, but eagerly, his mouth is saying he's very hungry but also very patient, and Stacey barely has time to think that she just knows that means he's going to be good in bed before the rest of her falls away and she is nothing but lips and a tongue and a sudden surge of moist heat.

MARK

        Mark watches in amazement as this dork in a purple suit kisses an incredibly beautiful, sexy woman. You think too goddamn much, he tells himself, and before he knows it, his right hand is traveling down her back, his left hand is sliding up from her hip to her breast, and he pulls away and whispers, "Oh my God, I've been dreaming of this since the first time I saw you."

Stacey smiles, and Mark finds he wants to stand here and just soak in that smile, but he also has to kiss her again or he will go completely insane. They kiss again, and he wants all of her, he wants to touch her everywhere, to lick her everywhere, he doesn't just want to fuck her right now (though he most certainly does want that, and he feels certain he could smash cinder blocks with his penis if, for some reason, he were called on to do so), he wants his whole body inside of her whole body, he wants to touch every inch of her skin from the inside.

Stacey gives a soft moan, and Mark realizes that in two more seconds he's probably going to have to tear her clothes off, and that would be a terrible idea with fifteen kids outside and would almost certainly result in the loss of Stacey's livelihood, and as much as he wants her, he wants to do this right, to be proud of it, to feel like it's his heart and not his dick that's leading him into this.

He pulls away. "Oh, wow. Oh, okay, uh, I'm getting to the point where I don't trust my brain to keep working, and right now it's telling me that there are fifteen children right on the other side of this door, and I think I probably should listen."

Stacey smiles. "You're right. You're a fantastic kisser. Really. Better than I dared hope."

Mark doesn't know what he did, but he likes the compliment. "And you are the sexiest woman on the face of the earth."

"Mmmm." She takes a deep breath, blows it out, and says, "Okay, I've got the ledger here, so let me just cut you a check, and then I guess you don't have to hang around for late-night hijinx with the six-year-olds . . ."

"But could I?"

"What do you mean?"

"I mean, could I stay? I have my eye on a plaster SpongeBob," he says, smiling.

"You know, I do know how tacky the plaster stuff is. I really do. It's just that—"

"I really don't care about that. I just don't want to leave. I've spent so many nights by myself that I'm not really in any rush to go spend another one."

Stacey smiles. "Great. I'd like it if you'd stay."

"Great."

"Okay, we're about to be missed, so let's get out there."

"All right. Can you direct me to the bathroom?"

She does, and they emerge from the office, and Mark is convinced that all the kids and the college bimbo will be pointing and staring, that Kelly Phillips will point an accusing finger and say, *You were kissing!* but nobody seems to notice, except the BU girl does kind of look at them, and Mark can feel himself starting to blush. What does she know? Was this a plan she was in on?

Mark goes to the bathroom and undergoes the slow and difficult process of trying to pee with an erection. Eventually he manages, and the process calms his groin down enough that he thinks
he can be in the company of children without scandalizing everyone. He just has to not think about her mouth . . .

He makes himself return to the plaster area, where he grabs a
SpongeBob off the shelf. All the kids have brushes and paint, but
Mark can't see immediately where to get them. He stops Kelly as
she is walking by. "Uh, excuse me, K Phillips, can you tell me where
to find brushes and paint?"

Kelly smiles. "Sure Mr., uh, Mark." It appears that his out-of-
school name to Kelly is going to be Mr. Uh Mark. How long will
she call him that? How weird is this going to be? What the hell is he
doing? This is crazy—the stakes are way too high. He's already broken, and one more disappointment might just push him over the
edge—if he gets dumped, he might as well go buy some Dungeons
and Dragons supplies, start eating prodigiously, and develop
strong opinions about which is his favorite X-Man, because he's
going on an express train back to seventh grade, where "I take the
Elfin Maiden to the room above the tavern, and I'm plus three to
hit, if you know what I mean" was the closest he got to a girl, where
Jean Grey was his favorite X-Man because she was so hot and so incredibly powerful, though he always thought it would be interesting to see what you could do with Rogue and don't get him started
about Kitty Pryde.

And even if he stays out of seventh grade, then there is still the
problem of Kelly. If the stakes were high for him, what would they
be like with Kelly? Would he ruin school for her? Would she hate
him for intruding into the cozy little world she shared with her
mom?

What the hell is he doing? This is crazy! His stomach feels sour
as dread bubbles up inside him. He looks up from SpongeBob,
scans the room, and finds Stacey. She smiles at him, and he realizes
she is his favorite X-Man, that her mutant power is the smile that

has the power to dispel doubt, that makes him feel an absolute certainty that he is doing the right thing.

The next hour goes incredibly slowly. All he wants in the world is to be next to Stacey, to be kissing her, to be talking to her, to tell her everything. He feels the infatuation high that is scarily like the infatuation high he used to feel before a school dance or a party where some girl he liked was going to be there, except this girl likes him, too, thinks he's a fantastic kisser, and makes all those girls look like hideous trolls.

Once Mark has painted his SpongeBob, he and James, who is apparently his new best friend, go over to the beading table. He makes a little bead bracelet with the letter beads that says s&k PHILLIPS LLC and gives it to Kelly, because he knows how proud she is of that, because she's mentioned it three times at Share Time.

"Thanks, Uh Mark," she says, and smiles, and then returns to being a tiny adult.

Finally Stacey tells everybody to get their sleeping bags, and Mark helps James get his brand-new EMS sleeping bag out of the stuff sack and unrolled, and then he helps a couple of other kids, and then Stacey says it's time to read a bedtime story.

Kelly goes up and whispers in Stacey's ear, and Stacey says, "Well, apparently we have someone here who is a more skilled reader than I am, so, Mark, perhaps you'd like to do the honors?"

"Sure," he says, and heads up next to the kiln. Stacey smiles, and their fingers touch as he takes the book from her hand, and her hand is so soft . . .

Mark reads *Miss Nelson Is Missing!*, then *Guess How Much I Love You* and *Goodnight Moon*, which he's sure Kelly at least thinks is babyish, but which is surely one of the most powerful narcotics on the planet. Six of fifteen kids are asleep by the end, and even Mark, who feels so hyper he could run a marathon (or, he thinks, engage in some other kind of aerobic activity that required strength and stamina . . .), begins to feel a little edge of fatigue.

Mark doesn't have a sleeping bag. Kelly brings him one. "We always keep a few extras for the sleepover," she says. "You can find a space right over *there*." She points to an unused patch of floor next to the painting easels and completely on the other side of the store from where Stacey is unrolling her sleeping bag with Kelly right next to her.

Mark does as he's told and lies in the dark for what seems like hours. When can he go to her? Can he go to her? Can they sneak into the office? Every time he thinks it's safe to move, he hears a kid turning over, or the toilet flushing, or a cough, or something that lets him know not everybody's asleep yet.

Finally, after an excruciating eternity in the semi-darkness (the lights in the strip mall's parking lot apparently stay on all night, so the room has a faint, sickly orange glow), Mark decides he needs to get up. Stacey must be asleep by now. He'll just head over to the checkout and look for a pen and a piece of paper, and maybe he can try to get enough light from the orange parking lot lights to write something for Stacey, though he really has no idea what he wants to say.

He reaches the Formica counter that holds the cash register and begins fumbling around looking for something to write with. He hears movement and curses himself—she'll certainly be pissed if he's woken up a kid who's going to demand attention, and he'll be pissed if he's woken up James, because then he'll be on duty to comfort him.

He looks out at the floor and sees somebody standing up. It's an adult . . . it's Stacey. She tiptoes through the sleeping children toward the counter.

"What, are you trying to rob me while everybody's asleep?" she whispers right in his ear, and the feeling of her breath in his ear makes him really want to maul her.

"No," he whispers right into her ear, and he can't resist because her earlobe is right there, so he gives it a quick, gentle bite, which provokes an "mmmmm" out of Stacey, which in turn causes the return of the raging erection, and he continues, "Uh, I was just looking for a pen. I thought you were asleep. I was gonna write you a note."

"Okay," she says, and turns on the flashlight she is holding. She hands him a clipboard, a piece of paper, and an official Kids' Creation Station pen. "Kel's a very light sleeper, so writing is probably a better idea than whispering." She backs up to the wall behind the counter, slides down, and pats the carpet next to her. "Sit. Write."

Mark sits down, back against the wall, knees up, and takes the clipboard. He can feel the entire right side of Stacey's body against the entire left side of his body, and she feels warm and soft, and this sensation completely wipes his mind clean. He can't remember why he wanted to write her a note or what he wanted to say—it was just that he couldn't stand lying there thinking about her anymore. But now she's right here, and writing her a note seems absurd. He stares at the clipboard, illuminated by the flashlight in Stacey's hand, for a minute, and then Stacey hands him the flashlight and takes the clipboard.

So what do you want to write? she writes, and passes it back to him.

I forgot. I don't want to write anything. I just want to kiss you.

Me, too, but your brain is correct that there are too many kids here for that. So tell me a story. Tell me how it is that a man likes rock_l.

It's a long story. It might take a while to write it.

Well, we have all night. Don't worry, I'll find a way to entertain myself while you write . . .

Mark takes the clipboard back and debates briefly where he should start this story. Should he start with the guitar? With "My Left One"? Or with crying about Janet in the hallway and having Raquel ask if he wanted to kiss her? His thought process is impaired by the fact that Stacey is running her fingers through his hair, down his neck, and pinching his nipple while he tries to write.

No fair! he writes.

She takes the clipboard, and he returns to biting her earlobe. *Toughen up,* she writes. *You can take it.*

Okay, he writes. *You know the song "My Left One," right? Where she sings about the horrible thing she did to some guy, and how she'd give her left one not to do what she did, and how she left him, he's her left one?*

Yeah.

Jesus Christ, she's doing that thing to his nipple again. He turns his head and gives her a quick kiss, and she kisses him back, and he pulls away. *That's me,* he writes. *We dated for two years in college. And then she went to LA without me and wrote a number one hit single about me. Which wasn't true, I hasten to add, and she's pretty clear about that in her song "That Stupid Girl." But so, yeah, there you have it, I am the famous Two Minute Man. I always used to wonder when I heard a breakup song about who the poor losers were who had that song written about them. And then I became one.*

STACEY

Stacey reads what Mark has written, and her stomach turns over. This is something they have in common that almost nobody else can understand. As if the kiss weren't enough of a thunderbolt, this pretty much confirms it. This is the right thing, this is the right guy, at long last she's made a choice that isn't incredibly stupid, Stacey has saved her virginity for somebody who deserves it.

But.

But she can't tell him, Me too, me too, I was also the subject of a breakup song that was a number one hit single, and I even had my face on the cover of a tabloid, boy do I ever know what you went through. Except I could leave the country, and you had to stay. And I can't tell you.

But she has to tell him. She does have an urge to flee, to write the whole thing off, to say forget it, because her whole life is a house of cards that is going to come tumbling down. But then he's doing that thing to her ear, and he has a hand on her thigh, and the idea of running away is just completely absurd.

He writes some more—about how the song ruined his chances

for a few years, about how his fiancée broke his heart, and all she wants to do is pour her heart right back out to him, but she can't do that here and now, and especially not on a clipboard, so when Mark writes, *I'm sorry. I guess I'm kind of monopolizing the "conversation." What about you?*

Stacey takes the clipboard, and how the hell is she supposed to write anything, to think anything when he is planting those soft kisses on her neck? How is she supposed to get through till morning, till whenever they can actually be alone?

I have a long and tragic story. I swear I will tell you the whole thing, the whole uncensored version, but I can't do that tonight. Okay?

Mark takes the clipboard. *It's okay. Whatever you want to tell me whenever you want to tell me is fine. The only thing you need to tell me now is if you don't really feel like Stacey is who you are, and you have to go far away and be somebody else.*

No, Stacey thinks. I did that already. But what she writes is *I promise you that is not going to happen. But you'd probably take off way before I got a chance anyway.*

Why would you say that? Are you really a man?

Stacey stifles a giggle. *No, but I'm older than you, and I have a kid who's not yours, and I'm damaged.*

So am I. I need . . . I obviously don't know your whole story, but part of what I like about you is that you seem so alive despite whatever horrible thing has happened to you. I feel much older than I am, and I need—I don't want somebody who doesn't understand how awful life can be.

Well, I certainly know about that. And suddenly she needs to kiss him, so she leans over and they kiss for a long, long time, until Mark finally breaks away and grabs the clipboard.

New topic, he writes. Stacey nods, and then watches as Mark writes *Tell me if this is too much information, but I feel like I am going to go completely insane if I don't get to go down on you. Any idea when that can happen?*

She looks at him. Is he serious? She couldn't possibly have lucked out this much. Could she? She stares at him. She shines the flashlight on his face. He's blushing.

I'm really sorry, he writes. *It's late, and my brain is not* but Stacey grabs the clipboard away and whispers in his ear, "Soon."

Mark and Stacey return to their respective sleeping bags at five and pretend to sleep, and at six the kids start waking up. Mark goes next door to the Dunkin' Donuts and picks up Stacey's order, which both she and Katerina appreciate tremendously, because Jean-Jacques who manages the Dunkin' Donuts is a creepy horn-dog who hits on both of them relentlessly whenever they go in there, so it's very nice to have a man go in there to pick up the doughnuts without any creepy looks or comments.

Mark returns with the doughnuts and says quietly to Stacey and Katerina, "I'm by no means sure about this, but I think that guy was hitting on me," and they laugh hysterically while Mark looks at them trying to figure out what the joke is.

"I . . . uh, well, I guess ol' Jean-Jacques is an omnivore," Stacey says.

While the kids are being picked up, Stacey summons Mark to the office again and kisses him quickly. "Call me early and often," she says.

Mark smiles and says, "I will."

When they emerge from the office, Kelly is standing there looking impatient. "I thought you cut him a check last night," she says, and Stacey has a moment of panic, but Kelly isn't suspicious, just annoyed. "Can we *please* go home now? I really want to watch TV," she says.

Mark smiles, looks at her, and leaves. Stacey actually sighs aloud, like she is so dainty she needs to go to her fainting couch, and Kelly says, "What's wrong, Mom?"

"Just tired, sweetie. I had a hard time falling asleep last night."

"Not me. I slept like a rock!"

"That's good. You were a big help last night, Kel, I was really proud of you."

"Does that mean I can have ice cream today?"

"Yes. If you let me nap." What the hell, doughnuts for breakfast, ice cream for lunch. Stacey isn't going to be winning any mother of the year awards for today, but she really, really doesn't care.

MARK

Mark stands in front of the mirror in what he calls his "fashion boy clothes"—the smartest of his smart casual wear. It still doesn't feel real: the seventh-grade kid with the level-ten Chaotic Good Elven Thief playing dress-up because he actually has a date with a beautiful woman. And a *second* date at that, after their beautiful, white-frosted ice-skating date, which seemed like it was over before it even began because Stacey had to pick Kelly up.

What feels especially unreal is the fact that he's been behaving so unlike himself—asking her out, writing her notes about her smile, kissing her first, telling her that he wanted to go down on her before they'd even had a real date. Jesus, did he really do that? Yes, and, shockingly, it worked out fine. He wishes he could say that it's just a case of willpower that he made a decision to stop being so passive with women that trumped his natural shyness, the insecurity that bloomed in seventh grade and flourished under rock_l and Rebecca's tender care, but that doesn't appear to be the reason for his sudden attack of boldness.

Part of it is certainly that he just feels so powerfully that Stacey is a kindred spirit, that she understands, that she accepts him, that she's on his wavelength in a way nobody has been since the first few months with rock_l. But even this is incomplete and too noble. The other part of it is just that he wants her more than he's ever wanted anyone or anything ever before. His pathetic longing for Becky was a ripple compared with the tsunami of desire that washes over him and drowns his caution, his insecurity, and all of his horrible memories every time he sees Stacey.

He just doesn't know who he is anymore. Was this guy always inside him? How would seventh grade, eighth grade, hell, his whole life have been different if he'd known he could be this confident? What kind of life would he have had?

More important, though, what kind of life is he going to have? He is having dinner at Stacey's tonight, with Kelly in attendance, which makes him nervous—he figures this must be the single-mom version of meeting the parents. Except he already knows and adores Kelly, which will hopefully make it easier, except that it's one thing to be her teacher, and it's quite another to be trying to step into the shoes of her Sainted Dead Dad. And Stacey told him that Kelly's reaction to the whole "I'm dating your teacher, sweetie" talk had started at anger and moved to wondering if he was going to be her dad. This freaked him out, and him freaking out freaked Stacey out, and then he had to spend fifteen minutes on the phone telling Stacey that yes, she should have told him that, it's important for him to know.

Ugh. He's nervous. And he doesn't know what to bring—you don't show up at the home of somebody who doesn't drink with a bottle of wine. And you also don't get to have a quick glass of wine before dinner to calm your nerves. Well, when all else fails, try pie. He goes to the bakery and gets an apple pie that looks incredible.

He considers whether he should make a joke about the pie he's still waiting to eat when he presents the pie, but he decides that might be too cheesy. It's only been six days since the sleepover, and he realizes that they are still well within anyone's definition of *soon,* but he feels like he's lived three weeks since then. And in a way, he has: he and Stacey have been talking from nine till midnight every night, and once he's done talking to her he's usually too horny and excited to sleep, so it's usually at least one before he falls asleep. He can't sustain this schedule and continue to be a teacher, but for now it feels great—despite the lack of sleep, he's not exhausted. He wakes up every day feeling as hyper as the day before. He knows there's a crash coming, but it's not here yet.

He reaches the big Victorian house where Stacey and Kelly live and, as instructed, he goes around to the side door. He's about to ring the bell when Stacey appears and, without a word, begins kissing him hungrily. They kiss in silence for a minute and a half, and Mark is very unhappy that he's holding a pie, because his hands have far more interesting ideas about where they'd like to be, but they're stuck.

Finally Stacey pulls away and Mark exhales. "Whoa. Wow," he says. "Wow." The language center of his brain seems to have shut down, and he's only capable of making monosyllables.

"I had to sneak out and kiss you, because Kelly's a little edgy on that point, and I knew there was no way I was going to be able to stand to be near you and not kiss you all night."

"Wow."

"Yeah. You really are a spectacular kisser, you know."

"Uh, you, too."

"Hmm . . . ," she says, "I guess you were serious about liking to eat pie, huh?"

He looks down at the apple pie and realizes he probably could have made the joke. Oh well.

"Listen. In one week, Kelly has a sleepover. Can you wait a week?"

Can he? Of course, it's been months, of course he can wait a week. And yet he feels sure that his brain might explode if he has to wait a week.

"Well, it's gonna be hard."

"I'm counting on it," she says, and suddenly her hand is finding evidence that it is, in fact, hard. There's nothing else to do with a kid inside and an apple pie in his hand except kiss her really hard, so he does, and ten years later, the kiss ends.

"Okay," Mark says, "I need a cold shower or something."

"No can do. We're just going to have to compose ourselves. I'm going to go inside, you stand out here until things calm down and then ring the bell. Kelly is adamant that she's going to answer when you get here."

"Uh, okay," he says, and then Stacey is gone. Mark stands on the stoop trying to get his language center back on, trying to think of anything but how much he wants to make Stacey come. His brain conjures up an image of Principal Inez Jackson droning about how she hated to put this letter in his file, and she would be forced to make extra visits to his class, and this pretty much does the trick.

He rings the bell, and Kelly comes to the door. "Welcome to our home," she says, and smiles.

"Thank you, Kelly," Mark says. "I, uh, brought pie."

"Great! I love pie! I hope we still have ice cream!" Agh! He showed up with an apple pie and no vanilla ice cream! What was he thinking? Well, it's too late now, though he supposes he could run to the Store24 if there's a real ice cream emergency. "Well, come in. I'll take your coat," Kelly says, and Mark gives her his coat.

"Wow. It smells great in here," Mark says. Garlic frying in olive oil.

He sees Stacey standing at the stove and says, "Can I help you with anything?" Oh, my God, do I want to help you with something.

"Yeah. Do you want to chop some eggplant?"

"Sure," Mark says, and heads into the kitchen. He stands there chopping, watching Stacey, looking at her electric smile, and making dumb small talk that seems doubly dumb after the conversation they had outside.

Suddenly he hears a door slam. He looks around for Kelly. "Uh, what's happening?"

"Well, remember that anxious mom who called you back in the fall about how her little angel was an occasional little demon at home?"

"Yeah, I remember that."

"Well, that was the little demon. I think she's . . . well, she has two problems. One is that she really likes you and doesn't want to share you with me, and the other is that she both loves and hates me but doesn't want to share me with you. So there you go. I'm really sorry. She promised me . . . ," and Stacey is suddenly biting her lip, with tears filling up her eyes. "We talked about this a lot. And she promised me that she could be polite . . . God, I just want to kill her sometimes."

"Is it . . . can I . . . I mean, would I be overstepping if I went and talked to her? I mean, I can understand if you don't want her to think that this behavior is buying her what she wants, but I do have some experience dealing with kids who are upset, even if I've never actually had to do that with Kelly . . ."

"I couldn't ask you to do that. She's my problem, I can't . . ."

But, Mark thinks, she could end up being my problem, at least I kind of hope so, oh my God, do I really hope so? "Well, I . . . I mean, if you think I'd make it worse, I don't want to, but if you're worried about imposing on me or something, please don't."

"I don't . . . it's just . . . it's my problem, and I have to be the one who deals with it."

"Okay." He chops in silence for a minute and watches Stacey stir stuff in the pan and fill up a pot with water. He wants to help her, to comfort her somehow, but he doesn't know what to do.

"I mean," she finally says, "well, yes, okay. I'm sorry. It's hard for me to accept help. But yeah. I'm way too mad at her to talk to her right now, so if you think you can do something, by all means do."

"Okay," he says. He walks around the counter and gives Stacey a hug.

"I'm sorry," she says in his ear. "I'm a mess."

"Me, too," he says, and walks over to Kelly's room.

He knocks on the door. "What?" Kelly says in a hostile tone he's never heard before.

"Uh, Kelly, it's Mark. Can I come in?"

"Okay," she says, in a much quieter voice.

He opens the door and sees Kelly on the floor of her room with a Barbie in each hand. "Hey," he says, kneeling down. "I forgot to ask you for the grand tour. I'm sorry about that."

Kelly looks at him for a minute, puts the Barbies down, and says, "That's okay. It's not like there's really very much to show. Our house is really really small and the windows are all up really high. It's kind of embarrassing."

"At least it's clean and nice. I used to live in a place that was twice as big as this, but there was paint peeling off the ceiling, and sometimes rats came out of the toilet."

"No way. Not really."

"Well, I'm exaggerating. It happened twice. And it might have been the same rat."

"That is disgusting!"

"Yeah, it made going to the bathroom kind of an adventure."

"What did you do?"

"Well, Kelly, there are really only a couple of things that people usually do in the bathroom."

Kelly laughs. "No! I mean what did you do about the rat?"

"Are you sure you want to hear this?"

"Yes!"

"Well, I came into the bathroom in the middle of the night, and there was this wet rat just climbing out of the toilet. I was terrified and I was in my pajamas, so I just grabbed the plunger and started beating it. I think it was still a little stunned from swimming through poop or something, because I got several pretty good shots in, and it stopped moving. I used the dustpan to scoop it into a garbage bag, and I put the garbage bag into the Dumpster."

"Really? Is that something that really happened, or is that like the way you're always telling Kadeem you're going to call his grandmom even though you never do?"

"I talk to Kadeem's grandmom three times a week!"

"Really? Then why is he still bad every day?"

"If you figure that out, make sure to tell me. So what game are you playing?"

"Oh," Kelly says, and looks kind of embarrassed. "Well, this Barbie is really rich, and she's being mean to this one, who is really poor."

"Can I play? Can I be the rich one?"

"Well . . . okay," she says, and for the next fifteen minutes Mark has Kelly in hysterics as the evil rich Barbie who suddenly develops an uncontrollable flatulence problem.

Eventually Stacey pokes her head in. "Dinner's ready," she says. "Kel, go wash your hands please."

"Okay," Kelly says, and bounds out of the room.

"What on earth did you do?" Stacey asks.

"Well, you can't go wrong with fart jokes," he says. He expects Stacey to be happy, but instead, she looks sad.

"Why is she good for everybody but me?"

"I guess it's probably because you're the only one she feels safe enough with to let her bad feelings out."

Stacey looks at him. "I guess that ought to make me feel better, but it doesn't."

"I'm sorry. I can only imagine how hard it's been to be grieving and raising a little kid and dealing with her grief."

Stacey pauses for a moment, then says, "You do what you have to do. I've done a lot for her, but she's done a lot for me, too. She saved me from a really bad life." Stacey gets that look she gets sometimes—like she's said too much when it's not really clear she's said anything at all.

Mark wonders briefly what her deal is, why she won't talk about Bobby or her life before Kelly. Is it just too painful? He understands that—rock_l was like that about her mom, but then, rock_l was crazy as a bedbug, and he doesn't think Stacey is. Is she?

He looks at her and says, "Well, should we eat?"

"Absolutely," she says. "But Kelly is in the next room, so dinner is probably a better plan." She smiles that smile that wipes all doubt from his brain, and Mark knows in that moment that whatever it is, whatever Stacey was in the past—petty thief? Murderer? Junkie? Prostitute? Bisexual drug-addicted folk singer? Corporate counsel for an evil corporation?—she's the key to his future.

STACEY

        Mark manages to sneak a kiss as he leaves after dinner while Kelly is in the bathroom. He kisses Stacey's neck, then whispers, "At this time next week I'll already know how good you taste."

Stacey's knees threaten to buckle, but she remains standing and then tries to paste a professional face on as Kelly emerges from the bathroom.

The next week lasts five years. Kelly has already married them off, and starts talking about the new house they'll have when they're married, and how each of the three of them is going to decorate his or her individual bedroom.

She considers trying to gently break down Kelly's wall of denial, saying something about how you know how Aunt Phoebe and Uncle Steve share a bedroom, and that's what married people do, and if we were to get married, we'd share a room, but she's happy enough that the idea of Mark in their lives is not causing continuous tantrums that she decides to just let it lie. All she offers when this comes up is, "You know, Kel, it's really way too early to be thinking about that kind of stuff," but even this sounds incredibly feeble, because of course Stacey is thinking about it all the time, too.

How can she possibly be thinking that? How is it that just a few months ago she was resigned to living single for the rest of her life, and now she wants to marry a guy she hasn't even slept with yet?

Speaking of which, the mental countdown to the big day has made every day torturous. On Monday, when he's taking the walkers out, Mark looks at her, raises a palm, and mouths the words *Five days*. She feels her face get hot and realizes that she's actually blushing.

They still talk on the phone every night. Much of what they talk about is just the kids and parents who have either been delightful or else gigantic pains in the ass on that particular day, and Stacey is amazed at how nice it is to just be able to tell someone all the stupid things that happen in a day. She finds herself thinking, *I can't wait to tell Mark about this,* when something happens at work.

Once, she rattles on for twenty minutes about a glitter spill, a late delivery, and a projectile-vomiting four-year-old, and finally she realizes she must be boring Mark to death. "I'm sorry," she says. "I must be boring the shit out of you."

"No, not at all. It's actually pretty entertaining."

"Oh, come on. You're just saying that so you can get in my pants."

"Well, I do want to get in your pants, but I'm also completely sincere. I love talking to you and listening to you." Stacey still can't really believe it. She's never been with anyone she would have felt comfortable talking to like this, she's never been with anyone she would have wanted to talk to like this . . . well, she's never been with anybody, she corrects herself. Philippa had never been with anybody like that.

Philippa. That bitch is starting to seem like a bigger and bigger problem. Stacey doesn't know what to do about it. Mark has been so open with her, he's told her about Janet, about "Two Minute Man," and about how rock_1 broke his heart. Stacey had felt these ridiculous stabs of jealousy—how could he want her after he'd doubtless had all kinds of three-way orgies with rock_l and various women?—until she'd asked in a kind of joking way if he'd ever shared her with a woman, ha-ha, isn't it funny that I'm asking this ridiculous question about the famous bisexual. "Well, I suppose I'd have to say probably, but never simultaneously and never that I knew of, if that's what you're wondering."

"Ha-ha, no, I was . . . yeah, okay, I did wonder that." How could she be jealous of anybody in his past, when he'd had sex with the same number of people by age twenty-nine that she had by age seventeen? Except that wasn't her—that was Philippa. She was an untouched virgin.

Ugh. Philippa. One night he tells her the whole story of Becky/Rebecca, of how she humiliated him and he wrecked the apartment, and she wants to say, Oh Jesus do I know about humiliation, do I know about heartbreak, do I know about cursing yourself for ever getting into a bad situation, for being blind to who somebody really is, oh, baby, I know, I know exactly. And it stings when he says, "I mean, I don't know what it's like to be in your situation, to lose somebody like that, but the worst part of what happened to me was knowing that I did it, that I made the stupid choices, that I fell for the wrong person, and it was her fault, but it was my fault, too, because I didn't know who she was, or I didn't let myself see who she was. This is awful, and I'm sorry to even say this to you, but I kind of feel like if she'd died I wouldn't have to hate myself about it."

She has to tell him. She never really thought this through—since she never thought she'd be with anybody, she never thought about having to tell anybody, and if anybody had asked her what her plans were, she would have said that whoever wanted her would just have to accept that certain chapters of her life were closed, that nobody was ever going to have access to Philippa, because Philippa was dead, and Stacey was born, full-grown, nine years ago.

But there is no way she is going to tell him before they have sex, because she wants him so bad her brain is completely addled. It's gotten to the point that the sound of his voice on the phone makes her body tingle, and she masturbates with the vibrator every night after they get off the phone, and it used to be that a session with the vibrator would quiet her libido for at least a week, and now it's not even twenty-four hours, she's dreaming of sex with him every night and waking up hornier than she was when she went to bed.

On Wednesday night the talk turns to sex, as it frequently does, and Stacey tells him that she's going to come over to his house as soon as she drops Kelly off at Grace's house, and that she is going to come over to his apartment, and that they are going to have to have sex before they have dinner, and she's going to want him right there on the floor, that she's going to want them both to get rug burns, but that it's really important that they actually make it to the bed, and that there be candles. Because I'm a virgin, she doesn't say, and I want it to be special.

After this, Mark says, "Uh, listen, it's, uh, it's close to midnight, and I'm going to have to go to sleep soon, but you've made it impossible for me to sleep unless I handle things over here."

"Yeah," Stacey says, "I've got something I need to handle over here before I'm going to be able to sleep."

"So I was thinking . . ."

"Yeah?"

"I was thinking that if we're both handling things at the same time, it doesn't make a whole lot of sense for us to not be on the phone."

Stacey doesn't know what to say. The idea makes her incredibly hot, but how can she possibly? She feels like she'll be far nakeder than she's ever been in her life.

There's a long pause while Stacey thinks it over, and Mark says, "I'm sorry, bad idea I guess, I just—"

"I think it's a great idea. It makes me nervous, but it's a great idea." And so Stacey finds herself—Stacey, you're awfully saucy for a virgin, she thinks—describing in detail exactly what she's doing to herself and just letting loose and moaning, and listening as Mark describes all the things he's going to do to her, all the ways he wants her, and his nice, sensitive, mellow voice gets all rough and fierce when he's coming, and the whole experience doesn't do anything to make her want him any less, though it does help her fall asleep faster.

MARK

It's Friday. He hasn't slept well in two weeks, and his body keeps sending him these signals that he's exhausted that his mind keeps overriding with excitement about tonight. And fear.

He's terrified. Not because he's afraid he's going to live up to the song written about him, though that fear is playing in the back of his mind. He's hoping the sensation-dulling effect of a condom will offset his insane, ravenous desire for her. But what he's really afraid of is what this changes. He's been happier in the last two weeks than he can remember being at any time since Janet was alive and Becky was still Becky and hadn't blown anyone but him. And part of what's fun, what's making him happy, is this incredible unfulfilled lust.

What will be different tomorrow? Will the whole thing become less urgent? He's worried about this, but not, of course, worried enough not to do it. He tries, during the day, to focus on workboard, to focus on read-aloud, to focus on anything but tonight. He hasn't noticed any change in Kelly in class since last week's dinner—they have always had this relationship where they both seemed to be in on a joke that the rest of the class didn't really get, and that hasn't changed. Today, though, he finds it hard even to look at her for fear she's going to see it in his eyes, leap from her seat, point her finger, and scream, *You're gonna fuck my mom tonight!*

He even shuffles the reading groups so he doesn't have to meet with Kelly's group today. This backfires, because Kelly comes up to him later and says, "Mr. Norris"—she has never slipped and called him Mark at school, not once—"you said we were going to have reading group today, and we didn't."

"I'm sorry, Kelly—I got backed up with the other groups. They took longer than I planned. Monday, I promise." And hopefully Monday, the postcoital glow will have faded enough that she won't look at him and jump up and point and scream, *You fucked my mom!*

He takes the walkers out, sees Stacey smiling at him, and wants her right there up against the Bars of the Cage, but all he does is smile back and nod. Once all the kids are with their parents or babysitters or grandparents, Mark literally runs home and begins to clean. It's a disheartening affair. He's not the greatest house-keeper, but he's usually able to block out the condition of the apartment. Except when he starts cleaning. So now he's seeing everything that needs cleaning and realizing it's way way too much for him to clean everything that needs cleaning, prepare a dinner that is not embarrassing, and get himself showered and ready. He curses the dust on the baseboards and curses himself for never see-ing it before today. What is she going to think of him?

Oh God, when's the last time he changed the sheets? He digs around and finds clean ones and wrestles them onto the bed— God, they're totally wrinkled! Should he iron them? No time. He then scrubs the sink, then vacuums, then washes dishes, then scrubs the toilet, then attacks the baseboards with a cloth for the first time since he's lived here.

Finally he pronounces the apartment clean enough and begins

work on the spicy seafood soup, figuring that soup is a good call because it can stay warm for as long as it needs to and spicy is a good call because it's sexy. Once the ingredients are assembled in the pot, he realizes that he's forgotten to buy any bread to go with it. He curses himself again, runs out to the bakery, and returns with a gigantic sourdough boule.

He checks the clock—it's nearly five, and she's supposed to drop Kelly off at five! He takes a quick shower and stands naked in front of his dresser for five minutes trying to decide what to wear. He's never given any thought to which of his pairs of underwear might be sexiest, or indeed to whether any of them are sexy at all, because men's underwear always looks ridiculous to him, even when the ripped gay models on the box are wearing them. He settles on a pair of boxers with a decidedly phallic city skyline scene on them. He pulls on his best jeans and then irons his fashion boy shirt and puts it on.

Just as he's putting the shirt on, the bell rings. Shit! The ironing board is still standing there! Shit! He runs to the door.

His heart is hammering in his ears as he opens the door, and she is there. She steps into the apartment, drops her coat on the floor, and kisses him. They kiss, and kiss, their tongues frantically licking each other, and his hands roam all over her body. He's hungrier than he's ever been in his life, like he's poisoned and there is only one thing on earth that can save him and only one place in the world to get it. He kisses her neck down to the neckline of her shirt—a tight, hot pink, long-sleeved shirt that he grabs and starts to pull off, which of course can't happen with his mouth on her neck, but it's difficult to pull away, especially when she's saying "oooh" with every kiss. Finally he does, and she strips the shirt off, revealing that she's not wearing a bra and that she is in possession of what are surely the loveliest breasts in the universe.

"Oh, my God," he says.

"I searched in my underwear drawer for like an hour," she says, as he kisses his way down her chest to her left nipple, "and I . . . oh! . . . I . . . I couldn't find anything that was sexier than nothing."

Mark licks his way around her nipple, then sucks it gently and flicks his tongue against it. Stacey shudders and makes a sound—some kind of cross between a moan and a squeal—that he never in his wildest dreams of studliness ever dreamed he could cause in a woman. He returns to her mouth and kisses her hard.

Some amount of time passes, during which his hands are on her breasts, pinching her nipples gently, and he is so hard it actually hurts. Eventually she pulls away from him and slowly kneels down and reaches her hands up to his waist. "Belt. Button fly!" she says, fumbling with his button fly. "You're really gonna make me work for it, huh?" she asks, smiling. Mark curses himself for not thinking about easy access, rips open his belt and button fly, and steps out of his jeans and underwear. "Mmmm . . . ," Stacey says. "That's more like it." Suddenly, her mouth is all over him. He looks down at her, kneeling topless in front of him, with her head moving back and forth, back and forth, slowly at first but getting faster every second, and he won't even make it to two minutes if she doesn't stop, but he really really doesn't want her to stop. He forces himself to look away, because just watching her is going to do him in, and then he summons all the willpower he's ever had in his life and says, "Oh my God you have to stop or this is going to be over really quickly."

She smiles, stands, and says, "Well, that won't do. Where's your bedroom?"

"Follow me," Mark says, kissing her again.

He pads down the hall, feeling ridiculous wearing a shirt and no pants and with his erect penis bobbing up and down with every step. He certainly can't do anything about the latter, but he removes his shirt and drops it on the floor. He looks back and sees that Stacey has done the same with her pants.

"Elastic waist," she says, smiling. "You've gotta stop with that belt-and-button-fly chastity-belt thing."

"I think I can promise you that that will never happen again," Mark says. Once they reach his room, he feels ridiculous again as he fumbles with matches trying to light candles. He has six candles, but Stacey is lying naked on her back, with her legs hanging off the end of his bed with her right hand squeezing her right breast and pinching her nipple, and her left hand on her stomach and heading slowly downward, and he only manages to light two before he has to go to her.

He kneels at the foot of the bed, knowing that if he gets next to her, if he feels her warm soft skin next to him, he's going to come immediately.

"Do you remember what I told you on the phone?" he says to her.

"Mmmmm . . . I don't think so," she answers.

"I told you that I was going to kiss you on your right ankle like this," he does, and Stacey actually gives a little jump and moans as though he's done something much more spectacular. "And that I was going to lick you all the way up the inside of your leg," he does, though it's all he can do to stop when he reaches the top, "and then I was going to kiss your left ankle," she's completely nonverbal, and he has to try not to listen to the sounds she's making, or he'll be done before she is, and that wouldn't do—"and lick the inside of your left leg . . . And then . . . I told you . . . I was going to do . . . this." And he does. She keeps making these incredible sounds, and he wants to tell her that he's finally home, that he wants to be here forever, that she tastes better than anything ever in the history of the world, but he can't tell her any of that because his tongue is occupied and she is literally screaming at him that he is so *fucking* good oh my *God* don't stop.

She comes with a bucking, shuddering orgasm that probably has seismologists at MIT scratching their heads, and a cry that surely has mothers as far away as Canada trying to hide their embarrassment as they tell their children no, I don't know what that sound was, no, I don't think anybody's in trouble, everything's fine, hey, isn't it almost time for your hockey practice?

"Oh. My. God," she says. "I need you right now, right right now!" Mark stands, reaches for his dresser top, fumbles with a condom wrapper, and joins her on the bed.

"I want you on top," he says. "I want to look at you."

"Oh my God anything, any way you want it, anything at all," Stacey says. She climbs on top of him, reaches back and slides him into her. And now it's his turn to go nonverbal. Sounds are coming out of his mouth, but his brain is blissfully shut down by the perfection of this moment. Every nerve in his body is concentrated in one place, one place that feels better than anything ever felt. Her nails are digging into his shoulder, and her mouth is open and her eyes are closed, and she's making those sounds again. He watches her moving up and down, watches the look on her face and realizes that there is no way he can possibly hold back any longer, so he grabs her ass and pulls himself up into her as hard and as fast as he possibly can, as if he could get his entire self inside her if he only fucks her hard and fast enough, and then he is gone.

He comes and comes and comes and when he thinks he's done, he keeps coming, he's astounded that he's able to keep coming, he wonders if he is ever going to stop or if his body is just going to pump out every single drop of liquid he has. Stacey comes again and collapses on top of him.

"That. Was. Incredible," she says.

"That . . . that was . . . I've never . . . I mean I have never come like that in my entire life. You are an amazing, magnificent love goddess."

She smiles. "You're amazing."

He runs his hand all over her body, loving the softness, the warmth. They kiss, slowly this time, and they keep kissing, and then they just lie there. "I just don't know if I'm ever going to be able to walk," she says. "My legs have completely liquefied."

He reaches down and licks her on her left thigh. "I need some liquid. I think I am completely dehydrated."

She laughs. He reaches his hand out to hers and says, "I . . . I wanted you since the first time I saw you, I used to . . . well, I've thought about this night for a long time, but it . . . this was beyond even the best thing I ever imagined."

She kisses him. "I . . . I have no idea how you do what you do to me. I've never felt this way ever in my whole life. My body, my heart, everything. I feel . . . different. Better."

They kiss again, and Mark remembers everything that's just happened, and he realizes that he shouldn't have been afraid of what was going to change when he was finally able to have her, because now he's lying here and he doesn't want her any less than he did before, and, in fact, it doesn't feel any less urgent that he have her. He looks down and finds himself up to the task, and when she says, "Well, are you getting hungry?" he's able to reply, honestly, that he's famished, and slowly, slowly, he satisfies his hunger.

STACEY

After the second time, Stacey lies on the rug, exhausted, famished, and beginning to get sore. Her palms and knees hurt, and she can still feel the ghosts of Mark's hands gripping her hips from behind. "I really need some soup," she says, "but I don't trust my legs to get me to the kitchen."

Mark kisses her and says, "Me neither. My thighs have been replaced by rubber bands. And I'm starting to get cold."

She kisses him. "Yeah. It's a lot colder on the floor when you're not moving." He smiles, waves his arm around in the direction of the bed without taking his eyes off her. His hand eventually finds a blanket, which he pulls onto them.

"I hate that I can't look at you, but I can't have you freezing on my floor."

"Mmmm . . ." She snuggles up to him. "This is nice, but this floor is really not all that comfortable."

"Okay," Mark says, kissing her lips, cheeks, ears, and neck in the pauses between his words. "On . . . three . . . you . . . get up and . . . get in the . . . bed . . . and . . . I'll . . . get us some . . . food."

"Okay," she says, and kisses him.

"One . . . two . . . three . . . ," and he vaults to his feet. Stacey stays on the floor. Mark reaches his hand down to pull her up. She raises both arms, but makes no other effort to move.

"There's no way. My legs are not going to cooperate."

"Okay then." He reaches down under her arms and hauls her up, then deposits her gently on the bed. She scoots up to the headboard and sits up, watching him walk naked into the kitchen. She can't see him, but she can hear him from the kitchen. "I mean, I know there's no danger really, but there's a primal fear that comes from wielding a serrated knife when you're naked. At least from a male perspective. I think I'm glad I got a boule instead of a baguette."

She smiles, but something is already creeping into the cracks in her postorgasmic bliss. It's Philippa, of course. In her mind, Stacey sees a tiny Philippa perched on her shoulder, wearing a Barbie-sized Clash shirt, hair dyed jet black, and sporting Doc Martens that come almost to her knees.

"You *have* to tell him about me. You know you have to. He deserves it."

"He *deserves* it? He deserves to find out he's picked another crazy lying bitch? Just like Kelly deserves to know her father is alive and probably beating the shit out of a wife and kids somewhere in Ohio right this minute?"

"It's different with Kelly. You know that. What Mark deserves is as much of you as you have of him. That includes me."

"It does not! I killed you! And since when are you my conscience? I'm *your* conscience, and I had to kill you to get you to listen to me!"

"Well, you tried to tell me the right thing to do for years. Now I'm returning the favor. The longer you wait, the worse it's going to be for him. And he might kick your lying ass to the curb, but I don't think he will. And if he does, well, maybe you'll know something about how to do this right next time."

"There's not going to be a next time! This is the guy! I know this is the guy!"

"If this is the guy, then treat him the way he deserves to be treated. Tell him."

Grrr. Philippa has some nerve being right after all this time. Where the hell was all that good sense when she needed it? She might be alive today if she'd had even half as much before.

Mark returns to the bedroom with a big plate holding two bowls of steaming soup and several slices of really delicious-looking bread.

"Whoa. What's wrong?" he says.

"Nothing. What do you mean?"

"It's on your face. You look really sad all of a sudden."

"I . . . ," and she starts to cry. And then she gets mad at herself for crying, and suddenly Mark is next to her with his arm around her, and she finds herself leaning into him and really liking the way that feels even as she hates the way it feels. She cries and cries, and then thinks of something funny.

"I don't always cry after sex," she says. "I read about that in *Cosmo*. Some women . . . ," and then she cries again. Mark does not annoy her with questions, though she kind of wishes he would, because if he asked, she'd have to tell him, if he said tell me what the hell is wrong with you, psycho bitch from hell, she'd say, no, psycho bitch from Cincinnati, but close enough, ha-ha.

"Eat something. Crying gives you low blood sugar. You'll feel better if you eat something. This carbohydrate-intensive bread, for instance. Let's eat, and maybe you can tell me when you're done."

Stacey takes a bite of bread and suddenly realizes she's starving. She dips it in the soup, and the soup is delicious. "Wow. Spicy," she says.

"Yeah, I think I might have overdone the cayenne, it's a little—"

"No. It's perfect. Sexy."

"That's what I was thinking."

They eat their soup and bread in silence, and Stacey's tears recede to the point that she thinks she can speak.

"Okay," she says, and she looks at his eager eyes, looking full of love and lust, and she takes a mental picture of this adoring face, because she's about to bring the whole thing crashing down, and nobody's ever looked at her like that before, and probably nobody will ever again.

"I . . . I've never told anyone this story. Ever. And before I tell you, you have to promise that you will never tell anybody else. This story is only for you."

"Okay," he says, and it's gone already—the adoration has been replaced by fear and dread, she can see him thinking, Oh, shit, here it comes, I knew it was too good to be true. Shit. He's so sweet, and she can't stand to be the one to hurt him again. But she has to tell him. But she can't bring herself to think of Philippa as herself, and she can't just say, *I changed my name and I've been living a lie ever since* without explaining everything that came before, all the reasons why Philippa had to go. So she starts at the beginning.

"Okay . . . there was this girl. Her name was Philippa. She lived in Cincinnati with her alcoholic mother who used to fly into unpredictable rages and call her a stupid cunt, a fucking slut, and a cocksucking whore as soon as Philippa developed breasts, which was when she was thirteen."

She talks about Philippa going to London in the summers, about punk rock, and about Trevor and Christian and "Philippa Cheats."

"I know that song," Mark says, quietly.

She tells him about Andrew the tabloid reporter, about how Philippa fled the UK, about how she worked for years as a waitress and did way too much coke and dated one asshole after another. She sees the question in his eyes and says, "I don't know why. It's partly that she had no idea she deserved better, that there was anything better out there, that it was possible for somebody not to treat her like complete shit. You know? Do fish know they're wet? When it's all you've ever known, you just believe that's normal. And she was high or drunk a lot of the time, which didn't help her make good decisions. And she was a fucking idiot."

Mark doesn't say anything, but he reaches out and holds her hand.

She starts to tell the story of Ken and the Flying Baseball of Destiny, how she struck out swinging at ball four, went after a pitch that was way, way, way outside and moved in with Ken when she should have fled. She's never told the story before, not to anybody, and putting it into words gives it so much power, so much that she can't tell it without crying, so much that she stops referring to Philippa as *she* and starts referring to her as *I*, and that hurts even more, because it wasn't somebody else who got herself into that shit, who fucked up so badly, it was her, it was her all along. To speak that truth aloud hurts so much she can hardly stand it, like somebody's shoving her guts into a wood chipper, grinding them up, and shoving them back in so they can do it again.

She can barely talk for crying, and she can't look Mark in the face, can't see the shock, the disgust, the hurt that she knows are there replacing the adoration that was there such a short time ago. His hand is still holding hers, though, and he didn't say, *Hey, you said* she, *but now you're saying* I! So maybe that's a good sign.

"And when I . . . when I found out I was pregnant, I left. I . . . I obviously didn't care about protecting myself, but there was no fucking way I was going to subject an innocent kid to that. And that is the only smart thing I ever did when I was Philippa. I took a bus to Atlanta with my getaway money, then went to Nashville and changed my name and became Stacey and killed Philippa for good, because as much as I hated Ken, and I did hate Ken and I still hate Ken, and I hate Trevor, too, and Andrew and everybody else, I didn't hate any of them as much as I hated fucking Philippa, and it felt so good to do her in, to just kiss that person good-bye, because I couldn't stand being her anymore, and I can't stand it now, and I can't stand that she's going to ruin this. This is . . . I have never felt this way about anyone before in my life, or in Philippa's life. And that was . . . I can't even say the best sex I've ever had, because that doesn't even cover it, it's like I've been watching black-and-white TV my whole life and you just showed me that there is such a thing as color. But you are really a wonderful person, and I don't deserve you, and I'm sorry, I'm really sorry, I'm really—I never thought it was going to be a problem to live a lie, because I never thought I'd feel like this about anyone, and I can't do it, I can't lie to you. Jesus, Mark, I'm so sorry."

She's still looking down. He kisses her on the forehead. "I should go," she says.

"It's one A.M. Don't be silly. You can't walk home at this hour. You'll get mugged right before you freeze to death. You have to stay." His voice sounds all weird and flat. She looks up at him, finally. She can't read his face at all.

"What are you thinking?"

"I . . . I don't know. I don't want to say anything right now. Let's try to sleep," he says. He gets out of the bed, pulls on a pair of pajama pants, and takes the dishes to the kitchen. She hears the sound of him brushing his teeth, and he finally comes back to the bedroom and climbs into bed. His face is a mystery. The adoration is certainly gone, but she doesn't see any hatred there, either, and he didn't say you lying whore get the hell out of my apartment. He didn't even say I need to sleep on the couch. He didn't say it's all okay, I love you anyway, be my wife, but he's here, he's next to her, and he's warm.

He leans over, turns out the light, and kisses her. "I really hate that story. But thank you for telling me," he whispers to her. "It was the right thing to do."

"I'm sorry," she says.

"I know," he says. He kisses her again before turning his back to her.

MARK

Mark hears Stacey's breathing deepen and regularize very quickly. He guesses she's exhausted from telling him all that. Well, he's exhausted from hearing it, but it's clear that he's not going to be doing any sleeping.

He turns onto his back and looks at the ceiling. He felt himself go cold when she was telling her story, and he hasn't really warmed up. It was as though he just numbed up inside, like he got a shot of emotional novocaine to protect him from the drilling as Stacey told him, *Bzzzzzzz . . . I'm a liar with a name that's not the name you know me by . . . bzzzzzz . . . loser . . . bzzzzz . . . we all lie, that's what we do, that's who we are, bzzzzz . . . and I might not cheat anymore, but I damn sure lie, and if I ever do cheat, you'll never know because you fall for women's lies every single time . . . sucker . . . Bzzzzzzzz . . .*

At least, that was what he took away from what she said. And he told her some nice thing when he turned out the light because he knew that was what she wanted to hear, and yeah, maybe that made him a liar, too, because he wasn't so sure he was glad she told him. If she hadn't told him, they could have just continued on like they were forever. It really was incredibly selfish of her to tell him.

Now she gets to feel virtuous for telling the truth, and he has to deal with the fallout.

He chews on that for a few minutes, turning back over onto his side. He knows he should just get up, that's what you're supposed to do when you can't sleep, but despite it all, he wants to be in this bed with her, because if he stays in bed, his options are open, and he still wants to keep his options open. He might want to flee, but if he doesn't, he doesn't want to have "the night you rejected my confession" hanging over him for the rest of their time together.

His mind is a jumble of thoughts, his heart is beating fast, and his stomach feels tight and sour. And his dick hurts. But that, anyway, is a good thing, he thinks, smiling. She said it was like the difference between black and white and color, which seems pretty apt to him, like rock_l and Becky were great, fine, just like the beginning of *The Wizard of Oz,* but here was Stacey in stunning Technicolor saying, *Ding dong the witch is dead and welcome to Munchkinland.* But was that passion for who she really is, or for who he thought she was?

But who did he think she was? Before, he knew everything about her for the last seven years, and he really liked that person. Oh hell, he can admit to himself that he loves her, or loved her, or something, though he couldn't possibly tell her that, not this soon, that would be tantamount to just lying down in front of the door with WELCOME painted on his stomach.

So what's different now? What's different is that she filled in the gaps, that she told him about who she used to be. And it's not worse than the worst thing he could imagine—he has seriously been testing his reaction to the junkie/whore scenario, but in that fantasy he always told her that her past didn't matter, that what mattered was the future.

But it turns out the past does matter. And, he has to admit, he wouldn't have been satisfied not knowing. He didn't know why, but he had to know. He pestered and pestered Becky about the guys who fell between the last two times he saw her at Camp Service until he finally got her to give up names. Why? Because he couldn't stand her keeping secrets from him. Because he kept nothing from her, and it seemed petty to him that she held back something so stupid as the name of a guy she went out with. It doesn't matter, Becky said, and he'd said, It does matter, or else you would tell me. And she told him.

But she held back a lot more than that, it turns out. Still, the point was—he really has to pee all of a sudden. He looks at Stacey and hopes that she won't wake up while he's in the bathroom, because then he would come back from the bathroom and say he had really been in the bathroom, but she would think he just couldn't stand being in the same bed with her.

Which is not the case. When he comes back from the bathroom, he finds he loves the sight of her in his bed. His mind is flooded with memories of what happened before she told him about Philippa, and he's hard again. He remembers all their phone calls, he remembers spinning around the ice with her holding her hand, and he remembers how wonderful, how right everything felt just a few hours ago.

Is that gone? She lied to him. Just like Raquel, just like Becky. She lied to him.

Except she lied to everybody, and that was at least partly to keep herself safe, to protect her from some murderous asshole she had somehow once been in love with, or anyway had slept with. Why would she have done that? How could this woman, this treasure, allow herself to be treated like trash? How could a guy like Ken get a girl like her when Mark spent so many years being alone, watching all the good girls go out with the assholes? He finds himself angry at Stacey, at Philippa, at whoever she was at that time and before. How many nice guys, he wonders, crossed your path, and you didn't even notice them because they didn't do drugs, because they were kind to you and you didn't like that?

Well, there's no point hating Philippa, because Stacey obviously hates her plenty. And anyway, the thing about her lying is that, now, she lied to everybody *except* him. He's the only person on earth who knows the truth about her. The only one. He isn't the only one who doesn't know, standing there stupid with his dick in his hand while she chews carpet in LA for the amusement of some aged Australian, while she blows a co-worker and accepts a ring she never intends to keep. No, this time he's on the inside.

And this time, he has somebody at the other end of one of these name-change scenarios. She did run away and change her name and become a different person, but that's the person she is now, the person he . . . hell, the person he loves (but he has to stop even thinking that, because then it will tumble out of his mouth, and he can't have that), and before he'd always been stuck with the person on the front end of that kind of transformation.

And he admires what she did. He's mad, but he still thinks it was smart and ballsy of her to pick up and start over, and he thinks about sweet, smart, wonderful Kelly and how her face would look after her psychotic dad struck her, and how hard and cold she'd be on the inside when somebody like that was finished with her, just as hard and cold as so many of Mark's students who were abused. With her lie, she bought a life for Kelly that was immeasurably better than the life she would have had. It was a big price to pay, especially when you considered that Kelly would never know the enormity of what Stacey did for her. She would never grow up with an abusive dad, and so even if Stacey one day told her the truth about Ken, Kelly would never really understand what her mom's lies had saved her from. Raquel and Becky had bought nothing with their lies, and both of them, with their career success and all their soul searching and personal transformations, look trivial and pathetic compared to this mighty woman asleep next to him.

He thought that they had shared something, a bond of understanding about grief. He thought that when he was crying to her on the phone about Janet, he was crying to somebody who understood what it was like to have someone you loved just disappear from your life forever, how it wasn't till much later that you realized that they lost not just the life they had, but the future they never got. He thought when he told her that he hated college students even more than most Bostonians because Janet should be one of them, and was so much better than those pretty drunken idiots who clogged the streets of Allston, that she understood, that she thought of every birthday party of Kelly's that Bobby didn't get to see, of everything Bobby didn't get to do and should have.

But she had no idea. She said she thought of Philippa as dead, but that wasn't the same. And yet she did share so much more with him. She knew what it was like to curse yourself for falling for the wrong person again, she knew what it was like to be humiliated, and, most of all, she knew what it was like to have a whole country reveling in somebody else's version of your breakup, the one that left out everything bad that they did, that they were.

She lied to him, okay, but she couldn't keep it up. Raquel and Becky had no difficulty at all lying to his face continuously, and they didn't even have a good reason to lie to him. Stacey believed he was special enough to tell the truth to. She trusted him so completely she told him a story that she believed, rightly or wrongly, put her life and, probably more important, Kelly's life at risk. That wasn't the same as Raquel and Becky—it was the complete opposite.

He turns over and glances at the clock. Three hours have passed since he kissed her good night. He finally feels tired, but he can't go to sleep now, because if he's asleep when she wakes up, she might run away, and he is not going to have another woman he loves telling him she's somebody else and running away from him.

No, he's got to keep her. It terrifies him, because she's a mess, but so is he, and after three hours in the dark, what he realizes is that it's scarier to think about being without her. He had already been planning their life together, and he wonders if this makes him, on some level, a woman. Well, he certainly felt like a man earlier this evening. Possibly he's a lesbian trapped in a man's body. In any case, everything he's dreamed for them, everything he wants for him, for Stacey, for Kelly, for baby makes four (would she go for that? He hopes she would), all of that is still possible. They have fucked-up pasts, and okay, hers is more fucked up and continues to fuck up her present in some important ways (what about her dad in London? Wouldn't he like to know she's alive? Surely that line of communication is beyond Ken's reach), but they might also have a future, and hopefully that won't be fucked up.

He wishes he could play his guitar without waking her up, but he knows he can't. So he lies in bed looking at her sleeping and writes her a song in his mind.

STACEY

Stacey wakes from a dream of falling. She's confused for a second—things feel different, and she doesn't know where she is. Then she opens her eyes and wishes she could regain her confusion. Everything drops on her at once—the fantastic, amazing sex, and stupid Philippa, and Mark's face all blank saying, *Let's try to sleep.* She was light when she was confused, and now it all feels so very heavy.

Or maybe that's the arm that's wrapped around her—not the usual seven-year-old arm she's used to seeing when she wakes up. So he's still in bed with her. That's a good sign. And the erection pressing on her back is most certainly not what she's used to waking up with. But this might or might not be a good sign. Even if it doesn't just mean he has to pee, it could be that he's after some hot breakup sex before he shows her the door.

She finds that the idea actually kind of excites her, even not knowing if he's about to dump her. What is it with this guy? How does he do this to her? She's tempted to roll over and plant a big wet kiss on him, but she needs to know first. She's pretty sure they could probably have hot breakup sex even after he dumps her, and she has to know if it's ending here, if last night was a wonderful interlude in the life she'd made solitary with all her mistakes (yes, her mistakes, not Philippa's, not some dead girl's fuckups: hers) or the wonderful beginning of a life that didn't have to be solitary. The answer really matters to her, and she's suddenly nervous and jittery, and her stomach is suddenly sour and tight. She has to know right now.

She rolls over and does not kiss Mark. His eyes are wide open. He leans over to kiss her, and she pulls away.

"I . . . I'm sorry, I really want to kiss you and more, but I just have to know if this is going to be breakup sex."

"Breakup sex? What the hell is that? I mean, I guess it's pretty clear what it is, the phrase is pretty self-explanatory, but, I mean, I guess the times I had breakup sex I didn't actually know I was having it, if you know what I mean, since I was blindsided both . . . I'm sorry, I've been awake all night thinking, and there's just been so much going through my mind that it's very hard not to babble."

Stacey smiles. He's really cute and funny, but why won't he get to the goddamn point? Why doesn't he just say, *Of course it's not breakup sex, my darling, please be my wife*? She thinks she knows what he's going to say—after all, he's still here, and he's talking to her, but maybe that's just how nice guys break up. She wouldn't know. "So? What were you thinking all night?"

"I was thinking a lot of stuff." He sits up and leans against the headboard, and Stacey thinks that if he says something kind, she's going to just lean over and blow him while he sits there. She then wonders who this sex-crazed animal is and what she's done with Kelly's mom.

"I was thinking . . . well, I mean, do you want me to walk you through everything, or should I just skip to the end? I think I should just skip to the end, although, you know, you set off all my alarms with the name-change business and everything. And I really want to say that none of it matters, but I really had a hard time— I mean, I'm having a hard time in that I think you are this fantastic amazing treasure, and I don't get how you let yourself—how you could not see that about yourself. And—"

"You know, you're not really skipping to the end."

"Oh. Yeah. I guess it turns out I can't just skip to the end. Anyway. I was also jealous, which I know you're going to think is stupid, but like, I'm always—I guess I did something stupid in terms of falling for Raquel, but when I was young and stupid I didn't do anything wild and crazy and stupid. You know? Like, if I was feeling really rowdy, I might rent *two* vampire movies. And now it's just—I don't know. I don't regret many things I did, but I regret a bunch of things I didn't do, and, like, that ship has sailed. It's just not me. I went to this bar a few months ago . . . well, I'm sorry. Babbling. Can I kiss you? Please? I'm not breaking up with you. I just need to kiss you."

"See, now that's jumping to the end," she says. She slides up and kisses him. She hears a strange sound and realizes it's coming from her. She made no effort to cover up with the sheet like someone in a movie who's not getting paid enough to show her tits on screen, so she's topless, and Mark's hand is on her left breast. She enjoys that feeling for a moment before pulling away.

"Tell me why."

"Why what?"

"Why you're not dumping me. I lied to you, especially—I feel like shit about the widow thing. Like . . . I just felt like the lowest piece of shit every time you talked about Janet."

"I . . . can I . . . ," and now he's kissing her neck, ". . . *please* tell you later? I promise I will, but I can't possibly keep talking right now."

Stacey tries to consider this, but now he's found that spot on the back of her neck, and she's just going to have to hear about it later.

She does hear about it later—Mark's whole rationale about which end of the transformation she's on, about breakup songs . . . he goes on, and she eventually just stops him with kisses. Because it turns out not to matter. Whatever his reason, she still has him, and today is the beginning of something, not the end.

He makes coffee and says, "I tried to write a song. I mean, I had this whole idea of how you were going to wake up and I was going to serenade you with this song, and you would know everything was okay."

She wonders what this would have been like. She thinks uneasily about what kind of song this might be. *You're a lying bitch but I like you anyway* or something? She's a little leery of being the subject of another song, but she really wants to know what it was like.

"So why didn't you?"

"Oh. Well, I . . . I had more . . . I just didn't think it was good enough for you. When you mostly write songs about poop, it's kind of difficult to switch gears and write about something so huge."

"I want to hear it."

"Oh, I couldn't. I mean, I really . . . I think it's no good at all, and I'm not sure I'm going to remember the tune I came up with at three thirty. I mean, I guess I could show you the lyrics, but . . ."

"I don't want the lyrics. I want you to sing it."

"Aagh, but it sucks!"

"I don't care. Is it mean?"

"No, it's not mean, it's just not good."

"Okay. I'm going to take a shower. When I get out, I want to hear the song."

"Ugh. Okay."

She kisses him and heads to the shower. She glances at the clock and sees that she really has to go pick up Kelly, but she doesn't want to, she's impatient with life. She feels like she can see where this is going—now that Philippa is out of the way, she thinks, they can go straight to the happily ever after (mostly. Hopefully. If Kelly lets them), and she doesn't want to spend all the time it's going to take for him to propose, all the time it's going to take to plan a wedding, she just wants him to come home with her and tell her he's home at last and never ever leave.

She towels off and heads to the bedroom. Mark is sitting there with his guitar. His face is all red.

"Are you really sure you want me to do this? It's . . . you have to promise not to dump me for writing such a crappy song."

"Will you just sing it already?"

"Okay," he says. He starts to play, and it's clear that he's going to sing this song to the floor—he's still blushing and staring at some apparently fascinating spot on the rug.

"I . . . uh . . . I felt kind of bad for the dead girl. Kind of a thing with me, I guess," he says. "I was gonna call it 'Sympathy for the Dead Girl.'" And then he begins to sing.

She told him I lied I guess she was right
She told him I cheated late last night

She told him she hated me for the guys that I chose
And the booze in my guts and the coke up my nose

I'll never meet you.
Won't you guess my name?

She said she was glad that the stupid bitch was dead
But I'm why she's asleep in this bed

I gave her strength and beauty and my art
I gave her brains and my big broken heart

I'll never meet you
Won't you guess my name?

And nobody mourned me the day that I died
No one held a funeral nobody cried

And no one remembers my name today
But some record store clerks in the UK

I'll never meet you
Won't you guess my name?

She told him that she hated everything I ever did
But I killed myself to save her kid

And she'll never meet me
She'll never know my name

She'll never thank me
She'll never know my name

Stacey begins crying quietly at the first chorus, and by the time the song is over, she's sobbing uncontrollably. What the hell did he do? She never thought she was anything but happy to do away with Philippa, but it turns out she does feel bad for that lost kid, for the girl who didn't know how to be loved, the little kid crying in her room because her mother was drunk and screaming, the girl who made such a mess of everything, but not because she was bad, just because she didn't know any better. There's a whole life she cut off, and she always focused on Ken and the baseball, told herself that Philippa was just too fucking stupid to live, it was just natural selection, but it wasn't that simple. There was a lot that she liked about Philippa, and Stacey didn't exist despite Philippa, she existed because of Philippa, and how the hell had he seen that when she hadn't?

Somewhere, she hears Mark saying, "I'm sorry. It's doggerel, and I upset you."

"It's not . . . it's not that. I'm just upset because I miss her and I feel bad for her, and I don't understand how you could have such compassion for her and I don't, and it's me, and the whole thing just makes me . . . what's doggerel?"

"It's bad poetry," Mark says, and suddenly he's got his arms around her, and she feels so happy and so sad and so scared and so excited and so naked that all she can do is cry.

KELLY

Kelly worries a lot once Mom's boyfriend is Mr. Mark Norris, which is how she thinks of him in her mind so that she doesn't mess up and call him the wrong thing in the wrong place. She tells Mom that they're not allowed to kiss, and Mom says, "Well, Kel, for the time being we won't do that in front of you, but that's not really a decision you get to make."

This makes Kelly kind of mad, but not as mad as when she gets out of bed one night when Mr. Mark Norris is over for dinner, and he's leaving and Mom is kissing him good-bye at the door. She tries to do one of Karen Behavior's tricks, so instead of screaming at Mom she just yells, "I'm really angry at you!" and slams the door to her room and gets her broom and P. P. Swimmer, which is the stuffed rat she got Mom to buy for her, and beats on that instead of throwing stuff.

And in the morning Mom says, "I'm really proud of you for not name-calling and not throwing anything last night."

It's really hard to stay mad at her, but Kelly tries. "You said you wouldn't do that in front of me."

"Well, you were in bed. It wouldn't have been in front of you if you had been doing what you were supposed to."

This makes Kelly mad all over again. She's allowed to get out of bed! That's what she does!

But then one day they are at Mr. Mark Norris's house for dinner, and he serves her smiley fries, which are way better than anything Mom ever cooks, and then when they are walking down the hall, Mom says she forgot something and runs back to Mr. Mark Norris's apartment. Kelly follows her and sees them kissing, and it doesn't seem like such a big deal for some reason.

School is still hard, though. Mr. Mark Norris says, "I know it's awkward, Kelster"—this is what he calls her when he is being Mark, and one time in class he almost slips, and he calls her *Kel* . . . y—"but it's only for a few more months and then I will never be your teacher again. I am sorry, because I know this part is pretty unfair to you."

"Writers' workshop is the worst part."

"Why's that?"

"Because now we do so much stuff together, and I want to write about stuff, like the time that we were riding bikes in the arboretum even though it was actually still way too cold for that and your bike skidded on dog poop."

Mr. Mark Norris smiles. "And you don't want to write about it because then everybody will know that you were with me over the weekend and they'll tease you and be mean and stuff."

"Yeah. And also it's dumb to write it to you because you were there and you know it already." The good thing about Mr. Mark Norris is that he really understands the way a kid's mind works way better than Mom does. That's because he is a professional.

"Well, you could just change the names or something."

She looks at Mark like he is stupid, because that is a really stupid thing to say. "But that would be *lying*."

"I see your point. Well, I guess you'll just have to have a lot of fun with Grace and try to write about that."

"That's a pretty weak answer, Mr. Mark Norris."

"I know, Ms. Kelly Phillips. It's the best one I have, though. I'm sorry. I know this part isn't fair to you."

"Well, you just better not give me a two for writing just because my stories are boring."

"Deal."

She is afraid of being embarrassed, but at the same time she really likes feeling special in class because she knows stuff about him that nobody else knows and because she heard him saying *Son of a bitch* when his bike slid on dog poop. But there are still times when she has to shove him out of the way because he is hogging her mom, and she's Kelly's mom and he shouldn't hog her.

They keep going to Karen Behavior, and she makes them keep these Anger Logs for themselves where they have to write down a time when they were really angry and what they did. She likes the way Karen Behavior makes Mom keep one, too, so she has to admit when she said, *Goddammit, Kelly, I said get your shoes on.* Even though when she explains that she has to tell Karen Behavior about how they were ten minutes late to school that day because she wouldn't put her shoes on.

Karen Behavior says that big changes in your life are stressful, and she thinks Kelly is doing a great job of dealing with a big change in her life and nobody's perfect.

Finally school is over, and Kelly feels way better about everything. Mom and Mark sit down with her one night, and Mom looks all nervous, and she says, "Uh, Kelly, we've got something to tell you."

"You're getting married?"

Mom and Mark look kind of shocked. "Uh, yeah," Mom says.

"Well, duh. What else did you have to tell me?"

"Um, well, uh, I guess just that, you know, if you want to talk about anything, or you have any questions about what that means, you know, you can talk to me."

"Geez, Mom, we already talk to Karen Behavior every other week. You know, we don't always have to be talking about stuff."

"Uh, okay."

Kelly thinks it's kind of funny that they thought they had some big surprise for her when she knew they were going to get married the whole time.

One day Mom says they are all going to this festival in the cemetery and they are going to take a picnic. A festival in the cemetery sounds like just about the dumbest thing Kelly can even think of, and she tells Mom that.

"Why can't we do something *fun*?" she asks.

"Well, this might be fun, Kel, just give it a chance." She still thinks it's really dumb, but Mark brings over good picnic food that she actually likes. One thing about Mom and Mark getting married that she put on the Pro List that Karen Behavior told them to make was that the food was going to be a lot better because Mark is a professional who knows the kinds of things kids actually like to eat.

They go to the cemetery, and it is pretty boring with lots of music and dancing and stuff that is really not that interesting, but they do get to make these little lanterns, where they use markers to write stuff about dead people on pieces of paper that they put around these floating lanterns with candles inside. Kelly writes BOBBY PHILLIPS on hers and draws lots of stuff that she thinks her dad might have liked, even though she doesn't really know. So she just draws trucks and a football and other boy stuff.

Mark's lantern says, JANET NORRIS, and he's trying to draw some stuff, but he's crying. It is very weird to see your teacher cry, even if he is your mom's boyfriend or fiancé or whatever. Mom is making one, too, and Kelly thinks it's going to say something about Dad, but instead it says PHILIPPA JANE STRANGE on it, and there is a guitar and a melon on it. Mom is crying, too.

Kelly feels like it's embarrassing to have the grown-ups crying, so she puts a hand on each of their backs, just to try to get them to stop. They both look at her and reach back and try to hug her at the same time, which is weird and embarrassing, but maybe kind of nice.

When Mom looks like she's not crying too hard anymore, Kelly says, "Mom, who is that?"

"It's . . . she was my best friend." That's so weird. Why didn't Mom ever mention that before? She guesses it's like Dad, where she always just says Kelly I'm Sorry But It Just Hurts Too Much I Can't Talk About It.

Later they are sitting on the blanket and Mom goes to the port-a-potty. Mark digs out the cookies and offers her one.

"Can I ask you something?" she says.

"Yeah, okay."

"Why do you think you can talk about your sister and Mom can't talk about Dad?"

Mark looks at her for a minute and doesn't say anything.

"I guess it's just too painful for her. I think that what happened with your dad hurts her so much, she can't talk about it without it hurting again."

"She told me she threw all the pictures away after the funeral. I wish I knew what he looked like."

Mark looks kind of sad. "Yeah. That is too bad."

"I was thinking something crazy."

"What's that?"

"I was thinking that maybe like since they are all on their lanterns there, maybe my dad and your sister and Mom's friend could maybe like meet in heaven or wherever and keep each other company or something."

"I don't think that's crazy. I think that's kind of a nice thing to think about," Mark says, and he looks out at the pond in the cemetery for a minute.

Mom comes back, and it gets dark, and they go down to the pond with the million other people who are there and light their lanterns and push them off into the pond.

Mom and Mark are crying again, and they watch the lanterns for a minute until they all blow together into the center of the pond and you can't tell which one is which anymore. It's like all the dead people are hanging out together like Kelly imagined. She's kind of glad that they have people to keep them company because she feels happy to be here with Mom and Mark, and she'd feel bad if she felt like Dad was lonely.

Mom holds her hand and also Mark's hand. Janet and Bobby and Philippa and a whole bunch of other people who are dead all hang out together, floating on the pond, and Kelly and Stacey and Mark hold hands and walk away, back to the car, back to their regular life.

Liner Notes

Words and music by Brendan Halpin.

Written and revised in Boston, MA, USA, June 2004–September 2005.

Edited by Bruce Tracy.

Agented by Douglas Stewart.

Rock_L appears courtesy of El Rock Records.

National Hate Service appears courtesty of Shutchergob Records.

Lyrics from "Two Minute Man" by kind permission of Calvinist Songs.

Lyrics from "My Left One" by kind permission of Omnivore Music.

Lyrics from "Philippa Cheats" by kind permission of Pints for Music.

Lyrics from "Pukin' My Guts Out" and "Sympathy for the Dead Girl" by kind permission of Scatalogical Doggerel Music.

Brendan Halpin uses Apple computers and Samsung printers.

Thanks:

Suzanne Demarco, Rowen Halpin, Casey Nelson, Kylie Nelson, Andrew Sokatch, Daniel Sokatch, Dana Reinhardt, Jessica Yurwitz,

Deborah Bancroft, Trish Cook, Belle and Sebastian, JP Licks, the Boston Public Library, the Underground Garage (Sirius 25), Edinburgh (the city and the university), Cincinnati (just the city), Chris and Rob (and Handsome Clem and the Hockey Punk) on WAIF, the YMCA of Greater Boston, Peg Halpin, David and Cynthia Shanks, the Olson family, Steve and Eileen Cooney, the Cooney/Sullivan family, the Maranci/King family, the Shanks family, and everybody else who's supported my writing.

About the Author

BRENDAN HALPIN lives in Boston with his wife, Suzanne, and their children. Find him on the Web at www.brendanhalpin.com and at www.myspace.com/brendanhalpin.